IMPERATOR, DEUS

The Wars of CONSTANTINE THE GREAT and the
FOUNDATIONS of the CHRISTIAN CHURCH

JOHN R. PRANN, JR.

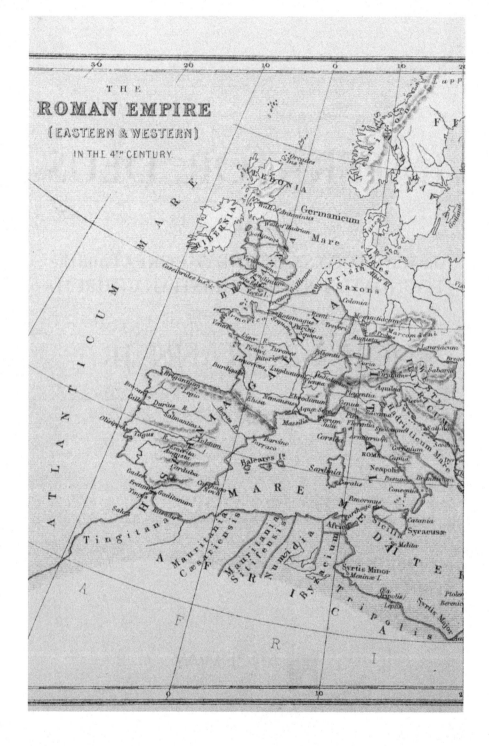

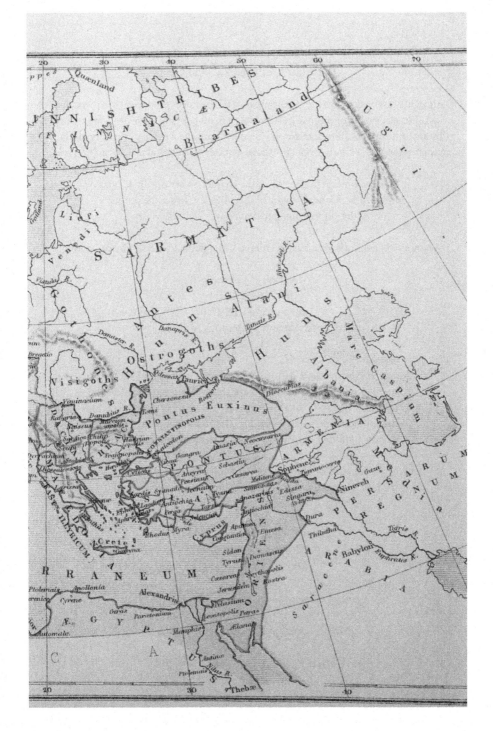

This is a work of fiction. All of the characters, names, incidents, organizations, and dialogue in this novel are either the products of the author's imagination or are used fictitiously.

Archway Publishing books may be ordered through booksellers or by contacting:

Archway Publishing
1663 Liberty Drive
Bloomington, IN 47403
www.archwaypublishing.com
1 (888) 242-5904

Because of the dynamic nature of the Internet, any web addresses or links contained in this book may have changed since publication and may no longer be valid. The views expressed in this work are solely those of the author and do not necessarily reflect the views of the publisher, and the publisher hereby disclaims any responsibility for them.

Any people depicted in stock imagery provided by Thinkstock are models, and such images are being used for illustrative purposes only.
Certain stock imagery © Thinkstock.

ISBN: 978-1-4808-3740-9 (sc)
ISBN: 978-1-4808-3738-6 (hc)
ISBN: 978-1-4808-3739-3 (e)

Library of Congress Control Number: 2016916771

Print information available on the last page.

Archway Publishing rev. date: 12/02/2016

Dedicated to;

Mom
Rich
Whitey
Tom
Bob
Roger
Jim
Lenny

All of different faiths
All of whom have preceded me
All of whom are far better than me

Acknowledgements

This book probably would not have been written if it were not for one glass too many of Chardonnay. In a dinner in Chicago after a Board Meeting late August 2013 with my good friend and CEO of Impact Products, Terry Neal, we were both feeling positive. Impact, owned by the Pritzker Group, was doing well and the prospects, with new products being introduced, were even better. I had recently torn my Achilles tendon so on a personal note I was walking around with a large boot, waiting for the inevitable surgery. Just before the main course was being served, Terry asked me what my normally active life was going to be like with no bike riding, motorcycles, water skiing, snow skiing, and boarding. My response was immediate, encouraged by the two glasses of wine I had had, 'I think I will write a book!' Terry politely asked the requisite questions, realizing that probably the wine was talking, and then changed the subject. In my conversation with my wife, Cheryl, that evening, I mentioned that I felt a bit like a turkey at Thanksgiving, having made such an announcement, I was now committed.

Charles Overby has the distinction of being one of the nicest men I have ever met. He influenced me the most on this project, in spite of the fact that he is not a fan of 'ancient news'! I owe more than a debt of gratitude to David Hart and Kerry Moynihan of ZRG Partners, an international search firm. Without David's and Kerry's introductions and encouragement, I might never have attempted to publish this book. The same is true of Jim Walsh's help and a special thanks to my son in law, Darren O'Day and to my friend, Wayne Thompson, for their thoughtful edits. I also thank my brother, Cris, and Mary-Lin Hoyer, sister, Charlotte Cassity, Bob Pigeon, Tom and Chris Kroeger and my Aunt, Jean Prann for all of their encouragement and enthusiasm.

Much credit also belongs to my grown children and wife. Of my children, Elizabeth advised me to keep it simple and not to lecture, Justin wanted more battles and less theology and John wanted more pictures, telling me the future was comic books. Cheryl would frequently remind me to get out of the Fourth Century, it was time for dinner.

Mostly I thank you the reader, my hope is you enjoy the book as much as I enjoyed writing it.

PREFACE

My first introduction to Arius was in my twenties. In a book about early Christianity, he was portrayed as a monk who was very popular who got involved the leading controversy of the time. A controversy that would be eclipsed only by Martin Luther over a thousand years later. Arius seemed like a sympathetic figure who I continued to pursue.

It was through my interest in Arius that I learned more about Constantine. Although my first impression of him was from reading about the Council of Nicaea, it is impossible to ignore his success on the battlefield. He justly deserves to be one of the Greats, certainly on the par with Alexander and Julius Caesar.

With the age of the internet, there is far more information available concerning Arius' controversy. His ties to Constantine and to Constantine's family were not as clear thirty five years ago as they are now. He still remains a sympathetic figure to me. Not because some of his beliefs are contrary to most organized Christian religions, but because many of them are the similar to mine. In spite of that I still consider myself a Christian, albeit an extremely skeptical one. The historical Jesus is convincing to me and his Father is forgiving, versus the more vengeful God of the Jewish faith and the more bellicose faith of the Muslims. All of these great religions have the same God and came from the same man, originally Abram of the Jewish faith, so one would think we would all get along better than history has proved.

There is also an irony that this controversy was almost entirely generated in what we now consider the Middle Eastern countries. Although the friction and violence from the controversy would last for almost one thousand years, the countries and cities where it all started would be Islamic in a third of that time. The irony is compounded by Islam's strict monotheism, one of Arius' arguments. It seems reasonable that part of Islam's early explosive growth and acceptance may have been fueled by conversion of Arian Christians.

I have tried to keep the historical facts as consistent as I could, while still filling in the blanks of history with what might have been. This book is my imagination of what happened almost two thousand years ago. It is not gospel to either history or to Scripture. All of the dates that are generally agreed to by historians have both the Roman Calendar Ab Urbe Condita (AUC) (From the founding of the City) and Christian (AD) in bold letters. If the Christian date is not bold, the date of the activity described is either unknown or my fiction. All of the letters, or portions thereof, are as referenced. There is very little original writings remaining from Arius, most of what is available is through Athanasius' letters, which usually isn't favorable. Where there are names of historical figures or Latin wording that have multiple spellings, I have chosen the ones that I am most familiar with.

IMPERATOR, DEUS

Flavius Valerius Aurelius Constantinus Augustus no longer felt like the invincible god his enemies—and some friends—thought he was. Some mornings, his whole body ached. He was 40 and just beginning to notice the effects on a body that had been at war for most of his adult life. His father had died at 56.

Looking south from his position on one of the rocky foothills above the Tiber River, Constantine could see the bright light of the rising sun on the Aurelian Walls of Rome. His troops were encamped directly below him on the plain, several hundred cubits from the river bank. He registered the chill of the October morning, thankful that it wasn't raining—as it often did in Rome, this time of year.

The Milvian Bridge was clearly damaged. Next to it was a makeshift bridge, constructed of wood planks laid over barges floating in the Tiber. A rushed job.

His enemy, Maxentius, had legions encamped on the south side of the river. But they were starting to cross the makeshift bridge and position themselves on the north side. Constantine watched intently as they took positions. Their forces were impressive. A hundred thousand or more. Twice as many *legionari* (foot soldiers) as his army had.

He studied the centurions directing Maxentius' legionari and *sagittari* (archers). Something was amiss. They moved too quickly.

Their haste wasn't quite a panic but it was…anxious.

Constantine knew that every defense had weak spots and he was starting to recognize Maxentius'. Meeting with his senior generals the evening before, he had focused on where his *equiti* (cavalry) should be deployed. They had agreed it was likely that Maxentius' weakest legions would be to the west. Farthest away from the center point of engagement. They had tentatively agreed that the equiti would ride west and flank the weaker troops after the sagittari and the legionari attacked center to the bridge. But, this morning, Constantine wasn't so sure. Maxentius' Centurions seemed to be focused slightly to the west of center. The flanks were drawing little attention.

"Vibius, summon my Generals!" Constantine snapped.

Vibius shifted uneasily and then hurried down to the camp while the other four *palatini* (bodyguards) stood at attention. Constantine smiled. Vibius was like a brother and would do anything Constantine asked. But, on the day of a battle, Vibius liked to keep close.

Like many of Constantine's troops, Vibius had once fought against him. In Vibius' case, the fight had been in Syria. Vibius was an African archer, enslaved by the Persians and then sold to the Syrians to fight the Romans. He had a tattoo on his neck that read "*taxo pensus.*" Taxes paid.

After the Roman army had defeated the Syrians, Constantine could have killed Vibius and the other prisoners. Instead, he'd asked for their loyalty and sent them to distant areas of the Empire to prove their worth. Vibius had been sent to fight for Constantine's father, the Emperor Augustus Constantius, in Gaul and Britannia. There, Vibius had earned the tattoo on the back of his right hand. This one was an eagle surrounded by a wreath above the letters

SPQR—standing for "the Senate and People of Rome." He was a Roman soldier!

A few years later, Constantine joined his father's army. By then, Vibius had become a well-rounded warrior. He had learned both the javelin and the sword—which was Constantine's favorite weapon.

Constantine had a daily routine of practicing all weapons. While in the north, he frequently chose Vibius as his sparring partner. This was unusual. Constantine's four palatini were all experienced weapons instructors, and it was expected that he would spar with one or more of them. But anyone with eyes could see that Vibius was more athletic—and a keener challenge for Constantine.

Initially, the four had been critical of Vibius but, in time, all five became close. The sintering of battle drew them together. So did the love and laughter of the man they protected. Here, at the Milvian Bridge, they had been fighting together for almost eight years.

"I have returned, Dominus. Your *Dux* (Generals) are directly behind me," reported Vibius as he ran back into position, shadowing Constantine.

Vibius' behavior on the day of a battle was well known to the other bodyguards, who nodded slightly and smiled as he shuffled next to Constantine. The Emperor was moving across the rocky plateau to get a better view of his opponent's line.

Vibius believed Constantine was as close to a god as a man could be. His life prior to meeting Constantine had been a miserable mix of slavery, threats and submission. He had been merely a body, a very tall and athletic body, but no one would have thought twice about him if he'd been killed in battle. Constantine was different, a great general who had granted Vibius—and many others—life rather than death. Who had given Vibius the freedom to become as good a soldier as his physical limits allowed. Who had allowed an African archer to become a sparring partner of the Emperor and a member of his palatini. And he wasn't just any palatini, he was a *Herculiani*, the top of the corps, a respected figure. Vibius had a good life, honor and prestige.

"Dominus," said Dux Gaius, addressing Constantine as he climbed the ridge of the rocky plateau, followed by Dux Tiberus and Ablabius. Constantine turned from the battleground to Gaius, stopping first to look Vibius hard in the eye and then toward the other palatini. Vibius recognized the signal and walked slowly, head down and shoulders slumped, to the far side of the plateau where the other palatini were standing.

Gaius, the Praetorian Prefect, was a bulldog of a man. And an aging one. Nearly bald and barrel-chested with disproportionately large arms, he was clean-shaven with large, muscular jowls. Most of Constantine's military staff copied their clean-shaven Emperor. But many lacked his square jaw.

Gaius was in command of all the armed forces, including the legionari. Tiberus commanded the sagittari, and Ablabius the equiti.

Tiberus was the tallest and leanest of the Dux. Ablabius was the only Greek—the other two were native Romans—and the only Dux who had a beard, which he groomed meticulously with a custom set of scissors, wood comb and a gold-backed glass mirror. Ablabius' eyes gave the impression of sadness, belying his almost constant good nature. That melancholy look also hid what was, in Constantine's opinion, the best strategic mind among his generals.

"Gaius, how do you read the formations?" Constantine addressed all his officers by their first names, a casual and close manner.

"Yes, Dominus. We were watching," Gaius pointed to the ridge to the west of their position. "Ablabius and I feel the build-up has most attention to the direct north of the Bridge. Tiberus worries that it is a feint. He fears that Maxentius is setting us for a direct assault and hiding his strongest legions behind the hills between the city walls and the Tiber. They would have immediate access over the bridge, once we attack."

The Emperor nodded his head slightly. "Tiberus, look at that bridge. He can't move two legions over so weak a structure in an hour. Not in half a day. Ablabius can overpower the center and start a rout before they cross." Years of building projects in the north of the Empire had given Constantine an eye for construction.

"I don't think Maxentius has the experience to position his army well here. And I don't recognize any of his Centurions from this distance." Gaius started to point but ended up waving his hand dismissively at Maxentius' forces. "After we killed his Praetorian Prefect—what was his name, Pompeianus?—at Verona, the only Dux who might stand with him now is Tiberius Aetius. And I know that man. He is more of a Tribune than a soldier. We won't see Maxentius today. We won't see him until we're inside the City." Gaius was only pretending not to remember Pompeianus' name. He had killed the man himself. Singlehandedly.

Verona had been one of the early battles in Constantine's march southward to Rome. As the fighting waned, Constantine's army was clearly victorious. Pompeianus ordered his army's horns to sound the retreat. The terrain was hilly, with several natural paths to and from the main battlefield. Gaius, who'd lost his shield in the fighting and had only his sword and dagger, had positioned himself astride the path closest to Pompeianus. The Prefect, who was on horseback, would either have to ride past Gaius or make a wide detour.

Pompeianus, thinking that the short, overweight opponent was merely a confused legionari and an easy kill to end a disappointing day, charged. Slamming his shield down on Gaius' arm the force sent Gaius' sword flying through the air and far out of reach. But it also sent Pompeianus' shield down into the dirt. Pompeianus turned his horse quickly to finish Gaius with his long sword—but the stocky old man was surprisingly nimble. He stayed in front of the horse and kept both hands free. Pompeianus started to turn his horse and swung his long sword to the right. In the same instant,

Gaius jumped to the left, grabbed the front of Pompeianus' four-post saddle with his left hand and lifted himself eye-to-eye with the stunned Prefect.

Gaius' right hand grabbed Pompeianus' larynx with such force that the Prefect gasped blood. Gaius let go of the saddle and fell back to the ground, pulling Pompeianus off of his horse. By the throat.

As Gaius' feet touched the ground, he pulled his dagger from its sheath—with his left hand—and planted it in the back of Pompeianus' neck. Through it all, the bulldog had never let go of the Prefect's throat.

For the soldiers of Constantine's army, Gaius' killing blow at Verona had become legendary.

"I agree, Gaius." Ablabius responded slowly and deliberately, catching everyone's attention. His eyes stayed fixed on the battlefield.

Constantine's camp was the standard rectangular formation, with tents filling the square forms and paths methodically constructed between. Each legion had its mess area and responsibility for its transport mules and horses. And there were many horses. Constantine believed in a large cavalry, but that made space a premium.

The center of the camp was a meeting area, a larger mess area, a medical staging and the generals' personal tents—including Constantine's. The entire camp was fortified by earthen walls, which were built on the first day that they arrived. On the far end of the camp, the engineers had dug trenches for fresh running water and water for the latrines, draining back to the Tiber.

Outside of the walls was Constantine's field command tent, which faced the battlefield almost directly across from the Milvian Bridge. In front of this tent, troops had taken positions and the Centurions were constantly moving soldiers, fine tuning their lines.

The archers were all in position as were the equiti. This was all standard.

What had caught Ablabius' attention was the position of Maxentius' army. Something looked wrong to him, just as it had to the Emperor. "Their position is too close to the river. How will they regroup when we break through their forward lines?"

"Yes!" the three others replied, almost in unison.

Constantine followed quickly with orders. "Gaius, move your initial deployments up 50 cubits before they realize their mistake. Tiberus, make sure there are several hundred archers positioned within bow shot in case Maxentius considers moving toward our camp. Good eye, Ablabius."

"Maxentius isn't the tactician his father was," said Tiberus, as he hand signaled new orders to his archers. "But it's unbelievable to me that there is such confusion. In the center of his army. Almost seems like a trap. Have we heard anything from our spies?"

Gaius grunted a sort of laugh. "Spies. Of the three I trust most, two have been killed. And the one who's left is having trouble getting to us."

Constantine watched the crowded middle of Maxentius' front line. The soldiers were still moving restlessly, as if they sensed their poor position. "We need to move. Soon."

This was a civil war—and the lines, on all fronts, were complicated. Maxentius was Constantine's brother-in-law. His father, Maximum, had been a good general and a friend of Constantine's father. As a sign of allegiance, Maximum had given his daughter Fausta to Constantine in marriage.

But Maximum's desire for power was greater than any allegiance. A few years later, he took command of a division of the Roman army, telling the officers and soldiers that Constantine had died. The deception was easily proved and Maximum was arrested. Though he had been an able tactician on the battlefield, Maximum was not so sharp when it came to politics. With his time running out, he plotted to assassinate Constantine. And tried to involve Fausta. She chose loyalty to her husband over loyalty to her father and warned Constantine.

Constantine was prepared to try his father-in-law before the Senate. But he offered the older man the option of suicide and keeping his family's honor. Maximum accepted.

Maxentius shared his father's poor political instincts. He lived off of his father's reputation, did little or nothing for his people and had never learned to be a soldier. As evidenced by the battlefield on which they were about to engage. The ablest Emperors had always been soldiers first.

Constantine turned back to look at his battle armor, which the servants were polishing and preparing. Leading troops was simple, compared to politics. His position as Emperor was part of a complex power-sharing arrangement. Before he died, Emperor Galerius had named him Emperor of the Western Empire and two men—Licinius and Maximinus Deia—shared the title of Emperor of the Eastern Empire. But even this had left some Romans unhappy. Maxentius, consumed by jealousy, declared himself Emperor of the West. He vowed publicly to avenge his father's death by killing Constantine.

None of Constantine's military advisors or soothsayers recommended a war with Maxentius. They advised Constantine to finish building his military in Gaul before marching to Rome and handling the usurper. Constantine would have none of that. He took a small army, crossed the Alps and beat the usurper's units at various locations between the Alps and Rome—Sequsium, Turin, Brescia, the brutal battle at Verona, Alguileia, Modena and Ravenna. After each victory, Constantine forbade his soldiers to loot, pillage or rape. This was still the Empire. He said that accused rapists would be castrated. And his soldiers knew that he had enforced that penalty in the past.

The march south from the Alps had done more for Constantine's reputation than any victories he'd won in Gaul. After his rout of the usurper's forces at Ravenna, he'd moved his small army slowly to the Milvian Bridge and the walls of Rome. This allowed time for fear and unrest to fester inside the city walls.

He realized he'd been quiet for a long time. And his generals were still waiting for his final word. "Tiberus, I disagree with you. This isn't a feint. We'll follow our plan in a…straightforward way. I want your sagittari to concentrate just north of the Bridge, perhaps half your bows. Ablabius, after the archers exhaust five rounds, charge with a legion into the center. Spread your others through the flanks, but your center charge must be your best. As we have discussed, we must break them quickly."

He turned to Gaius: "We will start the assault with our three lines, but spread wider. We can't have them flank us. Have all the Shields and Standards been painted with the CHI RHO?"

"Yes!" the three generals answered together. They were getting ready to go.

"Good. I look forward to reviewing them shortly."

"Dominus, clubs or swords for the equiti?" Ablabius asked. "Clubs were most effective in Turin."

"I like iron tipped clubs for the horseman. Along with their lances. The clubs have better weight against opposing riders. I think we should keep with all swords for the legionari. The swords are lighter. It appears from the size of Maxentius' lines that we could be fighting for a long time, so lighter swords will be a benefit." Constantine particularly liked the newer swords. They were lighter and sharper. "It is done. Let us get to advancing our lines."

Ablabius had one last question. "Dominus, should we employ our remaining molossus for the first assault?"

Molossus were large, armed attack dogs, bred from ear-lier Roman military attack dogs with English Mastiffs from the

Britannia campaigns. They wore spiked and sharpened collars and ankle rings and were trained to be vicious fighters.

Constantine hesitated for a moment. "I think not. With the large field between our position and Maxentius' lines, his sagittari will be deadly for the molossus. Plus, we have so few left. I doubt they would be effective."

Constantine walked to the edge of the plateau as his Dux left for the battlefield. Vibius and the other four palatini—Appius, Sevius, Titus and Quintus—surrounded him. "Dominus, do you plan to fight today?" asked Titus.

"Only if needed," Constantine answered.

As he turned to walk down the ridge, Constantine nearly collided with Vibius. The Emperor was of above-average height and muscular but appeared small next to the African. Appius, from Northern Africa but of lighter skin, laughed. "Vibius, you wish to dance with the Emperor?"

"No, Appius, he just wants to hold his hand," joked Sevius.

"Stultissima!" barked Vibius, using the feminine form of "you idiots" for effect. They all laughed. But stayed close to the Emperor.

The sun's rays were just beginning to strike the ceiling of Maxentius' Great Room in his Lateran Estate in Rome. The former home of the Imperial Horse Guard, the Great Room was extravagant. Huge silver and gold candelabras and elaborate oil lamps illuminated it at night. There were leather-bound seats for hundreds. Thick tapestries with gold detailing covered the walls. The massive arches supported the high domed ceiling—high even by Rome's standards. The Mesopotamians may have invented the arch, but the Romans had perfected the keystones necessary for such massive structures. In a corner of the Great Room, Maxentius sat on a cushioned purple and gold chair while many of his court mulled about, eating snacks of grains and fruit. He had summoned his soothsayer and his prophet. While he ate, he sought their counsel.

"Seer," Maxentius teethed, exaggerating the first letter of the title. "The gods have always been favorable to me, for which I am grateful. But what signs from nature portend the outcome of the battle today."

"The signs are all quite favorable, noble Augustus. Only the enemy of Rome will die in this battle. Today is the anniversary of your ascension to the throne. And the blood of our sacrifices by the river flowed toward Constantine. All of the entrails of the sacrificed animals had no abnormalities. Perfect in every way, obviously favoring your cause. In fact, I have bought the liver from one of the lambs, so you can clearly see the fullness of the lobes and brightness of the—"

The Seer reached into a woolen sack by his feet for the bloody liver.

"No, no! That is fine, Seer. I need not personally examine the lamb's liver. Prophet, what do the Gods say the result will be in my battle with the bastard of Constantius?"

"You will not be harmed in the battle and anyone that tries to harm you will be the one that suffers. The gods have aligned the stars so that they point to a stunning victory, as they were for your ascension, indicating the gods most certainly are in your favor."

Maxentius stood tall and turned dramatically, so everyone in the Great Room would notice. "Counsels!" Again, he exaggerated the first letter of the word. "It is my temptation to join the battle. I wish to watch the death of this child of a whore, who brutally murdered my father. Have you seen any omens that would caution me against such an appearance?"

"None," they both responded slowly, looking at each other. The question was a surprise that neither expected.

His strategy in the past had been to wait out any siege within the walls of Rome. He had given every indication that this time he would do the same. He had stockpiled several months' worth of grain and wine from Carthage. There would be enough food and drink for the entire city—well into the spring.

But this time was different. He was not a popular Emperor and even he knew it. A self-centered man, he had no ability to walk and talk to the plebeians. In a recent event in the Coliseum, he had been jeered and taunted about his likely loss in the looming battle with Constantine. No one inside the City walls—or outside—expected this heavy-set man with no military background to face an experienced fighter on the battlefield.

"I believe it will improve my stature within the City, for the citizens to witness me participating in the death of this rabid canine. And avenging my father's death. Once we capture him, I will kill him with my own hands. I will talk to my Dux shortly." It was a bold statement.

Maxentius didn't mention that his father had made a similar boast, years before.

The usurper had some reason to be optimistic. Aside from an overwhelming manpower advantage, he had some skilled soldiers on his side—seasoned fighters who'd supported him when he'd declared himself Emperor, including his Praetorian Guard. And he had some good generals. Tiberius Aetius commanded his troops here in the city. Pompeianus had defeated forces loyal to Constantine in Carthage—which explained the current wealth of Carthaginian grain and wine.

Of course, Constantine's army had killed Pompeianus at Verona. But Maxentius was convinced that some subterfuge had been involved there. Perhaps the followers of the Nazarene had poisoned the Prefect prior to battle. There were many Christians in Verona and they were loyal to Constantine, as they had been to his father. Christians.

Tiberius Aetius was standing to the side, looking concerned. This was a familiar thing. Whenever Maxentius planned to be on the battlefield, his generals worried. Maxentius tilted his head, inviting the general to speak. "Augustus, I am confident we will prevail today. Our forces are vastly more numerous, better trained and better rested. They are eager for the victory. I have no doubt that you would be a source of great encouragement on the battleground, but a battleground is a dangerous place to be. Even in full armor an errant spear can be—"

"I'm well aware of such risks. My mind is made. I will cross the bridge mid-day and station myself above the fray. Don't be worried, general. My Praetorian Guard will stand by me."

"Augustus—" The general wanted to explain that both the place and the time Maxentius mentioned were not optimal.

"Enough!"

The mid-morning sun was high in the sky but the air retained its chill. Constantine, gleaming in his Imperial battle armor, walked with his five bodyguards along the front of the lines of his legionari. He registered the temperature and thanked the gods. Heat could drain the energy of his troops—and they would need a lot of energy to overcome the number advantage of Maxentius' side.

He had instructed all shields to be turned toward the rear of the guard rather than toward the enemy, hiding what they had painted on them.

Infantry fighters carried a lot of equipment. First, every infantryman got a shovel. When not fighting or practicing fighting, they were building something. Their fighting equipment consisted of two or three javelins, a shield, a sword, a large dagger and armor consisting of a breast plate, arm and leg pieces and helmet. The front line would often have lighter armor for freer movement.

Typically, Constantine's infantry attacked in three lines. Each line was staggered slightly, so that the enemy could see no open space between soldiers. The lines would tighten up as they approached, which made them seem even more like one, solid wall. The formation was like the herringbone pattern of brick or tile that made the best road surfaces.

This formation's method for killing was to use the javelins to incapacitate the enemy through their shields and then to stab at them using simple but powerful sword thrusts. After the front line had struck, the next line was prepared and intact.

This formation had proved more flexible than the Greek phalanx formation made famous centuries earlier by Alexander the Great. The phalanx formation was vulnerable to breaching and flanking, the Roman formation allowed reinforcements to either breach or flanking maneuvers. It also allowed for an increased use of cavalry because it was a three man line. Relatively shallow with an ability to open and close the line quickly. Phalanx formations typically had many more lines, making them deeper and—again—less flexible.

As a battle drew on and the formations deteriorated, the manner in which the soldiers used their swords changed. The discipline to remain in formation was strict but, inevitably, legionari needed to be trained to fight out of formation. And this meant more slashing than straight thrusts. Constantine admired the sword because it was, in his mind, the fairest form of combat—one on one, loser dies.

Of course, shields could be offensive weapons as well as defensive. His army's shields were built with sharp protrusions opposite the handle that could incapacitate enemies.

As Constantine walked amidst his legions, he held his helmet in his left hand. His helmet was unique, only having a ridge where the colored horse hair plume was on most Roman helmets. The latest design. It was obvious he was close to his troops. When he came close, the younger soldiers would drop to their knees. The older ones would often shake his arm, each grabbing the other's forearm above the wrist—a Roman handshake. Occasionally, an older soldier would hug him.

All the while, Constantine looked relaxed and thankful to his men. Many had fought for him and his father. Many were Franks, who had a strong allegiance to him due to his family's long rule in the North.

Each of the soldiers had painted the first two letters of the Greek word for "Christ," symbolizing the crucifixion of Christ, on their shields. Constantine made a point of looking at as many individual shields as he could. He'd had a dream on the road from Ravenna that he should fight under this Standard rather than his family standard. In his dream, a voice said, "with this sign, you will conquer." The sign was a vexillum, a military banner standard, with the Greek letters CHI and RHO on it. With the CHI-RHO, the standard became known as the Labarum.

The Nazarene's teachings had struck a chord in Constantine. The concept of a single God made more sense to him than the multiple gods of the Roman history. Pagan gods had always seemed one dimensional and petty—like men and women. Of course, that may have been the point of pagan gods. If one's interest was for personal improvement and insight, then one studied Greek philosophy of Socrates and Plato. To Constantine, Christianity fulfilled both needs—a noble God and a coherent philosophy of the meaning of life.

His mother, Helena, had been responsible for introducing him to the teachings of the Nazarene. Constantine had been born in Naissus, Moesia, south of the Danube. His mother, a commoner and concubine with Constantius, was a strong believer in the Nazarene's lessons. And this faith had helped her maintain grace throughout the hardships in her life.

Concubinage was legally accepted in the Empire. Roman law still gave preference to monogamous marriages. And even to divorce and remarriage. A man might divorce his wife to marry another woman of higher social status or having more child-bearing years. But a man— especially a young man with bright prospects— would not be inclined to marry a woman of lower social status. In that case, concubinage was an alternative. The downside was the concubine's children might not be recognized as the man's legal heirs.

As a rising young officer, Constantius had been a young man with bright prospects. He'd met Helena, a waitress, during a temporary assignment in a provincial garrison town. Helena had always spoken well of Constantius, telling their son that they'd been wildly in love and that she'd been happy to be his concubine. In fact her father had strongly encouraged it!

Constantius left her to marry the Emperor's stepdaughter and to assume his expected place among the elite in the Capitol. Helena had raised Constantine through his early years.

In time, his father summoned Constantine to finish his education and to serve in a number of military and court positions in Rome and Nicomedia. Constantius always spoke lovingly about Helena—but he said that he regretted she had never found someone else to share her life. Her rebuttal was she had found the Nazarene.

When he served under his father's command in Gaul and Britannia, Constantine had learned the importance of building goodwill from the conquered, strict morality and a constant dedication to improving his skills, both militarily and politically.

And then Constantius died. At an early age.

After reviewing the legionari, Constantine reviewed the sagittari. He was less familiar with the archers; but, to them, Vibius and Appius were like demigods—so all the Emperor had to do was let the bodyguards speak and nod approvingly. He was back in his element when they moved on to the equiti. He inspected their shields closely, compared the club to the long sword and promised to share wine after the battle. This was important. Constantine had increased the number of his equiti to over twenty percent of his army.

Following at a distance and talking quietly with the troops was Ossius of Cordova, a Christian Bishop, dressed in a full-length undyed wool tunic and a small wooden cross hanging from his neck.

Constantine had met this priest years earlier in Diocletian's court in Nicomedia, where Ossius had come to plead the case against persecution.

After the troop review, Constantine walked toward his command tent on the outside of the encampment. He looked directly up in the sky. The sun was at its peak and the temperature was just right. It was going to be a fine day for battle.

Constantine's officers signaled that the troops were ready to attack. Maxentius' long line of troops was mirrored by Constantine's. The archers were nestled in with the third row of foot soldiers—for protection of their shields and to allow the fastest return volleys of arrows.

The Dux were uneasy that Maxentius had not attacked yet. Each was eager to get the advantage of the first blood. But neither side was striking first. Constantine's army was waiting for his command. Combat medics were placed were they would be most active, behind the center of the lines.

As they'd agreed the night before, Constantine remained by his command tent with his palatini and their horses nearby. Also nearby was the trumpeter, waiting to sound the buccina and start the battle. Constantine watched. And Ossius approached. "Imperator Constantine, my friend, may God be with you." He placed his hand on Constantine's shoulder. Ossius was one of the few people close enough to the Emperor—other than his troops—to touch him.

"Thank you, Ossius. Thank you."

Constantine waved his hand to the trumpeter. As the buccina sounded, the recently-painted shields turned to face the long line of Maxentius' troops. The Standard Bearers unfolded their vexilla, all displaying the Labarum—with their CHI RHO—above the purple standard of an outline of Constantine's profile.

An anxious buzz rose from Maxentius' troops. Soldiers were superstitious—and many were wondering whether these were the same vexilla that Pompeianus had faced in Verona. Before he died. Was he strangled and stabbed at the same time, in battle? And their other comrades, at Turin and Modena, did they see this vexilla? Before they were routed. Were these signs why Constantine was invincible?

While the buzz was still rising, Tiberus' archers let loose their first volley. The sound was almost musical, like the bass tone of a stringed instrument followed by the whistle of the arrows rushing through the air. The end note was either the metallic ping on a shield or a dull thump in human flesh. Then, a chorus of pain.

Tiberus had ordered three volleys before the other side's sagittari returned their first. The legionari shields faced the sky in unison, as the sheet of arrows descended. On their side, there were many pings and few thumps. Quickly, Tiberus ordered the fourth volley. And, for the first time, Constantine's troops started to move, leaving three large lanes in their center for Ablabius' equiti.

The lanes forced the legionari into a "V" formation, which would fill in as the last horse charged by. Another wave of arrows descended from both sides. As Ablabius' equiti started their charge through the troops, Maxentius' archers would not have an opportunity for another volley for fear of hitting their own equiti—which had also started their charge.

As his horse was gaining stride, Ablabius saw a purple standard crossing the wooden barges next to the Milvian Bridge. His adrenaline turned to anger. The only two people that could have a purple Vexillum were Constantine and Maxentius—and he had just saluted Constantine a moment ago. This was his opportunity.

To Ablabius, Maxentius was a pig and coward. When Galerius— who'd been one of the Emperors of the Tetrarchy before his death a year before—had challenged Maxentius with a siege on Rome, Maxentius refused to fight. As a result, Galerius had raped and pillaged the surrounding towns—including Ablabius' home. His wife and parents, who'd recently moved from Crete, died in the chaos.

Constantine saw the purple vexillum being held across the bridge at the same time his cavalry general did. But Constantine also noticed the standard of the Praetorian Guard beneath the purple. Tiberus' warning about a tactical feint came back to him. Behind Maxentius were thousands of elite fighters waiting to cross the floating bridge. Praetorian Guards had originally been body-guards for the early Emperors. Over time, they'd become strong enough—and politically powerful enough—to choose their own Emperors. They'd virtually controlled the Empire for decades, mixing an iron-fisted police force, a domestic spy network and a signature political viciousness. Most ordinary Roman citizens detested the Praetorians. But the Emperor had a more diplomatic relationship with them. Maxentius kept an uneasy partnership with the Praetorians by paying them off. He'd pledged that a large per-centage of all stamped gold coins would continue to flow into their coffers. And he'd struggled to keep that pledge. But the Praetorians realized that Constantine would not be their ally—and would likely outlaw them—if he gained control of Rome.

Constantine set off toward his horse.

"Imperator, please!" stumbled Titus. "The battle is yet to be-gin. Let us at least observe its engagement before you change your plans."

Constantine stopped, about halfway to his horse, and turned back toward the battle. "Yes, Titus. Observe. Thank you. I'll be patient and see how it takes shape."

Maxentius approached a tree to the right of the Bridge. Ablabius was riding toward him, too far in front of his own men. His pace should have been measured until he was closer to the enemy, giving time for the legionari to close. Ablabius wanted to kill Maxentius. But his bloodlust made him vulnerable.

As if he had heard Constantine's worries, Ablabius slowed enough that his equiti caught up to him. "Good. Good, my friend. Not so angry. Let the battle take shape."

Normally, Ablabius would fall back several lengths to avoid the worst of the initial impact with the enemy's riders. But, this time, he remained in the middle of the lead horses. He was intent on getting to the purple standard. He drew a javelin, brought it back and—in time with his horse's hooves—hurled it forward. The throw was true. Before Maxentius' cavalry lieutenant could raise his lance, the javelin pierced his horse's chest. In an instant, the horse was on the ground and the lieutenant's life was ending under hundreds of hooves.

Ablabius used his second javelin to deflect an incoming spear, something he had done only once before. He reached for his last javelin. Again, in time with the gallop, he threw his third javelin— this time, into one of the enemy equiti instead of the horse. Immediately, Ablabius grabbed the club he'd been holding with one of his legs and knocked another of Maxentius' riders two cubits out of his saddle.

Constantine knew why Ablabius was enraged. Most of the army knew the story, as well. No one would have stopped the Greek from seeking vengeance for his family. But Constantine was pleased that Ablabius seemed to be letting his mind command his heart. The legionari were now directly behind him. That was the right tactical position. Everything was now in sync.

Because the equiti had charged so hard, they'd broken through the third line of Maxentius' infantry. This was an early advantage for Constantine's army. But reinforcements from the Praetorian Guard were pouring over the makeshift bridge. They were effectively stabilizing the breach.

As the battle settled into hand to hand combat, Gaius' lines remained intact. They were taking ground, foot by foot. Constantine sighed. This was good—but his troops needed to move faster to have a true rout. With Praetorians still coming over the bridge, the middle could stall. Plus, the riders' arms had to be burning from the weight of those heavier clubs. He quickly checked the west and east flanks. They looked secure. Both sides seemed to know that this battle was going to be won in the center.

Suddenly, Ablabius' horse dropped. That was enough. Faster than his bodyguards, Constantine was on his horse and charging toward where he'd last seen Ablabius.

From the roar of the hand-to-hand combat, Gaius also saw Ablabius fall. But he was too far away—150 cubits or more—and facing the wrong direction to reach the rider quickly. Tiberus was closer to Ablabius; but not close enough. Constantine was across the battlefield in a moment. Vibius had caught up and, in fact, was slightly ahead. Appius, Titus, Sevius and Quintus were close behind. His standard bearer with the Labarum was far behind.

Constantine could see that Ablabius was still alive. The Greek had taken up his longer cavalry sword and, with several of Gaius' legionari, was fending off a steady stream of enemy foot soldiers. That stream was being fed by new fighters coming across the bridge.

Gaius was positioning himself in front of the bridge with several units of his best fighters to shut off the flow of Praetorians. They were making headway—but weren't there yet.

In the meantime, Ablabius and the handful of legionari fighting with him needed help.

Something whizzed by Constantine's head. A javelin? An arrow? He couldn't tell—but he realized that, on his horse, he was too tall and made an easy target for the emerging Praetorian Guards. He had about 50 cubits of human carnage to pass to get to where he could help Ablabius. Riding there would be slow and he would be too vulnerable, so Constantine launched himself off of his saddle and aimed for the largest Praetorian in front of him. The Guard raised his sword and quickly stepped to the side—and Constantine hit him with a glancing blow instead of direct hit. The Emperor tumbled to the ground for a second and sprang up to continue his attack. But the big Praetorian was already dead and falling to the ground, a javelin stuck deep in his chest.

Vibius had thrown with such force that the javelin had pierced the Praetorian's shield and armor as if it were a child's tin toy. Constantine cursed Vibius for throwing so close—but, really, for killing the enemy first. Vibius smiled.

The other bodyguards arrived within seconds and immediately all six fought in unison. They moved with an almost fluid precision, like a wave of death washing over the enemy legionari. Bodies and parts of bodies sprayed blood, up and down. Many of Maxentius' soldiers—slow to move or with their backs to Constantine's onslaught—lost their arms, when they raised to strike but hesitated for even a heartbeat. Constantine's standard bearer struggled to keep up, climbing over horses and bodies. The noise was deafening. Screams, horses, metal hitting metal, metal hitting muscle, warnings, orders, pain, death. All louder than any sporting event, mixed with the unmistakable sound of pain. Almost no one on the battlefield heard it.

Within minutes, they had reached Ablabius.

The Greek acknowledged them with a brief bow of the head— and then quickly returned to his goal, less than three hundred cubits away: Maxentius' purple standard.

Everyone was aware of Constantine's vexillum. The Praetorian Guards were streaming from the bridge toward Constantine, trying to press to a position where one might deliver a fatal blow. But Gaius' legionari were blocking the way with swords and lances.

In many places, Gaius' lines were still in formation—keeping them extremely effective. Gaius was trying to move these lines toward the Bridge, where they could stop the flow of Praetorian Guards. Constantine and his bodyguards were advancing toward Maxentius' purple standard. They were some two hundred cubits away but moving steadily. Suddenly, Ablabius—still slightly ahead of the others—screamed a warning. Maxentius' standard had started to move back toward the Bridge. He was retreating.

Ablabius turned to match the usurper's new direction. But the angle didn't favor pursuit. There was too much fighting in the way. Constantine screamed, "Stop! Stand down, Ablabius."

Overcome with exhaustion and the realization that he wasn't going to reach the coward who he blamed for the death of his family, Ablabius fell back, to his knees.

With Maxentius' retreat, the tenor of the battle started to change. By the time the usurper approached the Bridge, the lines of his legionari had begun to crumble.

Constantine and his guards surrounded Ablabius as the Greek fell in behind them. The rout was on. Maxentius' legionari had begun to withdraw to the water where they didn't have enough space to regroup properly. The main parts of Gaius' lines were close behind and pressing. Thousands of the usurper's men were soon to have no choice but to jump into the deepest part of the Tiber. Others were already dropping their weapons and begging for their lives, which were seldom granted.

Space cleared around Constantine's unit, as the fighting around them waned. Ablabius was still distraught, muttering curses at himself and the gods. Constantine saw this and tried to assure him: "My friend, we have tomorrow—for you have lived today. When we capture the usurper, he will be yours."

"Thank you, Imperator." And he turned to the others, "Thank you all...."

The others were watching Vibius, who had picked up a bow. Maxentius was near the midway point of the makeshift bridge— slightly more than a two hundred cubits away. The shot would test the accuracy of a very good archer, but it was possible. Vibius quickly chose the best arrow from a fallen archer's quiver. In one motion he tested the tension of the string and loaded the arrow. Then he arched his entire body to account for the trajectory and released.

Midway through the arrow's flight, Vibius said, "It will be short, by a couple of hands."

He was right. The arrow was short of the usurper's head. But it was not short of the usurper's horse. Half a pes of iron, wood and feathers lodged deep into its haunch. The horse reared to a nearly vertical position on the less-than-stable bridge and fell to its side, throwing itself and Maxentius into the Tiber.

The soldiers screamed with joy. But kept watching. The Praetorian Guards at the side of the Bridge pulled the wounded horse from the water and led it away. But they didn't see the usurper—or any other man—climb out of the water.

"No one swims in full armor," said Gaius, walking up them. His large chest was still heaving, his body and armor were covered with the enemy's blood. He'd seen the shot. "Vibius, I want you with me when I am being pulled into the depths of Hades!"

There was still some fighting going on around the near side of the Bridge. But it was dying down quickly. Constantine watched for a few more minutes then decided to go back to the command tent ahead of the Centurions. They would be reporting back with estimates of the casualties—and questions about when Constantine planned to enter Rome.

"Gaius, when you've gathered your breath, go down to the Bridge and retrieve Maxentius' body. I want to be sure that that fish didn't get away. And make sure no glory-seekers decide to come back across."

"By your order, Imperator."

Constantine signaled that the horns sound to order reassembly of the legions for headcount. He sent his standard bearer holding the Labarum ahead to the command tent, so the centurions would know where to report.

As his bodyguards gathered their horses, Constantine bent over to draw in the dirt a sketch of how he felt the army should march into Rome.

Fifty cubits away, on a small hill, one of Maxentius' archers shook his head as he awoke. He'd been hit by a club and his leg had been broken by a charging horse. Part of shin bone was exposed. His head and leg both throbbed terribly—but he was alive. As he looked around, he saw mostly bodies. Men and horses. He sat up a bit, against a dead horse. There was a Christian priest nearby. Some medics were farther away. And there was a group of Constantine's soldiers beyond that. One of them looked important, perhaps a dux. His armor was finer, but bloody. He was kneeling, drawing in the dirt. He couldn't be too important, though, because there was no standard bearer and his helmet didn't have a dark red or purple plume. Next to the kneeling one was a large black sagittari, holding a bow.

The archer knew he was likely to die—either from his wounds or his captors. He had no way to escape. So he would shoot the dux and receive the glory of Apollo. He had two arrows left. He slowly pulled his bow up to his midsection.

Constantine finished his explanation and stood up, forcing the ever-too-close Vibius to step back.

As the archer pulled back his arrow in the bow, Vibius caught the motion he recognized immediately from the corner of his eye. In a flash, Vibius was in front of Constantine—and pushing the Emperor to the ground.

The arrow hit Vibius below the shoulder blade and came out a half a pes from the center of his chest.

Constantine sprang up, running towards the archer, screaming obscenities.

The archer reached for his other arrow, bungling it slightly. He was disappointed that he'd shot a fellow African and surprised to see the Priest running toward him to his side. By the time he looked forward again, his time was over. The dux was upon him.

Constantine grabbed the archer by his chest armor, picked him up and threw him against a nearby rock, screaming at him the whole time. The archer made a sickening moan and rolled to the ground. Ablabius and Quintus took turns beating him and then dragged him back to where Vibius lay.

Constantine was already back, next to his fallen guard. "Vibius! Vibius, my brother. Talk to me!"

Vibius' eyes opened for an instant and he said calmly, "Owed to you, Imperator. Owed to you." His eyes shut and he was gone.

Constantine cried like he hadn't since he'd been a child. As the tears poured down his cheeks, he made the sign of the cross over the guard's body, as he'd seen Ossius do so many times.

As he stood, he looked up at Quintus—the quietest of his guards, holding the offending archer. Tears streaming down his cheeks, as well. Constantine then turned to Ossius, "I would like Vibius to have a service, as the Nazarene would have."

Ossius paused, at first not sure what Constantine meant. Then he realized he meant a Christian service of final rites. He said in a quiet voice, "Of course, Imperator. But Vibius was not baptized."

"Then baptize him," Constantine said curtly.

The Emperor turned back to the archer, held up by two of his bodyguards. "Before the hour is out, you will beg for death. Quintus, nail him to the large horse stake by my tent."

The sun was fading and an October chill was evident. The day was still bright but the orange tinge of fall was developing.

All four palatini looked forward to nailing the archer's hands to the tall stake not far from Constantine's tent. After tying a rope around his chest, Quintius held the archer's hands behind the post. Appius drove a large stake through both hands into the wooden post. The screams from the archer had just begun. A long line had developed of all ranks from the army who had heard of Vibius' death. But the Dux and Constantine's guards were to go first.

Gaius started. He used his dagger to cut off the tip of the hated one's index finger so that in the afterlife he wouldn't be able to hold an arrow. Ablabius punctured one of his eyes. Tiberus used a sharp arrow head to cut an x on his chest over his heart so that the gods would have a bullseye. The object was pain without a tremendous loss of blood. They didn't want him to die quite yet.

The rest of the troops started to file by, leaving their mark on the hated sagittari.

Constantine met with his Dux and the senior centurions with the cries of the archer echoing in the background. Constantine's losses were less than 2,000. The other side had lost as many as 20,000. The majority of Maxentius' loses were due to drowning in the Tiber—as Gaius' legionari had pursued the retreating troops to the water's edge. Three centurions who knew the Dux of Maxentius were dispatched inside the walls with instructions for how the other side could retrieve their dead. They also were to discuss preparations for tomorrow's grand entrance. Constantine's dead and any that were unclaimed were to be burned in funeral pyres which would start that evening.

All equipment from the soldiers, dead or alive, was to be cleaned, inventoried and extra equipment warehoused.

Constantine would enter Rome mid-morning the following day, following all his troops. He would attend a public victory ceremony at noon. Then, there would be a meeting on the Senate floor afterward. Several hundred senior centurions would circulate in the crowd to ensure none of the remaining Praetorian Guard would attempt to kill Constantine.

As they discussed their plans, the archer's cries faded to groans.

After over an hour, the meeting finished. There was still no sign of Maxentius' body. Troubling. Constantine walked out of the tent and glanced at the blood-covered mass held up by the gleaming red rope. He kept his eyes on it, watching to see if the chest still rose for air. It did.

There were over a thousand of his troops, mostly sagittari, in a line stretching down into the camp. Each man waiting for his turn to make a small cut. Constantine looked down the line and recognized a tall, mixed-race North African holding a javelin. It was Jonas, a distant relative of Vibius—cousin or nephew, he couldn't remember which. But Jonas had revered his Vibius.

"Jonas, I am sorry for our loss. More sorry than you can imagine."

"Yes. Dominus." The young man said, nervously. He had only spoken to Constantine once, with his cousin nearby. He wasn't used to being addressed by a living god.

"Jonas, are you as good as Vibius with a javelin?"

"No, Dominus."

Constantine chuckled at his honesty. "Are you good enough to hit a target at 20 cubits?"

"Yes, Dominus." Jonas wasn't sure what 20 cubits were. But he followed Constantine's eye and immediately understood what the target was.

Constantine reached for the javelin of one of Jonas' companions. He lifted it and found its balance point. Then he stretched his arm, feeling the muscles in his forearm and below his shoulder. He nodded toward the archer and told Jonas, "You aim high. In the chest. I will aim lower."

They threw simultaneously. A uniform thud indicated that each had hit his mark. The troops roared.

A thin sliver of the moon could be seen in the Eastern sky, as the sun's glow was still barely noticeable to the West. Thousands of soldiers watched as Ossius washed Vibius' body, poured holy water over his brow, anointed him with oil and prayed for all to hear that God would accept him into His Kingdom. After the sacraments, Vibius' body was placed on a pyre. It was consumed by fire in a few minutes.

Although Ossius preferred burial for Christians, Constantine had decided—and he had agreed—that cremation with his fellow fallen soldiers was appropriate.

The battlefield was aglow with mass pyres burning, consuming the dead. Pyres would be burning for several days. Carcasses of the dead horses were also burned, after any edible meat had been butchered by the cooks. Aniketos, the knife-wielding senior cook, could butcher a horse before most men would finish the first cut.

Three days was the usual time. If the bodies were left for more than three days, the stench of the rotting flesh would be overwhelming.

After solemn ceremonies at their dead friends' pyres, many of the soldiers were celebrating with food and wine. Constantine seldom participated—other than a quick swallow of wine when a bottle was presented, as a sign of goodwill.

As Ossius and Constantine walked back to the encampment, the Emperor asked the priest, "Where is Vibius? With that prayer, does he enter the Kingdom of the Nazarene?"

"I don't know, my Imperator."

"Why not? What is the delay? What do your holy rules tell us?"

"As we have discussed, it is written in early manuscripts that Jesus rose three days after being crucified. He sent his apostles to spread the word of His resurrection and then returned to Heaven. In order to join Him there, one must recognize Him as our Lord. And live a Christian life."

"And a Christian life would be?"

The priest hesitated for a moment. They had been over this many times. "Obey the Commandments of Moses. And, more important, follow the teachings of Jesus. Particularly His instructions that we honor God. Forgive others. And treat others as we would want ourselves treated."

"Yes. Good words. Vibius may have heard of the Nazarene, but he didn't know much of His teachings. So, it is impossible for Vibius to enter His Kingdom?"

"It is actually His Father's Kingdom."

The Emperor flashed an impatient glance at the priest, who nodded instinctively.

"No one knows. My own belief is that it is unlikely that a non-Christian can enter the Kingdom of Heaven. But I also recognize that there is another interpretation. In the translations from the early scripture, it is impossible to tell when one must recognize and follow Jesus. It may be at the very instant of death. Vibius may have died, immediately met Jesus and Satan and chosen to follow Jesus. In what seems to us like a blink of an eye. Certainly, his act of self-sacrifice would commend him."

"Then I believe he is in God's Kingdom." Constantine responded.

They walked along in silence for a few steps. Constantine looked back at his bodyguards, who were trailing father behind than usual and in deep conversation. Then, he said to Ossius, "By the way, thank you for this afternoon on the hillside. You diverted the archer's attention. Is that how a bishop is taught to act?"

"I was upset."

This time, the Emperor nodded. "Tell me, if you had reached that archer before the rest of us, what would you have done? Hit him with your cross?" Both laughed.

They entered the camp and separated for their respective tents. Before he'd settled in his tent, Constantine grew anxious and decided that the he wasn't tired enough to sleep. He would return to his command tent and watch the pyres. This usually had a calming effect on him.

As he walked toward his command tent, he noticed the archer was still hanging on the post. He tensed in anger. He'd told the palatini that he wanted the archer's body thrown to the army's pigs. He prepared to berate the guards but, as he walked closer, he saw that the archer's body was gone. It was merely the bloody ropes that gave the appearance of a body still nailed to the post. A trick of the eye. It had been an exhausting day.

The servants moved his wicker chair, as he instructed, to the entrance of the command tent. And he wrapped himself in a heavy cloak and sat. He watched the ghost-like figures of his caretakers throw bodies on the funeral pyres. Some of the bodies were still surrounded by fellow soldiers giving their last respects. The light from the pyres was not as bright as it had been an hour earlier, but it was brighter than the moon.

The distinctive, sweet odor of burning flesh filled the cool night air. And a mixture of sounds echoed against the city walls and across the plain. Some revelry, some moaning, some bits of conversation. He could hear flashes of his name mentioned among the troops.

He wondered how his troops had won such an overwhelming victory against a massive foe. He'd prepared. He'd studied the battlefield. He'd trusted his generals. But the victory felt...hollow. Though the priest would disagree, the Emperor felt more lucky than blessed.

He knew this hollow feeling well. He'd felt it when his father left to marry Theodora—the sense of overwhelming loss, the taunts and jeers from the garrison soldiers who called him a bastard child. Those jeers were constant. They'd motivated him to improve himself. Make himself stronger. Master the sword and, ever so slowly, earn the respect of the soldiers.

His father returned a few years later, as a general. And, in time, as one of the Augustus—co-emperors. But the happiness didn't last. His father sent him to study and learn in Emperor Galerius' court. It was a rare opportunity; one that confirmed how much influence his father had. Constantine enjoyed learning languages, math, law and— especially—the military training. He was good at it.

There were other lessons, too. Far less enjoyable lessons. Galerius was an unpredictable and brutal emperor. He was an ugly, thick-featured man, who'd come from humble origins in rural Dacia. He ruled by fear, which he used indiscriminately. He would instill fear in Christians by having them massacred—some by wild animals, some by fire, some by soldiers and some by poison. And he always insisted that surviving Christians watch their fellows die.

At his cruelest, Galerius sentenced people to death almost randomly. It wasn't just Christians. Common people that he disliked or for whom he developed distrust, real or imagined, would often end up dead at his whim. He couldn't prey so freely on senators or other elite Romans, but he could terrorize them—justice, he claimed, for the way Trajan had treated the Dacians generations before.

Later, near the end of his life, Galerius would stop terrorizing Christians. To maintain his political power, the old man would want to be seen as tolerant. A laughable proposition.

There were times when Galerius tried to humiliate the young Constantine in court, calling him a hostage and a pawn by which he could manipulate Constantius. When Constantine refused to be baited by these insults, Galerius looked for other ways to plant fear in him. Because Constantine had developed a good reputation with the sword, Galerius would order him to "spar" with seasoned soldiers and gladiators. But these fights were not sparring. The weapons were real—and the loser usually died.

Later, even more dangerous: Galerius would send young Constantine out into the streets of Nicomedia or Rome to arrest individuals suspected of sympathizing with the political opposition. These individuals could be citizens or non-citizens. They had little to lose in trying to kill an imperial agent. Constantine detested these orders, particularly when they involved arresting whole families. And children. He knew their fates would ultimately be death—as would be his, if he didn't complete the mission.

When Constantine took his father's place as one of the Augustus, he vowed that he would not rule by cruelty and fear, as Galerius had. He would support the laws and the institutions that had made the Empire great. He would work with the Senate, seek its counsel. Not try to terrorize its members.

Personally he would keep his son, Crispus, close to him and give the boy the love, support and training that he'd wanted from his own father. Crispus was 12 years old—and Constantine could remember clearly when he'd been 12 years old. His father had left. And the pangs of the hollowness had come.

The hollowness wasn't always with him. Sometimes, he felt blessed. A few years before, he'd had a dream—a vivid dream—in which the Nazarene had spoken to him. Had told him to protect those who needed his protection. Had it been merely a dream? Or, as Ossius argued, had the Nazarene communicated with him through the dream? And, if Ossius was right, was Vibius with the Nazarene now? Could Vibius also communicate through a dream? Ossius had said the Kingdom wasn't like the Greek afterlife—but why not?

A loud crack came from one of the pyres. It made him jolt up in his chair. He'd been drifting into half-sleep. His neck was stiff on one side and he could feel the muscles down the opposite side of his back. And his knee, again.

His groggy thoughts about the Nazarene and Vibius led him to one conclusion. His Mother was right, the visions he had and his victories proved it. He needed to pay more attention to the Nazarene's teachings. He needed to understand them. Even to support and promote them. But that would take time. The Nazarene's faith was merely a cult throughout most of the Empire, not like the politically supported and organized religion of the Roman Gods.

He stood slowly, looked once more at the orange pyres, registered the pain of missing Vibius, and headed back to his bed.

Rome, Italia
Morning, October 29, 1065 AUC (312 AD)

Constantine woke before sunrise with some stiffness, a headache… and the feeling of hollowness still lingering in him. For a moment, he expected to see Vibius standing outside his tent. Instead, it was Quintius—quickly joined by Appius.

They walked to the latrine. None felt like talking. After relieving himself, Constantine splashed his face with fresh water. Dawn was just overcoming the darkness as they walked to the mess area. Aniketos had prepared piles of thinly cut cooked meat, grains, fruit, yogurt, juice and diluted wine. Most of the legions prepared their own food. But it would be supplemented by Aniketos' staff— particularly when meat was plentiful.

"Aniketos, only you can carve like this!" Constantine yelled to the Greek cook, holding up a wafer-thin slice of meat on the point of his dagger before placing it on his metal plate.

"It is in honor of your great victory yesterday, Imperator!"

Constantine walked with his food to the highest point in the center of the camp and sat on the ground. Quintus and Appius sat on their side of him. In a few minutes, they were joined by Sevius and Titus—even though Titus had guarded Constantine's tent most of the night. As they ate, they watched the waking troops start their morning preparations for the entrance into Rome. Soldiers were cleaning their armor, touching up the CHI RHO insignia on their shields and sharpening their swords and javelins.

Rome had been the center of the Empire for centuries but had fallen in political importance over the last hundred years. Constantine—like most soldiers—considered Rome a place of weak men, whorish women and lying politicians. The century after Marcus Aurelius had been known as "the years of decadence" and that decadence applied to the rulers and general population alike.

Sexuality in the Empire focused on dominance and wasn't confined to gender or even species. As long as the male was dominant, he could have sex with whomever or whatever he chose— excluding fellow Roman citizens, their wives and children. Any others, slaves, prostitutes, entertainers, non-citizens or conquered armies were all acceptable objects of a citizen's carnal attention. With various emperors, the list extended to sisters, brothers, children and a variety of animals.

Most Roman men considered it shameful to be on the receiving end of a sexual tryst. But there were a few sodomites in every crowd—and more than a few in Rome.

Rome was also considered decadent because it had seen so many severe Christian persecutions. While the rest of the Empire was usually more tolerant of all manner of cults and religions, Rome had remained tyrannical against the followers of the Nazarene.

Constantine knew this history well. Nero enjoyed the evenings around his Imperial residence in Rome at night, lite by the burning bodies of Christians on stakes. After Nero had burned down the City and blamed them, Christians had been persecuted throughout the Empire. The persecutions had reached their climax during the rule of Diocletian, over 200 years after Nero. At that point, the Empire had become so large—and tyrannies so commonplace—that the Emperor decided that it could not be ruled by one man in one location. The senate tentatively proposed a solution in which the Empire would be ruled by three emperors, the Augustus', who would serve as checks against each other's excesses. The Roman elite called this solution the "recovery of the Empire." Diocletian had accepted the arrangement, and he claimed it had been his plan all along.

Diocletian's successor was the brutal Galerius.

The geography of the Empire had changed since Nero's time. It had spread all directions, but particularly north and east. Rome was now in the western portion of the Empire. Nicomedia—where Galerius' court had been and where Constantine had studied Latin, Greek and philosophy—was closer to the center. In many ways, it was more cosmopolitan. On the other side of the Bosporus from Nicomedia was the Greek town of Byzantium.

The Empire's economy had changed, too. Manufacturing and trade had become more important than farming. Building materials, road construction, iron, jewelry, wine and food were major industries. All were taxed heavily. But even those taxes weren't enough.

In relative terms, the government—especially the Roman Army—dwarfed other employers. Its expenses were massive. Without conquests, and the plunder that resulted, the Army couldn't pay its soldiers. So the Empire expanded into new territories. The Army's size required either that or taking the property of wealthy citizens. Or other Emperors.

As they finished their meal, Quintus broke the silence.

"Imperator, we need to discuss your protection."

"Yes, Imperator." Sevius agreed. "We are too small a group to keep you alive. Yesterday was dangerous. Even if Vibius were still with us, we would need more guards."

"Appius. Titus. I assume you agree?" Constantine asked, making quick eye contact with each.

"We do," they responded—almost at the same time.

"We discussed this last night, after you went to your tent," Titus said. "There were a dozen times yesterday that I thought the surge of the Praetorian Guards would overpower us, Dominus. They recognized you and were clearly trying to kill you."

Appius interrupted: "Perhaps we need more traditional palatini. Perhaps some mounted sagittari, like the Persians use."

Constantine nodded while his guards spoke. Then he stood up and stretched his back. And his right knee. "I am not sure about the mounted archers. But you are all correct about yesterday. We will increase our numbers. I have been thinking about creating a special guard unit for the Labarum. Perhaps our new guards could come from that." He stretched his neck—and then fixed his eyes on the main gate ahead of them. "Let us discuss it more after today's events."

Appius stepped toward him. "Dominus, I believe strongly that we should use mounted sagittari. We have discussed this among ourselves many times. Vibius was for the idea. And I agreed with him."

"That is because you have no clue how the Army actually works," Titus jeered. "We are as strong as our legionari are trained!"

"Wars change," Appius snapped. "And you, on your feet, are no match for a horse. Or an arrow."

"Enough!" laughed Constantine, to diffuse their anger. "I understand both of your points. If and when we face the Persians again, we will revisit this."

Gaius approached them from the mess area, his wide gait betraying his minor injuries from the day before. "Where have you four ghosts been hiding our Imperator?" the general demanded. "I had to ask the damn cook where you had him."

"I'm impressed, Gaius, that at your age you even remember who our Imperator is," Appius said, still choleric from his exchange with Titus.

"Mind your words, you little cricket. I remember many things. I remember when you were a runt of a soldier, just learning how to fight. And I may still snap your neck." Gaius reached one of his huge arms toward Appius, who—even four feet away—still backed away slightly.

All the palatini and most of the *hastiliari* (weapons instructors) had had to train with Gaius. He was an excellent but unforgiving teacher and almost impossible to beat in hand-to-hand combat. Even though he'd seen more than 50 summers. What he lacked in height, he made up with width. And his stout body showed the scars of innumerable wounds—some from training. He'd bellowed the same lesson to generations of soldiers and instructors: "Better that I beat you here in camp than an enemy beats you in the field." If someone got bruised or cut in the exchange, so be it.

Only Quintus and Sevius would spar with the old general these days. And Sevius warned anyone who would listen to stay away from his hands.

"This is why I look forward to retiring. There are no men left in this Army," Gaius said with mock dejection, as he looked at Appius.

"I understand your pain, Gaius," Constantine answered. "But, in retirement, you'll become a bodyguard, too. You will protect my Mother." Gaius was fiercely loyal to Constantine's family and worshiped Helena.

"I am undeserving of such a privilege." Gaius said. "The reason I was looking for you, Dominus, is because we found Maxentius' body at first light. It was wedged between the boat and the old bridge. What do you want us to do with it?" Gaius asked.

Constantine thought for a moment, looking at the gate again.

"Cut off his head and put it on a lance. I'll carry it in the parade."

"I will get a medic's saw," Gaius suggested.

"No." Constantine cut him off quickly. "Hack it off with a sword. I don't want it to look pretty. I want a reaction. I want Rome to see that he was killed as brutally as he ruled. And I want them to know that the same will happen to anyone else foolish enough to confront us."

"Consider it done, Dominus," Gaius answered with enthusiasm. As he started to walk away he stopped and turned back to Constantine. "Dominus, we had a great victory yesterday. By the gods, I am grateful for it. But we suffered a tremendous loss. Vibius was one of the best soldiers I have ever seen. And I hate it now that I never told him how good he was."

"You speak for all of us, Gaius," Constantine said. His guards nodded or murmured in agreement.

"May he be blessed, wherever he is." With that, Gaius headed back toward the river.

Constantine knew that Gaius had meant to be encouraging. But, as he walked back to his tent with Quintus to put on his freshly cleaned armor for the parade, sadness swelled within him again. He did not look forward to the parade. Nor the meeting with the Senate. He said "too many people with their hands out," and Quintus looked confused.

Constantine nodded in the direction of the City walls. Then Quintus seemed to understand.

An hour later, standing by his command tent, Constantine watched the formation of the legions assembling on the battlefield. They would cross the Milvian Bridge and enter Rome. Gaius' engineers had repaired the damaged span of the original bridge with large wood girders. This would support the troops crossing—and they wouldn't have to rely on Maxentius' narrow makeshift bridge.

He walked down to the battlefield and the near side of the formation, where Gaius had his chariot. Closer to the field, the smell of burning flesh was still strong. Dead bodies were still being fed to the funeral pyres. And the vultures of death had arrived, seemingly thousands of them, picking at anything edible on the battlefield. He stopped short of the chariot and called to Gaius, who was about ten cubits away standing with the other Dux. They seemed to be making fun of Ablabius, who was dressed in immaculate and polished armor and whose head didn't have a hair out of place. A Greek.

"Gaius, why did you choose this?" Constantine asked.

"My apologies, Imperator. I assumed you would ride in it. Most other Emperors I have served preferred chariots for parades. Your father did."

Constantine didn't say anything. He was thinking that there was something…Greek…about riding in the chariot in a parade.

"But your horse is here, if you want to take him."

Before Constantine could reply, a centurion arrived on horseback with Maxentius' head on the end of a lance. Gaius and Constantine looked at it and then at each other.

"This is good, Gaius. And I think it will be even better if I am higher, so let's take the horse. Plus, the horse was in the battle. He also deserves some recognition!" He ran his hand along the horse's flank. It was wet. The horse was tired.

"Yes, Imperator!" Gaius answered, grinning.

Several buccinas sounded, and the legions started to move over the Milvian Bridge and toward the walls of Rome. The legionari marched first through the large gate, called Porta Flaminia, in the Aurelian Wall. They were followed by the sagittari then the equiti. Constantine, led by his generals and guards, was last to enter the City.

The sound was a striking thing. Constantine heard the cheers—felt them, really—from outside, as the first soldiers marched into the City. It sounded like roar of lines charging in a heated battle. And it grew louder as each unit entered. By the time he and his generals passed through Porta Flaminia, the roar was almost deafening. He had to use hand signals to keep the Dux at an even pace.

And those signals weren't easy. He held the lance with his right arm, its butt resting between the two front posts of his saddle. And he tipped it forward a bit, so that people on all sides could see the usurper's head.

It was difficult to make out any single thing amidst the roar—but he heard a few words. "Jupiter." "Hercules." "The Macedonian."

Their route passed the original Circus Maximus and then turned north to the Coliseum. As they rode, Constantine became more relaxed. He waved with his free hand, in the manner that his mother had taught him when he'd been a small boy. Chin up. Look forward. Hand open, palm forward for all Romans to see.

He showed no sign of his headache—which lingered, dully, at the back near his neck.

The roar receded a bit, as they proceeded through the City. But it never died away. Wine was everywhere. They were drinking it in simple cups and fine chalices. Bowls. Gourds. And it wasn't diluted. Full strength, fueling their adulation. How many barrels had they drunk? And how many had they spilled? There seemed as much wine on the ground as in their bellies.

They slowed their pace as they passed the Coliseum. Constantine practically stopped. He made sure to sway the usurper's head slowly from one side to the other, to allow ample viewing. The roar rose again.

He allowed himself a slight smile. Some said speeches were politics. He didn't agree—*this* was politics. He started toward the Senate Curia.

The streets between the Coliseum and the Senate Curia were packed with people eager to see—and touch—Constantine. Initially, he didn't mind Romans reaching out to his horse. Or his legs. But the crush of the crowd soon made moving difficult.

Gaius followed his battlefield instincts and ordered a legion of soldiers to march in front of Constantine in wedge formation and part the crowd. This made it easier for the Emperor, his generals and bodyguards to pass. The procession stopped while the soldiers cleared the street to the Curia.

Although the Senate was still an elected body, it was largely powerless. Ever since Mark Antony ordered the death of Cicero, over 300 years earlier, power had shifted to the Emperor. Constantine's plan was to give some power back to the Senate. This plan didn't follow from any great reverence for old men in gaudy tunics; it followed from his realization that he would need a bureaucracy supporting him—especially because he planned to spend little time in Rome.

Like most soldiers, Constantine had no patience for bureaucracy. But one of his generals had a gift for working with politicians. Ablabius. The Greek. The man who'd tried so hard to kill Maxentius. In a room of politicians, Ablabius became a different man.

And the other generals knew this. Outside the Coliseum, while they waited for the streets to be cleared, Constantine handed off the lance and cleaned Maxentius' blood from his arm, he barked out orders to several centurions. "Have this paraded around the

City while we meet with the Senate. Then deliver it to Carthage to remind them that I expect their loyalty."

Gaius said, "Ablabius, you used to live here. You know some of these Senators. Tell me, which will you sweet-talk? And which should I take care of with my sword?"

Tiberus laughed. "You will need a lot of help, old friend. I've yet to meet a Roman politician who didn't deserve the sharp end of your sword. It is a strange profession that lives off of empty promises!"

"We need them," Ablabius said. "They manage the purse strings. They pass the laws and preside as magistrates over trials. They are the gears by which this City—and the Empire—works."

Gaius almost hissed, "You could get the crossing sweepers that followed our horses today to do a better job than these anus cavus."

The Greek smiled at Gaius. "I didn't say they did a good job. I said we need them. If we concentrate on the ten or twelve senators who have the most influence, the Emperor's plans will go smoothly."

"The citizens will expect a lot of promises," Constantine said. He'd cleaned most of the usurper's blood from his arm and straightened his tunic to prepare to address the Senate. "They will want to hear about new public building projects—which is the tradition. But there's more. They want a new money system. They want legal reform. The usurper acted like a tyrant. There are three things I must do to cure this wound. One: I will dissolve the Praetorian Guard and confiscate all of their property. This will be a popular change. Two: I will return property taken by the usurper to the rightful owners. Especially Christians. Three: I will decree religious freedom as law in the Western Empire."

"The Senate will agree to your points, Imperator. And quickly," Ablabius said. "You have unlimited political power right now. But getting these things implemented may be more difficult."

"What do you suggest we do, Ablabius?"

On Constantine's hand signal, the procession started to march to the entrance of the Curia as the legionari opened its doors.

Ablabius kept talking, paying no attention to the soldiers and cheering citizens all around them. "As I said, there are about a dozen senators who are the most influential. It is important that each of us spends some time with each of them. I will point them out while the Emperor is formally welcomed. Perhaps we should have dinner with these 12 influencers. They will be even more agreeable after several bottles of wine. Then, they will debate the points—and vote for them in a day or two. I will keep in touch with them to make sure the Senate votes...properly."

"What's this dozen?' Tiberus asked, frustrated. "I thought there were over a thousand senators."

"Diocletian cut their number to about 600. And there are usually only about 200 active. Of course, we'll probably see more than that today because all of them want something from Constantine. The important thing, Imperator, is that you don't engage in any political debate. Greet them in a friendly way—ask about their wives or children. But don't discuss proposals or ask them for their support. Let us do that. Such details are beneath you." The Greek was becoming a bit self-impressed.

"We've introduced Senate bills before." Constantine mockingly stated, looking over to Quintus, whose only reaction was to raise an eyebrow. Then the Emperor said, "But we will follow your lead, Ablabius. And I have asked Ossius to join us. To help persuade the Senate on the religious issues. Those old men have a history of patronage to pagans. There is probably a good amount of money changing hands in those matters. Now there will be...less of that. And the owners of those hands may be unhappy."

As they headed into the Curia, Constantine looked around and caught a quick glimpse of Maxentius' head on the lance. He had a fleeting thought. Would his wife, Fausta, blame him for the deaths of her father and—now—her brother, too? Probably not.

Unlike many aristocratic women, she'd always been a loyal wife. He couldn't see her turning against him.

The Senate meeting went smoothly. The Greek's strategy of isolating and engaging the influencers worked. The project that was most important to the Senate was a substantial increase in the size of the Circus Maximus. It would be costly. But it would make an impression on the City and the citizens. Constantine agreed to support the project. The Senate also approved a commemorative Arch of Constantine to be built facing the statue of Sol Invictus, the relatively recent incarnation of an all-powerful pagan sun god. This version was a patron of soldiers, so the association made sense. Constantine accepted the honor with humility. He had never been comfortable receiving accolades like this—but he had learned to tolerate them, as an important ritual.

It was also resolved that new coins would have Constantine's profile against a background of Sol Invictus' aura, a halo.

The Senate also passed Constantine's religious freedom proclamation, though this matter involved some debate. Quite a few of the old men still were distrustful of followers of the Nazarene. Constantine agreed to declare, with Senate approval, that once a week there would be day honoring Sol Invictus when no one but farmers would work.

The Senate seemed relieved that he didn't make demands or act like a victorious tyrant. He'd never been that kind of winner or Emperor. His father had taught him to treat people kindly. That made it easier to incorporate them into his forces.

After an extravagant dinner with his generals and several of the influential Senators, Constantine and his company walked the short distance to the Lateran Estate where the usurper had been living. It would now be his palace when he was in Rome.

Adiutor Aelius, the chief of his domestic staff had spent the day removing Maxentius' more extravagant furnishings and preparing the palace in the simpler manner that Constantine preferred.

A company of legionari had been waiting outside of the banquet rooms where the Emperor and senators had dined. The soldiers shuffled into formation, surrounding Constantine, his generals and his bodyguards. Amidst the soldiers, the generals and bodyguards formed a smaller circle around Constantine and Ossius— who walked together.

"Ossius, are you satisfied with the proclamation?" asked Ablabius, walking a step ahead of the Emperor and the priest.

"I am satisfied with the words, Ablabius. My sense of the Senators is that they believe this is just one of those idiosyncrasies of the latest leader. And that it, too, shall pass."

Constantine cut in: "That would be their mistake."

"Lack of faith is human nature, Imperator," Ossius said. "Only time will show them the power of our Lord. Of course, one would expect that, after three centuries of persecuting Christ's followers, the Senate would give more credit to the tenacity of His message."

They walked for a few paces and then Ablabius asked another question: "Would it have helped to have Pope Miltiades or perhaps Sylvester—his Presbyter—at the Senate today? I don't know the Pope but Sylvester is a great priest. A persuasive man. He baptized me."

To Constantine, this sounded like a political discussion masquerading as a religious one.

Ossius answered Ablabius: "He is a great priest. And he has been extremely supportive of Miltiades through his illness. But neither he nor the Pope is comfortable with how they should interface with the political system. Sylvester has said this to me, directly. But he believes that religious freedom must be throughout the Empire, not just in Rome. Otherwise, Christians can simply be shipped off to the countryside to be persecuted."

Constantine followed quickly with a question of his own. "What if we can convince Emperors Licinius and Daia to embrace the same concept of religious freedom for the Eastern Empire as we have now in the West?"

"That would be incredible. Unbelievable. I say this as someone who remembers the persecutions in the East—only a short time ago. It would a miracle, really," Ossius said. "But, from all that I've heard about Emperor Daia, even less likely."

The group entered the Estate's courtyard. It was clean and free of Maxentius' decadent décor. Constantine's efficient Adiutor Aelius was waiting with staff people who showed each guest to his bedroom. Constantine bade his Generals good rest and saw that his bodyguards were prepared for their nighttime shifts. Some of the ordinary soldiers encamped in the courtyard; others stood watch around the Estate's walls. A few took leave and headed out into the City.

It was very late when Constantine finally closed the doors to his chambers. They were elegant. The bed was large and fine. There was a private latrine with flowing water. The staff had left fruit and wine. The figs caught his eye but he was too tired to eat them. He was even more tired than he'd been the night before—after the battle. At least the headache was gone.

He usually bathed before going to sleep, but the long dinner had taken all that time. He'd have a bath in morning. Instead, he barely managed to strip off his sandals and clothes before he collapsed on the bed. He slept soundly for the first time in many nights.

Milan, Italia
February, 1066 AUC (313 AD)

Emperor Licinius relaxed in an upholstered chair near the fireplace in the large study of the palace. It had snowed the night before and now, although it was mid-day, the palace was not warming up. Licinius did not like cold weather. And he made sure everyone knew it.

It had been warmer two days before, when he'd married Constantia, half-sister of Constantine. She was an attractive woman, less than half his age. So Licinius considered himself lucky. He'd seen political marriages much worse than this.

Marrying Constantine's sister had turned a rival into something closer to an ally. And this new alliance would likely keep Maximinus Daia on the east side of the Bosporus. There was no way that pagan would risk invading Licinius's part of the Empire now. Word had spread about Constantine's crushing victory over Maxentius. No one, not even Daia, wanted his head paraded around on the end of a lance.

Galerius, who has been Licinius' mentor, had made only one mistake in all his years in power: He should have killed Daia. He'd said as much himself. But he'd hesitated. Perhaps he'd feared Daia, whose reputation for brutality had given many men pause.

Licinius and Constantine were unlikely allies. And this bothered Licinius. He was a big man—older, taller and considerably heavier that Constantine. While Constantine had retained a soldier's spartan lifestyle and demeanor, Licinius enjoyed living well and had accumulated great wealth from the Eastern Empire. He didn't spend on public works, as Constantius had taught Constantine to do.

As Licinius watched the fire and mulled his political circumstances, he heard laughter echo in from the hallway. A few moments later, Adiutor Aelius and Ossius walked in.

"What is so funny on a day that no one can get warm?" Licinius demanded.

One of the men was chastened by Licinius, one was not. Ossius responded casually: "Our friend and host Aelius was commenting that bishops are easy guests to take care of—and was inquiring whether there were any positions available in Cordova."

"You must never have had Constantine's cousin Eusebius as a guest then," Licinius sensed that his response was too angry. He needed to match the priest's levity. "I have never seen such a bishop. He never seems to sit still." He ended with a somewhat forced laugh.

Ossius nodded for a moment and then accepted Licinius' effort at good will: "Indeed he is, Augustus. And, now that you've mentioned him, why isn't restless Eusebius here?"

Licinius sat up in his chair. It was as close as he would come to standing, in recognition of a priest and a servant. "Apparently a bishop in Syria died. And they needed Eusebius there to help install the replacement."

An awkward silence followed. Aelius recognized the opportunity to break in with small talk: "Augustus, is there anything I can get you from the kitchen? You have not had any lunch."

"Just more heat," Licinius said—ending, again, with a forced laugh. "I will wait to have something to eat until Constantine gets back with the women."

Aelius stoked the fire and added a small log. Meanwhile, Ossius sat in one of the chairs next to Licinius.

"I'll have them bring in some more wood for the fire, Augustus. And I'll send word as soon as Constantine and the other approach." He nodded and left through a back door.

Ossius looked at several scrolls that he had been carrying. He'd come in to talk business.

But Licinius would have preferred to be left alone. "Riding horses in the snow. I have no idea what they were thinking."

"Some enjoy riding as sport." Ossius said, distractedly and almost in a whisper. Then he found the scroll he wanted. "Dominus, I have rewritten the Edict we discussed after the wedding. And I reviewed it with Emperor Constantine last night. I would like to read it to you to make sure you are in agreement with its current form."

"Fine."

Ossius began,

When I, Constantine Augustus, as well as I,
Licinius Augustus, fortunately met near Milan,

and were considering everything that pertained to the public welfare and security, we thought, among other things which we saw would be for the good of many, those regulations pertaining to the reverence of the Divinity ought certainly to be made first, so that we might grant to the Christians and others full authority to observe that religion which each preferred—

Licinius raised his hand. "Can I see that part?"

Ossius handed him the scroll. He knew that Licinius did not read Latin well, so the gesture seemed somewhat false.

"Why do you mention 'the Divinity' here?" Licinius asked, pointing to the word. "Our purpose is to call for tolerance of all religions. Doesn't this point only to the Christian God?"

"Yes. It does," Ossius said, impressed that Licinius had noticed. "Constantine wanted that included for his specific faith. If you think it is exclusionary, we can discuss the matter with him."

Licinius laughed again, less awkwardly. "Maybe later." And he handed the scroll back to Ossius. "Go on."

Ossius continued. Partly through the second paragraph, Licinius raised his hand again and asked Ossius to reread one sentence.

Ossius did:

And since these Christians are known to have possessed not only those places in which they were accustomed to assemble, but also other property, namely the churches, belonging to them as a corporation and not as individuals, all these things which we have included under the above law, you will order to be restored, without any hesitation or controversy at all.

"Who pays for all of this, priest?" Licinius asked.

Ossius cocked his head at the question. It sounded like a trap. "Well, I believe the intent is that the Imperial Treasury will ultimately be responsible."

"Oh," Licinius laughed, sounding disappointed this time. "Go on."

Ossius finished the last few sentences without interruption. Just as he finished, Constantine, Fausta and Constantia burst into the study and headed directly to stand in front of the fire.

"You make this room like ice!" Licinius barked. "Can't you go to another fireplace? Constantine, you are covered with snow. What happened?"

"The guilty parties have been identified. Two females. They will suffer my wrath," Constantine laughed, as he shook snow and slush from his outer tunic.

"My brother has gone mad. He thinks he is an Emperor. Fausta and I had to show him his place," Constantia unwrapped the long scarf from her head and neck and turned her back to the fire, so she could face her new husband. "He's forgotten how our father taught us to treat people who take themselves so seriously."

"You should live with him, sister," Fausta said, archly. "He only relaxes like this when you are around." She smiled when she spoke.

But her tone was less playful than Constantia's.

"We had fun, Licinius. You should have come." Constantia said, kneeling at the side of her husband's chair.

"Fun for you two." Constantine retorted, rubbing his hands at the fire the snow melting and dripping to a pool on the floor by his feet.

Constantia looked back at her brother and Fausta, who were standing on opposite sides of the fireplace. "It's harder to get you to play, brother, than it was to convince father. But I do love it when you finally relax. In those moments, you remind me of him."

"Yes. He was always looking for the bright side of things," Constantine said, turning to face Constantia and Licinius. "It's true that I'm less jovial. And less forgiving. I watched him forgive enemies—who later turned against him again."

Licinius realized this last comment was directed at him. "I knew your father. I met him numerous times in the company of Galerius. He was an easy man to like. Quick sense of humor. But I never doubted that he was formidable. I would have thought long and hard before crossing him."

"All true," Constantine said, somewhat defensively. "My father accepted people's…faults…graciously. He forgave easily. This made him popular. And I have benefited from it. But I don't accept… things…as he did. My father accepted that Galerius kept me as a hostage and a pawn for several years—I would kill anyone who tried to keep my children from me."

Constantia sensed that her brother was getting agitated and tried to calm him. "Brother, you have gifts that go beyond even our father's abilities. He told me so himself. You notice small details on the battlefield and in the Senate that the rest of us miss. And, because of all that, I love when you still play in the snow with me."

"That doesn't look too smart to me. That snow is cold. And it's already cold enough in here next to the fireplace," Licinius replied, with another nervous laugh.

"I told Aelius to bring us something to eat," Constantine said, ignoring Licinius' mock complaints.

Just as Constantine spoke, Aelius and three of his staff entered with large serving plates piled with carved meat, bread and fruit. While they prepared the long table in the center of the room, there was a sound of a single horse—and then several horses—galloping into the courtyard. The sound of men's voices followed; but it was impossible to make out what they were yelling about.

Constantine nodded and Aelius ran out to the courtyard. The others had questioning looks. Constantine, still dripping from the snow, shrugged and turned back to the fire.

Aelius returned shortly with a centurion from Licinius' army. The centurion was surrounded by Constantine's palatini—behind them was a small man wearing a white toga with purple hems.

The centurion spoke first: "Hail, Augustus Licinius. May you have a long and happy married life!"

"Thank you," said Licinius with a laugh. "What news do you bring?"

Constantine's bodyguards stepped back, instinctively, from the centurion. The news was going to be bad.

"Imperator, Emperor Maximinus Daia has crossed the Bosporus from Asia Minor to Byzantium with his army of 60,000 troops."

"What!" Licinius howled in disbelief.

"Yes, Imperator. We rode the day our troops reported it. Three days ago."

Licinius stood, his face red and his fists clenched. "We leave immediately! I will crush that perverted pagan infidel!" He turned to Constantia and took a deep breath before he spoke: "My Dear, I know we had planned to be here another week. But I must leave. You can stay, if you like, and join me after this matter is resolved."

"No, Licinius. I will follow in a day or two. After I have had a chance to get my things organized," she answered. She noticed a long stare from Constantine after she'd answered. So, she took Licinius' arm.

"Licinius, brother. Is there anything you need from me?" Constantine asked.

"No. Not at this point. Daia's brutality does not necessarily translate to an efficient, organized army."

Constantine thought a moment and replied, "Good observation."

As Licinius was leaving the room, Ossius handed Constantine the scroll containing the Edict. Constantine called to Licinius, "Do you want any changes to the Edict?"

"No. It is fine with me," Licinius answered with another nervous laugh. He and Constantia left. His centurion followed them.

Constantine turned toward his palatini, realizing that in the turmoil he had forgotten the small man in the toga. "Magistrate Cato, I am sorry to have ignored you."

"Dominus, it is I that must apologize. I seem to have a habit of appearing at inopportune moments."

Constantine gestured to the long table. "Please join us for lunch. But allow me to postpone our business until tomorrow morning so that my wife and I can help my sister prepare for her travels. Aelius will arrange a room for you."

The guards stayed in the room and positioned themselves near the doors. Constantine and the others took seats at the table.

"Fausta, this is Cato, the Magistrate of Pola and a retired Roman Senator. He is here to discuss judicial cases that are sensitive or out of the ordinary. Ossius, I believe you know the Magistrate." He handed the scroll back to the priest and tapped it briefly in the exchange.

Within a few months, after Licinius' victory over Daia, the Edict of Milan would become law and mark the formal end of the policy of persecution and slaughter of Christians throughout the entire Roman Empire.

Milan, Italia
Next Morning, February, 1066 AUC (313 AD)

Eating his grain cereal breakfast, Constantine sat across from Magistrate Cato. Cato didn't say much. Judicious. Constantine preferred the easy banter of soldiers. "I am sure I have asked you this but have forgotten, Magistrate. How is it that you became the legal guardian of cases that are considered sensitive to the Empire?"

The magistrate took a moment to gather his answer. "It started almost ten years ago, when I was a Senator. Diocletian looked favorably on me, as he did on both your father and Galerius. He saw that the judges could be a significant political force. So, he sought to control them by ordering that they bring cases which could negatively affect the Empire to the Emperor for consultation."

"My father often said that Diocletian was a perceptive man."

"Yes. Very much so. Soon after that, as you know, he reduced the size of the Senate. I took that opportunity to retire and moved to Pola. But my service to the Empire was not finished. Diocletian appointed me Chief Magistrate. And he ordered specifically that I would be the one who briefs the emperors on these unique cases." He said the name "Diocletian" reverently.

"So that is why Ossius and I saw you at Galerius' court."

Cato nodded. "Yes. Diocletian and your father were easy to work with. Perceptive, as you say. Galerius was difficult. Almost all of his rulings were death sentences. Which may be swift justice in the moment but can cause...complexity...in other regards for the Empire."

The Emperor looked hard at the judge. Although he had vowed to avoid Galerius' harsh brutality, Constantine appreciated swift justice. It was effective, especially in ensuring a compliant populous.

Cato seemed to understand that he'd overstepped a boundary. "Augustus, when you were focused on the north, you and I had few occasions to speak. Now that you control Rome, we will have more. Many more."

Constantine smiled. It was predictable—when politicians erred or overstepped, they scurried behind the protection of "Augustus." The title meant they knew their place. "And you sent me three in your letter. That's why we are here. I read your letter, but I read dozens every day. Summarize each of these cases for me again and we will do something about them."

"Certainly. The first one will likely be the most difficult. It involves a group of young men. Twelve of them, between the ages of 18 and 22. All sons of citizens. Four from prominent Roman families. Three others from...reputable...families in the border towns by the Black Sea. These young men traveled as a group and, in their travels, they befriended relatives of Aliquaca. One of the chiefs of the Goths."

Constantine nodded impatiently. He knew very well who Aliquaca was.

"The twelve protested for months, all around Rome, that the Empire should have a better relationship with the Goths. But few listened. The city authorities viewed them as a just fringe group." Cato saw the Emperor's impatience and spoke more quickly. "Two months ago, the twelve went to the border and met with Aliquaca's son and several of his lieutenants. The local military authorities raided the meeting. Aliquaca's son got away. But we captured the twelve and two of the Goth's lieutenants. Under interrogation, they admitted that the twelve had agreed to sneak the Goths into a nearby garrison town. Of course, the barbarians would kill everyone in the town if someone let them in."

Constantine sat back in his chair with his chalice of fig juice.

"The parents claim that the young men are just idealistic. That they were hoping to demonstrate common human understanding. The Roman magistrates and I find their actions dangerous and perhaps treasonous. The four wealthy parents have made it clear that they will pay whatever fines the courts stipulate. For the entire group. Almost all of Rome is talking about this case. I recommend significant fines and hard labor or military duty."

Constantine shook his head slowly as he finished his fig juice. "I don't agree, Cato. I have fought the Goths, personally. I have watched Roman soldiers die at their hands. They are brutal and unforgiving. All citizens of Rome should understand how dangerous the Goths are. How much they hate us. To me this is treason. These men should all be hanged."

"I would certainly recommend death, but for their ages." Cato responded. Cautiously.

"They are all of age. Most women their age are married. And have children. I sympathize with the parents but these aren't little boys. Besides, where were the parents when these young men were protesting? That was the time to act. I don't mind that people protest. The Jews have protested for centuries—within the walls of their cities and outside of the walls. But the next step--the meeting--the agreement--was treason!"

"Death by hanging?" asked Cato.

"Yes."

The magistrate wrote some notes onto his parchment scroll.

"I assure you, Cato, I do not want to be viewed as a new Galerius. But, if the common man thinks the rich can pay for treachery that might have killed soldiers or citizens, our moral fabric deteriorates. I will personally sign this decree, so no local magistrate feels tempted to take a payoff from any of the families."

"Yes, Augustus. That will settle the matter clearly. The next case involves the divorce settlement between a prominent merchant and his wife."

"This is Spurius?"

"Yes, Augustus." Cato answered. "Do you know him?"

"I have met him. And I know his reputation. He wanted to speak with me after our Senate meeting last year. But I declined."

"Undoubtedly, he wanted to discuss this case," Cato responded. "He declared a divorce from his wife of 25 years through one of his slaves. Some months later she informally requested, through two city magistrates, that she needed a residence. He had thrown her out of all of their homes and she was living with friends. When she didn't get any results, she formally petitioned the court—"

"This irritates me," Constantine interrupted. "We have laws that are supposed to protect divorced women. How many residences does Spurius own in Rome?"

"Four, I believe, in the city. Several more in the country."

"So many! How did he make his money?" Constantine asked.

"Wine, mostly. He owns several large vineyards north of Rome, some in Gaul and even some in Britannia. And he has a contract for supplying wine to the Army."

"Yes, that's right. Wine. And your recommendation?"

"The law is clear. He divorced her, so he must support her. And return her dowry."

Constantine sat forward in his chair. "Inform this little Bacchus that he will give her the residence of her choice. That residence will be hers free and clear, no mortgages or legal tricks. And he will pay all expenses to support her. Furthermore, if the courts hear of this case again, she will get another of his residences in the city. And any contracts he has with the Army will be terminated. Make sure this order is read to the public at the Forum."

"Yes, Augustus. The last case involves a Senator and daughter of a Ship Captain who aspires to be a Plebian Tribune."

"So. Class politics?"

Cato nodded wearily. "Apparently, the Senator got inebriated at a café next to a small dress shop that the Ship Captain's daughter owned. He entered the shop, looking for coitus. She denied his advances and he killed her. There are multiple witnesses who saw him enter the shop. And leave it, with blood on his clothes. He denies everything. She was a talented seamstress and engaged to be married. Her father, the Captain, filed suit against the Senator. Before trial, the Senator offered to pay damages to settle—but he would only pay a quarter of the amount the Captain demanded. He justified this by claiming that the Captain's wife is not a free-born citizen, and therefore their child was only worth the amount of a slave girl. This case, like the first one, has been the topic of much gossip in Rome."

"Who is the Senator?"

"Marcus Remus Tertius."

Constantine shrugged. He'd never heard of the man. "Is there proof that the Captain's wife was born a slave?"

"Not definitive. It would appear that, at best, she was a freed woman but not a citizen when they married."

"So they had a wedding. That's something. Any dowry?" Constantine asked.

"They had a public reception. But no formal dowry recorded," Cato answered.

"Your recommendation?"

"Difficult. The local magistrate is inclined to give the Captain just a little more than what the Senator has offered. But the magistrate and the Senator are friends. I would recommend more. Perhaps half of what the Captain has demanded."

"Is the Captain's demand reasonable for the death a female citizen?"

"Yes. Other cases for citizen's murders have settled for similar amounts."

Constantine spoke slowly. "So, the Captain knew what he was doing when he filed suit. And his claim may be correct. There is no question that he is a citizen. And he accepted this daughter at birth as his child. He didn't reject her by leaving her on his door step, a sign for her to be taken as a slave. So, regardless of the mother's status, his child would have rights of a female citizen. Of course, I'm not an attorney. Is there anything wrong with my reasoning, Cato?"

"Nothing, Augustus. The courts have, on a historical basis, favored the patricians in these sordid cases. The fact that the Senator is willing to pay something is viewed by the magistrate as positive. In such cases, the courts tend to seek compromise." He held out his hands, like balancing scales. "If you rule for the Captain, the plebeians will celebrate. But the patricians will be critical."

"Oh, the patricians," Constantine smiled. "I know their criticisms, Cato. My father was a general, then an emperor. My mother was a plebian. They never married. She would have had no dowry. The Captain is to get his full demand for the death of his daughter."

Again, Cato scratched notes into his scroll. This time, he seemed to smile a bit as he did.

Constantine wondered, for a moment, whether the clever judge had encouraged him toward this conclusion. "I don't remember any other cases from your letter, Magistrate. Am I forgetting something?"

"No, Augustus. These were the critical ones. I will plan to write you three or four times a year to keep up on these types of issues. And perhaps we will meet once or twice a year?"

"Very good." Constantine said, pushing his plate forward and motioning to one of the attendants to remove the breakfast. "We are finished ahead of time. I will go find my mother and my son. Gaius told me he plans to start training the boy today. I want to watch one of Rome's great soldiers training a 12-year-old!"

Constantine offered his arm to Cato when they both stood. Cato seemed startled. "I've never shaken the arm of an Emperor."

Alexandria, Egypt
April, 1071 AUC (318 AD)

Presbyter Arius of Alexandria had risen early and walked to his church to say his morning prayers. As he knelt, he reflected on the work that lay ahead of him. There was a lot. And it proved he was a beneficiary of Constantine's Edict. He had been ordained as a priest shortly after the Edict was been announced; in the five years since, Christianity had expanded dramatically. The church in which he was kneeling was one of four surrounding the original Christian Church in Alexandria. In just the last few years, it had grown in members and in physical plant. Alexandria was considered by Christians as the Rome of the East, its Bishop equal to and referred to as the Pope.

Arius' church comprised about one fourth of Alexandria's population. It was wealthy—which afforded Arius the time to do the Lord's work. His days were spent praying, helping those in need, innumerable church services and studying. His knowledge of early religious texts was one of the best. Any free time he had, he spent in

Alexandria's great Library. It was the largest and most complete in the Empire, in spite of several fires and looting over the centuries.

With the Church's growth came some changes that Arius did not like. Money-hungry scribes were recreating parts of the Holy Scripture for popular distribution. Those recreations were often sloppy and not true to the original sources. Even more troubling, some included new teachings that certain Church leaders favored—but were still controversial and didn't remain true to the Scriptures.

On the positive side, Arius liked that the popular Scriptures—though flawed—were diminishing the influence of more radical interpretations of the Lord and warped interpretations by self-serving charlatans. The written word had power over the spoken word, even for people who couldn't read.

And there was a drive among the churches to develop a unified set of Scriptures. A New Testament Bible. Most people including priests, attributed this movement to Constantine; Arius knew the Emperor had, in fact, little to do with it. But he wasn't inclined to quibble over small matters. Because someone of the Emperor's stature believed in the Lord and favored a unified set of readings, some good would come.

Arius had met Constantine when he'd visited Alexandria, right after the Edict had been announced. The priest had been impressed with Emperor—and hoped that Constantine would eventually find a way to replace Licinius. The two had been at war twice in the five years since the Edict. And most people in the Empire expected more fighting before their differences would be resolved.

Another reason that Arius favored Constantine was Eusebius, Constantine's distant cousin and the recently-appointed Bishop of Nicomedia. Eusebius was Arius' guest, currently sleeping at his residence near the church. He'd come to Alexandria for a few weeks to study in the Library and glean some of Arius' knowledge of early Scriptures.

Arius and Eusebius had been students together under Lucian, who had been martyred—beheaded—by Emperor Daia near the end of the official persecution, six or seven years earlier.

After his prayers, Arius had a small meal of grains, an apple and fig juice in the small church kitchen. Then he strapped on his sandals and prepared to walk to the original church in the center of Alexandria. His Bishop, Alexander of Alexandria, was going to give a sermon today. Easter Sunday. But even this day stirred debate. Learned priests and scholars did not agree on when, exactly, Christ had been crucified and rose from the dead. Tradition tied Easter to Jewish Passover; some took exception to tradition.

He sighed and adjusted his robes. For the moment, Arius would just enjoy his walk. It was a glorious, bright day.

Libyan by descent, the tall and rangy Arius had never been married. In the very earliest days of the Church, this would have inhibited him from becoming a bishop. St Paul, however was a devote celibate, while the majority of Apostles were married. Paul recommended in one of his Epistles that he preferred celibacy for all men. In another Epistle he recommends that bishops be married, but to only one woman. In that Epistle he advises that if a bishop can't run his own house well, how could he be expected to run his church? Gradually, particularly with the age of persecution, Paul's Epistle on celibacy was prevailing. Who could have a family when sudden death was a daily reality? In addition, celibacy had become a symbol—*the* symbol, really—of dedication to Christ.

Arius was content to live alone, to dedicate his days to serving others and his studies.

As he walked towards the entrance of the old church, Arius attracted a following of people—young and old. He was quick with a quip and a verse; people were naturally drawn to him. He picked up the young child of one of his parishioners with little hesitation. No one in the group would have guessed that their priest was nearly 60 years old.

"Abba, abba. Where are we going?"

"To hear our Bishop speak to us about Easter Day and the risen Lord."

In the western part of the Empire, centered in Rome, Christians accounted for perhaps a quarter of the population. Most favored the pagan gods. In the eastern part of the Empire, including Alexandria and Nicomedia, the Christian population was much larger—half or more. The Apostles, particularly Paul, had been most active here; and the eastern Empire had more Jews as part of their population.

Saul of Tarsus had come from a prominent and devout Jewish family. He was a citizen of the Empire who received an excellent education and finished by studying under the senior Rabbi in Jerusalem. For a couple of years after Christ's Ascension, he was a feared prosecutor of Jews who believed that Christ was the Messiah. Then, traveling to Damascus, he'd been struck blind by a light and a voice had asked him why he so vehemently persecuted Him. When Saul asked who was speaking, the voice said: "I am Jesus, the one you are persecuting! Now get up and go into the city. And you will be told what you must do."

Three days later, Saul was baptized by Ananias of Damascus. And his sight was restored. From that point on, he was known as Paul. And an Apostle for Christ. He was Arius' favorite saint.

Paul ended up calling himself the "Apostle of the uncircumcised"—that is, gentiles. His made three long apostolic missions, each lasting several years and taking him to all corners of the Empire. But most of his work concentrated in the East. And he was a prolific writer. His letters and other correspondence made up the largest part of the Scriptures that priests like Arius and Eusebius studied.

In the earliest years of the Church, the Apostles had framed Christ's teaching within Mosaic Law. This required a strict dietary regime, rigid prayer and circumcision.

Those requirements—especially the last one—were not viewed favorably by gentile converts. Paul was one of the first to identify this problem. After his first mission, he met with Peter, Jesus' brother James and some other Apostles for the First Council of Jerusalem. They decided that new members of the Church did not need to be circumcised but did need to follow the dietary requirements of Jewish law. In time, though, he relaxed even the dietary requirements.

As Paul continued his missions, he refined his understanding of Christ's teachings. And his message to potential believers. Paul focused on the lessons of forgiveness, of treating people as one would want to be treated, of resurrection and of the coming end of time. This became the Christian faith that priests like Arius embraced and taught.

During his third mission, Paul was arrested in Jerusalem for preaching Christianity. As a Roman citizen, he appealed "unto Caesar"—which allowed him to appeal to the courts in Rome. He was sent to Rome, were he was held for two years by the Praetorian Guard. When he lost his appeal he was beheaded. A lesson for all Christians.

But his many writings survived.

Arius led his people into the old church and had them stand together, just inside the inner walls. Then, he hurried back and joined the other priests in the sacristy to prepare for Mass.

For most of the Mass, Arius sat in one of the small pews behind Alexander and his Deacons. The first part of the Alexander's service was standard. The most quoted scriptures described the resurrection of Jesus. Prior to the sharing of the Eucharist, Alexander gave his sermon. The bishop quoted heavily from Athanasius, his most trusted Deacon...and a man with whom Arius had many differences.

> Who that has heard the words of John, "In the beginning was the Word," will not denounce the saying of these men, that "there was a time

when He was not"? Or who that has heard in the Gospel, "the Only begotten Son," and "by Him were all things made," will not detest their declaration that He is "one of the things that were made"?

For how can He be one of those things which were made by Himself? Or how can He be the Only-begotten, when, according to them, He is counted as one among the rest, since He is Himself a creature and a work? And how can He be 'made of things that were not," when the Father saith, "my heart hath uttered a good Word," and "Out of the womb I have begotten Thee before the morning star"? Or again, how is He "unlike in substance to the Father," seeing He is the perfect "image" and "brightness" of the Father, and that He saith, "He that hath seen Me hath seen the Father"?

And if the Son is the "Word" and "Wisdom" of God, how was there "a time when He was not"? It is the same as if they should say that God was once without Word and without Wisdom. And how is He "subject to change and varia-tion," Who says, by Himself, "I am in the Father, and the Father in Me," and "I and the Father are One"; and by the Prophet, "Behold Me, for I am, and I change not"?

For although one may refer this expression to the Father, yet it may now be more aptly spoken of the Word, that though He has been made man, He has not changed; but as the Apostle

has said, "Jesus Christ is the same yesterday, today, and forever." And who can have persuaded
them to say, that He was made for us, whereas
Paul writes, "for Whom are all things, and by
Whom are all things"?

Arius prayed for patience and forbearance as his anger caused
him to fidget, like a child. He rushed through the Eucharist. He
tried to humor himself by recounting Paul's complaints 300 years
earlier of drunken Gentiles. They mistook the meaning of the
Eucharist by overconsuming wine while Paul preached.

Rather than waiting to speak to Alexander and the parishioners
who had greeted him earlier, he rushed out after the service and ran
back to his small home.

"Eusebius! Are you here?" he called out.

"I am here in the courtyard. I just got back a moment ago. The
service was wonderful. You have such nice people in your parish."

"Yes. I suppose. I can't think of my parish right now." His voice
broke as he said it.

"Good Lord, Arius. Are you ill?"

"No. Upset. It was Alexander, his Sermon. It was as if he was
attacking me, personally. So foreign to the Scriptures. I can't stand
it. This is lunacy!"

"Arius, calm down. Please. Let us go inside to your vestibule.
And talk there."

Arius nodded in agreement and they walked inside. His
breathing slowed and his muscles relaxed a bit. They sat, facing
one another, on the woven benches in the small entrance room
of his three-room stone house. He took a deep breath and spoke
slowly, "Alexander's sermon concerned the nature of our Lord,
Jesus Christ."

"Good," said Eusebius, encouraging more.

"Not so good. He ignored the early Scriptures, all of the legacy
history of our Lord. And declared Him to be equal to God, our

Father. This is an attack on those of us who believe, through the evidence of the early Scriptures, that Jesus was begotten by the Father, at some later time." Arius could feel his words speeding up again. "He denies that there was a time when the Son was not. He relied on philosophical reasoning. And on the Gospel of John, the glorified musings of some romantic Greek who heard of Jesus third-hand from one of Paul's converts. Not an eyewitness. Not an Apostle. That…story…should not be considered one of our sacred Scriptures."

Eusebius held up a hand and smiled in what he meant to be a calming manner. "Please, Arius. Be careful how you account for my namesake." This was a bit of humor. Some scholars speculated that the Gospel of John had been written by the Greek mystic Eusebius of Ephesus. "Besides, the Gospel of John gives you some of your strongest evidence of Jesus' admission that he was not equal to God. He says:

> "I go away, and I will come to you. If you loved
> Me, you would have rejoiced, because I go to the
> Father; for the Father is greater than I."

The Scripture reference didn't put Arius at ease.

"Besides, Arius, you are in a very small minority that does not consider the Gospel of John as a sacred text. You know that most believers hold it in high regard."

Arius flinched. "We are at a crossroads for the future of our faith. It has been evolving away from the Word of our Lord to… to I'm not sure what. Some image taken from the Roman gods. We will be worshiping two equal gods, God and Jesus. Three, if they include the Holy Spirit. Is this the price of Rome's acceptance of Christianity?"

Eusebius shook his head but tried to keep a positive demeanor. "Rome doesn't have any concern with theology or metaphysics. Rome only cares about taxes, politics and war."

They sat silently for a moment. Then, when he'd gathered his thoughts, Arius resumed his argument in terms he thought Eusebius would appreciate: "Jesus was a Jew. A pious Jew, as were his Apostles. And God's first Commandment to the Jews—handed to Moses— was, 'I am the Lord, thy God, thou shall have no other gods before me.' Jesus never challenged this law. And the Scriptures written by those actually knew Jesus—Luke, Mark and Matthew— all portray Him as a humble servant of the Father. The Son of Man, not an equal to the Father."

Eusebius didn't seem convinced.

Arius fell back on some of the simple arguments he'd used when teaching younger students. "Jesus was begotten to be God's divine human Son. There can't be a Son without the Father existing first. On the cross, He asks, 'My God, my God, why have You forsaken me?' Surely, if He was equal to the Father in heaven, Divine as human, He would know He was going to be in paradise soon. He wouldn't need to plead with the Almighty if He *was* the Almighty."

Eusebius sighed, as if he'd had this conversation many times. "The common argument, Arius, is that with time we have grown to appreciate more fully the significance of Jesus' life, death and resurrection. Now we understand that He was indeed God on Earth, but while on Earth, He was indeed human. The early writers didn't have that perspective. They couldn't have it. They were too close to the actual events."

Arius wasn't so weary. He answered immediately: "I disagree. Time has only diminished the real message of Jesus. Meanwhile, these vulgate writers—Greeks and pagans—have created a myth based on what they call 'rational thought 'starting with the 'Word' in John's Gospel. And they miss Jesus' message. In a time more brutal than our own, He spoke of peace and goodwill toward all men. He taught us to do unto others as we would have others do unto us. He blessed and prayed forgiveness in His Father's name. He said that the end of the world was near—and that we should follow his teachings and his example. He was Divine and each of those messages was revolutionary."

"And each still is."

"Yes. Yes, each still is. But this is my point: We do not diminish Jesus to worship God and follow Jesus' example. We diminish Him when do what God commanded the Jews not to do. Worship false gods."

"Arius, your words come close to heresy." Eusebius warned.

"Then my words fail me. I worship Jesus. I try to live as He instructed. As I said, I believe that He was a divine man and is Divine now. I believe that He proved Himself to be stronger than Satan and, thus, more glorious and divine than the Angels. But I do not believe Him to be equal to the Almighty. Neither did Paul. Or the early writers. Or Irenaeus, or even the great Origen. They all believed that Jesus was the Son, but not equal to God. Now, Alexander is using Greek reasoning to argue that Jesus is equal to God. But who are we to assume that God uses reason? How can we imagine what God thinks?"

Eusebius nodded slowly. "I agree. But I don't see it as definitively as you do. There are many phrases in the early writers that have several meanings. And the confusion is compounded in translation. Origen, in particular, created complexity in his translations. He was a brilliant man, but eccentric. Perhaps that came from castrating himself...or perhaps it's *why* he castrated himself. In any event, eccentric or not, Origen's idea of the Trinity is close to my own. I believe that the Son and the Spirit are restricted wills of the Father."

"Restricted wills. Yes. I remember that term," Arius said. "Origen has written so many volumes, it is difficult to keep all of them front of-mind. His writing on the preexistence of souls is fascinating."

"Yes. Another controversy. So, Arius, what would you like to do? Should we meet with Alexander?" Eusebius asked. His close ties to the Emperor made Eusebius a formidable man, regardless of his official rank in the Church.

Arius thought for a few moments. "Alexander's beliefs are opposite of mine. That's one issue. But there is also the issue of Alexander's Deacon, Athanasius. Another influential man. I suspect he writes many of Alexander's sermons."

"Two are always more difficult to persuade than one."

"Exactly my concern. Perhaps the correct thing is to have an informal conversation with Alexander, so that he is aware of my concerns," Arius concluded. "And I don't need to involve you in this."

"Good. One bit of advice," Eusebius cautioned. "Be wary of mentioning the depth of your thoughts on how the Scriptures have modified the image of Jesus. Alexander is well aware of such teachings. Claiming they were written by mystics or romantics will only divert attention from the important point. I would focus on the writings that define the nature of God and the nature of Jesus."

"Of course. You are correct," Arius answered. He was much less agitated than he'd been earlier. "I will write you after I've seen how Alexander reacts to my objections. In person."

That meeting was cordial but brief. Arius had been directed into the bishop's private chambers, where Alexander reclined on a day bed.

He greeted Arius warmly, gave him a short blessing and waved him to one of the chairs facing him. "What brings you here, stern Arius?"

Alexander was older than Arius and not in good health. He breathed with difficulty. Like Arius, Alexander had witnessed persecution—at the hands of both the Romans and local pagans—first-hand. He'd lived through the deaths of friends and predecessors. His immediate predecessor, Achillias, had ordained Arius. At the time, it had been a controversial move. Other priests thought that Arius was too unforgiving, some even dismissed the strict Arius with the harshest term in their vernacular: "not Christ-like."

"Master. I've come to discuss your recent sermon—"

"Yes. You don't like that I described Christ as one with the Father."

"That's correct. Forgive my insistence, Master, but I believe this is an essential point...."

Alexander smiled benevolently while Arius explained his essential point. He thought Arius was an excellent shepherd for his parish but not a forward thinker. Arius' hard focus on the earliest Scriptures was heart-felt. It was also evidence that he didn't see the broader direction the Church needed to go. This was a constant tension: some priests could see broad issues, some priests could tend to flocks. It was a rare priest who could do both.

When Arius had finished, Alexander nodded and said questions of Christ's nature—and God's—were difficult. And that they should both pray over the matter. "In time, I believe the Creator will show us answers. For now, let us ask for His grace in these matters. And in all things."

After Arius had left, Deacon Athanasius approached Alexander— making no effort to hide the fact that he'd listened to the private conversation. "This is a significant breach of Faith, my Overseer."

"Perhaps."

"Arius is a hard man. He shows little mercy for others, so it is just that he is held to a hard standard. His beliefs oppose Church dogma. He must recant these beliefs or be excommunicated."

Youth, thought Alexander. Athanasius was barely 21 years old. "Quiet, my son. We will consider Arius' beliefs and let some time pass. Arius speaks respectfully. And he is a knowledgeable priest."

This was a gentle reminder to Athanasius that Arius ranked above him in the Church's hierarchy.

Alexander lay back in his day bed and rubbed his sides, above his hips. He prayed that this pain would pass, as it had so many times before.

Sirmium, Pannonia
Spring, 1072 AUC (319 AD)

Ossius sat in a landscaped courtyard, reading a long letter. He took several breaks while he read. The contents of the letter were troubling, but the day around him was pleasant.

Constantine had moved the Imperial Court to Sirmium after his last skirmish with Licinius. He wanted to be closer to his mother and to expand the Empire to the Northeast. He also vastly preferred the cooler, less humid weather. Late springs and summers in Rome could also be pungent. It was a large city with no garbage collection, such waste being thrown on the streets.

Ossius had spent most of the last year with Constantine. It seemed even longer since he'd been back to Cordova, where he remained Bishop.

Discord was growing within the Church. It had started as a dogmatic debate among several priests in and around Alexandria. They argued over whether Jesus could be both God and the son of man. Ossius was not usually interested in such metaphysical musings—but this seemed to have the potential to cause deep division within the Church.

The trouble wasn't just dogma. It also involved personalities, of course. Athanasius, the young deacon serving under Alexander of Alexandria, had been relentless in his arguments against a group of priests and scholars who cited the early Scriptures to argue that Jesus was a man and not One with God the Father. Eventually, the young deacon persuaded Alexander to make an example of Arius, one of the discordant priests. Arius was removed from his parish and excommunicated.

The controversy did not end there. Arius was a close friend of the Bishop Eusebius, Constantine's distant cousin. Upon notice of his excommunication, Arius had written Eusebius:

> To his very dear lord, the man of God, the faithful and orthodox Eusebius, Arius, unjustly persecuted by Alexander the Pope, on account of that all conquering truth of which you also are a champion, sendeth greeting in the Lord.

> Ammonius, my father, being about to depart for Nicomedia, I considered myself bound to salute you by him, and withal to inform that natural affection which you bear towards the brethern for the sake of God and His Christ, that the bishop greatly wastes and persecutes us, and leaves no stone unturned against us. He has driven us out of the city as atheists, because we do not concur in what he publicly preaches, namely, God always, the Son always; as the Father so the Son; the Son co-exists unbegotten with the God; He is everlasting; neither by thought nor by any interval does God precede the Son; always God, always Son; He is begotten of the unbegotten; the Son is of God Himself. Eusebius, your brother Bishop of Caesarea, Theodotus, Paulinus, Athanasius, Gregorius, Aetius, and all the bishops of the East, have been condemned because they say that God had an existence prior to that of His Son.

Through Eusebius, news of the controversy had reached Ossius. And Constantine.

Ossius had read enough. He put down the scroll and stood up to walk. Sirmium was located close to the Sava River, the largest tributary of the Danube, which supplied water through a large aqueduct. For over 25 years, Sirmium had been the northernmost of the four Capitols of the Empire.

The walled Capitol Complex incorporated a Hippodrome, a Coliseum for horse and chariot racing; a large public bathhouse; several barracks for the army; private houses; eight churches and the Imperial Palace. Although the area surrounding Sirmium may have had as many as 100,000 residents, fewer than 10,000 of those lived within the Complex. Ossius had developed a regular path that he walked, just inside the walls of the Complex.

The Imperial Palace was built adjacent to the Hippodrome. A multi-level structure made primarily of fire hardened brick (with radiant heat from its floors), the Palace had been built with a large area for the administration of the Empire's business. This included offices for ranking officials from various parts of the government—but the majority of the space was for the Quaestors, the imperial accountants. Since the days of Octavius Augustus, the Empire had kept detailed financial records. Over everything. Ossius could hear the clicking of abacuses when he walked past the accountants' space.

The administrative quarters also included public areas and large sitting areas where the Emperor and his bureaucrats could meet, in groups large or small.

The private part of the Palace was a series of apartments that made up the residence of Constantine, his family and close servants, many of them eunuchs. Frescos, tapestries and statues were displayed throughout the Palace. To Ossius, they seemed ostentatious—and unlike the Emperor.

Ossius stopped in front of the statue of one of Constantine's distant ancestors. To a passerby, the priest would seem to have been studying the artwork. In fact, he was thinking about imperial politics. There was more than just Church trouble simmering in the Eastern Empire. Licinius was quietly starting to persecute Christians, in violation of the agreement he'd made with Constantine in Milan some years earlier. Apparently, Licinius was taking wealthy Christians' homes and belongings—even absconding funds from wealthier parishes.

Constantine's army had faced Licinius' forces twice in recent years, over minor territorial disputes. Constantine had prevailed both times; but he'd allowed Licinius to remain Emperor. Of an increasingly small territory. A violation of the Milan Agreement would be cause for something greater—which didn't make sense. The balance of power had moved decisively in Constantine's favor. Why would Licinius provoke a violent confrontation?

Eusebius of Nicomedia had recently returned to Constantine's court after a two-month absence. One of the first things he did was visit Ossius—whom he came upon studying the statue. "Esteemed Ossius, you look well." Eusebius greeted.

"You are losing your sight, my friend. My prayers are that God has been with you during your busy days."

The two Bishops knew each other well. Both had the Emperor's respect and trust. Eusebius, a blood relative of Constantine, was critical of those who used proximity to his cousin for personal gain—but he did not think Ossius was one of those.

Ossius was impressed with Eusebius' ability to gain trust and affection quickly with whomever he encountered. He viewed it as a God-given gift.

But the strongest bond between the men was their shared faith—which was honest and true.

They walked into the courtyard of the Imperial Palace. Spring had taken a hold and the budding trees were fully bloomed with a sweet smell of pollen in the air. From a distance, it was obvious that both men were priests.

A closer observer would see that Eusebius was the taller of the two and was wearing a dark nettle tunic. Ossius wore his signature undyed wool tunic. Each wore a rope cincture around his waist. Each had a cross hanging from his neck—Ossius' was wood and Eusebius' was metal with a small Lamb in the center. Both men were slim. Ossius was slightly less well-kept, his hair and beard a bit disheveled.

On special occasions and holy days, both men would wear an omophorion—a Y-shaped scarf that distinguished them as bishops.

But this was not one of those days.

Eusebius, the more talkative of the two, pushed the conversation forward: "Is my cousin causing you hardship? Still making your life intolerable?"

"Our Imperator is always challenging. But ever fair. Have you seen him yet, Eusebius?"

"No. And I suspect he will disown me when I do." Eusebius gestured toward a stone bench in the courtyard. They both sat. "I have a problem that he will not appreciate. I sent you some of the letters surrounding the controversy."

Eusebius relayed the entire saga to Ossius, holding back nothing. He started describing his conversation with Arius in Alexandria, almost a year earlier. He explained that his Diocese was currently hosting Arius. And he explained that he and Eusebius of Caesarea had issued a letter to the eastern Bishops, stating Arius was blameless.

Ossius took a few moments before responding. Then, he asked: "This would be a problem—particularly with Meletius—that could cause unrest within sectors of the Empire?"

"Yes," Eusebius replied with a rueful laugh. "That is a diplomatic way to put it."

Ossius nodded. "Constantine will not like this. He feels strongly that consistency and orthodox rules keep stability within the Empire. And there are practical considerations. The fact that I have only recently heard of this matter means it is still primarily an Eastern Empire conflict. Licinius should resolve it."

Eusebius shook his head. "Licinius is ignoring the Edict of Milan—again—and claiming the wealth of many of the Christians in the East. I have tried to persuade him against these actions. But his judgment is…suspect. Constantia is very worried."

"Her brother will like it even less. Tell me, Eusebius, the conflict over the nature of Jesus—is there ground to be gained if Constantine intervenes?"

This time, the prolix Eusebius took a moment to think.

"Doubtful. Although I am biased toward Arius' perspective, I believe both sides are firm in their positions—which will make a compromise difficult…and a diktat intolerable."

"And, in reality, neither side knows the nature of God with certainty," Ossius offered.

"No. There is confirming and contradictory evidence on both sides of the argument. One would think a common ground might be available, with so little evidence for either position. But, as we know, sometimes we humans can't see the benefit of compromise."

Ossius saw some movement inside the Palace. "Isn't that why people die for their beliefs? Isn't that why it is called faith?"

Both priests got up from the bench and headed for the large stone archway that served as the main entrance to the Imperial Palace.

"Welcome, your eminences." Adiutor Aelius was standing just inside, flanked by several Imperial Guards. Having seen the two Bishops talking on the bench in the courtyard, he prepared a small meeting room down the hallway from the personal residence. The room had one large upholstered chair at the end of a rectangular table with five other wood-and-wicker chairs surrounding it. Tapestries hung on two of the walls, keeping the room secure for sensitive conversations.

As Aelius ushered the bishops into the meeting room, he was surprised to find Constantine already seated in the larger chair reading a papyrus scroll with a bucket of scrolls beside him. He was dressed simply in a white tunic—his breakfast robes—but didn't seem to mind. He rose to greet his guests.

"Dominus, I had intended to come get you—"

"Aelius, all is well. This was a good place for me to get through some of this correspondence." Constantine said. "Ossius. Eusebius. Good to see you both." He gave each a Roman arm shake and a brief embrace, which interrupted their bows. "Sit, my friends. Sit. You both look perplexed. Cousin, you a little more. What news?"

The bishops sat on either side of Constantine. There was a moment of awkward hesitation and then—against anyone's expectation—Ossius took the lead and began to talk. He explained the earlier conversation with he'd had with Eusebius. He described the Edict of Milan's erosion. And the dogmatic discord over the nature of Jesus and God.

Constantine listened intently, concentrating his attention on Ossius while he spoke.

Eusebius, on the other hand, felt his attention wandering. His mind drifted to when, as a boy, Constantine would intercede with the adults and get his younger cousin out of trouble.

Then Constantius left to marry Theodora and things changed. Constantine withdrew from his cousins, spoke much less and began training with his sword.

At Helena's urging, Constantine had visited the local priest for spiritual counsel. Eusebius often tagged along. The priest provided little help to Constantine—who felt cheated and betrayed by Constantius—but had a much greater effect on Eusebius.

Constantine's rare bright moments came when his father began his occasional visits. Eusebius remembered the flurry of excitement when Constantius and his detail would ride into town. He seemed bigger than life on his horse and wearing the brightest armor anyone had ever seen. He remembered the playful threats of burnishing the broad side of his sword toward the back end of all the children that would invade the small house when he visited.

"Cousin, some things never change. When we were children, you caused me problems—and, here, you still do." Constantine said, bringing Eusebius back into the moment. "I need some proof of what Licinius is actually doing. Telling me that you've heard reports is not enough. Have the priests who've been affected give me written reports. If they are concerned for their safety, then summarize their reports and send those to me. Have other bishops do the same. Licinius would not be so foolish to threaten or harm you."

Ossius and Eusebius both nodded in agreement—but said nothing.

Constantine sat back in his chair for a moment or two. "I am surprised that he would be so brazen as to persecute Christians. Perhaps he has calculated that he can challenge me, taking the pagan side. By persecuting Christians, he will attract those that have the most to gain from making our personal conflict into a holy war. It seems to me that that would have narrow attraction, particularly in the East. Are you still close to Licinius, cousin?"

Eusebius answered instinctively: "I spoke with him, and your sister, less than two months ago. Constantia is worried and prays for peace between you."

"My sister is a good woman. I will grant her that peace if her husband keeps to our agreement in Milan. If not…." His sentence faded into a regretful shake of the head.

Another silent moment passed, and then Constantine concluded: "This matter of the nature of Jesus appears to be a minor thing. As Ossius points out, no one really knows the correct answer. Tell me again the name of the bishop who's stirring up this quibble?"

"Alexander, the older bishop you met when you were in Alexandria after your victory in Rome. He is Pope Sylvester's counterpart in Alexandria," Eusebius answered nervously.

"Of course, he runs the school there, by the Library. I certainly don't view him as…favorably…as I do Sylvester. "Constantine rubbed his eyes. "Then this Arius would be the tall priest that wanted the old scriptures from Rome sent to the Library."

"Yes, the same."

Constantine sighed and fidgeted with a small child's toy that had been hidden somewhere in the folds of his tunic. "Why is it that God endows man with intelligence and reason—that man casts aside so quickly? Why does an Arius fight his bishop on a matter that has no certainty? Why does Arius' bishop condemn others on matters they cannot prove? Why does Licinius challenge me, when he must know he cannot prevail? He has fought me twice in the last several years, yet I have let him live. Now he tempts me a third time? What has God put inside of us to abandon reality? To rattle sabers, based on insignificant matters and improbable odds?"

Ossius looked at Eusebius before he answered. "We spoke of this earlier, Imperator. We believe that it is based on faith. Regardless the nature of the faith, it seems that if one believes in something he will die for it. Perhaps it can be the greatest nature of man or the definition of sin."

Constantine cocked his head, as if perplexed by the answer.

"Well, I continue to pray to both the Nazarene and the Father that they grant me the wisdom to see the correct way. And the strength to follow it. I hope that this Arius matter will die down. But, if it doesn't...if something does develop—any unrest, any change in either side's position—let me know."

One of his bodyguards came into the room and whispered something to Constantine. He nodded quickly and gestured to the door. "I must be going. I wish we had more time to sit and talk."

As the three men walked out of the chamber into the main hallway of the Palace, Constantine pointed with his index finger—a habit he had, when giving orders—and said, "Ossius, when the opportunity presents itself, visit both Alexander and Arius. I would like to hear your impressions of each man."

"Yes, Imperator."

Eusebius seized that moment to say something. "Imperator, you mention your prayers for wisdom and strength. With such prayers, isn't it time you were baptized?"

"As always, Eusebius, you press. I've told you before that I intend to wait until the last possible hour to be baptized. I need all the sins I have—and continue to accumulate—to be washed away by the sacrament."

The priests smiled a bit nervously, unsure of how serious the Emperor was about his plan.

"I will make sure you are available to baptize me when the time comes, cousin." He smiled, too. Cryptically.

Constantine's mother, Helena, approached the three men from the residential end of the hall. "Eusebius? Dear cousin." She ran to the priest and hugged him affectionately.

Helena was a tall, slim woman. Dressed in a light yellow tunic with a small wooden cross around her neck, she looked as attractive as she had 30 years before. Nearing her seventieth birthday, she showed no evidence of decline—in health or enthusiasm for life.

That enthusiasm had seen her through hard times, like the year or so after Constantius had left her. An attractive local woman with a bastard child was considered little more than chattel by Roman soldiers in a garrison town. Many women in circumstances like hers turned to prostitution. Helena never did that.

Her circumstances improved when Constantius was elevated to governor and then co-emperor and made his intentions concerning his son clear. Constantius recognized Constantine and arranged a stipend for his former concubine. Although she was not a fixture at his court, Helena had access to Constantius when she needed it. And people knew that.

And now, a fixture in her son's court and a wealthy woman in every measurable way, she showered attention on Eusebius. "You look well, cousin. How long are you going to stay? Let's sit down and have something to eat. I need to talk to you about Jerusalem."

"Mother—" The Emperor started to chide his mother, with mock exasperation.

"This needn't bother you, Constantine. It's a godly matter." Then, turning back to Eusebius: "I want to join one of the expeditions looking for Jesus' cross."

"Mother, it's not the time."

"Constantine is right, cousin. It's not the time," Eusebius agreed. He held both of her hands and looked intensely into her eyes. "But, when it is, we can arrange things for you. The bishops in Caesarea and Jerusalem are Eusebius and Marcarius. I will write them and inform them of your intentions."

She seemed happy with that news. She greeted Ossius with a hug and headed toward the dining room arm-in-arm with both bishops. Constantine enjoyed the image for a moment and then headed away to one of the formal meeting rooms and his Generals.

Alexandria, Egypt
Summer, 1072 AUD (319 AD)

The dark of the evening had settled in but Athanasius was still bright with anger. He paced back and forth between his apartment and Alexander's office, 20-odd steps down the hallway. As he walked, he gently hit his hand with the scroll he'd just received from Clodius.

He was starting to lose momentum. For every two bishops that offered support, three were defecting. Eusebius was the problem—he was an effective advocate for Arius among the elite. Without Eusebius, Arius would be stuck with his *Thalia*, his poems explaining theology to the plebes.

And now Clodius—his friend from their student days and a deacon under Ossius of Cordova—had written him, saying that Eusebius was visiting Constantine. No doubt, pressing Arius's side with the Emperor. Clodius had tried to get details about the meetings; but all Ossius would say was that they involved "a number of issues." Of course, Ossius hadn't gained the Emperor's trust by sharing sensitive information with underlings.

Eusebius was clever. He wouldn't use his kinship with the Emperor—at least not at first. He would let Ossius do most of the talking. Position himself as the careful counselor. Position Arius's heresies as a reasonable compromise, the sort of solution that would make sense to a soldier.

He hit the scroll hard enough that it stung his hand.

Athanasius's disdain for Arius was growing. This debate was unnecessary. The glory of God was an obvious matter—it satisfied the mind and the heart. God's glory did not just to reflect off of Jesus—it emanated from Him, as it did from the Holy Ghost. Three equal pillars, supporting one another. Not a complex archway of God, with one large opening and two small ones.

Some of the early teachers had actually used that convoluted image. So, Arius and his fellow heretics were at best living in the past. They didn't see the magnitude of Jesus's life on earth and His sacrifice. They were too closely tied to the "Jewish" heritage of the early Gospels. They didn't comprehend the magnitude of the miracles, the virgin birth, and the resurrection—the full effect of God's love. The mystery that God had been on earth as He was in heaven.

Their heresies would have Jesus be some angel or pagan-like lesser divine being.

And the Scriptures supported the truth as Athanasius saw it. From the old Hebrew Bible to the new Scriptures. The Scriptures were the Word of God. Although some of St. Paul's letters could be ambiguous, John's Gospel was not. In it, Jesus declared in His own words that He was God.

The synoptic Gospels didn't address the matter. It was not their purpose. Their authors testified as eyewitnesses; they could not be expected to delve into the deeper questions of God's nature.

Initially, Athanasius had assumed that it would be easy to convince the bishops to see these theological points the right way.

Looking back, he understood he'd been naïve. Not all Bishops had the foresight of Alexander—and Church politics were as complicated as Imperial politics.

The key to succeeding at both was still Alexander. He was trusted beyond reproach in the Eastern Empire, with the possible exceptions of the two Eusebiuses, Meletius and a few others. As for the Western Empire, it would be best to keep those bishops out of the debate entirely. They were unpredictable. They had distaste for the multiple gods of the pagans—and they might see the Trinity as three separate Gods and therefore side with Arius.

To prevail, he was going to have to get his bishop more involved. So far, Alexander had been far too passive—a short letter here, a comment there, a sermon or two, but no strong statements. He needed Alexander to favor the idea of the Trinity with more vigor. More persuasion. His impulse was to go to the bishop's bedchamber...but he realized Alexander would be fast asleep.

After a few hours of fitful sleep, Athanasius had his best chance to address the matter with Alexander when they had their after-prayers breakfast.

In his younger years, Alexander had been a big, athletic man. But age and gravity were having their ways with him. His frame was thin, now, and seemed to have difficulty holding up his large head. His beard, once vibrant and full, had faded to grey and wispy. His eyes were still sharp—but they looked tired, even after a full night's sleep.

Impatient, Athanasius started talking before Alexander had started to eat. "Your Holiness, I was disturbed to receive a note yesterday that Eusebius of Nicomedia had lunched with Ossius of Cordova and Emperor Constantine in Sirmium recently."

"A note? Who wrote this note?" Alexander asked. He seemed more interested in the dry fruit on the table than intrigues.

"A deacon friendly to our cause, who studies under Ossius."

"So, clever Ossius is back again from Spain," Alexander said, inspecting a piece of flat bread. "What was the purpose of their meeting?"

"The deacon does not know. But can there be any doubt?"

"There can *always* be doubt, Athanasius. One never knows what goes on in a politician's mind. Constantine trusts Ossius because they have gone into battle together so many times. And he trusts Eusebius because they are cousins. Grew up together," Alexander said, like a teacher lecturing a student. "This Emperor is a soldier, first and last. His relations with those two are not defined by theological matters."

Athanasius seemed even more impatient than before. "Your Holiness, we must address this controversy over the nature of Jesus, and eventually the Trinity, in a more aggressive manner. We have given Arius freedom to promulgate his heretical beliefs. Now, we are letting the machinations of Imperial politics define the nature of the life, blood and sacrifice of our Lord. I can give you a list of the bishops that should side with us—but are siding with serpent-tongued Arius. Bishops, swayed by heresy! We cannot allow this. It is a battle, just as fierce as any Ossius has seen at Constantine's side. If we lose, God will hold our souls to account."

Alexander swallowed some dried fig and took a sip of water.

"What do you suggest, Athanasius?"

The young deacon leaned forward, over the table. "Give me leave and Letters of Recommendation to all the bishops of the East. I will visit each one to convince them the danger of what is before us. And the Glory for them, if they choose the right path. When I've spoken with all of them, we call a council—where we announce to the Empire the unanimity of our position. And we demand the exclusion of those that do not acknowledge the truth."

"What of the bishops in the West?"

Athanasius sat back again and a thought for a moment. "It would be best if they are spared involvement in this conflict. Their troubles have more to do with pagans than heresies."

Alexander nodded. He didn't say anything for a few moments. This discord over God's nature and Jesus'—was not going away, as he'd originally hoped. And his Deacon was correct, it would eventually include the Holy Ghost, thus the Trinity. This young Deacon was impetuous; but he might have the will and temperament to end the discord.

The older man rubbed his thinning beard. And then pushed his breakfast plate away. He looked at his student with resignation and said, "Draft that letter, Athanasius. Allow me some time to study it. And we shall try to resolve this matter."

"Yes, your Holiness," the younger man answered. With a smile.

Nicomedia, Asia Minor
Fall, 1073 AUC (320 AD)

Nicomedia, where Licinius and Constantia lived, had been the Capitol of the Eastern Roman Empire for several generations. It was almost twice the size of Sirmium, although the walled part of Nicomedia—the real core of the city—had a population of only about 12,000 people. Still, Nicomedia had the prestige and accoutrements of a first-class city: three coliseums, four libraries and seven bathhouses. It was a wealthy place, full of wealthy people. Eusebius had been preceded as bishop by Anthimus of Nicomedia, who was beheaded by Maximinus Daia during the persecutions. Anthimus was a godly man. He had welcomed and fed the soldiers sent to arrest him.

After Anthimus' death, Eusebius petitioned several friendly bishops to recommend him as Bishop of Nicomedia. Most of the Church leaders were aware of his relationships to both of the Imperial families—especially, his blood ties to Constantine. And he didn't hesitate to inform the handful who weren't aware.

The position in Nicomedia gave Eusebius significant opportunity to influence the politics of both the Church and the Empire. The only problem was time. He always felt he had too little of it. It had been more than a year since he'd met with Constantine and Ossius and he still hadn't documented Licinius' new persecutions and sent them to Constantine. There was no time.

Even with several priests assisting, he was consumed by the day-to-day work of growing his church.

In truth, there was another reason—probably the main reason. He was trying to keep peace between Constantine and Licinius. By serving both Emperors, he truly served neither. Both sensed this; and neither liked it. Eusebius sincerely loved and respected Constantine— and loved and respected Constantia, who was loyal to Licinius. The bishop realized this put him between Schylla and Charybdis, between a rock and a very hard place.

Eusebius thought about all these things while he sat in his sparse office, adjacent to the cathedral, and stared at a scribed copy of a letter from Alexander to all the bishops in the Eastern Empire.

> To our beloved and most reverend fellow-ministers of the Catholic Church in every place, Alexander sends greeting in the Lord:
>
> Since the body of the Catholic Church is one, and it is commanded in Holy Scripture that we should keep the bond of unanimity and peace, it follows that we should write and signify to one another the things which are done by each of us; that whether one member suffer or rejoice we may all either suffer or rejoice with one another. In our diocese, then, not so long ago, there have gone forth lawless men, and adversaries of Christ, teaching men to apostatize; which thing, with good right, one might suspect and call the precursor of Antichrist. I

indeed wished to cover the matter up in silence, that so perhaps the evil might spend itself in the leaders of the heresy alone, and that it might not spread to other places and defile the ears of any of the m ore simple-minded.

But since Eusebius, the bishop of Nicomedia, imagining that with him rest all ecclesiastical matters, because, having left Berytus and cast his eyes upon the church of the Nicomedians, and no punishment has been inflicted upon him, he is set over these apostates, and has undertaken to write everywhere, commending them, if by any means he may draw aside some who are ignorant to this most disgraceful and Anti-Christian heresy; it became necessary for me, as knowing what is written in the law, no longer to remain silent, but to announce to you all, that you may know both those who have become apostates, and also the wretched words of their heresy.

Later in the letter, Alexander stated that he was confident that nearly one hundred bishops sided with him. They were planning a synod in Alexandria, where they would excommunicate all that believed in the "Arian heresy"—including, most importantly, Eusebius of Nicomedia.

Eusebius tried to understand how he could have been so ignorant, so blind. He had been traveling constantly, primarily in the West. He'd focused his attention on Constantine and Licinius, as their relationship deteriorated. He had heard talk that Alexander's deacon, young Athanasius, had been visiting several bishops.

Now that Eusebius saw what the young deacon had been circulating—and how—he had to admit it was a brilliant tactical approach. By personally meeting so many bishops, as the emissary of the most powerful cleric in the East, Athanasius had been able to cajole, threaten and promise with no paper trail. Once he had enough positive responses, Alexander could call for a meeting—giving gravitas to their position. The rest of the bishops would probably fall in line. As would Constantine.

Constantine, the proponent and supporter of orthodoxy for the stability of the Empire, was not likely to overturn anything the majority of "learned men" supported.

Eusebius opened the first scroll of the letter again. Even the title—"Catholic Epistle"—sounded authoritarian and noble. The letter itself was full of strong language. It's Theology, the comparisons of Eusebius to the Antichrist, the threat of excommunication. In terms of Church law, the charges were over-reach. But Eusebius acknowledged to himself that now he was on the defensive.

Caesarea, Palestine
Late 1073 AUC (320 AD)

Three hundred years earlier, Pontius Pilate had ruled the Province of Judea from Caesarea in a palace originally designed by Herod. That palace had been built on a stone breakwater constructed to form one end of the town's harbor entrance. Clear blue Mediterranean water nearly surrounded the structure.

Now the foundations of that palace stretched towards Eusebius of Caesarea's church and residence—perhaps the most beautiful see in the world, seeming to float in the westernmost Mediterranean.

Arius was impressed. And he was excited to be meeting the Caesarean. This Eusebius was a well-known man, a respected priest and prolific writer. He had written several commentaries on the Gospels, discussing the critical differences among them, and an *Ecclesiastical History* from the death of Christ to the current era.

Another favorite topic of this Eusebius was the early theologian Origen, who had spent many years here in Caesarea. Origen had written extensively about the difference in nature between God and

Jesus. Both Origen and Eusebius of Caesarea favored the concept of subordinated distinction between Jesus and God. "The Father" was primary and Jesus—while beloved—was secondary.

This was the reason that Alexander and Athanasius had been careful to ignore this Eusebius of Caesarea, in their "Catholic Epistle." They didn't want to give credibility to the Arian side in the theological debate.

Arius and the two Eusebiuses were meeting in Caesarea to decide how to respond to Alexander's "Catholic Epistle" and how to counter Athanasius's campaign. They dined together as soon as Arius and Eusebius of Nicomedia had arrived. Now, they were sitting on a balcony, watching ships come in and out of the harbor. Servants had cleared their table of everything but their wine.

They had talked of small things through most of the meal.

Arius thought the time had come to speak to important business. "Eusebius, if our position is weakened by Athanasius's politics, can we recover some ground by petitioning Constantine?"

He'd meant the question for his Eusebius—of Nicomedia—but both men answered "No" at the same time.

The host drew a taut smile. "This will go on and on. Call us by our places. Nicomedia," he nodded to his guest. "And Caesarea."

Nicomedia smiled more warmly. "Better, I suppose, than 'This' and 'That.' Constantine's immediate goal is to expand the Empire to the east, taking territory from the Goths. But his long-term goal, I suspect, is to keep his troops sharp for a final resolution of his differences with Licinius. His mind is focused on war and politics. Approaching him on this will only invite his wrath. He has made it clear that Ossius speaks for him on Church matters."

"Is Ossius favorable to us?" Arius asked.

Nicomedia took a sip of wine and paused for a moment. Then: "Ossius is favorable to what is best for Constantine and the Empire. He is personable. But he has two roles: the personal confessor of the Emperor and the rector of Empire's relationship with the Church."

Caesarea pointed toward Nicomedia, "You share that first role—personal confessor."

"Perhaps. To a small degree. But my relationship with the Emperor is different. We're cousins. Friendly but not very close. Ossius has gone into battle with him. They are more like brothers."

"So, Ossius protects Constantine?"

"Yes. He is also a good priest. A loyal servant of God. But, in places where the Church has conflict with the Empire, I believe he thinks of Constantine—of the Empire—first."

Caesarea nodded. "I know them both, slightly. But I yield to your deeper knowledge. If Ossius thinks first of protecting Constantine— and if Constantine is thinking of other things— then it seems to me that the best way to influence them is to reduce the size of this quarrel. Solve the dispute for them. This task becomes more difficult because young Athanasius has put us at a tactical disadvantage."

Arius added, "It's a sorry thing. Our position is supported by the historical record. But that doesn't seem to be enough."

Caesarea agreed. "Yes. They set the frame of the debate. So, let us respond by focusing on where we agree. When I read their Epistle, I noticed—aside from the unnecessary vitriol—that there are some points that may be areas of common ground. Perhaps a new letter to Alexander, emphasizing those similarities, may give us time to gain the support of others in the Church."

"It is a start," said Nicomedia. "But do we have any idea what has been promised? Has Athanasius gathered commitments from bishops' *quid pro quo*? Alexander has a wealthy and influential podium."

Arius groaned, "This is unseemly."

Caesarea smiled again. "Perhaps. But, if their support is built on promises, we have very little that we can counter."

Nicomedia laughed ruefully. "I have not heard of specific deals but—knowing the age in which we live—it is safe to assume there are *quids* outstanding. The poorer parishes will seek money and the wealthy ones will seek sabbaticals in Alexandria. We will have trouble matching that. Our greatest advantage is the strength of our beliefs."

Caesarea sighed and looked out at the ships.

Arius offered the best solution he could think of to summarize their talk: "I will write a letter describing our mutual understanding of faith this evening. And we can review my draft tomorrow."

The following morning, the three priests worked on Arius' letter at the same table where they'd had dinner the night before. The two Eusebiuses were both rested and seemed calm. Arius was more anxious. He hadn't slept much.

After they'd reviewed the letter several times and made some corrections, Arius read it out loud:

> Our faith from our forefathers, which also we have learned from thee, Blessed Pope, is this: We acknowledge One God, alone Ingenerate, alone Everlasting, alone Unbegun, alone True, alone having Immortality, alone Wise, alone Good, alone Sovereign; Judge, Governor, and Providence of all, unalterable and unchangeable, just and good, God of Law and Prophets and New Testament;

Arius took a brief break.

"I think that turned out well," said Nicomedia. "It gives us the common ground of what we all believe concerning our Father. I can't see that Alexander would disagree with what we have written so far."

"I agree," said Caesarea. He looked at Arius—who continued reading:

> who begat an Only-begotten Son before eternal times, through whom He has made both the ages

and the universe; and begat Him, not in semblance, but in truth; and that He made Him subsist at His own will, unalterable and unchangeable; perfect creature of God, but not as one of the creatures; offspring, but not as one of things begotten; nor as Valentinus pronounced that the offspring of the Father was an issue; nor as Manichaeus taught that the offspring was a portion of the Father, one in essence; or as Sabellius, dividing the Monad, speaks of a Son-and-Father; nor as Hieracas, of one torch from another, or as a lamp divided in two; nor that He was before, was afterwards generated or new created into a Son, as thou too thyself, Blessed Pope, in the midst of the Church and in session has often condemned;

Caesarea chimed in again. "Alexander and Athanasius should also agree with this section. Particularly the condemnation of Sabellius. Of course, they don't see their equation of Jesus with God as… dividing…the Monad. Of dividing God into parts."

Arius nodded in vague acknowledgment and continued:

but, as we say, at the will of God, created before times and ages, and gaining life and being from the Father, who gave subsistence to His glories together with Him. For the Father did not, in giving to Him the inheritance of all things, deprive Himself of what He has ingenerately in Himself; for He is the Fountain of all things.

Caesarea interrupted again. "I don't think there will be disagreement on this section, we are merely… defining…The Almighty again and what he gave to Jesus." Arius cleared his throat for the next section.

> Thus there are Three Subsistences. And God, being the cause of all things, is Unbegun and altogether Sole, but the Son being begotten apart from time by the Father, and being created and founded before ages, was not before His generation, but being begotten apart from time before all things, alone was made to subsist by the Father. For He is not eternal or co-eternal or co-unoriginate with the Father, nor has He His being together with the Father, as some speak of relations, introducing two ingenerate beginnings, but God is before all things as being Monad and Beginning of all. Wherefore also He is before the Son; as we have learned also from the preaching in the midst of the Church."

"I think this is where they will disagree most," said Nicomedia. "This is our belief, taught to us by Lucian before he was martyred. As he had learned it directly from the Apostles' scriptures."

Caesarea nodded eagerly, "I believe you are correct. From my perspective, this shows clearly that the Scriptures support Jesus' reverence, subservience and different essence from God. Some may not agree. Regardless, I think the letter is good." He seemed to plan to stop there. But the other two were looking for more. "And so, after you send this from Nicomedia, I will send Alexander a letter suggesting some corrections to the misinterpretations in his Epistle."

Arius and Nicomedia seemed satisfied with this response—but, now, Caesarea seemed unsatisfied. As if he had second thoughts about the letter. So, he said more: "I continue to believe it is best to let this quarrel subside. Until we see an opportunity to change many of the recent converts to a more...conservative...perspective."

Arius answered with what hoped would be soothing words: "Our prayers are that such an opportunity presents itself. And God knows that none of us controls the events that may forge that change. So it will be God's will."

"I agree, Arius. But I would feel more comfortable if we had better advantages to…ensure…God's will. Almost two years ago, in Alexandria, you cautioned me that we were at a crossroads. Your words are as pertinent now as they were then. We have lost ground. The beliefs of our fathers are being put aside for an image that is…attractive…perhaps, and makes sense to those that ascribe to Greek philosophy. However…however, they are not consistent with the early observers' descriptions of Christ. Nor to the actual words our Lord spoke. This is a tide…a tide that started in Egypt and is spreading through the Empire. It threatens to engulf us with its radical description of Christ, its adherence to a strict new orthodoxy, its continued glorification of celibacy, its continued exclusion of women. Women, who were so influential in the early foundations of our Faith. I lament that I lack the tools to stem this tide. Our future may be based on the pagan images of three gods instead of the One God that we, through our Jewish heritage, recognize as Our Father."

Caesarea smiled, nodded thoughtfully and said nothing.

Sirmium, Pannonia
Early 1074 AUC (321 AD)

Constantine felt his right arm flex with as much force as he had, when he slammed it down on Quintus' shield. He grimaced as his body lifted slightly from the power of the strike. He wavered for a moment and then regained his footing, using his shield as a counterweight away from his body. But this left his chest unprotected. Quintus' leg buckled as his arm tried to absorb the impact of Constantine's strike. Instinctively, from a crouched position, he spun around and aimed his sword at the Emperor's unprotected chest. But he froze instantly, when he saw the sharp end of Constantine's sword at his nose.

The three other bodyguards gasped. This was sparring. But the blades were real.

The Emperor didn't lower his sword but smiled at Quintus, who stepped back and bowed slightly. Only then did Constantine relax. Their small audience cheered for the victory. It had been a good match.

It had been almost five years since Constantine and his palatini had fought together in an actual battle. That last battle had been against Licinius, during the last civil war. The Battle of Cibalae. Constantine had flanked Licinius' troops and led a charge toward the center, routing the opposition decisively. Since then, the battles had been minor—and the Emperor's immediate attention hadn't been needed.

These days, they didn't practice as much or as intensely as they had prior to the battle at Milvian Bridge. With less exercise his knee pain had diminished. Constantine still exercised, now three times a week, but he hadn't found a sparring partner as challenging as Vibius. So, he rotated sparring duty among his guards—whose ranks he'd expanded to include several equiti.

And there'd been other changes. Gaius had retired after the victory at Rome and was in charge of the personal security of Helena. He had been replaced by Marcus, an outstanding centurion, to lead the legionari.

Constantine had promoted Ablabius to Praetorian Perfect. He had tried to stop using the Praetorian title and rename the position, Magister, but old habits made the name change difficult. Aside from the Greek's innate ability to assess a battlefield, he had a good sense for using horsemen effectively. And Constantine believed the tactical value of equiti was continuing to increase. A strong use of horses at the beginning of a battle intimidated the legionari. This intimidation helped win battles quickly.

As Constantine and Quintus relaxed and drank water, Titus was the first to ridicule his fellow bodyguard: "Quintus, I thought you had no fear. Why did you panic at the mere sight of a sword?"

Appius followed: "Q, I would say you fight like a woman. But you lack the strength of a woman. The Emperor has yet to breathe hard and you're trembling like a maiden on her first night of love."

In fact, both combatants were drenched in sweat and working hard not to be the first to sit.

Constantine smiled again at the ever-quiet Quintus and said, "It was a good fight, soldier. I have no idea how I got my blade up there. I was exhausted."

"Thank you, Imperator. It is an honor to spar with you," Quintus responded, stone-faced.

Ablabius had walked up to the group and heard the last bit of joking at Quintus' expense. He faced Titus, Appius and Sevius and said: "Why is it that every time I see the three of you, you are lounging about while Quintus and the Emperor are sparring? Are you eunuchs now? Have you assumed your proper place in the Empire?"

"Bold talk from you, pretty one," Appius sneered. "You've been on the back of a horse for so long, you've probably forgotten what it's like to fight. Hand to hand. Like men."

Titus raised his hand, so both Ablabius and Appius could see. The joking insults had gone far enough.

Constantine wiped his face with a towel and draped it loose around his neck. "What brings you here, General? I thought you were away to Rome."

Ablabius stood tall, separating himself from the jokes. "Dominus. We've received word from couriers that two of our northern outposts have been attacked by the Goths."

"Where?"

"North of Tomi. By the Black Sea," Ablabius answered.

Realizing the seriousness of the subject, the bodyguards gave Ablabius and Constantine room to talk privately.

"Goths," the Emperor grunted. And then he drank more water from his pitcher. "They are not diplomats. We have to respond with force. Either a reprimanding skirmish or full-fledged war. Do you have any idea how many troops they have?"

"No, Dominus. Details are few. Our forts held. And have already received some reinforcement. But they will need more. With your permission, I have two legions ready to leave. I will send a few reconnaissance units with them—and have those report back."

Constantine felt a soldier's impulse to strike hard at this latest opponent. But that was not the right response. Not yet, anyway. "Two legions sounds about right. Order them to engage the Goths with guerilla tactics. Skirmishes. Keep them occupied while we develop a plan to send an entire army there."

"Yes, Dominus. That will occupy them. The Goths are guerilla fighters themselves."

"The region around the Black Sea is trouble," Constantine said, between drinks. "We need to build a larger buffer between the Empire and all of the barbarians up there. It's not just the Goths. When we put them down, we can march west and break the Sarmatians. Move our frontiers north and east—and give Empire its buffer."

Ablabius rubbed his left thumb through the beard on the left side of this face. Constantine recognized this gesture.

"You have a concern, General?"

"Yes, Dominus. If we send an army, we will crush the Goths. But some will survive. They're sneaky bastards. And the survivors will try to regroup by finding a wealthy sponsor—"

"Licinius." Constantine finished, with a flash of anger in his voice.

"Yes, Dominus." Ablabius had already noticed that Constantine's temper was more volatile than it had been many years earlier. Or even a few years earlier. Most of the time, the Emperor reined in his anger but, occasionally, it led him to make snap judgments. This was a change from his younger days.

"The question, Ablabius, is: Who would you rather have fighting next to you? A Goth or a Frank?"

"A Frank. But chasing the Goths to Licinius' side helps him. As I said, they're sneaky bastards—but they are fighters. On the right battlefield and in the right conditions, they could be a challenge."

Constantine was visibly bothered by discussing Licinius. "God is with us, Ablabius. Not with Licinius. If we should line up against Licinius again, it will be our God—the true God—against pagan idolaters. And we will win. Again. So, dispatch our two legions and we will prepare to send an army to follow."

Ablabius believe that he understood the Emperor's frustrations. Several times, he'd had the opportunity to crush Licinius' forces and kill his rival once-and-for-all. But he'd always hesitated—which wasn't like Constantine.

Constantine started to walk toward his residence's bath house. But his general had one more matter to discuss.

"One more thing, Dominus," Ablabius started nervously. "Crispus has requested to join the two legions going north."

"Oh?" Constantine stopped abruptly. Ablabius had reason to be nervous. Crispus, Constantine's son by Minerva, his first wife—who'd died shortly after Crispus' birth, was a young man now. As a boy he had always been something of a lost spirit. He had shown some promise as a soldier. But he had a wandering mind. For the five years or so that Crispus had been in the army, Constantine had kept him close. A post in Tomi would be more dangerous. But it also might allow the boy to make his own way.

Constantine was pensive—not angry, as Ablabius had feared. The Emperor was thinking strategically about his family. His young wife Fausta, daughter of Maximian, had borne him several children but had never shown much interest in his oldest son. As a result, raising Crispus had fallen to Constantine and his mother Helena.

And Helena would not like to hear that her "precious one" was off fighting in some distant land.

Ablabius broke the silence. "I had thought Crispus might take control of the naval units. It is a small operation, but he has shown promise as a commander. We will need some naval presence if we attack Licinius. And, most of all, this will give him the experience he needs before he commands larger ground forces."

Crispus had commanded small ground units in the battles in the North Rhine. This was the next step in his training. "It's not the size of the force; it is the type of battle. You know this, Ablabius. The Goths are fast, fierce and unpredictable. They will attack anywhere they sense a weakness. In a large battle, I would not fear them. They wear light armor and are poorly organized. But, in guerrilla fighting, they are deadly to the unprepared. And Crispus has not experienced that kind of fighting."

Which was a reason he should go. And why Ablabius would then have him on the boats, away from the skirmishes but close enough to observe.

"Let him go for a season. And make sure he returns by summer's end. We will have the full army prepared to leave early fall. And I will have Crispus command our naval forces then."

"It shall be so, Dominus."

Sirmium, Pannonia
Late Fall, 1074 AUC (321 AD)

Constantine sat in his study within the Imperial Palace. It was late in the day and he was in a wretched mood. The weather was cold and rainy—and had been so for several weeks. The preparations for the war against the Goths were completed but it was impossible to move the army in these conditions. More precisely, the troops could move but the heavy wagons and supplies would get stuck in the poor roads to the north.

Earlier that day, in a meeting with Ablabius, Crispus, the Dux and senior centurions, Constantine had agreed to postpone the campaign until spring. Six weeks, at least.

Crispus had brought useful intelligence back from his time in the north. Their small forces had encountered the Goths numerous times; they'd skirmished, without suffering major casualties. And they'd gathered timely information on the land and its inhabitants.

Crispus estimated that the Goth army had more than 25,000 soldiers. That was more than they'd expected.

Constantine was encouraged with his son's development. Crispus was not a tactical genius—but he was becoming an able commander and he had the respect of his fellow officers. However, these good feelings were overwhelmed by his frustration at having to wait for the rains to stop. The Goths were a problem to be solved, not delayed.

Impatient with reading imperial agency reports from Rome and other cities—and feeling a bit like a caged circus lion—the Emperor decided to take a walk. The rain had lightened to a misty drizzle. But his spirits lifted when he saw Ossius and a deacon walking towards the chapel he had built next to his residence. He had not seen the Bishop in several weeks.

"Ossius of Cordova, why have you avoided me?" Constantine called.

"Imperator, I beg forgiveness. I have been in and out of Sirmium the last several days," Ossius replied, as he changed direction and approached. "Have I introduced you before to Clodius, one of my deacons?"

"No, I believe not. How do you do, son?"

"My Imperator," replied the deacon, with his head bowed as if looking down. However, his eyes remained strangely fixed on Constantine.

"How do the building projects in Rome progress, Ossius?"

"Well. I saw Pope Sylvester in my travels and he told me both basilicas inside the Aurelian walls—the Baptistery and the Croce—are completed. And that construction has begun on three of the eight planned for outside the walls. The secular construction of the Baths and Circus Maximus are nearly complete and, of course, your Arch is complete."

"Do the churches meet with the Pope's satisfaction?"

Ossius considered answering truthfully. But word had spread around the Imperial residence that Constantine was short-tempered lately. So, the priest answered diplomatically: "Imperator, all of our Bishops appreciate your Faith."

In fact, the Pope had noted several times that the size and locations of the churches were not comparable to those of the other building projects. Some of these subtle complaints were legitimate—the number of Christians in the Empire was expanding quickly, now that official persecutions were outlawed. And Constantine had given the Pope use of the Lateran Basilica, Maxentius' former residence. Nevertheless, if Pope Sylvester wanted to chide Constantine that the Church was being shortchanged, he could do it himself. Ossius wasn't about to.

"Ossius, have you heard of any further persecutions of Christians by Licinius since our meeting with Eusebius?"

Another difficult question. Ossius nodded to buy himself some time. Given the political sensitivity of this question--and the increased interest from his pupil—it was best to send speak with Constantine privately. "Clodius, please give us a moment to speak alone."

"Of course, Your Holiness. Emperor."

From across the terrace in front of the chapel, Clodius could make out only a few words. The Emperor's voice—higher-pitched than he'd expected—carried farther than Ossius' did. But Clodius had a clear view of expressions and gestures. As always, his bishop remained quiet and reserved, never raising his voice. On the other hand, Constantine's voice and demeanor showed clearly that he wasn't happy with the Ossius' answer. Constantine pointed at an imaginary list in the air—at least five accusations, each ending with a loud bark of Licinius' name.

Ossius managed to calm the Emperor for a few moments; but, then, a second crescendo came quickly. Something about a visit from Eusebius. Then something about Arius. Then Licinius' name again—this time, with Eusebius. And finally Eusebius' name repeated in anger, followed by the loud declaration "I could exile him!"

Clodius knew enough about the individuals named to put the pieces together. The Church's disagreements were combining with political disagreements—and the result could be trouble for everyone. As the afternoon grew dark and the rain started to pick up again, Constantine and Ossius separated with promises to revisit their conversation. As Ossius rejoined Clodius and they headed again to the chapel, Clodius couldn't help but ask what had so agitated the Emperor.

The question convinced Ossius what he'd been beginning to suspect—that Clodius was too interested in politics. His reply had a chill of admonition: "Imperial secrets should remain Imperial secrets."

Alexandria, Egypt
Early 1075, AUC (322 AD)

Before dinner and evening prayers, Athanasius lay on his bed in his tiny room reading Clodius' letter. Athanasius was buoyed by its content. His friend reported that, "Emperor Constantine was visibly angry with Emperor Licinius, to the point of beseeching to heavens, and my Master's prayers, to do away with the scourge that has infected the Empire's well-being."

There had been several documented reports of Licinius' continued persecution of Christians. Athanasius knew personally of several churches that had been ransacked and robbed by Licinius' henchmen. Some of their motive was fear of the Church's message; some of it was political—testing the limits of what Constantine would tolerate.

Athanasius suspected that those limits had been reached.

Like many, he considered it inevitable that Constantine would defeat Licinius finally, which would be a good thing for the Church.

Athanasius turned over on his narrow bed and re-read a sentence near the end of Clodius' letter: "The Emperor appeared agitated at the mention of the name of his cousin, Bishop Eusebius. Truly, his face turned red with anger whenever Ossius spoke either Eusebius' or Licinius' name."

During the two years that Athanasius had traveled the Eastern Empire speaking with bishops, a consistent image of Eusebius had emerged. He was a capable cleric, but more a politician than a priest. He had connections with everyone and particularly good ones with both Constantine and Licinius—a rare accomplishment.

And an opportunity. Constantine's personality and temperament demanded supremacy. He would not tolerate unresolved competition from Licinius—or anyone—over friendships and political allegiance. Constantine would force a resolution of his position. And, if Athanasius positioned the Church correctly, Constantine might help to resolve its uncertainty at the same time.

Athanasius was confident that his position, and Alexander's, on the nature of Jesus was accepted as theology by the majority of the bishops in the East. Although his stature was small, the strength of his faith and the fervor of his presentation were convincing. Very few bishops left their meetings staunchly opposed to his theology. Two or three in Libya, a couple in Egypt and a few in Palestine—a tiny number, overall. He estimated, conservatively, that over seven out of every 10 eastern bishops agreed that Jesus was equal to God. The only influential bishops he had not met with were the two Eusebiuses—Constantine's cousin in Nicomedia and the "other" Eusebius in Caesarea.

It was time to take the next step.

He approached Alexander that evening. "Your Holiness, I have good news from Sirmium. Our friend there indicates there appears to be a division between Constantine and Eusebius"

Alexander frowned, "And what could have caused such a division?"

"Imperial politics. We suspect that it has to do Eusebius' relationship with Licinius."

"I would be careful about underestimating Eusebius, my son. He is Constantine's cousin."

Athanasius nodded in agreement. "Of course, you're right about that, Your Holiness. Still, I am convinced that we are in a position to call a Council of Bishops and affirm our position on Jesus' divinity. We can resolve the matter once and for all. Formally renounce views that are antithetical. And an abomination to the will and nature of God." Alexander raised his chin and sighed deeply. He stared at Athanasius for a few moments before replying. And then:

"I have let this go too far. We have been too harsh, my son. These are not our enemies. These are Godly people who have some different views than we do. We are all of the same family, under the reverence of our Lord. The letters you have written for me, while effective, sometimes indicate a personal distaste for fellow believers because they differ from us slightly. On these matters of the nature of Jesus, yes, I agree they are wrong. They are mistaken. But our resolution must come through persuasion. Not by holding a Council to excommunicate our brethren."

"So, so..." Athanasius stammered, something he rarely did. He was red-faced and angry. "Your...Your Holiness, you wish to delay the Council? But we had agreed to hold the Council, once we were assured our theology would be...be embraced. Now, we are assured."

"Delayed, yes. For the time being," Alexander answered, with as much assurance as he could muster in his voice. "I have recently read Arius' *Thalia*. I think it would be entertaining and educational for parishioners, if lacking somewhat in substance—and obviously incorrect in its theology. But there are areas in which I believe we can make progress with Arius. Also, I reviewed Eusebius of Caesarea's letter and I am hopeful that we could make some progress there, too."

"*Thalia*? Poems for plebeians—not for...for clergy. As if plebeians will make the choice! God's will is not a matter for...for Athenian democracy!" Athanasius hissed when he said "democracy." His mind was racing. He'd already started making the plans. He'd already started spreading the word. "The Council must meet. I...I mean, we...I mean, the Church...we have already made the choice." He knew immediately that he'd said too much.

Alexander looked at him carefully and waited a few moments before responding: "No choice has been made, Athanasius. You and I believe that the Cross represents God and Jesus as equal, divine entities. Arius and Eusebius believe it represents one God and one lesser—but still divine—Son of God. We are correct. But this is a matter that the Church must consider and discuss. And conclude, over time."

Athanasius was even angrier than before, nearly spitting he asked, "So, even though we can win on this question—right now—you... you wish to delay?"

"For the time being, yes. Let us see how the Arians feel in a couple of months. As I said, I sense we are making some progress. We will revisit this in the fall."

Athanasius stormed out of Alexander's study.

He was so frustrated that he could barely think. How could this befuddled old man pass up the opportunity to crush these heretics? More importantly: How could God allows this delay? The circumstances were in place to clarify and strengthen His Gospels... and, yet...nothing? He threw himself onto his bed and cried uncontrollably.

As he wept, there was the sound of a ship's horn outside at the mouth of the harbor, being guided in by Alexandria's famous lighthouse, the Pharos. Even at night, Egypt's largest port and most prominent city was busy with merchant ships arriving and departing. The arriving ships carried goods from all over the Empire; the departing ones carried loads of glass and grain. Alexandria was the Empire's center of glass work, the Nile River valley produced the majority of the Empire's grain.

On board, the arriving ship's crew rowed to the cadence of one of the poems from Arius' *Thalia*. This sound wafted into Athanasius' room. And his tears gave way to rueful laughter.

Nicomedia, Asia Minor
Spring, 1075 AUC (322 AD)

Spring in Nicomedia was beautiful. The temperature was mild, the skies were clear and the sunlight had a golden quality that was unique to the region.

Eusebius' small villa was adjacent to the main church, nestled next to the foothill separating the Agora, the old city and the port from the new city on the hill. The church was near the Offices of the Empire's Administration but a distance from the Imperial Palace of Licinius. The Empire had recently rebuilt the entire lower city—making it larger, better organized and with running water from a new aqueduct.

Arius was busy planting some flower bulbs in the courtyard of Eusebius' villa. The bulbs were sent to him from a wealthy parishioner in Alexandria. He missed his work with those who had relied on him; intellectually, he missed his visits to the Library.

He had been working in the garden to take his mind off of other things. Somehow, in the push and pull of the last few years, he felt as is his life was no longer his own. He'd become, at best, a spokesperson for a cause. At worst, a pawn in someone else's game.

"Mastiff, stop!" Arius had adopted a small hound dog, a runt not satisfactory for hunting. They had become inseparable. As he planted, Mastiff would use her nose to push Arius' hand away from the bulbs. Grabbing a bulb with her teeth, she'd run to the other side of the courtyard. Arius would get up, retrieve the bulb and go back to his planting, only to have Mastiff repeat the theft a few bulbs later.

"Arius, you have quite the helper. She seems to be telling you to plant on the other side of the yard." Eusebius had returned from Rome during the night, but Arius had yet to see him.

"Welcome back, my friend. I am sure that, if I were the plant there, she would be bringing the bulbs here!"

"Undoubtedly," Eusebius said, as he held Mastiff's head and played distractedly with her long ears. "I bought you a present from Rome. The Pope let me have a dozen letters that had been copied from St. Peter and St. Paul's time, prior to their deaths."

"Very good!" exclaimed Arius. He stood up from his planting and stretched his back with several gymnastic twists. Then: "They have references to our early Christian fathers?"

"From what I understand. I didn't read them," Eusebius responded, still focused on the dog.

"How is construction going in Rome?" Arius asked.

"Well. Well, indeed. I think Constantine will like them. But we will probably need larger ones in the future. With the persecutions over, our numbers are growing quickly."

Arius felt a twinge of jealousy at not having seen the larger crowds. "He is planning 10 more churches in Rome?"

"Unclear. Most of the talk is that he's planning to build a new Rome—a new capitol city—somewhere here, in the East. And his energies will be focused on that."

That was as much small-talk as Arius could muster. He moved on to the real purpose of Eusebius' trip: "Did Sylvester bring up our controversy?"

Eusebius let the dog go and turned his attention to Arius. "He mentioned it. But we didn't spend much time discussing it. He is more concerned about the rioting and fighting between followers of Alexander and our followers in Palestine and Libya. He referred to it as 'an Eastern Empire conflict.' He doesn't view it as urgently as we do. He told me that it's a regional issue and that we in the East should come up with some compromise to resolve the fighting. He said exactly this: 'Use some words that are ambiguous but satisfy both sides—and be done with it.'"

Arius was vexed by Sylvester's response. "Be done with it? They don't understand."

"No."

"So, perhaps we should involve the Western Bishops?"

Eusebius shook his head and shrugged his shoulders at the same time. "I think they would be more inclined to our interpretation. But involving them expands the controversy to the entire Empire. Constantine made it clear to me six months ago he didn't like the division within our faith. His conclusion is not much different than Sylvester's. But he would like it even less if we involved the West."

Again, the thought occurred to Arius that the debate had become a political game beyond his control. Or even understanding. "We need to convince one of them that this is a serious matter. Something that will shape the Church profoundly."

Eusebius shrugged again and looked out at the water. "I'm at some risk with Constantine because of my relationship with Licinius. If he heard I was coaxing western bishops into a theological dispute, he might have my head. Regardless of family ties. We've reached a lull in the debate. Perhaps we can convince Eusebius of Caesarea to write something that is a compromise—something that Alexander would find satisfactory. Constantine suggested a Greek word, homoeanian. Maybe that will work."

North of Tomi, Thrace
Summer, 1075 AUC (322 AD)

Constantine stood next to his horse, on the top of a hill overlooking the battlefield. His palatini were far enough behind him that he felt as if he was alone, surveying the last stages of the battle.

The battle had gone as he had expected. The Goths, confronted with a trained and disciplined army, weren't as effective as when they fought in random skirmishes. This battle had taken place on a warm summer day on a hilly plain near the coast of the Black Sea, south of the Dniester River. His army had broken their front lines and then pursued the retreating Goths across the battlefield—until the Goths felt they had the advantage of higher ground.

That advantage proved illusory, quickly. Constantine had a legion of his equiti flank the Goths while two other legions attacked their center—followed closely by several legions of stout foot soldiers. The result was Goths found their forces split in two, and their command never gained control of both sides. Marcus' legionari set about purposefully decimating their opposition.

The battle was over in less than two hours.

This confirmed his choice of increasing the number of equiti.

The horsemen were extremely effective, flanking and breaking the ranks of the Goths almost immediately. He was pleased with all his troops. They were as well trained and seasoned as any force that he had led.

He pitied Licinius, who'd lost more than the Goths had this day—even though he was nowhere near this battlefield. His most likely ally was crushed.

And he was proud of Crispus. His son was good on a horse, better than Constantine himself. Better balanced on the four-post saddle and very quick to shift weapons, while keeping his shield positioned. Like the best riders, Crispus' horsemanship seemed more instinctive than practiced. And he still was not as skilled a swordsman as Constantine wished—he wasn't strong enough yet. But Constantine was confident his son's strength would improve.

Ablabius rode up the hill toward him: "Dominus, the day ends well! We have fewer than 500 casualties. Yet the Goths are over-whelmed. More than 4,000 dead, perhaps 6,000."

"Thank you, General."

In a moment, Ablabius had climbed down from his horse and stood next to Constantine. "What's next? Shall we rest for a couple of days and then head back to Tomi? Or do you prefer that we head east and test the Sarmatians?"

Constantine rested a hand on Ablabius' shoulder. "East, General. We continue east, along the coast. We must control all sides of the Black Sea. This will give the Empire a buffer against the barbarians. The Sarmatians have always expected that we would approach them from the south. Their defenses are set up for that. If we go around the Black Sea, we will approach them from the north—and we'll have the advantage of both surprise and location.

"At the same time, send word to our remaining troops in Thessalonica to take a legion along the southern route toward the Sarmatians—but order them not to engage until we have attacked. Make that clear. Wait until we attack."

"Brilliant, Dominus," said Ablabius. And he meant it.

Constantine finally turned to Ablabius and made direct eye contact. "Let's get the Dux and the centurions together to discuss. Our route should remain a secret—as much as possible. It would be easy for a few Sarmatians to ambush us on the poor roads through the foothills. Also, the orders to the legion in Thessalonica should be sent with someone we trust. And not in writing. This is a stealth mission and the plans cannot fall into unwanted hands."

"How many shall we send to Thessalonica with the message?" Ablabius asked.

"No more than 20. Seasoned equiti—and only one should know the complete details of our plan. Locals will be watching. And spies."

"Who will this trusted rider be?" Ablabius asked, although he suspected that he knew the answer.

"Crispus."

Alexandria, Egypt
Summer, 1075 AUC (322 AD)

Alexander summoned Athanasius to his study after lunch. Both master and student dreaded this meeting.

Since Alexander had decided that they would not pursue the Arians, at least not aggressively, Athanasius has been out of sorts. The bright young man, practically a genius in so many ways, was acting like a petulant child. He avoided eye contact and answered questions with short answers. Merely grunts.

He'd also begun to grow a beard, perhaps to show some growing independence and authority. Or maybe just to make his boyish face look older. He was even attempting to reduce his hand gestures as he spoke; at some point earlier, one of the other students had made a cutting remark about Athanasius' gestures being effeminate. At the time, Athanasius insisted he wasn't offended—but, clearly, the remark had stayed with him.

"The world is imperfect and we humans never have things as we wish," Alexander whispered to himself. It was an epigram that one of his teachers had taught him many years before. Young Athanasius was maturing. But he was not mature yet. He still hated compromise.

Now Alexander had a chance to help his brilliant student through this difficult place. To learn the art of compromise. Athanasius came into the study, looking down at the ground, and sat in the familiar chair across from Alexander's desk. Only then did he look up and make eye contact.

Alexander smiled as warmly as he could. "We have some news, Athanasius. A possible break in our impasse. I've received a letter from Eusebius of Caesarea proposing some wording that might alleviate our differences."

Athanasius was not enthusiastic. "Oh? What has the good Arian bishop proposed?"

"That we use a Greek word, a word from philosophy— *homoeanian*, to be specific—as the description of the nature of our Lord and God. He also suggests some others. He makes it clear he is not speaking for anyone but himself; and he hopes that we can reach an agreement that we can introduce, together, to the bishops. He said he got the idea from a letter written to him by the Emperor!"

Athanasius looked down again. "So, we're being instructed on theology by a profaner and a politician?"

Alexander shook his head, disappointed. "Athanasius, I am trying to include you into this process so that you can help make it sound."

The student made eye contact again. "I'm sorry. I appreciate that you summoned me. I will try to…help. I believe the correct word would be *homoousian*, meaning the same substance in different entities. *Homoeanian* is vague and allows that the substance in similar but not exactly the same."

Alexander sighed slightly and cocked his head. "Eusebius suggests *homoeanian* to replace *heteroousian*. It is an alternative, which conveys our preferred meaning, without contradicting their preferred term. Eusebius is reaching out and offering a compromise. I think we ought to explore it."

"I don't object to a reasonable compromise. But, clearly, *homoeanian* is the wrong word to describe the similarity between Jesus' nature and God's. The correct word is *homoousian*."

This time, Alexander snapped back quickly. "Athanasius! A compromise means both sides give a little. There is very little difference between the two words."

Athanasius' stare grew intense. "But these are God's words. Your Holiness, when my days here have ended, I don't look forward to having to explain to our Maker why I didn't stand up to heretics that wanted to diminish the nature of His only Son, Jesus Christ."

Alexander suddenly felt his age and physical frailty. He didn't have the energy to argue with Athanasius *ad infinitum*. "We will discuss this more. I believe a meeting with Eusebius would be fruitful. I will give it some thought."

As the student rose to leave, Alexander felt an even greater wave of exhaustion come over him. It felt like he was melting into his chair. He couldn't travel to Caesarea to meet with Eusebius. It would have to be Athanasius. At this point all he could think about is how nice it would be to rest, to sleep, to forget about this conflict.

"Athanasius, you must see beyond your own beliefs. You must see into other people's hearts. That's how you will become a great priest."

West of Archeaopolis, Asia Minor
Fall, 1075 AUC (322 AD)

Sarmatians had a reputation as fierce fighters. And they were very skilled on horseback.

Originally from Persia, the Sarmatians had gradually migrated north and west. They'd become the local rivals of the Goths and, at various times, had been both an ally and enemy of Rome. One year, they would beg for Rome's assistance against their neighbor barbarians—the next, they'd attack Roman garrisons over some minor dispute.

Sarmatian women had a strong influence. Not just in their homes, but in their army. Many of their soldiers were women. At a young age, these women would burn their right breast with hot iron, so that it wouldn't grow. They believed that, without the breast, their right shoulder and arm would grow larger and better handle a weapon.

Soldiers told the story that these maimed women were copying the Amazons from ancient legends. Constantine had seen this before—strange behavior of the present day justified by questionable historical connections. Myth used for intimidation.

But the myth hadn't worked for the Sarmatians this time.

Crispus had gotten to Thessalonica without any trouble. He then marched east, with over a legion of soldiers—and they marched slowly, both to ensure that they'd be noticed and to allow Constantine's army to march around the Black Sea. To delay even more, Crispus' army had made camp and spread rumors to the local population that Crispus had taken deathly ill. Two days before the battle, the Sarmatians realized that they were surrounded. Assuming that forces coming from the north had to be smaller than Crispus' army, they attacked Constantine first.

They marched into his trap and the results were horrendous.

The Sarmatians wore light armor because they didn't have much metal or skill at working it. So, what they did wear was made out of bone and horse hoofs. That made them particularly vulnerable to archers.

Also, Constantine had ordered his equiti to wield metal-tipped clubs, which would minimize the Sarmatians advantage on horses.

The Sarmatians' attack never got through the first line of Marcus' legionari. Ablabius' riders quickly flanked the Sarmatians, beating their opponents viciously with the metal-tipped clubs. And then Tiberus' sagitarii started shooting. The causalities were staggering.

Thousands—maybe 10,000—of Sarmatians dead. Almost their entire army. There hadn't even been time for a formal retreat; the few that survived had simply ridden or run off the field.

When the last arrow had been loosed and the last sword swung, Constantine rode onto the battlefield and viewed the carnage with disgust. Near his original front line, which had barely moved, he dismounted and walked into the bloody mess. Up close, he could see that nearly half of the Sarmatian dead had been women.

In 30 years as a soldier, he'd encountered some women fighters. Occasionally. No matter how brave or skilled, they were at a disadvantage in hand-to-hand combat on the battlefield. Amazon breasts or not.

"What sort of fool subjects his troops—and so many women—to total defeat?"

Crispus and the palatini were walking close behind him. But none answered his rhetorical question.

"How many prisoners did we take?" Constantine asked.

"About 400." Ablabius responded quietly.

"How many of those prisoners had rank, were company commanders or better?"

"Perhaps10, maybe 12." Ablabius again responded.

"Kill Them." Constantine ordered.

They crossed the width of the battlefield, around mounds of dead Sarmatians. The funeral pyres would be burning for days. Maybe weeks.

At times like this, his habit was to look for wounded Roman soldiers. But he didn't see any. So, he turned back to the small group following him. "This does not feel like a victory."

Rome, Italia
Late 1075 AUC (322 AD)

It had been ten years since Constantine's victory parade after defeating Maxentius and Rome was hungry for another public celebration. It was ready for festivities honoring the Emperor's victories over the Goths and Sarmatians—the barbarians.

This parade route started at the Milvian Bridge on Via Flaminia and went directly to the new Arch of Constantine next to the Coliseum. The theme was more jocular than it had been a decade earlier. Lighter, if not more joyous. Before the army entered the City, various troupes of clowns frolicked along the way. Mimes, fools and jesters drew the attention—and loud laughter—of the gathering crowds. Wine encouraged their raucous response.

As soon as the soldiers escorting a handful of Goth and Sarmatian prisoners crossed the Bridge, the laughing and hooting transformed into the familiar worshipful roar.

Constantine had actually brought fewer troops than he had before—a few legions, really. The rest of his army was back in Thessalonica.

After the prisoners, the foot soldiers marched into Rome, followed by the archers and then a few units of riders. Next, in a new element that he'd seen in the North, Constantine had a few older centurions march ahead of him, carrying in the fallen standards of the Goth and Sarmatian generals. The roar got louder. Then, the usual bearers with his standards, the now familiar Labarum. And the roar grew. Finally, he and Crispus rode across the Bridge in identical chariots, both wearing bright purple cloaks over their armor.

And the roar was deafening.

Citizens crammed the streets, many risking the ire—and fists—of the centurions lining the route. The people were trying to run into the street to touch Constantine, his deity status confirmed again. Wine made them bold. But it didn't make them strong enough or fast enough to get close.

At the end of the parade route, the troops had gathered in the broad streets that ran around the Coliseum, Constantine's Arch and the Senate Forum. The Emperor, his son and his bodyguards went into the Curia for a mostly ceremonial meeting with the senators. This meeting would formalize a few things—but also gave the reveling citizens time to disperse.

The Senate had received his letters and followed his orders. He and Crispus were both given victory garlands. And the Imperial Treasury would issue commemorative coins, bearing Crispus' likeness.

Once that meeting was over, the Senate recessed and most of the army troops were released. A large delegation of senators, dignitaries and several dozen of Constantine's generals and officers were to be given a walking tour the new buildings that had been completed since Constantine's victory at Milvian Bridge. This was somewhat difficult, because quite a few citizens were still partying. Several dozen legionari led the tour, clearing the streets of drunks and stragglers.

Constantine was most interested in two new churches along the inside of the Aurelian Wall. He slowed the tour at those points. They were well built and very attractive—but he agreed with the consensus that they were too small for the growing Christian faithful.

"I realize that it sounds absurd, to say that a growing Church is problem," Pope Sylvester said while Constantine examined the fine woodwork of the altar. "But we are having trouble finding places for all of the Romans who wish to attend Mass."

"I understand. In the army, we call this 'logistics.' Soldiers can only fight when the supply lines are working. And they have food and water. Simple things aren't always…simple." He turned to the Pope and nodded to Crispus. "Pope Sylvester, have you met my son—Flavius Julius Crispus?"

Crispus didn't say anything right away. He was still tongue-tied in social settings.

So, Sylvester spoke first: "All Rome has heard about the young general's ability on the field of battle."

Constantine tilted his head to Crispus, encouraging him to say something.

"Your Holiness, it is an honor to meet you. My father has always spoken highly of you. I don't yet share the intensity of my father's faith but I do admire it. And I hope to learn more. Over time."

It was a little too much—but nothing Crispus said was untrue. Soon after Sylvester had become the Pope, Constantine had walked through Rome leading Sylvester on his horse. It was viewed by the citizens as a sign of the Emperor's Christian faith.

Church leaders in Alexandria noted that Constantine had never shown such reverence to their Pope, Alexander.

Constantine had given much more to the Roman Church. The Lateran Estate—Maxentius' old Imperial Palace—was Sylvester's official Papal Residence. And Constantine gave Sylvester nearby land and initial funds to build a grand Basilica, to be named for St. Peter. *That* church would have enough room for thousands; but it would take decades to complete.

Behind all of this support was Ossius, constantly encouraging a close alliance between the Emperor and the Pope. Ossius and Sylvester had known each other for many years and had a strong mutual respect. Ossius thought of Sylvester as a Holy Father, both spiritually and literally. Sylvester returned the favor, holding Ossius among the most honorable of the clergy he had known.

After the tour of new buildings inside the City walls, Constantine asked to see one or two of the new churches outside the walls. There was a scramble to assemble enough horses and carriages to transport everyone. During this hubbub, Sylvester invited Ossius to ride in his carriage. Ossius had hoped to slip away, unnoticed; he had a letter to read that was marked "urgent." But he accepted his old mentor's invitation.

As they sat across from each other, Ossius was trying to read the scroll sent to him by an agitated Syrian bishop. The scowl on his face reflected the difficulty of both the letter's content and reading while bouncing over a Roman cobblestone road.

The Pope watched Ossius' face, like a parent watching a favorite child—realizing that no parent can insulate the child from life's inevitable pains. He had seen Ossius grow from a young idealistic and brave priest convinced he could stop the persecutions by traveling to Gaius' court; to a bishop who held the respect of the most powerful Emperor of their time. Finally, he asked, "Ossius, you are talking even less then you normally do. What troubles you, my son?"

Ossius put down the scroll. "Nothing, Your Holiness. I'm just a little tired, I suppose, of the responsibilities that God gives us. At the least opportune times."

"There are few in this world who have a greater burden than you, Ossius. You travel in many worlds—the Army, the Empire, the Church. Yet there is no one I have ever met who handles it all better. With more thoughtfulness. Or a more even temperament," the Pope answered.

"Thank you. But I am afraid I fall short of your compliments, my Pope. With Constantine, I am riding a bull with no bridle. He is a force of nature. Powerful, decisive and increasingly deadly. Blessed but cursed at the same time. I can't control him. And then there are issues that should be within my control," he held up the scroll, "but the Lord shows me no path to resolve them. This Arian controversy is one of those."

The Pope nodded. "You do not control the Emperor. So, indeed, you must guide where you can but feel no inadequacy about his free will. He will be judged by our Lord, as we all shall be. But his reverence to God, which seems genuine, should give him good stead."

"The Arian issue is more complicated.' The Pope continued. 'It doesn't seem necessary that mortal men solve the question of Jesus' godly nature. I'm content that it is a mystery whose full answer we will only know when we join Him in heaven. But this question is consuming many of the faithful. And we can't control the timing—when such questions confront us. I met with Eusebius of Nicomedia a few months ago and encouraged him to find a compromise. He is a good man."

Ossius frowned again. "It is becoming a schism to the Church in the East. And, with that, proponents for each side become hardened and distasteful of compromise."

The Pope breathed heavily. "Alexander has always struck me as a man of profound faith, who would not be drawn into quibbling. Is it the Arian camp that concerns you?"

"No. It is Alexander's camp. My sense is that Alexander personally would agree to a compromise. But he has a deacon who will not—and that deacon is influential. The deacon's name is Athanasius and he has helped spread the controversy throughout the East. Eusebius has done the same thing, to a lesser degree, from the Arian viewpoint."

"So. A compromise would be a description of Jesus' godly nature elegant enough to be acceptable to both sides—but you fear that no such description is possible within doctrines of our faith?"

Ossius smiled. "Elegant. I've never thought of the solution as elegant. I've thought of it as ambiguous. My shortcoming. But, yes, we need this elegant compromise soon. Without it, one side or the other will foment problems and divide the Church. We've already had deadly rioting in some cities in the East."

The Pope leaned toward Ossius. "God delivers problems on the plate of those who can handle them. I know you will handle this well. I don't have the solution you need to this Arian dispute. But I promise that, if you need me to get involved, I will do so in whatever manner you wish."

"Thank you, Your Holiness. I only wish this plate was on your lap!" Both men laughed.

The carriage stopped at the first church outside the Aurelian Walls. Sylvester followed Ossius down onto the dusty ground and looked at the crowd gathering by the entrance of the building. He could see Constantine and his handsome young son Crispus, surrounded by wealthy parishioners and the elite of Rome.

Looking back, he could just make out the walls of the City in the distance, shining in the late afternoon sun. He bowed his head and briefly thanked God for his blessings and asked the Lord to give strength and wisdom to Ossius. And then he heard Constantine's voice calling him.

Sirmium, Pannonia
Early, 1076 AUC (323 AD)

Constantine was angry! Blindly angry! He had received a letter from Licinius, lodging a complaint. Licinius claimed that Constantine had infringed his territorial sovereignty, as defined by treaty, when he and Crispus had engaged the Goths and Sarmatians. The complaint was lengthy and—from Constantine's perspective—a foolish provocation. Emperors had equal rights throughout the Empire.

Constantine found Ablabius by the stables and vented his frustration: "This idiot! This…buffoon…accuses me of infringing on his territory. I think the solution is to disregard that he has any territory at all and take what he has away from him."

"This would be Licinius, Dominus?"

"Who else could irritate me *ad finem*?"

"And he has written you?" Ablabius asked.

"Written to complain that we abridged our treaty. He claims we trespassed into his territory during the war with the Goths and Sarmatians."

"We have such a treaty, Dominus? I thought emperors could go wherever they wished within in the Empire."

"You are correct. Emperors can go anywhere within the Empire. I think it is time to start planning what we are going to do with the Eastern Empire."

"Shall we start adding legionari?" His General's question seemed sudden.

"Not yet. Planning first. I am concerned about the size of the army we will need. With the larger size will come problems in supplying them. And Licinius will surely dig in, when we've surrounded him. If we have a siege, it could become a very long war." The battle planning was already calming Constantine—as it always did.

"We will march east from Thessalonica?" Ablabius asked, looking back at his horse.

"Probably. Once we start building the army, Licinius will do the same. And we will watch where he goes. Our troops are well tested, his are not. I don't want to give him much time, once we've gathered our forces, to build and train his."

"Then we won't be fighting until the spring," Ablabius said.

"Correct. We have to plan, get supplies lined up, start building the troops over winter and we will be ready by late spring."

"It will be done, Dominus."

"And, Ablabius, get Crispus to the navy." Constantine ordered.

Constantine's efforts to build his army without Licinius' knowledge proved short-lived. Within a few months, Licinius sent a Proclamation of War.

Nicomedia, Asia Minor
Spring, 1076 AUC (323 AD)

Arius, sitting on a comfortable leather chair in the sitting room of Eusebius' villa, read the letter from the other Eusebius. Mastiff had tried to jump onto his lap three times but he was too deep in thought to allow the dog up.

The meeting between Athanasius and Eusebius of Caesarea had gone badly. Nothing in Eusebius' description gave Arius hope that there could be a compromise. Athanasius had ended the meeting with a tirade. He accused Eusebius of much more than just heretical views—he accused the bishop of womanizing, associating with people of ill-repute, being the product of adultery and worse.

Eusebius reported that he was dumbfounded and couldn't understand why the sudden change. He wrote that, the prior day, they had had a detailed discussion concerning the two Greek words, *homoeanian* and *homoousian*.

These words seemed to be the area that had the most potential for compromise. They had some difficulty translating the words to

Latin; but Athanasius had seemed reasonable at that point. They had a long discussion concerning the Scriptures' differences concerning Jesus being the "Son of Man" or "Son of God." They discussed the sometimes contradictory language and the reasons for those contradictions. Eusebius thought that day had gone well.

The next morning it was like Athanasius was a different person. He would not discuss the words and rushed to leave, as if he was trying to get away from the devil.

Arius knew Athanasius from his time in Alexandria. The angry deacon had been born outside the city and grew up wanting to be a priest. He'd been a very small boy, physically—with an attractive, almost angelic, face.

There was a story that circulated through the Church in Alexandra. As a boy, Athanasius had been playing in the water with several other boys near Alexander's residence. Looking outside, Alexander had noticed they were imitating the ceremony of baptism.

Athanasius was playing the priest.

Alexander asked Athanasius' parents to allow the angelic boy to pursue his dream of becoming a priest. They did. Soon after, Athanasius was living with Alexander. In his early teens, he had become the bishop's personal secretary. A few years later, a deacon.

Arius considered Athanasius pious, smart and aggressive…but mercurial. He could be reasonable one day and paranoid the next, as Eusebius described. Arius believed that having a parish would have helped him. Working with common people's problems rather than the pressing problems of Alexander's office would give him a more grounded perspective.

In fact, Arius was surprised that Athanasius had developed a contrary view to his beliefs. He remembered a very agreeable conversation he once had with Athanasius concerning Origen's writings. Origen had been born in Alexandria and lived there for more than half of his life. All the local priests and deacons had read from his extensive library.

Their conversation led Arius to believe Athanasius saw God in the same light as Origen did. But, clearly, Arius had been wrong. Or Athanasius had changed his mind.

Arius laughed to himself, finally letting the nagging Mastiff on his lap. "How did Origen do that self-castration thing?"

Alexandria, Egypt
Spring, 1076 AUC (323 AD)

Athanasius found Alexander sitting in the rear pew of the main church, arms folded in front of him, bent over so that his beard was nearly touching his lap.

The old bishop had come to watch a wedding officiated by one of his priests at the simple wooden altar in the front of the church. He enjoyed weddings, the start of a new life. As a young man, he had almost gotten married—but the call for celibacy in the clergy had given him pause. All his life he had harbored regret that he hadn't made that commitment.

He reminisced that his life had been more vivid when he'd been in love with that shop keeper's daughter, so much more laughter.

Athanasius had just returned from his meeting with Eusebius and sat in the pew next to him, upright and assured. As Alexander listened to his student's hushed and rushed description of the meeting, he found himself picking the cuticles of his fingers, stopping when he became aware of what he was doing. "Strange," he thought to himself, "I haven't done that since the persecutions."

Athanasius said that the Arians would only consider the less-exact version of the Greek word. They were so stubborn that Athanasius and Eusebius had a vicious argument, just as Athanasius was leaving.

Although Athanasius was unrelenting in his insistence that *homoousian* was the only word acceptable, Alexander was considering the lesser version. It would avoid the pending crisis—all of the charges and countercharges, the councils, the fights.

On the other hand, he was concerned about his own mortality. He knew he didn't have much time left in this life. How would he explain to the Almighty his compromise when he strongly believed God and Jesus were of the same nature? This might be the defining decision of his life. But he was tired of the day-to-day toils and would often fall asleep during the day. Sometimes he fell asleep, even while he was meeting with people. His mind wandered back to the wedding as the bride answered "I do."

"Your Holiness, I ask you again. What is your choice?"

"I am sorry, Athanasius. Choice of what?" Alexander asked quietly.

"Choice of a synod of our See's Bishops or a larger Council of Bishops of the Eastern Empire?"

Alexander answered in a whisper. "Athanasius, once we start that process it is irreversible. The conflict will rise to the point that there can be no middle ground. It becomes what Pope Sylvester and Ossius have requested that we avoid—a spectacle. Using Eusebius' Greek word is a reasonable compromise. One which satisfies all parties and avoids a potential impasse. Or a loss of our position, if the bishops were to decide against us."

Athanasius responded with a tight-lipped reply. "Your Holiness, there will be no loss of our position. I have been promised by a majority of our bishops that they will stay with us. In response to your suggestion of compromise, I ask you: did Christ compromise? He had several easy ways of escape. Did He choose those easy ways? No. He went forward and died on the Cross for us. And your intention now is to repay him by taking an easy escape?"

There were a few minutes of silence between the men. In that break, Athanasius decided he'd been too emotional. He needed to return to reason. "This is not a fight to death. It is a fight over the correct dogma. Over the correct way for the world to view our Savior. But that is important."

Alexander looked wearily at his young deacon and then looked away to gather his thoughts.

After a few more moments passed, he answered, again in whispered tones. "In many ways, I would rather this were a fight to my death. The havoc it will cause my Church may be much worse. Well, so be it. We will have a synod of the bishops and priests of only our dioceses—not of the entire Eastern Empire. We will plan for early fall, after the summer's heat breaks."

In perfect time, the horns blew from the front of the church announcing the new marriage.

Bay of Naples
Summer 1076 AUC (323 AD)

Naples had been the headquarters of the Roman Navy for several centuries. Located southeast of Rome, on the west coast of Italy, the bay was protected and secure. Most naval operations were managed in a harbor just northeast of the small island of Megaride, directly off the mainland.

According to Greek legend, the body of the siren Parthenope washed up on Megaride's shore after she drowned because she'd failed to lure the great Ulysses to his death. The reason for that legend's location was easy to see, Naples was beautiful, but rugged. The City was surrounded by jagged mountains. It was a natural naval fortress that had repelled even the great tactician Hannibal.

Crispus examined the fleet from his chariot. The larger ships stayed in the deep water near the close side of Megaride; the smaller ones were anchored closer to the harbor. Small transport boats shuttled back and forth, like water bugs on a pond.

When he looked at the fleet, he didn't see ships but small battle-fields—as his father had taught him. Perhaps there was a better way. But this was how the Empire had always looked at its navy, as an extension of its ground forces. Rome had been built on its legions, not its ships. It didn't develop significant naval power until it had been challenged by Carthage—led by Hannibal—two centuries before Christ's birth.

The first ships they built were large, oar powered battering rams that had a tendency to sink in major storms. By the time the Romans conquered Carthage they had perfected the design of large warships. Then, for several decades, the Empire was attacked by swifter, smaller pirate ships designed in the East. As a result, the navy Crispus now commanded comprised several dozen heavy galleys—mostly triremes—and over 200 smaller and lighter liburnians. He also was responsible for thousands of small transport and landing ships.

For movement, the triremes relied on approximately 170 oarsmen arranged in three levels. The liburnian ships were biremes which used 35 to 40 oarsmen arranged in two levels. Both types of warship used sails when conditions permitted.

Popular legend held that oarsmen were "galley slaves" forced into labor and shackled to their seats. This wasn't so—and hadn't been for generations. All crew members were free men, including oarsmen. They were shackled to their seats by pay, not chains.

Most of the warships' crews were Greek, Egyptian or Carthaginian. Their pay was less than the pay of soldiers in the Roman Army, even though the mortality rate for naval troops in combat was quite high.

In addition to their crews, the triremes could carry as many as 50 marines on the upper deck; the biremes, about 15. Some of the marines—about one in five—were archers. The rest were trained on naval weapons.

The upper decks of both ships were typically equipped with catapults to hurl heavy stones and burning pitch. Most ships also had mounted ballista, large mechanical bows that could shoot large wood piercing lances. They could also shoot grapples with ropes which were used to hook onto opposing ships and pull them alongside for boarding. Once a specially-designed boarding plank dropped, Roman marines would attack as ground troops might.

All the attack ships had large metal rams designed into their bows at the water line. The boats could ram if they needed to—but that practice had diminished as the Romans became more sophisticated with other naval weapons and tactics.

A question that Crispus had considered, as he watched the fleet, was how long to stay here. Or move. There was a smaller naval port on the Adriatic side of Italy, near Ravenna. And Constantine had started to build a major port on the Eastern shore of Greece, near his military base in Thessalonica. The harbor at Thessalonica was complete but the docks and administrative facilities were still works in progress. But either of the other locations was closer to where the war with Licinius was likely to take place.

Crispus climbed off of his chariot and walked along the dock where his liburnian—the fastest bireme he could find—was moored. Past the ram of his boat, he noticed a transport out the in bay with an officer waving at him. Thestor, he thought. He waved back and gestured to a point further down the dock.

As he waited for the admiral of the biremes to join him, Crispus marveled at the beauty of the coral blue water stretching out into the Mediterranean, surrounding Megaride and supporting hundreds of his ships. He wished his wife could see how beautiful it was.

He missed his wife; he missed their love. He knew he could have a prostitute. Or several. But his father was Constantine. And Constantine had an increasingly strict moral compass. There was no question his father would hear about any dalliances with prostitutes; and Crispus knew his father would be critical.

Crispus' wife and infant son would join him when he arrived at Thessalonica. But that seemed a long way off. His plan had been to train with the navy for several months in Naples and then sail a large portion of the fleet to Thessalonica. From Thessalonica it would be an easy distance to Licinius' fleet by the straits of Hellensport and Bosporus. But maybe that plan would change....

Licinius' fleet was led by Amandus, an established admiral who had more ships under his command than Crispus had under his. Amandus' fleet was comprised of some 350 triremes and biremes; and his attack ships were also larger. His biremes housed up to 50 oarsmen.

To compensate, speed would have to be Crispus' strength. He was learning his boats from first-hand experience. He had spent the last couple of weeks sailing and rowing the larger triremes. This had been the first full day he'd sailed on his liburnian—and he was amazed at the speed it could attain both on sail and with oars. And how quickly the smaller ships could maneuver.

As Thestor's two-oar transport pulled up in front of the ram of the liburnian, Crispus yelled to the older Greek: "Thestor, I am dumbfounded. These smaller boats are fast! And rowing them seems easier. I didn't get as tired as I did on the triremes."

Thestor was Crispus' favorite naval officer. As a young captain, he had taken Crispus' grandfather Constantius to Britannia. And he had met Crispus' father, the Emperor, several times.

"Yes. Different muscles. Bigger boats need oarsmen more like me, short and stout. Smaller boats we like longer arms, faster." Thestor answered, climbing out of the transport, nodding thanks to the two oarsmen and shaking Crispus' forearm—all in one fluid motion.

"Amandus' liburnians are bigger than ours. Are they as fast?"

"No, Caesar. Not as fast. We are lighter have less draft. But they have more oars. With wind in our sails, we win. Also with wind, we can ram more. The oars aren't as tired."

Crispus looked back at his boat. "So, if we were lighter still, had wind into our sails and could ram, we would be able to overcome heavier ships?"

"We will win regardless, Caesar. God is with us. But—" and here the sailor in Thestor trumped the officer, "—how would you make us lighter?"

"We could carry fewer marines. Take the ballista, catapults and heavy artillery stones off the ships."

Thestor looked at him with doubt. "A risky move. If you're boarded, you are dead."

"Then carry archers."

"Perhaps, Caesar. Perhaps."

Alexandria, Egypt
September, 1076 AUC (323 AD)

Athanasius was in his element. There were over 100 bishops as well as priests and deacons from the southern rim of the Eastern Empire assembled in the main church in Alexandria. For three days, they had discussed the same points of the Arian controversy that he had discussed with them individually. He was confident that his earlier efforts would influence the outcome of this larger gathering.

The evening before the conclusion of the synod, Alexander spoke with Athanasius and a Palestinian priest. They discussed what proposed remedies they should expect.

Athanasius had spoken boldly, as he usually did on this subject. "We should state emphatically what orthodoxy demands—insofar as the equality of our Lord and God. And those that we know to have beliefs otherwise should be excommunicated."

The Palestinian priest answered first. "I am not so sure we should be so strident, Athanasius. Many of the skeptics are just that, unsure that the equality is obvious. St. Thomas is referred to as 'Doubting Thomas' but Jesus didn't reject him. He loved the Doubter as much as all the other Apostles."

"I agree, Athanasius. Something less judgmental," Alexander added. He seemed relieved that the Palestinian had taken the lead in the exchange.

"I respect you both, eminences. But this is far different than what St. Thomas faced. In his time, there had never been a Son of God on earth. There had never been a resurrection from the dead before. These things have now become historical facts. They are cornerstones of our faith. Our belief in God living here on earth is no longer based on prophesy—but history. Therefore the only question is: Was that God on earth in human form a lesser being? You either believe He was God and you are a Christian or you don't and you are an Arian."

The next day, the synod concluded with a proclamation that God and Jesus were homoousian. And it listed several bishops or priests of the Eastern Empire who had written or spoken differently— and were, therefore, excommunicated. No longer allowed to take communion. Prominently listed among the excommunicated were Arius, Eusebius of Nicomedia and Eusebius of Caesarea.

Athanasius took great pride in the fact that he had maintained the strictest measures of faith for the Church. But some of his supporters, including Alexander, had doubts.

The bemused old bishop had indulged the process—and Athanasius realized this. He worried that he wouldn't be able to maintain such measures without Alexander's indulgence. He needed a way to expand his own influence, in his own right.

Bithynia, Asia Minor
October, 1076 AUC (323 AD)

Eusebius of Nicomedia was hosting more than 50 bishops, priests and clergy from Asia Minor, Syria and Libya. A large former pagan compound in a town south of his see had recently been converted to a church and retreat center; it afforded the room—and the privacy— necessary for this "second" synod.

On the night before the last day of the meeting, the day when most of the important matters would be discussed, Eusebius couldn't sleep. He sat on the edge of his bed, the room lit by the flickering flame on the wick of the oil lamp on his night stand.

Balanced on his legs were a flat writing board, his inkwell and a piece of writing linen. He was writing a list of things he needed to get done. He wanted to talk to Secundus and Theonus concerning their thoughts, warn Arius about digressing and decide what the main conclusion would be coming out of the synod.

He stopped writing and gently cursed at his pen as it leaked some ink onto his finger.

As he wiped his finger he re-read the last two items on his list. He loved Arius—but there was no question Arius was aging. His tendency to ramble often led him into subject areas better left alone. Eusebius would gently caution him, hoping that would stop some of his more radical outbursts.

The extent of how far the synod's conclusions should go was a far more sensitive subject. He had no doubt that he could recommend the excommunication of Alexander and his upstart deacon. He'd have the support of bishops Secundus and Theonus who disliked the Alexandrians immensely. In fact, all of this synod's participants were infuriated by Athanasius' uncompromising arrogance. But declaring the sitting Pope of Alexandria excommunicated might be too aggressive, even for this group.

Writing three other minor tasks on his list, Eusebius put the writing board down, blew out the oil lamp, said a brief prayer and turned into his bed.

The next day, the synod declared Arius and his followers to be reinstated and allowed to take communion. All priests in attendance were encouraged to support Arius' views. Those that couldn't would run the risk of being excommunicated in the future.

Adrianople, Thrace
December, 1076 AUC (323 AD)

Licinius prided himself as being a fierce competitor. This was obvious, as he walked the hill overlooking the Hebrus River on one side of the hill and the city nestled below on the other side. Yelling to his Dux and select centurions, he commanded where they should plan to put different barriers, what weapons should be used where and how far their lines should extend to repulse Constantine's coming attack.

He concentrated on every detail that he could imagine would give him an advantage over his rival. He was particularly attentive to arming the ridge of the hill overlooking the river with artillery stone catapults, ballistae and hundreds of scorpios.

Scorpios were a sort of stationary crossbow, an individually-fired sniper weapon that shot smaller stone "bolts" with fatal accuracy. And enough power to kill through armor.

Licinius and Constantia had chosen Adrianople as the place to confront Constantine's army. The city was easy to defend, lying slightly lower than the shallow ridge that surrounded most of it. The other side of the ridge sloped gradually to the Hebrus River.

On the opposite side of the river were miles of watery lowlands. The battlefield conditions were difficult for any army planning a quick attack.

Licinius' army was in the very early stages of fortifying the ridge between the city and the river. The defensive strategy was simple: Arm the ridge to inflict maximum casualties on any approaching forces. He had ordered the army to dig long trenches along the closer river bank, so that any horses that got over the river would have difficulty making progress up the hill.

While spies reported that Constantine had become increasingly pious and lived by a strict moral code, Licinius had no problem stretching moral standards to fit his desires. The proclamation he had made with Constantine in Milan—about religious freedom and ending the persecution of Christians—had been fine at the time. Now, ten years later, it didn't serve his purpose any longer.

But ridge fortifications and broken promises weren't Licinius' only problems.

One of his problems was a simmering concern that Christians favored Constantine. To have such people in the Imperial government created an advantage for Constantine. So, Licinius relied increasingly on pagans as bureaucrats. He removed Christians from public office whenever he could.

Another of his problems was money. Licinius needed it—and the wealthy Christians had it. So he ordered the looting of many churches and ostracism of wealthier Christians. Of course, that only made the first part of the problem worse....

And the biggest of his problems was time. Or age, to be more precise. Licinius was ten years older than Constantine. He knew he had less time than his rival—but the same ambition. To be the one, true Emperor of Rome. His wife had noted, trying to be helpful, that his habit of laughing nervously was increasing. He told her that he was afraid that he was running out of time.

His marriage to Constantia was one of the best things that had happened to Licinius. She was a true patrician. She didn't hate her brother, Constantine, or enjoy intrigues or treachery; she was simply loyal to her own husband. Her devotion was obvious. And she doted on their son, who was just five years old.

Which was good, because Licinius didn't care for children.

They had chosen this place to confront Constantine's army, knowing that Licinius didn't have to do anything to draw Constantine in. All he had to do was make camp and prepare the field for battle. The spies and court gossips would make sure that Constantine came to him. As he reached the bottom of the hill and the bank of the Hebrus, he gave his last command of the day.

"Destroy all of the bridges."

That evening, after a quiet dinner, Constantia sent the servants away so that she and Licinius could speak privately. "Husband, I know that you believe you must confront Constantine. I know this, but I dread it. I feel I would be failing you as a wife if I didn't ask you to consider all alternatives. Is there no way to make a lasting peace with my brother? A new treaty? An abdication?"

Licinius looked at her. They'd been married nearly ten years. Before this, he'd never stayed with the same woman for more than a few years. But this marriage was different. He admired her.

He started with a short laugh. "Ha! I would certainly accept your brother's abdication, Constantia. But I doubt he would offer it. Emperors do not abdicate. It has never happened in the Empire and isn't going to begin with me. If Constantine insists on taking more of my land, we will fight!"

"Negotiate?" Constantina replied, keeping her tone serious and imploring.

"There is no negotiating with your brother, my wife. He takes what he wants, does what he wants, and then demands you pay him taxes on what you have left."

"Husband, I will support you in this. But remember that every war has a winner and a loser. And, though his God speaks of mercy, my brother is not a merciful winner."

"Constantia!" Licinius said sharply, "I appreciate your concern. But if you think I will be the loser, you have not witnessed the beauty of our position here in Adrianople. I know this area. I have fought here before. And must I remind you of the wars I have won in the past against far superior foes. Maximinus Daia. The Sarmatians."

He left out the fact that he had unsuccessfully faced Constantine in battle. Twice.

"Husband, I do not in any way underestimate you. But I do fear my brother. He is…different."

"Different in that life does not defeat him? In that he is a god? No. He is just a ruthless soldier put on this earth to make my life miserable. While he waves his false religion in everyone's face."

Constantina let her husband's frustrations subside and then replied. "I don't mean that my brother is different than other men. I mean that he is different than he used to be. He seems…harder. Less kind. I hear this—and I see it in the short notes he sends to me. Perhaps, if you would allow me to speak to him, I could suggest a different conclusion than war."

"No, wife. That will not happen. You grossly underestimate my strength here."

Constantia got up from the dining table quickly, Licinius followed equally quickly. He reached out with his hand, to insure she didn't leave the room angry. She accepted his hand, slightly shaking her head. They walked to their son's room to check on him.

Alexandria, Egypt
December, 1076 AUC (323 AD)

Alexander and Athanasius walked toward the beach in the yard of the Pope's residence. The sun had fallen into the last quarter of its decent into the Mediterranean.

A servant walked behind them in the event the Pope needed any help. This part of the city was popular with residents, who often walked along this stretch of beach.

Both Alexander and Athanasius had just read the declarations from the Synod of Bithynia. Athanasius was, of course, infuriated.

"Really, Holiness, this is blasphemy! Does the former Bishop of Nicomedia not comprehend his own limitations? Does he not understand that a mere bishop does not command the Pope? Has God not blessed him with even the humility to realize his position? That his self-importance is so great that he dares to 'possibly recommend' the excommunication of a Pope? Does he not fear that God may strike him dead for his imprudence?"

"Athanasius, please. This is merely one move in the game that we play. Eusebius is a powerful bishop and his synod was simply a reaction to our synod. Did you expect that he would react otherwise?" Alexander replied, having reached the water's edge. He bent over to look at a shell.

"Frankly, yes. I expect that to be excommunicated is more than just a humbling experience. It is a removal from the benefit and blessings of the Church. Being without the sacrament of Holy Communion, being devoid of the benefits of Jesus' blessing for a life ever after. It would be devastating to me. You should communicate with Pope Sylvester in Rome, concerning this breach. I am sure he would excommunicate the Bishop of Nicomedia."

"I am not sure my counterpart in Rome would appreciate being part of this conflict. I suspect he's is content that it is a regional controversy."

Athanasius followed Alexander into the shallow water—not seeming to notice it. "Your Holiness, this is not just a regional controversy. It is a worldwide Church crisis! We in the East are merely the front line. We must communicate to all believers within the Church to warn them. We should confirm our position with a council including the entire Eastern Church. As soon as possible."

Alexander waved his hands in the water to rinse off some sand. "Athanasius, a civil war is brewing between Constantine and Licinius. An Eastern Empire Council is not going to happen. Travel is already difficult and, once the military hostilities begin, it will even get worse. Can you imagine how Ossius might try to communicate this to the Emperor? The bishops wish to have a convention, so please don't attack the pagan Licinius until we are through."

Athanasius was silent while Alexander walked back onto the sand. Then: "At a minimum, we must inform the other bishops. I have been working on a letter for your approval that summarizes and substantiates our position. Perhaps you can review it and we will send it to all the bishops?"

"Yes, Athanasius. That would be fine," said Alexander, as if the topic was of minor importance. He picked up a two shells handed them to his servant. Then he turned to head back to his residence. There was a low rumble of a thunderstorm in the distance. "Strange," he said—not really to Athanasius or his servant, but to himself. "We had rain yesterday. It's not often we have it two days in a row this time of year."

Thessalonica, Greece
Early, 1077 AUC (324 AD)

Crispus and his fleet arrived in Thessalonica late in the evening. This was unusual—but Crispus had pressed his sailors and ships to make good time.

Constantine, eager to talk to his son, arrived a few hours later in the bright morning. They walked along the main sea wall of the growing port, followed by a small army of bodyguards. Constantine wanted to know about Crispus' preparations. In detail.

"Every defense has weaknesses, Crispus. Always be watching for your enemy's weakness. Then attack it, even if that means changing in the middle of a campaign. The great generals have always been flexible once they have engaged in battle. Dynamic. This is more important than one's initial strategy."

"I understand, father. I have studied the famous battles of Alexander and Hannibal. And Julius Caesar. I have read all I can about Octavian's victory over Marc Antony in the Ionian Sea. I think I am getting there with Amandus. First, he is old."

"Not much older than I am." Constantine responded sardonically.

"I mean, he is an older, long-time admiral. With that, often comes complacency. In your case, father, you have never been complacent. In his case, however…he is. I have heard from more than one spy that their fleet practices infrequently. They spend a lot of time in port. Amandus is overconfident about facing an inexperienced admiral—me—and our smaller fleet. He also likes a bit of wine."

"Good, so far. What is second?"

"Our liburnians are smaller, lighter and faster than theirs. I believe, if we can get even more speed by getting rid of as much weight as possible, we will be superior."

"How do you get rid of weight?" Constantine drilled all his Generals like this. He wished there had been time to do it more with Crispus when he was younger.

"Fewer armed troops. Going through each galley to get rid of non-essential equipment—and some essentials."

"What essentials are you getting rid of?"

"Ballistas. Catapults. Heavy artillery stones," Crispus replied. He hesitated a moment before mentioning the last item. "And the landing platforms."

"The landing platforms? How will you board Amandus' ships?"

"We won't need them. Our strategy is to change the way we fight, from boarding and fighting as we do on a battlefield, to doing everything we can to sink our opponents. They won't be expecting our maneuvers—nor our ramming—because they will be focused on grappling and boarding," Crispus answered. His didn't waver.

He father thought for a moment. "If you have less weight, your ramming will be compromised."

"We've tested that. With sharper bows and faster speed, we are equally effective. Possibly more effective."

Constantine's next question came quickly: "How will you defended yourself if you are boarded? With fewer armed troops?"

"That is a risk. We need our best archers and perhaps two or three Marines per ship. But, again, our strategy is not boarding them. It is sinking them."

"Yes, a risk. Is there anything else?" Constantine asked.

"Yes. But I have not been able to address it, because I will only know on the day of the battle," Crispus said. "But this is it:

a combination of wind and confinement is my friend. Open sea is probably my foe."

"You are doing well, son. I am very proud of you." Constantine said, squeezing Crispus' arm. "You are thinking like a general."

"Thank you, father. It is an honor to serve under your command and to try to think like you!"

They continued their walk toward the pier where Crispus had moored the bireme he'd sailed from Naples. From a distance, there was no mistaking that the two men were father and son. They had similar builds, similar gaits and made similar gestures when they spoke. As they walked their shoulders would periodically touch, disturbing neither's gait. A touch both seemed to enjoy.

Nicomedia, Asia Minor
Spring 1077 AUC (324 AD)

Arius sat across from Eusebius. Trees along the edges of stone patio next to Eusebius' Church shaded them from the bright spring sun while they ate lunch. Arius had decided not to speak of Church matters, at least for one day. He'd planned to focus instead on a flock of birds that he'd recently noticed.

And then one of Eusebius' deacons brought them a letter. Eusebius looked at it quickly, shook his head and then handed it to Arius.

It was a carefully made copy of an original letter between the two Alexanders—Bishop Alexander of Alexandria and Bishop Alexander of Byzantium. It was, nominally, from one bishop to another. But Arius recognized its real author immediately. It was divided into fourteen sections. And strident from the first few words.

"Athanasius has outdone himself," Arius said.

Eusebius nodded and examined one of the olives on his plate.

"I've heard about this letter. I'd hoped I could avoid seeing it."

"Agreed. Yet here it is. Shall I read it?"

"I suppose. I'll try not to let it ruin my appetite."

Arius drank some water and unscrolled the letter to read the first of several pages.

> To the most reverend and like-minded brother Alexander, Alexander sends greeting in the Lord.

> The ambitious and avaricious will of wicked men is always wont to lay snares against those churches which seem greater, by various pretexts attacking the ecclesiastical piety of such. For incited by the devil who works in them, to the lust of that which is set before them, and throwing away all religious scruples, they trample under foot the fear of the judgment of God. Concerning which things, I who suffer, have thought it necessary to show to your piety, in order that you may be aware of such men, lest any of them presume to set foot in your dioceses, whether by themselves or by others; for these sorcerers know how to use hypocrisy to carry out their fraud; and to employ letters composed and dressed out with lies, which are able to deceive a man who is intent upon a simple and sincere faith.

> Arius, therefore, and Achilles, having lately entered into a conspiracy, emulating the ambition of Colluthus, have turned out far worse than he. For Colluthus, indeed, who reprehends these very men, found some pretext for his evil purpose; but these, beholding his battering of Christ, endured no longer to be subject to the Church; but building for themselves dens of thieves, they hold their assemblies in them unceasingly, night and day directing their calumnies against Christ and against us.

Eusebius had stopped eating. But that wasn't enough. He clicked his tongue. "Here we go again. I do all the work concocting these calumnies and heresies—and Athanasius gives you all the glory."

Arius laughed, drank more water and continued reading.

> For since they call in question all pious and apostolical doctrine, after the manner of the Jews, they have constructed a workshop for contending against Christ, denying the Godhead of our Savior, and preaching that He is only the equal of all others. And having collected all the passages which speak of His plan of salvation and His humiliation for our sakes, they endeavor from these to collect the preaching of their impiety, ignoring altogether the passages in which His eternal Godhead and unutterable glory with the Father is set forth.

> Since, therefore, they back up the impious opinion concerning Christ, which is held by the Jews and Greeks, in every possible way they strive to gain their approval; busying themselves about all those things which they are wont to deride in us, and daily stirring up against us seditions and persecutions. And now, indeed, they drag us before the tribunals of the judges, by intercourse with silly and disorderly women, whom they have led into error; at another time they cast opprobrium and infamy upon the Christian religion, their young maidens disgracefully wandering about every village and street. Nay, even Christ's indivisible tunic, which His executioners were unwilling to divide, these wretches have dared to rend.

Eusebius reached down to pet Mastiff. "Arius, you must be a consummate politician. You are now with disorderly women. Where are these women? Why are you keeping them from me?"

"Athanasius' writing is a bit extravagant," Arius allowed.

"Extravagant? He sounds like a hysterical child."

Arius shrugged. "It seems to be the style of letters today. Malign frequently. And often. I am sure he will give you some credit. Later."

"He sent copies of this letter to every Bishop in the Empire, East and West," Eusebius said, still paying attention to Arius' dog. "It's an embarrassment. I don't understand why he doesn't simply state the facts, as you did in your letter to Alexander. He should leave out the overheated rhetoric about how we have become subhuman. I suppose it's meant to scare people—make them fear that their names might appear in the next one, if they don't fall in line."

"Will it work?"

"I don't think so." Eusebius sighed, finally looking up from Mastiff. "I am sure you are correct. He will castigate me later in the letter. But, for now, I've heard enough. I'm going to walk your dog. After you have finished this epic, leave it by my door. I'll read it. Later."

"By the way, I meant to tell you that I heard some merchants in the marketplace singing the verses of your *Thalia*. The part: '… the members of the Holy Trinity share Unequal Glories.' I am sure they sing it whenever they see anyone in a Christian Tunic. But it was pleasant, nevertheless. I've heard that your verses are sung in the harbors throughout the East. Sailors discuss them on their voyages. You have given the common man a lesson in theology, Arius. One that he can understand. That is God's work."

Arius looked up from the scroll. "Thank you. But I'm not sure it makes any difference with the bishops and priests. I suspect Alexander will call a synod after Constantine defeats Licinius?"

Eusebius nodded. "Yes, I think you are correct. Nothing will happen until that war is over. And, unless something shocking occurs, Constantine will prevail."

"Have you heard from Licinius since he left for Adrianople?"

"No. But Constantia sent me a short note. She fears for the worst," Eusebius said. He looked distracted, as if he was already finished with this exchange. "She'd like me to talk to Constantine. But there's nothing anyone can do at this point. Except her husband. He could fall on his sword."

"She's an honorable woman. May God bless her and give her peace," Arius made the sign of the cross and bowed his head.

Eusebius did so, too. Quickly. And then, standing up, he started to follow Mastiff.

Thessalonica, Greece
May, 1077 AUC (324 AD)

In his bedroom of the Church residence near the Imperial Palace, Ossius completed a first draft of his response to Alexander's letter to the bishops. It was still rough—only partly done, really. He had started this letter earlier in the morning and then left it, face down, in a compartment to the left of his writing desk. When he'd come back, later in the day, he'd found the letter face up.

Someone had been reading his work. He concluded that Clodius was the likely suspect and wondered whether the matter was worth a confrontation. Ultimately, he decided it wasn't. Yet.

He was growing tired of Clodius' clandestine ways. Clodius never looked at him directly. He was shifty—literally, shifting his weight from one leg to the other so pronouncedly that he usually had a swaying motion whenever they spoke.

Early on, Ossius had decided that it would be better to keep this sneaky deacon close. But he was beginning to question that decision.

He wasn't one for out scheming schemers.

In the meantime, there was work to do and Ossius headed out to attend to that. Constantine had called his entire command staff to gather in the courtyard of the large marina he'd recently built. It had a scenic view overlooking the port and the nearby shipyards.

The meeting had a relaxed atmosphere, not as formal as battle-field staff meeting. Constantine wanted to discuss the logistics of the looming battle with Licinius. He stood in the middle of a circle of his commanders and asked each to describe what his units were going to do.

Occasionally, one of his trusted generals—Ablabius, Tiberus and a few others—might add questions that followed Constantine's line of thought. These meetings were standard, starting weeks before a campaign. They would become more frequent...and more detailed... as the departure date neared.

Constantine's main concern seemed to be Crispus' naval strategy. Crispus, who was still uncomfortable speaking in front of larger groups, had brought Thestor—the Greek admiral—as a spokesman. Thestor had tried to bow before Constantine, who prohibited that with a friendly laugh and shook the old sailor's arm.

Tiberus was the first to question Crispus: "Young Caesar, I applaud your focus on faster ships and am pleased that you have chosen to use more sagittari. I worry that you have chosen not to carry ballista on the main decks. They are not heavy themselves but they shoot large lances over twice the distance even the best archer can shoot. And they have good accuracy. I would also suggest that you keep the iron boxes for fire arrows on the deck. I've only spent a short time at sea. But I could hit a ship near the water line with a fire arrow at 150 cubits."

"Bragging!" laughed Ablabius. "But I agree with Tiberus. Having two or three ballistae one each ship does not add much weight. Now, I see that getting rid of the catapults and heavy stones is not as crazy as I thought when I first heard the idea. But, since you aren't going to have many marines on board, who will slice the ropes of grappling claws when they hit a ship?"

Thestor looked to Crispus, who stepped forward to answer. "The three marines on each of the smaller ships will have long-armed scythes. To cut the hooks and ropes. Since they won't be working catapults, they can focus on that cutting. As for the ballistae, I am having them reinstalled."

"Are you positive you are getting that much more speed with your cuts in arms and people?" Marcus asked.

Thestor answered this question: "We took five ships laden and five unladed, all using our largest sails. The five unladed won in a thousand-cubit race. We then switched the crews and raced back and the same ships—the unladed ones—won again."

"Impressive" said Ablabius. "And ramming is still good?"

Again, Thestor: "Yes, General. Better. We have sharpened the bows. At speed, we had no problem breaching the walls of old triremes we grounded."

"Will you use any of your triremes?" asked Marcus.

"Initially, not many. We will keep most of them in reserve. Several mille behind. We hope to have land flags to direct messages to the big ships, if we need them."

Then, Crispus stepped in to add: "We will not be certain of exactly what mix of ships to use until we see Amandus' fleet and the conditions we face. When we actually see what he brings to battle, we can change our forces as needed. Quickly, I believe."

After a short pause, Marcus said, "If we are finished with young Crispus, I have another concern about this campaign. And that is the food."

Many groaned. "No wait, hear me out! You others don't have the same problem I have. I have almost 80,000 legionari who get very ornery when they're hungry. And, during the campaign against the Goths, they were starved. We all know you can't run an army on empty stomachs."

Aniketos was the head of the food detail. He stepped forward to answer Marcus, "The battles with the Goths and Sarmatians had unexpected difficulties. We had initially planned to return to Thessalonica after the first battle. Instead, we kept marching. So, we were caught short with grains and we had problems getting the meat we needed. And it was warm, so we had spoilage issues. This campaign is easier for planning. We know the destination. We know how long it will take. There are much better roads with supply farms nearby, so food will not be an issue."

"Are we going to have ale? A third of our legionari are Franks."

"Yes. And we have plenty of wine, as well."

Another pause and Tiberus brought up the matter of the destination: "I haven't been to Adrianople. But I know many of us have. We have all heard what our spies have reported. The approach on the south side of the river is apparently lowlands and would be difficult for our legionari to cross. Is there any way to approach their position from the north?"

"We don't think so, Tiberus," Constantine answered. As soon as he spoke, the group got very quiet and everyone listened. "There are two rivers to cross to the west and one to the east. And all of the city's bridges have been destroyed. They are expecting us. I have some ideas to regain some elements of surprise—but we won't be able to make a good assessment until we get there.'

He continued. "From the perspective of the sagittari, there is not much concern. You will have dry ground and be well within your range. But, as you mentioned, it seems that it will be a challenge for the infantry. That is the riddle to be solved right now. That's my focus."

As the group started to break up, Fausta appeared with Constantine's youngest child, one-year-old Constans. And several attendants in tow. She was a striking woman—tall and elegant, with large and pleasant eyes. She wore a fashionable tunic. It was evident from her bare arms and the lines under the dress that Fausta still had a younger woman's body, even though she was well into in her 30s and had borne Constantine three children. She was renowned as one of the Empire's great beauties.

Although Roman citizens hated the idea of royalty, there was no other way to describe Fausta. She looked and acted like a queen.

This appearance was by design. It was politics. Constantine had arranged for his young wife and child to come out and embrace him, so that his staff would see that he was still a virile man. Ossius recognized this from earlier conversations they'd had. Constantine had a strong impulse to convey strength, especially to his lieutenants. He'd once told Ossius that he'd seen leaders undo themselves by conveying weakness among those they considered friends.

Fausta greeted every one of her husband's senior officers individually, saying at least a brief encouraging word to each. She moved and spoke like a woman who was accustomed to power. She wouldn't do this among the larger army; but it worked here.

Ossius noticed a slight awkwardness between Fausta and Crispus. It looked like the tension between a young man and his stepmother— who was much closer in age to him than to his parent. This was common in aristocratic families and one reason that the Church frowned on older men divorcing and remarrying.

The Emperor didn't seem to mind. He was either ignoring it or it was part of his plan.

Alexandria, Egypt
June 1077 AUC (324 AD)

Athanasius was surrounded by warm water, in the main pool of Alexander's private bath house. He enjoyed mid-morning baths because no one else was there. Few residences had private baths and Athanasius always looked for the opportunity to take one. It allowed him the privacy never afforded in the afternoon—when most of the clergy and select faithful would converge for social baths.

It also allowed him to avoid older male bathers, particularly Romans. Because of his youthful appearance, they'd often assume that he was a pullus—a "chick"—the vulgar slang term for a sexually available boy. These corpulent, pock-marked sodomites would proposition him. Or reach out and grab him under the bath water. A young boy might have to submit to that but not someone of Athanasius' stature in the Church.

Alone, Athanasius could relax. And he needed to. He had an aging pope. Clodius had written him that Ossius was going to demand participation of the western bishops in the next synod. Indeed, Ossius' letter to Alexander arrived a few days later, making just that demand.

The addition of the western bishops would change the dynamics of the next gathering substantially. The clever infidel wags were beginning to draw comparison between this theological conflict and the war between Constantine and Licinius. Both were long and drawn-out, lacking any clear conclusion. If it kept going like this, the day would come when the Church no longer had Alexander to uphold the equality of Jesus and God.

It would take time to get the western bishops educated. As a group, they tended to be politicians first; those that cared enough to have an opinion generally viewed the dispute as esoteric. He had the recurring thought that, if they had more participation, the western bishops might agree to treat Jesus, God and the Holy Spirit as multiple gods. These so-called "practical" men, little different than pagans.

Also, inviting the western bishops would benefit both Eusebiuses—because the Nicomedian was so close to Constantine and the Caesarean had written well-reviewed treatises on the Church's history. Alexander was not particularly well-known in the west. Nor appreciated. Sylvester, however, was. The Constantine-Sylvester-Eusebius relationships were close. Like an Empire-Church triumvirate.

Athanasius was the power behind Alexander, everyone knew that. The private correspondence he'd received after Alexander's letter to Alexander of Byzantium applauded the brilliance of his theology and rhetoric. But, without the prestige of his pope, the powerful pagans—Arius and Eusebius—might prevail.

There was no simple solution to this. He either had to find a younger sponsor...or become the next Pope of Alexandria himself.

The more he thought about it, the more it became clear that he had to be the standard bearer for the faith. Only he knew the intricacies of the theology. Only he knew all the bishops who had pledged loyalty to the pope—and what they had been promised. It had to be him. There was no one else.

First, he had to become a bishop. In order to become a bishop, he had to be elected by three surrounding bishops. And to be over the age of 30. Alexander wasn't likely to be alive until Athanasius reached 30. Perhaps, when the time got close, he would write a letter for Alexander—endorsing Athanasius, regardless of his young age.

Athanasius smiled as he got out of the bath and reached for a towel. Eusebius had done similar things to get his post in Nicomedia. But he had done it for personal political power. Athanasius would do it to assure the glory of Lord Jesus Christ.

His first order of business, however, was to deal with Ossius's request to involve the western bishops in the upcoming synod. That afternoon, he had the opportunity to discuss both letters with Alexander as they walked to the church for prayers.

"Your Holiness, I worry about the contents of the letters we received from Clodius and Ossius. Our brothers in the western Empire are not as versed on the intricacies of the Scriptures as we are. To involve them would, perhaps, delay our ability to confirm our faith under the umbrella of a single orthodoxy."

Alexander smiled, wearily: "I share your concern Athanasius. But Ossius is correct. The entire Church should give this issue a hearing and I have no doubt it will embrace our opinion."

"Surely, Your Holiness, you don't believe the bishops of Britannia or of the Rhine would have meaningful input into such a weighty subject?"

"No. I am not sure they would. But, again, Ossius is correct: They should have the right to do so. I believe we are correct, young Athanasius. But others must be given the choice to confirm their opinion."

Athanasius' whole body practically twisted, like Archimedes' screw. "Such a process could take many years. I mean, to educate and inform all parties. There will be confusion. The participants of today may not be here to be the participants of tomorrow. So our message may get diluted with time."

Now, Alexander was slowly shaking his head no. "The subject matter has little room for dilution, my son. Like all such conflicts, the leaders of the Church will ultimately make the decision. Ossius' point was only that the leaders of the west should be part of the process."

Athanasius wasn't sure what had gone wrong—but he was losing this argument. He had to regroup. "Perhaps to speed the process, we could invite Ossius to participate in our eastern Council first. He would gain the insight of our resolve. After hearing the facts, he can decide whether the entire Church should endorse the findings of the East. Perhaps he could chair the Council. He would be representing the western churches. Unless, of course, your Holiness would feel obligated to take that responsibility."

"No, not at all. Athanasius, your idea is sound. Write Ossius the invitation—subject to the end of the civil war—and I will sign it. The location should be accessible to him, near the Bosporus but not Nicomedia."

"Yes my Holiness, I agree," Athanasius responded, as they entered the vestibule of the main church.

Adrianople, Thrace
Late June, 1077 AUC (324 AD)

The summer heat was starting to build, even in the morning. Constantine studied the battleground before him. The Hebrus River ran toward the horizon, just a little off center on the wide plain. Two smaller rivers flowed into it—and Adrianople sat at the confluence of the three.

As the scouts had reported, the bridges crossing into the city had all been destroyed. On the other side of the Hebrus was one of the longest lines of troops he had ever seen. It seemed to follow the river to the horizon. He couldn't remember seeing such a large force. It had to be over 150,000 troops, far more than he had.

The ridge of the hill above Licinius' troops was loaded with artillery. The lower shore, full of obstacles and barricades. It was the usual variety to delay attacking legionari—tree limbs, bolted fences and long trenches. It was enough to give Licinius' archers and artillery ample time to decimate advancing troops. It was impressive but...conventional.

This was Licinius' great play, his strongest stand. If Constantine could win here, he would win completely.

He was going to have to be *un*conventional. And he thought he saw a way. Licinius' troops were many—but they were arranged thinly.

But the landscape favored Licinius. On Constantine's side of the river, a wide stretch of marshy sea grass and wetlands made the banks hard to see clearly. Behind the marshes, his army was camped in its standard rectangular formation. Some of his troops were in clear sight of Adrianople but more were hidden—or at least partly hidden—behind low, rolling hills. That was good.

Licinius was inviting him to cross the river directly. There was a small strip of dry land to his left, where one of the smaller rivers flowed into the Hebrus. That was the bait. Crossing there would be suicide. The dry strip would compact with the weight of his army with all the horses. It would become a quagmire and his men would be easy targets.

His eye kept going back to the long, thin line of troops. That was the key. If it started to collapse, Licinius wouldn't be able to reassemble his troops and hold.

This was a strategy Constantine had used before. But he didn't see an easy way to cause that initial collapse.

He sighed and shook his head. He had the pieces of the puzzle— he just hadn't put them together correctly yet. His bodyguards stood far behind. They knew Constantine could be short tempered at times like this. Ablabius, riding alongside a very large centurion, was the only one bold enough to approach him. "Dominus, cheers! I believe we have found what you are looking for."

Constantine nodded to the centurion and spoke softly, "Good to see you both. What is it?"

"A crossing. About ten mille up the Hebrus—perhaps a little less. Shall we ride there?"

"Yes. But go ahead a bit and meet me across the camp, behind the hills. We have an audience here." And he bent his head in the direction of the city.

Ablabius sneered across the river. "Yes, Dominus."

The riders left and Constantine and his palatini walked into camp, toward the mess tent—as if to get breakfast.

An hour later, Constantine got off his horse in a small forest of thin trees on the bank of the Hebrus. He gave his reins to one of the bodyguards, who stayed behind with Ablabius' riders. Constantine and the rest of his guard followed Ablabius and the big centurion through the trees.

The water ran quickly against a solid bank. Constantine kneeled down and felt the current with his hand. He looked up, down and across the river—and estimated they had a 40-cubit stretch where they could cross. It would be tight but better than any other available option.

He stood up and walked along the river's edge until he reached the big Centurion. He shook his arm. "Good work, Centurion. You're a Rhinelander, a Frank, if I recall correctly. So you know rivers."

"Yes, Imperator. You recall correctly. This place is very much like my home."

Constantine looked along opposite side of the river again, to make sure they had no company. Turning back to the Centurion, he asked "How deep?"

"About four feet, Imperator. Easy for horses but difficult for legionari. The river runs quickly."

Constantine looked back at his bodyguards and the others. "Let's see for ourselves."

He instructed the several men still on horses and most of the group on foot to forge the river. The water was cold and the current strong, as the centurion had said. But the bed was gravel—not many larger rocks, as he'd worried it might have.

When they reached the other side, he signaled to Ablabius and the centurion to join him as he examined that bank.

"Very good job, both of you. We will need rope guides when we cross. So that our legionari don't lose their balance in that strong current. But this will work."

He nodded to the men, to cross back again. Over the sounds of splashing, he said to Ablabius, "When we get back to camp, let's discuss how we'll organize this. We have to maintain the element of surprise. Have to maintain that."

Adrianople, Thrace
Midday, July 2, 1077 AUC (324 AD)

"Idiots! This is not how we drew the plans! The Emperor will have your heads!" Ablabius was up to his knees in mud and water. He screamed at the carpenters to tighten the ropes to the girders on the portable bridge. He knew that many eyes on the other side of the river were watching him as he laid into his workmen.

His workmen knew this was a show. For over a week, they had been playing at building this bridge. But the actual attack was being prepared elsewhere.

As with everything Constantine did, he prepared. And then prepared again, for good measure. For two nights, a legion of sagittari, 250 molossus and their handlers, three legions of equiti and five legions of legionari got up before daybreak. The first night, they marched two mille in the general direction of the actual crossing point. The second night, they marched all the way to the small forest of trees by the river bed—and a handpicked few actually crossed the river., all in a chilling silence. Combined, the men involved in these predawn exercises accounted for a slightly less than half of Constantine's fighting force.

The other half practiced looking normal and being seen. Specifically, they milled around the higher ground near the river and the portable bridge that was being built with theatrical delay. Some of those troops were dressed casually, without armor, others wore armor.

Ablabius threw up his arms, slapped the shoulder of the carpenter in charge and walked away, shaking his head.

Constantine met him on the other side of the hill. "You missed your calling. You should have been an actor."

"Do you think it was too much?"

Constantine laughed and shook his head. "No. I suspect our audience thinks we will be another week before that bridge is ready."

"It will be finished this evening, Dominus. It doesn't look like much, but it will function. And the men are ready. I have mats prepared, to cover the low ground by the base of the bridge."

"Those mats will hold up?"

"Yes, Dominus. That is the question. They're made of hemp, so they're likely to break up at some point. Sooner, if the horses and carts are moving slowly."

Constantine briefly closed his eyes, imagining the scene. "If the horses and carts cause serious delay, send the infantry at pace to our other crossing point. It will take some extra time—but it will be better than standing around waiting. Have you sent word to Crispus that he should be prepared to move the fleet?"

"Yes, Dominus. I also told him where Amandus is anchored. By the mouth of the Hellespont. A good location. For us."

"A *perfect* location. But Amandus will move, as soon as he hears about this," and Constantine pointed over the hill, toward the city.

"God may grace us, Dominus."

"God *has* graced us," said Ossius, as he approached. "And may He bless you both tomorrow."

Adrianople, Thrace
Evening, July 2, 1077 AUC (324 AD)

In a command tent overlooking the Hebrus River and most of Constantine's camp on the opposite side, Licinius stood listening to his Dux and three senior centurions. They were laughing confidently as they described the scene they'd witnessed that afternoon.

"Augustus, it is comical. This contraption they're building couldn't hold a kitchen boy and his dog, much less an army with horses. And they're proceeding like a bunch of women!"

"We watched the great Ablabius have a temper tantrum at the slow pace. He struck the carpenter in charge so hard that he fell to the ground. And favored his right arm the rest of the day!"

Licinius forced a smile. He was uneasy about laughing at Constantine—but he wanted to show his officers that he could be one of them. "So, when will this rickety bridge be ready?"

"I estimate three or four more days, Augustus."

Licinius looked out, toward the river. "Have all the walls and barriers between the river and our legionari been tested? In case this bridge is some sort of feint and Constantine crosses the river on boats at night? He's a deceitful bastard, you know."

"Yes, Augustus. The walls are secure. And we have seen no boats. There is no way they can cross at night without us knowing it. We have watches all along the Hebrus. And our archers are ready. If they attempt any crossing, we will have our way with them."

Licinius tuned back to his officers and nodded. "Good. Keep those archers poised. I'm going to spend the night in town with my wife. Send word to my guards immediately if there's any news."

After he'd climbed onto his horse—a fine Arabian—Licinius held the reins for a moment and took a hard look at the rickety bridge. It was empty of its carpenters and well-lit by the torches on his side of the Hebrus. It was wide enough to carry eight or ten men abreast. And, in truth, it didn't look so rickety.

He could order archers to rain fire into the bridge. But that wasn't the right move, tactically. Large armies were involved here; but this was really a battle between two men.

Licinius wanted Constantine to attack directly at the center of his line, his archers and his barricades. It would be strength versus strength—and, once and for all, that bastard would learn that Licinius was the stronger man.

But, as in the past, he had a nagging feeling that he might be missing something. He looked up and down the river. It was a marshy, muddy mess on the other side—as far as the eye could see. Constantine's only choice was a direct assault. Turning his horse toward town, Licinius reassured himself. "No more tricks. This time, I have the dominant position."

Adrianople, Thrace
July 3, 1077 AUC (324 AD)

The morning began for Licinius' troops as the last several had. It would be another sweltering day, with loud hammering and yelling down at the river. They could attack Constantine's bridge at any time but were under orders not to do so. The generals wanted to "invite" Constantine to cross at that spot.

Many of Licinius' men gravitated toward either end of their fortifications, to get away from the constant hammering. The soldiers on the left flank were doing what all soldiers did during lulls before battle—sitting around complaining. Because of the heat and humidity, few were wearing their armor.

A cloud dimmed the sunlight.

A few soldiers screamed warnings—but they were hard to hear, over the hammering and yelling down at the river.

The cloud descended. It was over five thousand arrows. And they weren't coming from across the river; they were coming from beyond the left flank.

Most of Licinius' left flank never got the chance to stand up. The arrows fell with nothing to stop them. The few survivors ran away from the direction of the arrows— most leaving their armor on the ground. A second round killed most of the survivors.

Tiberus had ordered his sagittari to jog forward 50 cubits, get into formation again and release another volley. Then jog forward, regroup and shoot again…. The challenge soon became slowing down to prevent the legionari in full armor from tiring out from all the jogging.

Panic set in quickly amongst Licinius' troops. His centurions tried to form a defensive line, facing left; but the long, narrow body of troops was hard to manage when one side was folding under multiple barrages of arrows. Finally, Licinius' centurions formed a line by killing many of their own retreating legionari.

As the defensive line was beginning to form, Ablabius looked to Constantine—who nodded. Trumpets sounded and the dog handlers raced past the archers, seconds after another cloud of arrows had launched. The handlers released the dogs fifty cubits from the defensive line.

Licinius was having breakfast with Constantia in her bedroom when they both heard the unmistakable sound of a battle. Screams of pain, screams of orders, the thud of impact, the vibration of hoofs. She didn't say anything—but cocked her head at him, skeptically. He felt nauseous.

"Guards! Guards! What the hell is going on?"

His Adiutor and two of his bodyguards met Licinius in Constantia's outer sitting room. None of them knew what was happening; but all of them recognized the screams.

Licinius grabbed the Adiutor's shoulder. "Get my wife and the child over to Byzantium and make sure they are secure in our friend's villa. Immediately!"

"Yes, Augustus."

He didn't say anything to the guards—but headed out.

As soon as Licinius was on his horse, a centurion—also on horseback—approached. "Augustus, Constantine has attacked. From this side of the river."

"*This* side? How many?"

"Don't know. He attacked our left flank with sagittari, many of them. And it appears more of his army stands behind them."

"Have his equiti attacked?" Licinius screamed.

"No."

"Good, then we are holding our formation." Licinius kicked his horse and started off.

"No! We have not yet held. The army is retreating into itself." The centurion yelled, galloping next to Licinius.

"What?"

"We have not held, Augustus."

Licinius, his guards and the centurion crested the hill just out of town, near his command tent. The battle came into view—much closer than any of them had expected. The dogs had met the forming defensive line. It didn't stand any chance of holding.

Molossus were trained to kill but not to eat until their handler gave permission, so they continued to attack—even though they hadn't eaten in several days. Since most of the dogs weighed as much as a soldier, their teeth, razor sharp collars and leggings had little trouble overpowering legionari who were already in retreat.

Ablabius' equiti had started their attack, following the dogs.

As soon as the standard bearer raised the Labarum for the equiti, Licinius' troops started retreating in even greater numbers. Some were literally running, with their backs to the dogs' teeth and the equiti's swords.

Licinius realized that his preparations for repelling Constantine were now entirely useless. Not a single artillery stone had been fired, not one bolt from any of his scorpios. And his long line of troops was folding like the bag of a bellows. Blood and gore were everywhere. Licinius felt nausea overwhelm him again. He leaned forward in his saddle and vomited his breakfast onto the ground.

Constantine, Ablabius, the four palatini and half a dozen extra equiti guards followed the charging troops toward Licinius' retreating legionari. Leading the small group was a standard bearer signaling Constantine's presence. The Vexillum was now constructed so that the Chi Rho symbol, the Labarum, was formed onto the top of the iron structure. Below that was a purple banner embroidered with three profiles of Constantine's head. This had changed from a decade earlier, when the Chi Rho had been painted on the cloth.

Constantine's bodyguards were wary of engaging directly in battle—but everyone noticed that, wherever he approached, the intensity of fighting increased and Licinius' troops turned from the sight of the standard.

Licinius' thin line continued to collapse on itself.

As the day progressed, Constantine took possession of the top of the ridge where Licinius' command tent had been that morning. From that spot, he could see the progress his troops had made in the first few hours of the battle. They had penetrated to almost the midpoint of the initial position of Licinius' army. They were less than two hundred cubits from the decoy bridge. And the lines were actually starting to solidify.

Per Constantine's instructions, there had been no activity from his side of the bridge. But now, he gave a signal and the buccina sounded a command to the remaining sagittari on the other side of the Hebrus.

Within moments, a legion of archers was in position next to the bridge. The horns sounded again and Licinius' troops were caught in crossfire. They weren't trained to form phalanxes. And it was impossible for any single soldier to hold his shield in two directions. Their lines began collapsing again.

Licinius had moved to another observation point—about a mille to the west of his original position. He could see that he had lost at least half of his left flank, perhaps 25,000 men. Although it was hard to calculate in the heat of battle, it appeared to him that the two armies were now at about equal strength.

He had to get his troops to hold at some solid point to stop the advance of Constantine's troops. There, they could rally and turn the tide of this battle.

Given the speed of Constantine's initial advance—and now his archers firing from the opposite shore—Licinius realized it was impossible to consolidate his troops near the decoy bridge.

His troops needed time to get some barriers up and formations, including their archers, in place. His commanders were waiting for orders. He chose a spot west of the bridge.

"Look. There," he yelled at one of his officers, pointing to the location. "Set fortifications there, near those carts. Put up barricades and get the archers in place behind them. Now!"

"Yes, Augustus."

The ground was high, there—good for making a stand. His troops would have time to fortify the area and to be out of the range of Constantine's archers. For a while, anyway.

Constantine saw Licinius' legionari dragging large wooden tree barriers and fences west of the bridge. Now was the time to test the effectiveness of the bridge. He gave the signal and the troops on the other side of the Hebrus mobilized. Within minutes, the bridge had several pontoons on the end closest to the river and a padded buttress on the far side that served as a yoke for horses.

Then, the surprise: The horses pushed the buttress—and the entire wooden bridge moved—from the wetlands toward the river. Carpenters placed hemp mats in front of the structure and the horses for stability. Within 20 minutes the bridge spanned the river. Constantine's remaining troops started to cross.

When he saw Constantine's fresh troops crossing the bridge, Licinius cursed himself. Another trick. His rallying point wasn't close enough to block the bridge—but it was close enough for his archers to make crossing difficult. "Order the archers to fire on the bridge. As soon as they're assembled. Focus on the front side. Seal it with bodies!"

Constantine signaled his officers at assemble for a quick meeting on horseback. Ablabius started the exchange: "Dominus, I don't think we should slow down and give them a chance to regroup. If we let Marcus assault from the river side with our fresh troops, I am sure I can circle over the crest of the hill with my equiti. And we'll have them surrounded."

Marcus nodded in agreement.

Constantine was worried that the assault from the river side was difficult because of both Licinius' new fortifications and the uphill march. "Yes. Marcus, attack their rallying point. But, Tiberus, I want your sagittari hitting the riverside. Right now! We have no time to wait. As many volleys as you can. It will be better when we have breached their fortifications and are fighting in formation."

They immediately fanned out. Tiberus' arrows were flying before Licinius' archers had assembled. The legionari fighting on the river side bogged down—the ground was even softer than either army had expected. Ablabius was successful in circling behind Licinius' fortifications, but his progress once there was slow and of little help to the legionari on the river side.

"They need help." And, with that, Constantine—accompanied by his regular palatini and extra units—left his observation post to ride into the battle on the water side of Licinius' fortifications.

The sight of Constantine's standard added incentive and the progress through the armed fortifications quickened. Constantine stayed on his horse, using a lance to stab opposing troops. His palatini and the equiti tried, with little success, to keep him from fighting; he found being on the horse effective because most of Licinius' soldiers would look away when they saw him. That made stabbing them easier, either for him or one of his men in the group.

After about an hour of intense fighting, the legionari from the river side broke through the fortifications and joined Ablabius' equiti inside Licinius' rallying point.

Some of Licinius' troops tried to surrender—but Constantine's men weren't taking prisoners.

As the enemy was being pushed back, Constantine raised his shield as a signal of good progress to his troops. As he did, an arrow aimed at him ricocheted off of the shield and landed deep into his right thigh.

Constantine stared for a moment in disbelief. If he hadn't raised his shield at that instant, the arrow would have hit his neck or his face. He yelled to Ablabius, "Our Lord protected me!"

"Dominus, go to the Medic and let us finish this business!"

"No!" Constantine broke the shaft of the arrow at his leg, held it up for a moment and then threw it onto the ground. A cheer went up and his men started fighting with even more intensity. They moved through the rallying point and pressed against the body of Licinius' army—forcing it, again, to collapse on itself. "We are the fire," he yelled to his troops, "and we are burning this candle to its base."

Eventually, his leg started throbbing. Constantine had been hit with arrows several times in his fighting life, but never this deep. He broke off from the fighting and climbed down from his horse so his guards could examine the wound. Climbing down was painful; but he made a point of walking around his horse, so that his men could see that the wound wasn't life threatening.

Then he went back across the river on the bridge to his command tent, where a medic waited.

The medics of the Roman army had developed medical procedures to minimize infection, primarily through cauterization, and to reduce pain, primarily through use of opiates.

The arrow in Constantine's leg was too deep to pull out by hand, so the medic started to heat an arrow extractor. He encouraged Constantine to drink a fig juice-opium mixture to reduce the pain. The procedure was going to be painful—it involved cutting the skin around the arrow and inserting red-hot metal thongs to extract the arrowhead and cauterize the wound. Then he'd close the wound with an ivory needle and catgut sutures.

Initially, Constantine refused the opium, insisting that he wanted to remain clear-headed. But, when the medic started cutting around the arrow shaft, he changed his mind.

Within an hour, the procedure was over. Constantine could walk, with some pain, and headed out to his horse.

As soon as he got outside, he saw Ablabius crossing the bridge. "Dominus, how is your leg?"

"Fine. I'd forgotten how much it hurts to get wounded."

"My apologies. Would that Vibius were still here."

"Yes. How is the battle progressing?"

"Licinius just left. Took a legion with him, headed towards Adrianople. I suspect he will keep running beyond that," Ablabius said. "His remaining forces are broken. It should take us another hour or so to finish them."

"It is getting late and I am sure the men are tired. Why don't we withdraw from the field?"

"Withdraw now, Dominus? Only a part of Licinius' army is left. Perhaps a quarter of the original number. We can annihilate them, if you give me another hour."

Constantine was confused by what Ablabius was saying. A quarter? Of what? "So, the battle is won?"

Ablabius was confused by the question but assumed Constantine hadn't heard him completely. "Yes, Dominus. Licinius' army isn't just defeated—it has been crushed. None of his troops want to face you again. In fact, they were told never to face you in the first place. Licinius told them to never look directly at your Labarum."

"What? Why did he tell them that?" Constantine asked, even more confused.

"He has always been superstitious, Dominus. Perhaps a pagan soothsayer told him not to look at it."

"How much of his army remains?" Constantine asked again.

"Fifteen legions, perhaps fewer. There are many desertions already. We can offer the survivors surrender...."

"Casualties?"

"Our chief field medic says relatively few for us—perhaps 2,500. Well over 30,000 for them. I think it is the largest battle I've ever fought, Dominus! Perhaps we should continue for another hour—"

"Fine. Sound the withdrawal. Take whoever joins us. And wait to hear when Licinius is going to surrender. If he does not want to surrender, get word to Crispus to start moving the navy. We need to control the Bosporus either way." Constantine replied, as if he'd heard nothing Ablabius had said.

Adrianople, Thrace
July 4, 1077 AUC (324 AD)

"Ablabius!" Constantine screamed, limping out from his tent— just as the sun was rising.

"Yes, Dominus?" answered Ablabius, as he emerged from the latrine behind Constantine's tent.

"We crushed Licinius' army yesterday."

"Yes, Dominus. A complete victory."

"No, I mean in the afternoon. After the medic extracted the arrow. We didn't stop. We finished the battle, correct?"

"No, Dominus. You instructed me to sound the withdrawal," Ablabius answered, nervously combing his beard.

"Ye Gods! Ablabius, the doctor gave me opium for my leg. I didn't know what I was thinking. We should have pressed his forces and crushed them. Now, he'll probably gather enough together to fight another battle. You had to know that!"

Ablabius dropped his head. "Dominus, I questioned you. Each time, you returned to wanting to withdraw."

"Damn it, Ablabius. I have had commanders put to death for less stupidity than this. This is extreme negligence. How could you. Damn it Ablabius, stop primping like a woman. Whatever madness I thought was a good idea yesterday, it was a…." Constantine limped back into his tent, leaving Ablabius speechless and looking at his comb and mirror.

Byzantium, Greece
July 5, 1077 AUC (324 AD)

Two days after the massacre at Adrianople, Licinius met with his officers in the large villa of Byzantium's wealthiest Christian merchant. His remaining troops were encamped outside the walls of the city, recovering.

Licinius sat in a large leather chair, looking out at the Bosporus Strait. His officers stood in a half-circle facing him.

"How could you not anticipate that Constantine would find a way to cross the river? He'd massacred our entire left flank before we fired the first arrow!

He continued. "I sat here last night, considering having all of you killed! Each one of you, standing here. Dead! But I have no time to find new commanders. That bastard will be nipping at my heels again in a few days. And let me tell you this, each of you had better be motivated to fight him now. And fight him viciously. Because, if you don't, then win or lose you will be dead that day. I'll kill you myself!"

He stood up and looked each of the in the eyes for at least a moment. Each of them looked down.

"Now, I have some other news. I have decided that the bastard brother-in-law of mine is no longer fit to be my co-emperor. He is an enemy of Rome! As of today, I am elevating Sextus Martinianus to be Emperor to the West. He has been my trusted bodyguard for several years. Now, he will rule the Western Empire, after Constantine's death."

"As for the rest of you—you're lucky you're still breathing. Get out there and sharpen your swords. Fix your saddles. Train your men. Prepare to defeat that bastard. Or die trying! Now go!"

As the others left quietly, Licinius motioned for Sextus to sit next to him.

Sextus pulled a woven chair facing Licinius at an angle, backwards, and sat down straddling the chair—his arms on the back, facing Licinius.

"Sextus, I don't think I've ever been so discouraged. What happened in Adrianople was inexcusable. We were in a far superior position and now we are defensive. Amandus has to buy us time and ensure we build our strength back up. What is our current troop count?"

"Not strong, Augustus. Perhaps ten legions. Fifty to sixty thousand soldiers."

"How many did we lose at Adrianople?"

"Difficult to know. We have about a third of our original deployment. So, we lost about a hundred thousand troops. Perhaps half of those were desertions. And the other half, casualties," Sextus answered.

"It was a massacre," Licinius sighed.

"It could have been worse," Sextus answered. "I wonder why Constantine didn't continue the battle. He sounded the withdrawal as soon as we left."

"Perhaps he got a new sign from his Christian God," Licinius said. This wasn't scorn—he believed in signs. "We need to enlist new troops as soon as possible. The Goths should be our principle allies. They hate Constantine. They're pagans. They should understand what an attack on their culture the bastard's God would be."

"Yes, Augustus. I know their chief, Aliquaca. Sent emissaries to him this morning, after you and I talked. He'll be a strong ally. But, even with his troops, we need at least another 30,000 legionari."

Licinius sat back in his chair. "Get word out throughout the Eastern Empire that this is a holy war. All those that remember the glory of the Empire as it used to be should fight with us."

After a short silence, Licinius continued. "Use that as our recruitment theme. We will need to build our strength quickly. I suspect the bastard has already notified his bastard son to start moving into position to confront Amandus. We must get word to Amandus: Avoid Crispus initially, at least, in order to give us the maximum time to rebuild our troops."

Sextus sneered: "Amandus won't have any problems with Constantine's fleet. It is far smaller than ours. It's mostly liburnians, mostly Greek commanders. Our ships are larger—with Egyptian, Persian and Syrian commanders. We'll hold the Bosporus. We'll block Constantine from attacking us on the Asian side. He won't be able to get his troops across the water to attack us in Chrysopolis or Nicomedia. He took Adrianople—but he's stuck where he is."

"I agree, Sextus. Our situation isn't dire—we just lost our dominant position." Licinius said, ending with a nervous laugh.

Sextus stood up and looked at the water. "Augustus, do you wish to keep our remaining troops here in Byzantium? Or should we build our strength on the other side of the Bosporus?"

"I'll stay here with a legion as a decoy," Licinius answered. "Take the rest to Lamseki, on shores of the Hellespont. Rebuild the troops there. I suspect that the bastard will attempt to cross to the Asian side either there or at Chacedon. I'll negotiate with him as a delaying tactic. Again, we need time."

"Good. I will be near Amandus and the largest part of our fleet."

Licinius stared at the water. It was muddy—almost red—not glistening and clear, as it usually was.

Thessalonica, Greece
July 5, 1077 AUC (324 AD)

Crispus heard the news of his father's victory that morning while waiting on the ship's deck for the final ballista to be installed on an older liburnian. He wondered about his father's injury—but the messenger, barely a boy, knew few details. He was also somewhat perplexed that his father had withdrawn his troops. It was not like Constantine to give up on an absolute victory. There must have been details missing from the report.

Regardless, it was time to get the fleet moving. The latest intelligence had Amandus' fleet split between the Bosporus Strait and the Hellespont, with over two hundred ships at the entrance of the Hellespont and the Aegean Sea. The remainder of Amandus' fleet, mostly the older ships, was located in the northern part of the Sea of Marmara by the Bosporus. An odd arrangement.

The Hellespont was a narrow strait that separated the Aegean Sea from the Sea of Marmara. It formed the southern end of the

Sea of Marmara; the northern end was the Bosporus Strait, by Byzantium.

The Sea of Marmara—from the Hellespont up to the Bosporus— was the demarcation line between the Western Empire and the Eastern Empire. Amandus was blocking both ends.

"How shall we go?" Thestor asked, when Crispus told him that the fleet had to move.

"I've spoken with the other senior captains," Crispus said, knowing that Thestor would expect him to do so. "They're concerned about storms if sail straight across the Aegean."

"That would be the straightest line," Thestor said, like a school master.

Crispus shook his head. "We're loaded for war. A strong storm could scuttle the fleet. We'll hug the coast of Greece and attack Amandus' fleet at the mouth of the Hellespont."

Thestor smiled. "It will add a few days to the trip. Amandus might have moved before we get there."

Crispus smiled, too. "I've sent word to our scouts to meet us west of Cape Helles, on the way in. They'll confirm his whereabouts then." He was beginning to feel like a commander.

A few hours later, the fleet had left Thessalonica.

Adrianople, Thrace
July 7, 1077 AUC (324 AD)

In the command tent overlooking the Hebrus River and the recently ravaged battlefield, Constantine threw Licinius' scroll to the ground. "This idiot claims that he should still control a portion of the Empire after losing over half of his troops in one day. I don't think he understands what 'defeat' means."

Ablabius was less talkative than he'd been a few days earlier. He didn't like being blamed for withdrawing the army when it should have attacked. Nor being threatened with death.

"A delaying tactic, Dominus."

"Undoubtedly, which means he is calling on the Goths and needs at least a couple of months to build a new army."

"Which will have never fought together. And they will be facing us at our best. We should strike soon." Ablabius picked up the scroll and scanned it briefly before putting it on a folding table.

"We can't be too confident. We have to flush him out of Byzantium first," Constantine said. "He's holed up in there."

"He can't build his army while hiding in Byzantium, Dominus. If we lay siege to the city, he'll be stuck."

Constantine shook his head. "It's hard to lay siege to a port city. All he needs to do is slip out some night on a skiff. His army is just across the Bosporus."

Ablabius let silence sit for a moment and then tried another approach. "There are different ways to attack, Dominus. Licinius always takes over the same villa when he's in Byzantium. One of our centurions has family members that have been servants during his prior stays. We could feed him some poison and end his lunacy."

Constantine thought for a moment. "I'm no Nero. You know I've never liked the idea of poisoning opponents, Ablabius. It seems like...cheating. Now, in Licinius' case, I am tempted. It would save the lives of so many of our troops. But I'm not sure.... Talk to this centurion and see what the risks to his family would be. Don't do anything until we talk again about it."

"Yes, Dominus." Ablabius angled toward the door of the tent. "We have made initial plans for a siege on Byzantium. We could leave in two days, if your leg has healed enough for you to ride."

"That will be fine. My leg is better every day. Any word from Crispus?"

"Nothing yet. I suspect he received our messenger two days ago and has set sail yesterday. Since Licinius doesn't appear to be willing to surrender, we need to control the straits to get across safety."

Constantine looked at the scroll and shook his head. "More than that. We'll need the ships to blockade Byzantium from the water, if our siege has any hope of working."

"Yes, Dominus."

Byzantium, Greece
July 17, 1077 AUC (324 AD)

The summer heat was in full force. And odors of horses and humans filled the humid air. Thousands of troops were working as earth movers. They were building huge mounds of dirt almost equal to the height of the city's walls. Carpenters had started to build bulwarks on which they'd mount catapults and ballista captured from Licinius at Adrianople.

If the citizens of Byzantium had been uneasy about having nervous Licinius as their guest when he first arrived, they would be terrified now that Constantine was laying siege to their city.

Constantine, walking with a slight limp, was examining the ground works with his palatini when Ablabius found him. "Dominus, I have word from Crispus."

"Where is he?"

"Three days out from Cape Helles. He needs intelligence about Amandus' position."

Constantine pointed to a low ridge, several hundred feet behind them. It was away from the noise. As they walked that direction, Ablabius noticed that the Emperor's limp was more pronounced than it first had seemed.

"And what is Amandus' position?"

"As of two days ago, he was in the same place he has been for weeks. By Canakkale. Half his fleet is there, with him, and the other half, the older ships, are up here by the Bosporus."

"And their army? Where are they assembling their troops?"

"Sextus Martinianus is rebuilding their army near Lamseki."

"Who is Sextus Martinianus? And why Lamseki?"

"Martinianus is Licinius' new co-Emperor."

Constantine sneered. "By God's grace! I've been replaced?"

"Not God's grace, Dominus. By Licinius' word. This new 'Caesar' was one his senior guards. Promoted because of loyalty more than brilliance or skill. And I have no idea why Lamseki, unless Licinius thinks you will try to cross into Asia there—because of their famous docks."

At the ridge, the palatini set up a folding chair for Constantine—who sat with a thud. One of the guards gave him a damp cloth, which Constantine put around his neck. Another guard handed him a cup of water, which he drank quickly. "Well, Caligula made his horse a senator. Ablabius, get our scouts to the Cape soon, in case he gets there early. And why is Amandus staying in the straits? The open sea would give him more room to maneuver and evade...."

"I don't know. Naval tactics have never made sense to me."

Ablabius waited for a few moments, to make sure the guards weren't listening. They were trained to attend to the Emperor—but pay little attention to the details of his conversations.

"I do have word from our centurion concerning that... business...with Licinius."

"Ah, yes. The basket of asps. What news?"

Ablabius spoke carefully. "He thinks he can get into Byzantium by boat and deliver the package to his sister, who is very trusted. They do not think Licinius has any doubts about them and they would be safe."

Constantine nodded—but was looking at the workers on one of the bulwarks. "I am still not comfortable with this. I would kill him in an instant if we had swords in our hands. Give me a day to think about this. Let's make a decision on this in a day or two."

"Yes, Dominus." Ablabius bowed slightly and quickly walked back toward the earthen mounds. He'd spotted a worker starting to put a ballista foundation facing the wrong location.

Cape Helles, Greece
July 20, 1077 AUC (324 AD)

It was a warm, late afternoon. Crispus, Thestor and several of their senior commanders listened to three scouts describe the location Amandus' main fleet. They were on the beach at the southernmost shore of Cape Helles—and the scouts had sketched in the sand the locations of the Amandus' triremes and the smaller liburnians. They had drawn their location, where the Hellespont narrowed, not far from the town of Canakkale.

There were 50 of the big ships, the triremes. Many more liburnians—half of which were located north of the big ships, half south. They estimated there were 200 ships in total. It was a large fleet, poorly arranged.

Thestor immediately questioned the report's accuracy. "No disrespect meant, my friends. But are you sure Amandus has this half of the liburnians north of the triremes? Why would he leave his big ships vulnerable from the south? There is no risk of our fleet attacking from the north. There is no way for us to get there without engaging the triremes first. It doesn't make sense."

"The ships are as we draw them, Great Thestor. We all saw them from different locations just yesterday."

Crispus craned his neck to study the sketch more closely. "Is it a ploy? A trap being set? How long have they been in that position?"

"For over a week."

"Amandus is no fool. Is there a reason he would want part of his fleet to be able to go north quickly?" Crispus asked.

Thestor understood the point his young admiral was trying to make. "Only if Sextus needs some of the fleet. Or if there's a problem confronting the remainder of the fleet by the Bosporus."

"And Sextus is in Lamseki?" Crispus asked the scouts.

"Yes Caesar."

"And all this my father knows?

"Yes, Caesar."

As soon as the scouts got their money and left, Crispus sighed and scratched at the sand sketches with a stick. "Thestor, they must be worried about Constantine's army crossing the straits. More worried than they are about us. Which is good for us. Since we will have the wind behind us, we will attack tomorrow morning with 80 of our fastest ships—and keep the remaining 100 or so here by the Cape.

"The Hellespont is narrow where they're moored. And the wind will be behind us, giving us full advantage. If we are agile and fast, and they are slow to protect their cumbersome triremes, we will sink many of them in the first few hours." Thestor repeated.

South Narrows of the Hellespont, Asia Minor
July 21, 1077 AUC (324 AD)

In his stateroom on his newest trireme, Amandus arose early with a minor headache. At night he liked his wine undiluted and he tended to have one cup too many.

He rationalized that it was a reaction to his frustration at taking conflicting orders from Licinius. Being told to delay any conflict with Constantine's fleet and to be fully available for Sextus were mutually exclusive.

To delay would mean he should be located in the Aegean Sea, where he had room for the big ships to move. He could then attack when they had the advantage of wind or speed. To be fully available for Sextus meant being in the Hellespont, ready to move north at any sign of Constantine's approach.

Not that it mattered; he didn't expect much problem from Crispus' fleet whenever they arrived. So here he stayed, less than five mille from the Aegean and 15 from Sextus.

Walking into the small mess area he debated to have a cup of fig juice or watered wine, and choose the fig juice. Following the stairs to the upper deck, he scanned the horizon to the south, past his liburnians. It was clear. He nodded to some of the marines leaning against the starboard rail and finished his juice, slightly cutting his lip on a chip from the clay cup's rim. It was a bit windy and the clouds were low and large. Storms in a day or two, he thought.

Looking south again, he saw what he thought might be a sail. He kept his gaze, his heart beating a little faster, and focused on what looked like another sail. He threw the empty chipped cup into the water and yelled at his young signalman to sound the buccina. The horn's deep bellow indicated to the fleet that Amandus was communicating. A series of trumpets followed, sounding the alarm. Other signalman raised the ready flag.

Crispus' heart was also beating faster. He could see the Amandus' fleet in front of him. For a moment, he questioned his choice of bringing only 80 liburnians. Two hundred opposing ships looked intimidating at three mille. But it was too late to question. The crew was making last-minute preparations. And the oarsmen weren't rowing, because the strong wind was carrying them. The die has been cast.

Amandus' liburnians were starting to tack and row toward them. They would be easy to avoid, given his greater speed and maneuverability—and, particularly, because of the wind.

The fleet's sails had the Chi Rho painted on them with a smaller Labarum flying off of their sterns. Crispus was on a ship captained by Akakios, a close friend of Thestor. Thestor's ship was sailing to his port side. Thestor had encouraged Crispus to sail with Akakios, a wary sailor. Thestor was convinced Crispus would be safer there. True to form, Thestor was the first to draw fire. Cutting off Akakios and taking a grapple fired from a liburnian, Thestor's marines cut the grapple rope as it spun their ship almost 90 degrees—and headed directly at the opposing ship.

"Strike! Strike, lads!" Thestor yelled at his oarsman to pull at their full strength and 20 seconds later the first of Amandus' liburnians was sinking.

Crispus was watching Thestor's successful attack when a grapple slammed into his ship. Akakios turned the ship to starboard, giving it more drag and making it harder for the liburnian that shot the grapple to pull it close. Before Crispus had time to give an order, one of the marines cut the rope connecting to the grapple. Everyone was moving more quickly than Crispus had remembered them training.

As Akakios turned the ship upwind, it accelerated past the ship that had shot the grapple—and one of Akakios' marines fired a burning lance from a ballista. Because they were so close, the lance hit high amidships. And another of Crispus' ships took advantage of the stalled liburnian and rammed it.

"Two down," thought Crispus.

In the first hour of battle, Akakios had yet to ram any ship but had acted as a decoy for his fellow captains at least five times. Crispus had lost count of the how many ships his fleet had sunk but knew they had only lost one ship so far. He'd seen a large artillery stone from one of the triremes hit one of his liburnian's bow, tearing off the entire ram. It sank instantly.

Amandus was trying to get his liburnians north of his triremes into the battle. The narrowness of the straits and the difficulty of moving the big ships, also trying to avoiding Crispus' quicker liburnians, were frustrating the Amandus' captains. Several of the big ships almost rammed each other—and, when their crews rowed backwards to avoid each other, they were rammed by ships with Chi Rho sails.

Early in the afternoon, Akakios sailed out from the center of the fighting. He had his eye on a larger liburnian whose sail was down and its crew was rowing against the wind toward shore. It appeared the captain wanted to row downwind, tack and have the advantage of the wind in his sails. When he realized Akakios was tracking toward him, he knew he had to turn quickly. He turned and dropped his sails—but didn't have enough time to get to any speed before impact.

Both ships lurched. Crispus nearly lost his footing but grabbed a mast line just in time. The bow of his ship split a three-cubit hole near the stern of their target. Immediately, Akakios ordered his oarsmen to row backwards. The deck was littered with enemy arrows.

Amandus' marines were swinging onto Crispus' ship. Their ship was already sinking. For what seemed like an eternity—but was really less than a minute—both boats remained linked. Finally, the efforts of the oarsmen were rewarded. Cripus' boat slowly separated from the sinking liburnian. Several enemy marines had boarded. Crispus didn't hesitate. He drew his sword and buried it to the hilt in the closest marine. He pulled it out just in time fend off a blow. And then sliced the neck of another attacker. His archers killed the rest.

Flush with adrenaline, Crispus turned around and noticed the oarsmen were rowing forward. Thestor's ship was behind him now. He made eye contact with Thestor, who pointed a shaking finger at Akakios. Who shrugged. Crispus realized what was happening: Akakios had been ordered not to ram enemy ships for his safety.

As both ships headed back toward the center of the Hellespont, where most of the fighting was going on, Crispus ran to Akakios at the stern of the ship. "Next time, you ram!"

Akakios didn't say anything. He just pointed at a large trireme heading toward them.

They would be easy prey for the catapults and ballistae of the big ship in open water. So Thestor was attacking. He took the lead using both sail and oars heading towards the starboard side of the big ship. Akakios ordered his sail down and cut to his starboard. He crossed Thestor's wake and was moving as far away into the wind from the two ships as he could. Crispus realized what they were doing. "How can I help?"

"Get to the mast with the marines. Use scythes."

As Akakios turned his ship into the wind and raised his sails toward the trireme, Crispus saw two grapples hit Thestor's ship a few hundred feet away. Instead of trying to cut the ropes, Thestor ordered his oarsmen to row with all their strength.

Akakios ordered his oarsman row toward the other side of the big ship, adding to the speed of the sails. As the large trireme slowed to a stall from Thestor's ship pulling on the grapple ropes, their entire weak side was exposed to Akakios' ram. Realizing his vulnerability, the captain of the trireme ordered the ropes cut and the artillery to focus on Akakios' ship.

It was the right order—but it confused his crew. The men on the upper deck had been focused on Thestor's ship. They cut their own ropes and started to row. But they couldn't move the ship fast enough. Or far enough.

Their comrades at the catapults also had to move fast. And they also were slightly confused. They launched their stones before they were able to set properly.

As two huge stones missed to either side, Akakios rammed the trireme at full speed. Crispus had time to secure himself—and he still fell to his knees. This was the sign that he still wasn't a true sailor. They never seemed to fall, even during impact.

The strike from the smaller ship barely caused the trireme to move. It just shuddered slightly as Crispus' ship punched a large hole in its side.

Immediately, Akakios ordered the oarsmen to row backwards from the trireme. Their deck was hit with several grapples at once. Crispus and the marines cut two quickly—but one was hooked high above the deck, on the mast. One of the marines climbed toward it but was hit by an arrow. At nearly the same moment, another was hit with a lance. The third...Crispus couldn't see the third. He jumped on the pegs on the back side of the mast and climbed toward the grapple. While he was climbing, he felt the stern of his ship rise. He reached the grapple on the mast and slashed the rope with his sword in two cuts. His sword was still wet and red from the earlier fighting.

But his ship was still rising in the stern. "Get down, Caesar! Get down!" Akakios screamed, running toward him.

He did. In three quick jumps, Crispus was back on the deck. And now he could see what was happening. Their bow was wedged in the sinking trireme. It was going to pull their boat down as well.

The oarsmen were abandoning the ship. Marines from the trireme were jumping aboard the upper deck of his liburnian. Akakios and the team of six archers had assembled at the base of the mast and were picking off enemies as fast as they could. Crispus saw that they were retreating gradually toward the stern. He fell in with them. He didn't have a bow, so he picked up a shield and held it over the heads of two of his archers. Akakios nodded in agreement and did the same.

Arrows were flying in all directions, but their group stayed calm and kept the enemy marines on the other side of the ship. Crispus could see water starting to fill the front of the deck. They were secure in their position—but they didn't have much time.

Thestor had lowered his sail and was rowing toward the stern of the sinking liburnian. Akakios yelled to Crispus and the others: "We'll hold them off as long as we can, Caesar. Thestor can't stop with so much going on. He'll just slow down. We've got to swim to him."

"We'll follow your lead, captain." Crispus yelled back.

The archers kept shooting. They did a good job, killing several more enemy marines. Thestor's ship drew close—and the archers kept shooting. Crispus looked at Akakios, who nodded. Thestor's ship was passing. Akakios was still calm. The archers got in a last volley. And then:

"Now, gentlemen. Let's go!"

He and Crispus dropped their shields, the archers dropped their bows and all eight dove into the water. It was cold. They swam as quickly as they could toward Thestor's ship, which was dragging dozens of trailing lines in the water. All eight men—plus several surviving oarsmen—grabbed the ropes and pulled themselves toward Thestor's ship.

Crispus had a firm grip on his line, so he made sure that his men got aboard Thestor's ship first. By the time the sailors helped him onto the deck, the trireme and his liburnian were gone from view, with only the mast of the trireme still above water. He was out of breath from the water—so he just nodded to Akakios, who was also still out of breath and nodded back.

A few minutes later, Thestor came back to see them.

Crispus stood up. "So, you and Akakios had an agreement to keep me safe?"

"Caesar, your father told me to take care of you. And you ram a trireme!" Shaking a finger at Akakios. How would I explain this to our Imperator? He would have my head. I am lucky that Neptune has smiled on me."

As they returned to the other ships, the battle was waning. Crispus walked toward the middle deck with Thestor and did a quick count of the sails in sight.

"I count 29 of ours and about 60 of theirs."

Thestor nodded. "Yes. But there are many ships on the other side of the peninsula that we can't see. Let us sound the horns. We will have tomorrow to finish the job."

Amandus heard the horns of Crispus' fleet and sounded his own. His headache—which the passion of battle had dulled—returned. He hadn't lost everything, but he'd lost badly. Crispus' smaller, faster fleet had sunk three of his ships for every one of theirs he'd sunk. Their ships had managed to keep the wind at their backs most of the day. And they were fast, much faster than he remembered. And constantly ramming.

With the narrow water, they had more opportunities for their more agile ships. The strait was wider north by Gallipoli, near where Sextus was located. By the rocky shores of Lamseki. It would be best to meet them there. He still had over one hundred ships left; Crispus couldn't have more than 50. He could still prevail, given better conditions for his ships and adjustments he'd make to his defenses.

The main adjustment would be to bomb Crispus' ships with more artillery.

He would delay sending a report to Licinius and Sextus until after tomorrow's battle. And drink less wine tonight.

North of the Hellespont, Asia Minor
July 22, 1077 AUC (324 AD)

Amandus searched the horizon again from his ship's deck. Still no sign of Crispus' remaining fleet. Clouds had started to darken the midmorning sun and the wind from the south was strong. Good weather for Crispus coming up the strait; poor weather for accuracy of the artillery from heaving decks.

He had his fleet in a good position in the widest part of the straits, south of the city of Gallipoli. By the final count, he'd lost 77 ships the day before—about a dozen of those had been triremes. All of his liburnians were now in front of his triremes, whose broadsides were perpendicular to Crispus' approaching fleet for movement and best artillery deployment.

His liburnians were facing the direction that Crispus' fleet would be approaching.

He looked again—and, this time, he saw something. A row of sails. He gave the signal and the horns and trumpets sounded alarm. Within 20 minutes, the sails had become more evident, the Chi Rho's visible to the eye. But the most disturbing part was their number:

There were well over 100 ships. Crispus had kept forces in reserve.

Amandus' first instinct was to retreat. But he couldn't. Abandoning Sextus at Lamseki would violate Licinius' direct orders—and make it easier for Constantine to find a crossing point. Besides, where could he retreat? If he sailed north into the Sea of Marmara, Crispus' faster ships would pick them off individually, particularly with today's strong winds. If he crossed to the Bosporus, Crispus' faster fleet would have an easy time picking off the older ships stationed there.

His best option, which wasn't good, was to stay and fight.

From Thestor's ship, Crispus watched Amandus' fleet shift formation. He yelled to Thestor, who was speaking to the helmsman:

"They didn't realize how many of us were coming to the party, Thestor. Now they're tightening up their liburnians."

Thestor walked amidships and studied Amandus' fleet quickly. "No matter, Caesar. If they don't want us to use the front door, we'll come at them from the sides." He yelled to his signal mate and then ordered the horn command to split the fleet into a pincer formation. A flag went up the mast indicating the same thing.

The fleet split, turned and attacked to the left and right of Amandus' defensive formation.

Within a few hours, the battle was developing just as it had the day before. Crispus' fleet had sunk over 30 of Amandus' ships and lost fewer than 10 of its own. Because of the heavy seas, Amandus' artillery tactics were practically useless. And the weather continued to deteriorate, with strong gusts coming from the south and west.

By mid-afternoon, Crispus and Thestor were starting to worry. The wind was overpowering—too strong for either fleet to raise sails—and the entire western sky was as dark as night.

Crispus was the first to suggest a retreat. "Thestor! I think we should retreat to the west side of the strait. This wind is brutal."

Thestor thought for a minute and then yelled back. "I agree, Caesar. We should be able to row against the wind. It will be very difficult. Thank God we are in small ships."

The horns sounded—but some of the ships had started turning already. As if in unison, the fleets disengaged. And the dark clouds approached more quickly. They brought a collapsing wall of howling wind, rough waves and pounding rain. Amandus' triremes suffered the worst effects. Their larger hulls began to act as sails and, regardless of the power the oarsmen put into their oars, the big ships were pushed in the direction of the wind.

Because of their smaller size and lower profile, Crispus' ships made slow headway toward the west side of the strait. Still, the oarsmen were struggling. Thestor ordered the marines and sagittari to help. Soon everyone was at an oar with the exception of the helmsman.

Within an hour of the storm striking, Crispus' fleet was halfway to the western shore. Amandus' fleet was losing its battle with the wind. One by one, his ships were driven onto the rocks on the Eastern shore.

Two hours later, the storm had passed as quickly as it had come. All but four of Amandus' ships had been thrashed onto the shore of the east side of the Hellespont. His flagship was one of the many wrecked. He'd had to swim to the rocky shore.

In two days, Licinius' fleet had lost 196 ships. A crushing defeat.

Byzantium, Greece
July 24, 1077 AUC (324 AD)

From the top of a wooden bulwark overlooking the besieged city of Byzantium, Constantine watched Licinius' forces scurrying about the banks of the Bosporus. They'd scrounged together every old ship in Licinius' fleet to ferry soldiers, horses and armaments across the strait to the Asian side.

They were trying to reposition—and retreat—before Crispus' fleet arrived, sometime in the next day or so.

Constantine was frustrated. He knew there was nothing he could do. Although his catapults were ready, they couldn't reach the ships in the strait. Bombarding the city would only harm the residents— which was pointless. They would surrender in a few hours. Storming the gates was a possibility; he'd be in Byzantium sooner. But his spies told him that Licinius had abandoned the city earlier that morning.

He'd been one of the first across the Bosporus.

As he expected, the city's residents opened their gates that afternoon. They were celebrating, joyous that Byzantium had been spared. And infatuated that the living god was now their Emperor.

Constantine walked with a slight limp through the city, toward the water of the Bosporus. Ablabius and his bodyguards formed a loose cordon around him. When an arrogant-looking man tried to approach the Emperor, that cordon snapped tight—and the palatini drew their weapons.

The man's demeanor changed immediately from haughty to frightened. He raised his hands above his head and waved one that was holding a scroll. Ablabius recognized the man and whispered to Constantine, "Shipping merchant. Very wealthy. Turns with the wind. But he's a Christian."

Constantine nodded to Ablabius, who barked out an order. "Let him approach."

"Great Imperator, I invite you to use my villa. If you would like a comfortable place to stay."

Constantine made eye contact with the merchant "Thank you, friend. I may do that."

"Licinius left this letter. It's for you"

"Thank you." Constantine broke the seal and started to read the contents of the scroll. He shook his head. In a voice only heard by his palatini he whispered, "Poison." And he started walking again toward the Bosporus.

As they approached the wharf that had been so busy earlier that day, Constantine—still holding Licinius' scroll—the Christian and Ablabius started to get ahead of his palatini. They'd quickened their pace, wanting to see the other side of the Bosporus before night settled in.

Near the wharf, two men approached Constantine—one on either side. Subtly, Appius and Titus moved toward one; Quintus and Sevius moved toward the other. The other palatini stepped around Constantine just as the two men drew daggers and lunged at the Emperor. The bodyguards pushed the Christian merchant toward one attacker and Ablabius toward the other.

In a movement almost too fast to see, Appius and Titus both drew their daggers and stabbed the first attacker. They held him up for a second, blunting his momentum, and then let him fall to the ground. His last words were a hissing curse.

Quintus and Sevius knocked the other attacker to the ground, kicking the dagger out of his hand and slamming his face on one of the street's cobblestones. Quintus grabbed the man's head by its hair and slammed it back on the stone, to make sure the attacker was disabled.

All four senior guards looked back at Constantine, who'd barely moved. He looked at the surviving attacker and made a gesture with his head. Quintus and Sevius raised the man up to his feet, though he couldn't really stand. He mumbled something incoherent that included the word "bastard."

Constantine looked at Quintus and said 'Kill him'

Ablabius quickly put his hand up and turned to Constantine, whispering something to him. Constantine, obviously vexed and angry, repeated with vigor 'Kill him.'

Ablabius again whispered something and Constantine slowly shook his head in agreement as his anger cooled.

A crowd of onlookers was gathering. Constantine walked toward the attacker, whose face was bleeding profusely.

"Tell me, captive, what have I done to get this kind of a reception?"

"Roman. Die," the man mumbled.

"Do I hear a…Syrian…accent?" Constantine asked.

"Dog. Bastard. You hear nothing."

"Who paid you to kill me?" Constantine asked.

"All of them." And he tried to laugh. Quintus drew his knife to the Syrian's neck. But Constantine shook his head.

"If I promised you a chance of freedom, would you answer my questions?" Constantine asked.

"You'll never give me freedom."

"I said I would give you a *chance* for freedom. In order to earn that chance, you need to tell me who you are. Who this was," he pointed to the dead man. "And who sent you."

"What chance?" The attacker asked, his head clearing.

"You'll fight one of the men holding you. If you win, you are free to go."

"What weapons?"

"Swords."

"Shields?"

"Yes, you can use a shield. Are you a soldier?"

"Yes."

"So, do we have an agreement?" Constantine asked.

"If I can fight the small one."

Sevius bristled at the reference. Quintus and he were the best swordfighters in the palatini company. He was slightly shorter than Quintus—but the real difference was that he was not as muscular. He was however, notoriously fast.

"All right. Who are you?"

"Where are my weapons?"

"You have my word you will get them after you answer my questions," Constantine sounded like a schoolteacher who was losing his patience.

"My name is Ashar. That's my brother, Domara. We are soldiers of the true Emperor's army. And we know about you. Your atrocities, back to your invasion of Italy. You are the bastard usurper. You worship a false god. No one paid us. We would kill you only for glory."

"So, they didn't pay you. But is either Licinius or Sextus aware of what you're doing?" Constantine asked.

"I don't know or care. Sextus is close to our centurion. Now give me the weapons, so I can kill this man and go free."

Constantine nodded. Quintus and Sevius let the Syrian go. He staggered a bit but gained solid footing. He wiped the blood from his face, up into his hair.

Ablabius told one of the soldiers in the growing crowd to give the Syrian his sword and shield.

"Ablabius, may I use your longer cavalry sword?" Sevius asked.

"Of course." Ablabius answered, handing his sword to Sevius. "I just cleaned and sharpened it this morning."

"I was counting on that, my meticulous friend."

"Do you want my shield, Sevius?" Appius asked.

"No. Thank you, though," Sevius responded.

As the two squared off, the palatini formed a circle around them. A crowd now stood outside the circle, watching intently. Byzantium has just lived through a siege—but few citizens had seen any actual fighting. This would stand in for what they'd only heard about before.

The Syrian grasped his shield with one hand and sword with the other. Standard legionari battle stance.

Sevius stood in front of him, holding Ablabius' sword in his right hand and a small dagger in his left.

Appius turned to Titus and whispered: "The Syrian will be dead in one minute."

He overestimated.

The Syrian made the first move, using his shield as a battering ram and jabbing at Sevius. Sevius easily moved aside and, using his sword, hit the rim of the Syrian's shield—causing the Syrian to turn slightly and leaving his side vulnerable. Sevius made a lightning fast slash with the dagger, down the length of the Syrian's torso. It wasn't a deep slash—nor was it meant to be. But it was bloody. The Syrian glanced down at his wound, his shield dropping slightly. Sevius dropped his dagger to the ground. The Syrian looked down at it. He was confused. He then looked up. The last thing he saw was the flash of Ablabius' sword coming toward him. He had no time even to flinch. His head was quickly separated from his body.

The crowd cheered wildly. The Christian merchant gagged. Sevius bowed to Constantine and then reached into his tunic for a piece of cloth to clean Ablabius' sword.

Constantine nodded back to Sevius, "Very well done Sevius. Very fast with no wasted effort." Then, he turned to Ablabius, "Have a couple of your legionari emasculate both Syrians. Put their genitals in jars and send them to Licinius and Sextus. With a note that they are next. We need to communicate with these people in terms they understand."

In the next couple of minutes, while the crowd was still lingering and Constantine remained by the wharf talking with some city leaders, two soldiers appeared with a cart. Loading the dead brothers onto the wooden panel that was the rear gate of the cart, they lifted the tunics, cut off their loincloths and castrated them. Then they had a grim-humor contest to see who could throw the genitals into the earthen jars from farther away.

The Christian merchant, looking over Constantine's shoulder at the contest, had to bend over next to the cobblestone street and gagged again.

Byzantium, Greece
July 26, 1077 AUC (324 AD)

Constantine, Ablabius, Crispus and all of the Emperor's senior commanders were in the sizable sitting room of the Christian merchant's villa. They were standing around a table with a large map of the local area. All had read Licinius' latest letter with a weak appeal to end the hostilities—a rambling list of territories, waterways and residences he would control. The scroll was on top of the map.

"How will you respond to this latest fantasy, Dominus?" asked Ablabius

Constantine smirked. "I think we responded appropriately last night. We all know the letter's purpose is to give him time to rebuild his army. The question is how we get across the Bosporus in a reasonable time in order to defeat him once and for all." He picked up Licinius' scroll and drew an imaginary line on the map where the Bosporus separated Byzantium from Asia.

"Does he still have Sextus in Lamseki?" asked Tiberus.

"Our latest report confirms he's still there. But that information is two days old," Ablabius answered.

"Has Licinius joined him there?" Tiberus continued.

"Not that we know of. We know the soldiers he had here are now in Chacedon, directly across the Bosporus from where we are right now," Ablabius pointed to that spot on the map. "And we know the Goths are headed there."

Crispus observed: "Looks like he's stationed troops at the points where he believes we're most likely to cross."

"Exactly. Which is why we're not going to cross in either of those locations. The best crossing will either be somewhere north of the straits," Constantine pointed the scroll in that general direction. "Or on the south shore of the Black Sea."

"Ugh. That shore is steep and rocky," groaned Marcus.

"How will we transport the troops?" Crispus asked. "The liburnians have too much draft for that area. And our closest true transports are in Thessalonica. Not that it matters. They'd be too large, too."

Constantine scowled at the map. "Crispus, you and Marcus scout that shoreline for the best location. Ablabius, work with your carpenters to build as many transport barges as you can."

"How much time do we have, Dominus?"

"I'd like to know our landing location in a week. And have all the transport barges in a month."

"A month? I'm not sure we will have enough barges by then, Dominus," said Ablabius.

"So be it. We'll get started and delay later if necessary. Giving Licinius more time only helps him. The Goths will be with him in a week or so. And we know he's offering big bonuses to anyone signs on for this battle. He'll be watching the Bosporus, of course. He never learns. We'll let him think he's right. We will even send some 'scouting parties' down near Sextus to alarm them. And we must keep his forces separate from Sextus to the south. That's essential." While Constantine spoke, Licinius' scroll cracked slightly in his hand.

Chacedon, Asia Minor
September 1, 1077 AUC (324 AD)

Sextus joined Licinius in a private villa in Chacedon, on the water directly across the strait from Byzantium. After shaking arms, they sat on the patio overlooking the Bosporus to develop a strategy to defeat Constantine.

"Augustus, other than some decoy scouting parties, we see no sign of activity from Constantine. He's hiding. I think he's being clever. Perhaps we should consolidate our forces here at Chacedon? I got a gift a couple of weeks ago that doesn't make me feel comfortable with passively waiting for Constantine. I worry that we need more training together to withstand his inevitable, aggressive assault."

Licinius shook his head. "He's a hypocritical bastard. I got the same gift. I assume that was all that remains of the Syrian brothers you told me about?"

"I assume so as well," Sextus answered.

"I wish they'd killed him. Here's the thing about Constantine: He's reactive. We need to draw him here to Chacedon. When you're facing a clever fellow, be the opposite. Be simple and you can deliver the fatal blow," Licinius punctuated his answer with a nervous laugh.

Sextus shook his head. "Amandus' failure hurts us here, Augustus. Crispus controls the straits, so Constantine could land virtually anywhere. I'll say it again: We should bring our troops together and train for a more defensive strategy."

"How can he cross anywhere? The only good dockage is where you are and where I am. I can watch his activity from this chair. His ships are so small we'll see them crossing. They'll have to ferry back and forth for hours. Days! He still believes I'll surrender. That will be his demise. I'll stall him another couple of weeks we'll have enough troops to repulse him—even if he flies over the Bosporus with his Christian wings." Licinius ended, again, with a laugh.

"True. We will have more strength. But we have the Goths here now and my troops are down south. We must train them to fight together, Augustus."

Licinius shrugged. He was full of himself. "If we don't see any activity in Lamseki in two weeks, we will bring your troops here and leave scouts there to warn us when he starts crossing."

Both men turned to look over the Bosporus towards Byzantium. There was almost no activity. Crispus' fleet looked stagnant, its masts barely moving with the calm waves. As if on cue, Licinius and Sextus both shook their heads.

For different reasons.

Byzantium, Greece
September 1, 1077 AUC (324 AD)

Constantine was having his daily meeting with his officers in the sitting room of the Christian merchant's residence. For the first time in many weeks, Ossius joined them.

"In 10 days, we should have enough barges to make the crossing. The liburnians will push them to the sandy area Crispus and the locals have found. We're constructing cradles that attach the barges to the ships—and we have tested the ones we've completed. They work," Ablabius reported. He used a thin reed pointer to show where, on the map, each part of the plan would take place.

"But what does Licinius see?" Constantine asked. "Is there any sign that his troops are surveying the area to tip him off of our intentions?"

"No sign of that, Dominus. We've landed at the crossing point by night. We've sailed by it—several times—by day. Nothing," Ablabius answered. "They can't see it from Chalcedon. It's too far north. And Licinius isn't looking."

After a few moments of silence, Marcus spoke. "I can second what Ablabius says. I've seen it with my own eyes. But I'm still concerned that we've shown our plans. Somehow. I think we should start the transport at dusk. That way, we will be able to build troop strength before dawn. We'll need at least five legions across before I'll feel comfortable."

"I agree," Crispus said. He was getting more comfortable talking in these meetings. "How many can we transport at night, Ablabius?"

The Greek held his hands in a balancing gesture. "If everything goes well, we could move two legions across each night. Maybe three. The problem is, with this kind of enterprise, nothing goes as well as you plan, particularly when you start."

Marcus shook his head. "So, two nights for five legions. And we're still vulnerable to a full-force attack from Licinius." He looked at Constantine. "I don't like it, Dominus."

Constantine didn't say anything. But he nodded, as if in agreement with—or at least understanding of—what Marcus had said.

Ablabius responded defensively: "Our latest reports still have half of their troops with Sextus in Lamseki. And none of them are in formation. If Licinius were to discover us, it would take him more than a day to get his troops—and I mean just the ones in Chalcedon—in position to confront us."

Constantine knew it was time for him to make a decision. Still, he took a few moments to visualize each of the options for attacking Licinius. Then, finally: "We stay with our plan but we will start at dusk. It is a manageable risk, as long as our landing spot is unknown to him."

He looked quickly at each of his generals. "One more thing. I want to organize a consort brigade for the Labarum. A group of perhaps 50 senior legionari who will be responsible for moving and protecting my standard. We saw how effective it was in motivating our troops at Adrianople. This special unit will move it wherever our army needs assistance."

Marcus spoke next. "As you command, Augustus. I'll choose those men myself. But I wonder whether the corpulent portentous Licinius will tell his troops to turn away—as he did at Adrianople. Surely, by now, he understands that was suicidal. And he can't afford many more mistakes."

"I don't know, Marcus. He's a bit of a nutcase," Ablabius said, laughing. And the rest joined him.

Constantine dismissed his commanders. As the group started to leave, Constantine motioned to Ossius to join him. They sat, looking out at the Bosporus, until the room had emptied.

"Ossius, we haven't spoken in so long. How is our problem with Alexander and Arius?"

"There is no change, Imperator. I believe I mentioned to you that I have been invited by Alexander to Chair a Council of the Eastern Bishops when this war is ended."

Constantine shrugged. "That should help. But I must tell you, I've gotten reports of deadly rioting in larger cities in Syria, Palestine, Egypt. Gangs of Alexander's followers killing Arius' followers. And vice versa. Over a theological quibble about the nature of God. This doesn't make things easier."

Ossius nodded. "No, it doesn't. And I'm sorry for any trouble this matter causes you, Dominus. Frankly, I doubt that this Council will resolve things. It will not be attended by Arius or any of his followers. I believe the true intent is to build a consensus favoring those who believe Alexander's position."

Constantine poured two glasses of diluted wine and handed one to Ossius. "No. That doesn't sound helpful. We will have to force a resolution on these quibbling clerics. As soon as this war is over— and I've crushed Licinius once-and-for-all and consolidated power within the Empire—I will call the meeting. And I'll count on you for advice on the best resolution."

"Yes, Imperator. I think that's the most practical answer."

Chalcedon, Asia Minor
September 15, 1077 AUC (324 AD)

Licinius howled at the news the centurion delivered. "How did this bastard usurper get across the Bosporus without us knowing? May the gods damn him to an eternity of sodomy!"

The centurion had seen Constantine's army himself. "No one knows how they got there—but his army on the very northern tip of the Bosporus on the Asian side. A place known as the Sacred Promontory."

"Sacred, eh? Figures. That would appeal to him. Is his entire army there?" Licinius asked, noticeably shaking.

"No one is sure what his 'entire army' is, Dominus. But it is a very large encampment."

"How far from here?"

"Nine or ten mille. At most."

"Get a messenger to Sextus. Tell him to get here as soon as possible. I believe he has already left Lamseki—so your men will have to find him along the way."

"Yes, Augustus."

Chrysopolis, Asia Minor
September 18, 1077 AUC (324 AD)

Constantine's troops had marched from the Sacred Promontory to Chrysopolis two days earlier than planned. They'd made camp and started building standard fortifications in the rocky ground. He was inclined to give them time to rest. At least for a few hours.

His spies had reported that Sextus was already en route; so, Constantine had calculated that today would be the best day to attack Licinius. Any of Sextus' troops that made it to Chalcedon early would be exhausted.

Constantine's troops were ready. Crispus, Ablabius, Tiberus, Marcus and the palatini were all prepared. But, for the first time in many years, Constantine was having difficulty making the decision to attack. He went into his new command tent to pray—and to get away from his commanders.

After several minutes, Ossius walked in. Constantine was on his knees, praying in front of a large metal cross.

"Imperator, may I pray with you?" Ossius asked, starting to kneel next to Constantine.

"Of course, Ossius. I'd hoped you would," Constantine replied

After a few minutes, Ossius asked, "My friend. Is there anything I can say or do to help you?"

"Thank you, Ossius. Your empathy is always…comforting. I am afraid I have no strategy for this battle, no grand scheme, and no brilliance. I don't think I will lose. But I am not excited about winning. For the first time in ages, I have doubts. I have doubts that I have been a good Emperor, a good father. And I certainly have doubts that I have been a good Christian. And then I go back to the fact that I have no strategy to win this battle. My mind is…in a spiral. I am consumed by an emptiness and hollowness that has plagued me so often in my life."

The old priest smiled. "For you Princeps, for you."

Constantine raised his head and looked directly at Ossius.

"Vibius' last words."

"Yes. And he was right. You are a great man, Constantine. And the world is about to become yours—in a way it's rarely been for any man. I believe this battle will mark the end of so many battles and will begin your time as the supreme ruler for whatever time you have left on earth. What you do after this battle will determine how you are judged. Not just as a general. Not as a politician. And not just by men."

Constantine laughed a little and looked upward. "Some part of me has dreaded defeating Licinius for just that reason, Ossius. Dreading the day after that day. Even good men with honest intentions make mistakes. How can God help me to avoid them?"

Ossius thought for a moment. Then: "It would be easy to tell you to live your life as our Lord teaches us. But Jesus also advised us to 'render unto Caesar the things that are Caesar's.' He knew that there are tensions between a man's spiritual life and his worldly life. I believe He was telling us that we don't have to choose one or the other. We should keep both in mind. Balance them as best we can. For you, the same is true, only more so because you are indeed, Caesar! Your spiritual life must follow the teachings of our Lord. Your worldly life must be guided by them—but it may not always adhere to them, strictly. But don't let the necessities of your worldly life make you ignore or abandon the most important tenets of your spiritual life. No matter what happens, you can always ask God for His forgiveness. And His grace. It's never too late for that, and hopefully that Grace will fill your feelings of hollowness."

"Thank you, Ossius. Thank you."

After a few more moments of silence, Constantine asked, "So how do you think Vibius would fight this battle?"

Ossius laughed. "*That* question is beyond the realm of my expertise. But I did know Vibius. Subtlety was not his style. I imagine he would attack Licinius as directly as possible—"

"You are right, thank you again, Ossius!" Constantine said, immediately getting up and leaving his tent.

He walked toward his commanders' quarters. Crispus was sitting in front of his tent, reading a scroll. Ablabius was standing by a fire, talking with some of the Dux. "Crispus, come here. Ablabius, send someone to get Marcus."

His bodyguards caught up with him. Everyone else stopped what they were doing and gathered around him. Within a few minutes, all of his commanders were present. They were unsure of what Constantine's plan was going to be.

"Gentleman, there will be no tricks in this battle. We are attacking Licinius and Sextus right now. Right now! In the straightest line possible. Gear up!"

With the horns blowing, Ablabius, Crispus and the other commanders organized their troops into a tight formation. They could see Licinius' army responding by assembling as quickly as they could. Licinius was hoping for a longer delay.

As he shouted orders, Ablabius tried to hide his concern. An impulsive attack was not like Constantine. Among other things, it meant there were no dogs—they would have been perfect to start this assault. And the soldiers did not have the normal time to prepare for battle, to get their minds into the fight. No review, no coaxing, no fine tuning of the lines, no buildup of high expectations.

After the sagittari loosed several rounds, Constantine's army pressed forward. After the equiti, the infantry engagement seemed to start of its own will. Each army was eager to prove its God greater— Constantine and Licinius had both told their troops that this was a holy war. But, to Ablabius, it seemed like a sloppy collision.

However, Constantine's army proved to be the more disciplined of the two. Licinius' troops fell out of their three-line formation within minutes. Constantine's formation, imperfect as may have been, pressed right through Licinius' lines.

Within an hour, Constantine's army had broken Licinius' lines into four or five pieces. When Sextus arrived with his forces, they had no clear formation to join. And they were quickly surrounded by several of Constantine's companies. The newly-formed Labarum Consort Brigade moved around the battlefield in an oval pattern. Wherever it went, Licinius' troops seemed to freeze—and Constantine's troops could either regroup or press to advantage. It was still working.

Constantine and his palatini rode back to his command tent and watched the battle from their horses. He could see two purple standards—one for Licinius, one for Sextus—on either side of most intense fighting. But they weren't able to assemble any coherent formation. They didn't even retreat. They were just being broken into smaller and smaller units.

Ablabius also returned to his tent, on a small hill a half mille from Constantine's. His horse had gone lame and one of his armor straps ripped. He was stained with the blood of Licinius' soldiers. His equiti stood guard while he cleaned himself up. While he splashed water on his face, he looked around. Across the field he could see that Constantine was watching the battle, still on his horse. But something was strange. A small brigade with a Labarum was riding from rear of the main camp toward Constantine's command tent. The Labarum they carried was not one of Constantine's—it was similar to the ones they'd used years ago.

"Look! Something is wrong!!" He was on another horse in an instant. And riding with his equiti towards Constantine. The enemy unit looked like about 20 riders. They were closer to Constantine then he was.

"Caesar! Caesar! Dominus!"

Standing near Constantine, Quintus noticed Ablabius riding and screaming. Was he celebrating? Quintus looked more carefully and realized there was some sort of danger.

"Dominus! Trouble!" Quitus screamed.

In an instant the four palatini and their six equiti counterparts turned their horses towards the oncoming riders.

Licinius' assassins rode, with swords drawn, up the small hill toward Constantine's command tent. The bodyguards formed a small double line of their own between the assassins and Constantine. They held their ground, waiting for the attackers. Close quarters would favor defense.

With only 10 guards against 20 attackers, the palatini did well to block all but three from getting near Constantine. After stabbing several assassins, Quintus jumped off his horse and grabbed two lances from the ground. He threw them at the assassins closest to Constantine. Both assassins fell—but that wasn't enough. Two more charged. And one of them stabbed Quintus in the back as he charged past him.

Constantine had his sword drawn and shield raised. He wasn't an easy target—even for several attackers. He reared his horse up and turned it hard in a circle, slashing with controlled fury.

Appius, who'd already killed one attacker, spun his horse in the opposite direction as Constantine. This would disorient the assassins and give him the best chance at unguarded arms or necks. One attacker was very close to Constantine, easily within the striking distance of a sword. Appius pressed toward him but, before he could get close, that assassin dropped from his horse—dead. Then another dropped in a similar manner, untouched by any of the guards.

"How the..?" Appius grunted.

Constantine charged the remaining close attacker, driving him into his command tent. The assassin's horse lost its footing and fell.

The rider collapsed into the tent's canvas and screamed in agony.

Sevius, Appius and Titus had killed more than a dozen assassins. The survivors tried to ride away—but Ablabius and his equiti were already upon them. They were dead in an instant.

Constantine jumped off of his horse to tend to Quintus. The stab wound on his back started just under his right shoulder and went down to his middle ribs. It was deep. But it wouldn't be fatal.

Appius and Titus were still on their horses, riding between Constantine and the two attackers who had suddenly dropped from their saddles. Ablabius arrived, leapt off of his horse and helped the Emperor remove Quintus' armor to have a medic clean the wound.

"Surely, this is Licinius' handiwork. He can't even get an assassination right." Ablabius joked.

The Emperor hesitated for a second and then laughed. Quintus laughed, too—though it made him wince.

"Was it by God's hand, Dominus that these men died?" asked Appius, still looking at the two attackers who mysteriously fell from their saddles.

Ablabius stood up and looked at the dead attackers. Then around and finally back to Appius. "God is with us, soldier. But I think your Angel of Death is over there." He pointed past the collapsed command tent, to the white-haired cook, Aniketos, standing several cubits away.

Aniketos held up two more knives. "And I have a trunk full of these, if anyone else tries to kill our Emperor!"

Constantine sent for a medic to dress Quintus' wound. He was getting ready to get back on his horse and return to the battlefield, when Ablabius called out.

"Dominus! Come see this."

Ablabius was standing in the mess of the fallen tent. He'd cut away some of the canvas and ropes. And discovered the rider that Constantine had pushed off his horse—impaled on Constantine's metal cross. "God truly is with us."

The battle lasted only as long as it took for Constantine's army to kill most of Licinius' 30,000 remaining troops. From the first minutes, when Constantine's army punched through the center of their line, Licinius' centurions were unable to get them to regroup. Their soldiers retreated in a chaotic manner. Most simply deserted.

Licinius fled the battlefield with a few faithful troops—less than a legion—and rode back to Nicomedia.

Chrysopolis, Asia Minor
September 20, 1077 AUC (324 AD)

In Constantine's reconstructed command tent, his sister Constantia had come from Nicomedia to plead for her husband's life. Constantine's senior officers were all present and standing, as Constantine sat behind a small folding table.

"Brother, I do love this man. You gave me to him in marriage. I have borne and raised his child—your nephew—whom I adore. He has been a good husband to me. His only fault is pride. Pride led him down this useless path. Please, let him live. In exile, if it must be. But let him live."

"Sister, I respect you for coming to plead for your husband's life. But I don't respect him. He doesn't deserve to live. As you know, before this war started, I offered him terms that would have been better than exile. And, even before this last battle, he could have sued for peace. Instead, he sentenced thousands of soldiers to death. And he tried to assassinate me, using weak trickery and one of my old standards. He has failed in every way that a general can fail. If I don't kill him, survivors from his own army will. This is the nature of war."

"It's pride. I tried to warn him," Constantia was politically wise enough not to mention her husband's name in her brother's camp. "Brother, you are now sole Emperor. You've restored the order of the Empire's greatest days. You are a god to the people. Surely, you don't need to take the life of a man you have so humiliated on the battlefield."

"Sister, the very order you speak of demands your husband's head. An Emperor can abdicate due to age or illness. He can surrender for his life before a battle. But he can't declare war, fight, lose—and then say 'I was just kidding.' Your husband may not be a threat now but, later, he could attract dissidents and foment unrest. Letting him live is an affront to order. Years ago, when I was in Gaul, I told a diplomat in your position, 'It is stupid clemency that spares the conquered foe.' Your husband must die. If not by his own hand, by mine."

Constantia fell to her knees, next to Constantine. She pushed the folding table aside, which caused Ablabius and the palatini to reach for their weapons. "Brother, it was not my husband who authorized the assassination attempt. He is too superstitious, of both the Labarum and of Christ's power. It had to have been Sextus."

"And which one of them will plot the next assassination attempt, Constantia?"

"There will be no next attempt. You can put him in a place that you control completely. Thessalonica. Is there anyone in that city that would imagine conspiring against you? It is not possible. You are revered there. You could keep our family there, in a house where we would be restricted. Please consider this, Constantine. Please, for me. In the name of our Savior, I pray to you."

Constantia at this point had fallen to her knees in front of her brother's large chair, pushing the table completely away.

Constantine rubbed his eyes. "Get up, sister. Stand up. You are an honorable woman. You don't need to crawl on the ground, begging. Like a slave."

She stood up and tried to stifle her tears. He gave her a handkerchief.

He sighed and thought for a few moments about his conversation with Ossius before the last battle. "Constantia, for you—and only for you—I will do this. Take this offer to your husband. Both he and his...aide...must come and surrender to me. In person. Both of them. They must prostrate themselves in front of me, like you just did, and beg forgiveness. They must renounce all claims and vestiges of their time as...officers...of the Empire. All of their lands and money, of course. And I will arrange exile for both of them."

Crispus, Ablabius and most of the other officers slowly shook their heads. No honorable man would accept such an offer. And any man who would accept was trouble.

Alexandria, Egypt
Late September, 1077 AUC (324 AD)

"Holiness, the war for Christianity has been won by Constantine!" exclaimed Athanasius, as he burst into Alexander's chambers.

Alexander was sitting on his chair next to his bed—still in his bedclothes, even though it was approaching noon.

Athanasius, surprised that his mentor's appearance, asked, "What is wrong, bishop? Are you feeling ill?"

"I've been feeling off these last few days. And today I had difficulty getting out of bed. Missed my morning prayers. Old age, I fear. Look forward to joining my martyred brothers in Heaven. Now, what was that you said about Constantine?"

"I pray you will be feeling stronger soon. Today, we have word that Constantine prevailed against Licinius in Chrysopolis. Pagan worship will now become a relic of the past."

"That is excellent news. Was his victory a bloody one?"

"For Licinius' army—not for Constantine's. And again, as in Adrianople and the Hellespont, the Labarum was instrumental in the domination of the pagan forces."

Alexander nodded. He was already considering the political effects of the battle. "Was Licinius killed?"

"No, he lives. Constantine granted him his life after he begged on his knees. He renounced his army, his belongings and all vestiges of being an emperor—his purple robes, standards and armor." Athanasius seemed to enjoy describing Licinius' humiliation.

"Well, God has smiled upon his people and we are the beneficiaries of that."

"We must call for the Council we have discussed. Shall I arrange to have it in Antioch?"

"Yes. I think that is the best location. Invite all the bishops in the East. And notify Ossius. Let us try to have this meeting after the first of the New Year."

"Yes, your Holiness." And Athanasius practically ran out of Alexander's bedroom.

Thessalonica, Greece
Early October, 1077 AUC (324 AD)

Constantine sat back in his chair, exasperated. "This is beyond any rational thought process, Ossius. This argument rages on, causing riots among lay people and dissent among priests. It is based—entirely—on rival beliefs that we can never prove or disprove. The early scriptures generally support the belief that the Nazarene was…lesser…in divine nature than God. But the later scriptures generally support the belief in an equal nature. So Ossius, tell me, which is the better belief?"

"Better?"

"Truer. Closer to the truth."

"I do not know, Imperator." Ossius was standing—and occasionally paced back and forth when confronted with a difficult question.

"Ossius, I've known you for more than 20 years. You're holding back. I have asked you for spiritual direction in this matter and you are deliberately denying my request."

"I do not mean to deny your appeal. But the matter is complex. With elements that could be pitfalls to both my Church and your Empire. Even if God gave me the Wisdom of Solomon, I doubt I could give you the simple answer you deserve. I don't think it exists." Ossius was clearly vexed—and the fact that the Emperor seemed entertained by his anguish only made matter worse.

"Will this upcoming synod in Antioch provide us with an answer?"

"I don't think so. I fear it will only deepen the division between Arius' supporters and Alexander's. This Athanasius," Ossius practically hissed when he said the name, "Alexander's deacon, has designed the meeting to minimize the Arians' position. That Jesus is something less than God. Arius himself is not invited, nor any of his strongest supporters. The whole thing is intended to convince me—and thus you—that the Church is united behind Alexander."

"If it is merely for the appearance, then don't attend," Constantine suggested.

Ossius shook his head. "By not attending, I—and thus you— send the message that Alexander's position is not correct. That perhaps we agree with the Arians."

"So be it. I'm inclined to agree with the concept of a single God. With a single nature. When we first met in Nicomedia, that is what you taught me," Constantine said.

Ossius nodded, somewhat distantly. "I probably did. These arguments—Alexander's and Athanasius' beliefs—are more recent. Even 20 years ago, most scholars believed in the Mosaic God, the Jewish God. After all, that is what Jesus believed. He was a devout Jew, a Rabbi."

"Yes, yes. I know this. Tell me again when the dispute started."

"Well, in some sense, it's quite old. Paul considered Jesus lesser than the Father. An early scholar, Origen, also considered that Jesus was lesser than the Father. Because the Father came first. But this remained something that only a few scholars concentrated on. That changed when Arius wrote his *Thalia*."

"The religious songs."

"Yes. And those songs repeat the phrase 'There was a time when the Son was not.' Many times. And those songs are extremely popular with the plebeians. Working men sing them in streets. Sailors, on boats. The vast majority of our populous believe Jesus is lesser than the Father. Now, if we take the position that Arius is correct, we ignore the recent developments of our Church's theology. We alienate many of the Eastern Empire's bishops and other learned men who've come to believe that Jesus shares of the exact same nature with God."

"But they don't know that," Constantine said. "No living person does. And God hasn't sent a scroll stating that He and Jesus are the same nature."

"No. But there are rational arguments and the wording of the scriptures gives many Christians comfort that Jesus was more than Divine—that he was Divine on earth and equal to God before and after his human life."

"So, what changed in the last 20 years?"

Ossius stopped pacing. "If you read the scriptures and religious writings from the earliest to the most current, there has been a slow change in the interpretation of Christ's nature. At first, He was a man, brought to earth by God, crucified and resurrected as an example for our redemption. Later, He was the Son of God, brought to earth to demonstrate His power and greatness—now seated at the right hand of God. The change has been subtle, but definitive."

"I must not be subtle enough—because it doesn't seem definitive." Constantine was growing disinterested with fine theological points. "Why don't you just choose the Scriptures that support one side of the argument and get rid of the others? Affirm either son of man…or Son of God, and build your orthodoxy on that."

"That would be fine, if we were an Empire. But we are a Church—a community," Ossius answered. "Besides, most of the scriptures support both sides."

Constantine shook his head and smirked. "Why aren't all these new religious scriptures in one place? One book, and in some sort of order?"

"That is coming. Over a century ago, Irenaeus suggested that the Gospels of Matthew, Mark, Luke and John should be the basis of a new Christian Bible. A 'New Testament' to go with the Jewish Old Testament. Later, Origen later suggested 27 sacred scriptures make up the New Testament. Today, most bishops are comfortable with about 20 scriptures that they feel should be in the New Testament. It is widely accepted that the Gospels of Matthew, Mark, Luke and John should be part of it. Most of Paul's letters are also generally accepted. But there are serious differences of opinion beyond those books."

Constantine yawned. "Seems to me it would be easier to build your orthodoxy around that New Testament. The way you are do-ing it now…puts the cart before the horse. Plus, you've also made it more difficult by having no one in charge. You have dozens of bishops—but they don't answer to anybody. They are centurions without a general."

"I am not sure how that could change. It would upend the Church."

"Well someone has to be in charge. That's why I have supported Pope Sylvester so strongly. You need someone like him, or yourself, who has the authority to say what must be done. Otherwise you have local power struggles. Hundreds of different interpretations. And disagreements. And here we are."

"Yes, Dominus. Here we are."

"I don't care if it is a religion or an army, it will falter if you don't have a hierarchy," Constantine said. Clearly, his interest in the subject was again waning.

Ossius started pacing again. "You may be correct. But many of our bishops would disagree. We have had three centuries during which the Church has survived—and grown—because of the bishops' autonomy and sacrifice, in many cases, with their lives. Giving that up will not come naturally to them."

"Well, they are going to have to get used to it, if you're going to have uniform orthodoxy."

"Perhaps uniform orthodoxy isn't what the Church should seek, perhaps God wants our faith to be left to some individual interpretation." Ossius said, plaintively.

"Perhaps," Constantine answered, a little more interested. "But I would wager that someday the Church is going to need it. You know, Ossius, I often hear Arius' *Thalia* being sung by my soldiers while they march. That's…powerful."

"Yes. I know. It is a very clever message. Far more popular than Alexander's and Athanasius' theological letters. Its cadence is infectious. But they are very popular poems and songs for the plebeians, not the educated opinions of the knowledgeable clergy. I am not sure they reflect what the truth of the Scriptures is," Ossius replied.

"I go back to my question, Ossius: Who do you believe has the correct answer?"

"And I go back to my answer, Caesar: I do not know. I am older and am fond of the early Scriptures, specifically the Gospels. They seem real to me because they describe events from the perspective of eyewitnesses. Mark, Luke and Matthew are like old friends. Regardless of who actually wrote those books, those testaments are authentic to me. On the other hand, the Glory of Jesus as the Son of God is beautifully described in the Book of John."

"That isn't an answer, Ossius."

Ossius stopped pacing. Again. "Then let me say it this way: Athanasius has done an effective job of getting his opinion to Alexander's bishops—either by cajoling or threatening. Or both. He has the majority of the Eastern bishops of his opinion. And it is an opinion that I also feel comfortable with."

"Why aren't the Western bishops involved in the controversy?" Constantine asked.

"Most think as you do: that it is an unanswerable question. And they feel the Eastern bishops, specifically the ones in the lands around Egypt, are fixating on a divisive issue."

"Good. How does Sylvester feel?"

"Much as I do. He will agree to whatever is decided to keep peace within the Church. He is grateful that the persecutions have ended and he is astounded at the growth of our Church— for that, he praises you. He feels the body of the Church should be concentrating on saving souls, not debating theology. He believes Jesus' message doesn't change if he is homoousian or homoeanian with God. Next time you see him, he will press you to build more churches throughout the Empire. He is a practical man."

"That's why I like him. And he won't have to press me very hard. I have plans for a New Rome, where churches will be prominent. Helena is headed to Jerusalem, where I understand there are few churches by the holy sites." The talk of building churches seemed to pique Constantine's interest again. He raised his hand for a moment, waving it while he thought. "I have another question. If the Eastern bishops are inclined to interpret the Nazarene and God as equal, what effect does that have on the Holy Spirit?"

"An equal to God and Jesus in the Trinity. Three separate entities, working in unison. Arius points to the writings of Sabellian—a priest who lived over a century ago. He felt that God, Jesus and the Holy Spirit were merely different facets of one God. Not three separate entities."

"Yes, that's getting closer to an answer," Constantine was looking for something while he spoke. "Whatever decision your Bishops reach, the Church's theology must be...embraced...by everyone. Human nature is fickle and flawed. The Church must offer order. Spiritual order. If we don't have that, these factions will be fighting for a thousand years. Politically, of course, it's best to have a compromise solution in mind before this synod begins. Compromise, Ossius. If you have winner and losers, the losers will feel...abused. And that leaves an opening for problems later."

"Perhaps I can have some private conversations with Alexander before the meeting. Find the theological common ground where both sides can meet."

Constantine finally found a tablet. "Yes! Good. And I will send a letter to both Alexander and Arius, emphasizing the importance of resolving this controversy."

Alexandria, Egypt
End of October, 1077 AUC (324 AD)

Athanasius and Alexander were riding in an open carriage to go to a market on the south side of Alexandria, not far from Arius' former church. Alexander wanted a new rug for saying prayers next to his bed; his old one was threadbare.

Athanasius was concerned that many of Arius' supporters were in this part of the city. He'd tried—and failed—to convince Alexander not to go to this market. So, he'd notified some of his fellow deacons about the trip.

As a result, seven young men in dark brown tunics walked alongside the carriage. Each wore a large wooden cross around his neck and carried a thick shepherd's staff.

As they rode in the carriage, Athanasius was reading in a loud voice, parts of Constantine's letter that was sent to both Alexander and Arius.

...now that I have made a careful enquiry into the origin and foundation of these differences, I have found the cause to be of a truly insignificant character, and quite unworthy of such fierce contention. I feel compelled to address you in this letter, and to appeal at the same time to your unity and discernment. I call on Divine Providence to assist me in the task, while I interrupt your dissension as a minister of peace. I have hope for success: Even in a great disagreement, I might expect with the help of the higher Power to be able without difficulty, by a judicious appeal to the pious feelings of those who hear me, to recall them to a better spirit. How can I help but to expect a far easier and more speedy resolution of this difference, when the cause which hinders general harmony of sentiment is intrinsically trifling and of little importance?

Athanasius couldn't resist commenting: "So, our good Emperor feels our disagreement with Arius is insignificant and trifling. The nature of God and our Savior is trifling? And, this from the most powerful man on earth! Is this the intellectual power of the Empire?"

"Athanasius, please. Just read the letter. I want to hear what he says."

Athanasius continued.

As long as you continue to contend about these small and very insignificant questions, it is not fitting that so large a portion of God's people should be under the direction of your judgment, since you are thus divided between yourselves. In my opinion, it is not merely unbecoming, but positively evil, that such should be the case.

"Is this a threat? Is he telling you that he will remove you if you don't make a deal with Arius? And what must Arius give up?"

Alexander seemed impatient. "You must listen without prejudice, Athanasius. This is a man who just consolidated all of the political power in the Empire. He's the first true Emperor in my lifetime. He's no fool. And we don't want to pick a fight with him. Keep reading."

> I say this without in any way desiring to force you to a complete unity of judgment in regard to this truly idle question, whatever its real nature may be. For the dignity of your synod can be preserved, and the communion of your whole body can be maintained unbroken, no matter how wide a difference exists among you about unimportant matters. We are not all like-minded on every subject, nor is there such a thing as one universal disposition and judgment.

"Fatherly advice from our great leader, that not everyone thinks the same. This is—"

"Athanasius! You are being disrespectful. To a lay person these matters may appear trivial. How many people pray to our Lord about their problems and wonder whether he is identical to God or merely almost like God? Not a one, I would venture."

Athanasius closed the scroll. "Regardless of the Emperor's pleadings, we are correct. Even if he resumes persecutions, I shall not compromise!"

As Athanasius helped Alexander out of the carriage, their brown tunic protectors relaxed in the shade of a nearby building. Alexander went directly to a vendor with a pile of rugs under a makeshift tent.

The vendor was an old man. They seemed to recognize each other.

"My friend," Alexander said, "it has been years! How is your wife? Your son?"

"Bishop, it is good to see you again," the merchant bowed quickly to Alexander. "My wife is no longer with us. My son is well—but he lives far away. He is a quaestor with the Romans in Nicomedia. He's always been good with numbers. Your priest, Arius, taught him well. Arius used to live right there," the vendor pointed a boney finger toward a small house down a side street.

Athanasius visibly bristled. But Alexander didn't flinch; he answered sincerely, "I am sorry to hear of your wife's passing. I will say a prayer tonight that her soul is at peace in our Lord's company."

"Thank you, Holiness. What brings you here, to this part of the city?" The merchant asked, aware of Alexander's guards. And of the riots that had occurred just a few weeks earlier.

"I need a new prayer rug, my friend. My old one—which I bought from you—has seen better days." Alexander responded, as if oblivious to any social discomfort.

As the two old men looked at rugs, Athanasius heard a catchy cadence coming from two streets away. For a moment, he couldn't place it. Then he realized that it was from Arius' *Thalia*. He quickly looked at Alexander who, although in conversation with the old merchant, smiled. He understood.

Two groups of young men—dressed in beige tunics, with crosses around their necks and staves in their hands—poured out into the main street. They outnumbered Alexander's guards three-to-one. Or more. And they surrounded Alexander's guards by the building.

Alexander paid for the rug and the merchant rolled it up, tied it and handed it to Athanasius. They started to walk back to the carriage. One of the beige tunics had tripped one of the brown tunics with his staff. Alexander's guards rushed and closed ranks around the old priest—which left their comrade on the ground vulnerable.

A beige tunic tapped his staff on the fallen man's chest and started berating him: "What are you doing here, pagan? Sodomite! We don't like your filth in our streets!"

Athanasius tried to push Alexander into the carriage. But Alexander ignored him and walked up to the screaming beige tunic. "Son, I can see you are a believer of the Church. You are one of our Lord's faithful. Why do you show this anger in the street? Why court violence? Jesus tells us to treat others as we would ourselves."

Another of the beige tunics—one of their leaders—pointed at Alexander, Arius and the men in brown tunics. He replied. "These men represent lies to God. The righteous priest Arius has been maligned and subjected to ridicule by the decadent Church elite for telling the truth."

One of the beige tunics walked up behind Athanasius—who'd followed Alexander part way—and nudged him in the back with his staff. "This one looks like a *puer delicates.* Maybe the old man's pullus."

Another leaned toward Athanasius and rubbed his face with the back of his hand. "Such soft skin. Maybe he wants to experience how a real man treats a pullus."

A third beige tunic jammed his staff into Athanasius' side and flipped up his tunic, baring him to his waist. Athanasius jumped forward with a high-pitched yelp, colliding with the one who'd rubbed his face.

"Hear that? He wants you! He cries for you!"

"And he's ready for you. He wears no loincloth!"

Alexander interrupted with a loud voice—that had surprising authority. "Do not do that. Even in jest. This man is a priest. My assistant. A learned man of faith. Leave him alone. Our great teacher, Paul, warns of dire consequences for coarse behavior like this. God watches you."

The beige tunics stood silent.

Turning to the entire group, Alexander continued: "I know of no lies to God that any of us have told. These men are students, just like you. As for this priest Arius, he is a righteous man. And that he means well for the Church. We've allowed our differences to grow too large. You have my word on this: We will seek a resolution. Now, I pray that you search in your souls to forgive us our trespass. If I ever return to do business with my old friend here, I will come alone."

The beige leader hesitated for a few moments. Then he nodded to his comrades—and they stepped back from Athanasius and the fallen sentry. "Go your way, old man. But remember: God watches you, too. And you have few friends here."

A few minutes later, when they were in friendlier parts of the city, Alexander looked at Athanasius and said simply: "That is what we have allowed to happen."

Athanasius, still shaking, started to ask whether Alexander had planned the trip to demonstrate his point. But he kept quiet. He knew the answer.

Nicomedia, Asia Minor
Late October, 1077 AUC (324 AD)

"Eusebius, I have received a private letter from our Emperor!" Arius held up the scroll.

Eusebius was walking on the cobbled street coming from the upper city, having just officiated at the funeral of a wealthy merchant and staunch supporter of the Church. The merchant, Plinius, had made his fortune mining and trading marble throughout the Empire. His family owned much of the land east of the city. He had been a well-known figure—and a character—in Nicomedia.

"Good news, Arius. I had heard from Constantine that you and Alexander would receive something. But I do not know its contents.

Let us get a glass of wine and discuss it."

As they walked, Arius asked: "How was Plinius' funeral? I assume there was a huge crowd."

"It was crowded." Eusebius replied. "Every notable was there. He was a good man—a pleasant mixture of fun and piety. He loved his family, his friends and our Lord."

"Do you think he was the exception to our Lord's warning that it's nearly impossible for a rich man to get into heaven?" Arius asked.

"I would think so," Eusebius answered pensively. "I have always wondered what Jesus meant by that image. Camel through the eye of a needle. It seems like a very high standard. Some who still speak Aramaic say that the correct translation is 'rope,' not 'camel.' Others say 'eye of the needle' was an idiom for a small gate. Lots of questions about that one."

"There are lots of rich men who want to enter the Kingdom of God," Arius said, ruefully.

"Yes."

"Perhaps the barrier should be high. The rich are easily diverted by material things. But.."

"Often, yes." Eusebius interrupted. "But Plinius was not like that. He spent much of his time—and money—on the poor and the sick. He organized with others to build hospitals. He was willing to hire undesirables as workers."

"To us, these things made him a good man. But we cannot know the thoughts of God, but I sincerely believe He is all forgiving. All forgiving for all walks of life, just as Origen believed." Arius smiled slightly. This conversation was heading toward well-worn path between them. "I'm just happy we live in better days that Jesus did."

"You hold proof of that in your hand. Constantine is a moral man. The emperors of Jesus' time—Tiberus and Caligula—were rapists and murderers. Let's hope that Constantine's restoration of the unitary Emperor doesn't lead us back to those depravities." They had reached the café. Eusebius pointed to his favorite table.

After ordering their wine, Arius handed Constantine's letter to Eusebius. Arius watched his friend as he quickly read its contents.

"He wants a compromise and he is pushing Alexander for it." Eusebius commented, "I don't like the number of times he mentions the trifling nature of the conflict. That will wound Athanasius' vanity. But I do like this part:"

> ...the cause of your difference has not been any of the leading doctrines or precepts of the Divine law, nor has any new heresy respecting the worship of God arisen among you. You are really of one and the same judgment.

"I wonder whether Ossius helped him write it," Eusebius said. "Probably not—he would have edited some of the 'trifling' out."

Arius nodded. "I agree that it puts pressure on Alexander. But I don't see it changing their position. Sylvester sought a compromise two years ago and didn't get one. I doubt Constantine will now."

"Agreed. As I said, Athanasius will not like this. It will make him even more strident. I have talked to most of the bishops. They are inclined to our position but feel pressure from Athanasius. He's threatened to include them among those to be excommunicated by Alexander."

"Would Constantine issue an edict commanding the Church to follow our position—and the teachings of the early gospels?"

"No, not a chance. He's quick to anger at suggestions like that. And I get nervous when he gets angry."

"He doesn't like being asked to make edicts?"

"He doesn't like being asked to resolve the Church's problems." Eusebius responded. "His goal is stability in the Empire, which he believes is aided by a single Orthodox Church. If that orthodoxy is different than what he, you or I believe in, he expects us to adapt. It is simple for him. More difficult for us."

"So who decides what's orthodox?" Arius asked. "I've seen in other letters mention of another Synod—which Alexander has called for in January in Antioch. We haven't been invited. Nor has anyone sympathetic to our position. I hope Constantine will not let Athanasius' hand-picked friends decide the direction of the Church."

"He won't. He knows that the Antioch Synod is going to be a one-sided affair. But I am not sure how he will have us determine the proper direction."

"I've asked this before—but can Ossius help our cause?" Arius asked, sipping some wine.

"As we've discussed, Ossius has become Constantine's personal confessor. His interests are too close to Constantine's. With most of the Eastern bishops against us, Ossius would make the political decision. Not the theological one. So, no—he wouldn't help us."

"What about Pope Sylvester?"

Eusebius thought for a moment, then shook his head. "Sylvester could change the entire argument, if he chose to. But, like Ossius, he's close to Constantine. He views this as a distraction from the Church's real business—of being everyone's parish priest."

Arius smiled ruefully. "So, we've advanced our cause little over the last few years. Other than with the plebeians. I wish I'd been able to convince the Church that Jesus preached as his Father directed. That He was divine—but begotten by the Father. I failed in exactly the area God best equipped me."

"This world is not an easy place, Arius. And God didn't design it to be so. He does not judge us by worldly achievements. He judges us by our hearts, efforts and love. If our efforts are sincere and moral—following the example Jesus gave us—God will grace us. If they are not, he may not. As I have said so many times, Arius, God's only promise to us is eternal life. Nothing else."

Antioch, Asia Minor
January, 1078 AUC (325 AD)

Ossius was tired. Alone in the Council's meeting room, he'd finally finished his notes and was slowly packing his scrolls in a wooden bucket at the head table. The Synod was ending—and it had gone exactly as he'd anticipated. Almost 100 bishops and priests from throughout the Eastern Empire described Arius as a traitor. Apostate. Heretic. And worse.

Athanasius had orchestrated the entire thing.

Alexander didn't attend the meeting. He'd taken ill. Ossius had visited him in Alexandria, before continuing on to Antioch. Alexander didn't seem particularly sick. But he did seem frail.

Before Ossius finished gathering his papers and notes, Athanasius came back into the room: "Bishop, I could not help but notice that the creed you shared with us did not include the wording I suggested. Specifically, you left out 'homoousian' in describing the nature between Jesus and God."

Ossius stared at Athanasius for a moment—until the younger man looked away—and then responded: "Alexander and I discussed the creed. We both approved the wording. We agree that the purpose of the creed is to establish the basis of belief necessary to be a Christian."

Athanasius looked confused.

"The basis, Athanasius. Not the fine details. Now, you're correct. We haven't included any descriptive wording concerning the exact nature of Jesus and God. It's not necessary. Our faith demands that Jesus was begotten by God. That's the important thing."

Athanasius seethed: "You must tighten that wording to include the exact nature of our Lord and His Father. Otherwise, those whom we rightly criticized during the Synod will undoubtedly establish themselves as Christians—in spite of the fact that they are heretics!"

"Perhaps that isn't a bad thing, Athanasius. Allowing some room for minor differences follows the recommendations in our Emperor's letter on this matter."

"The Emperor's recommendations are appreciated, Ossius. But a council of learned men, such as this Synod, should make an independent decision about the criteria necessary to be a Christian. Those criteria must include the belief that Jesus is, in every way, identical in nature with God. Otherwise, we diminish the glory God bestowed upon us."

Ossius chuckled, with a touch of menace, and then responded: "We'll see what wording the next, broader council agrees upon."

Ossius had finished packing his things. He took the bucket and starting to walk out.

"Ossius, one moment—" Athanasius had changed his tone. He sounded more plaintive. Perhaps he realized he'd approached the subject too aggressively. "I have just one more question."

Ossius, now by the doorway, turned back. "Yes?"

"I have given thought to a new Bible. A New Testament Bible. I think we need to develop it as canon as soon as possible."

Ossius stared again at the younger priest. Athanasius was full of schemes—and every suggestion he made had multiple meanings. Why was he shifting suddenly from the proposed creed to the new Bible? "I agree. But I'm not sure of how quickly we can do it. First, we need to agree on which scriptures are worthy of being included."

"I would like to present my ideas for the new Bible at that next, broader council you mention. We should include no more than 25 of the scriptures with which we are all familiar. One synoptic gospel. John's Gospel. Thomas' Gospel. Paul's letters, of course. Peter's letters. Revelation."

It was an interesting subject. And Athanasius was playing the part of the brilliant student, courting the favor of his teacher. Ossius cautioned himself about giving in to his vanity. But it was an interesting subject.

"Why would you leave out two of the synoptic Gospels, Athanasius? And which ones?"

"I would leave out Mark and Luke," Athanasius answered. He was a more confident again. "They are so similar, they're redundant."

"I'd find it disturbing to leave out their testimony," Ossius said. "And I would be suspect of Thomas' Gospel and the Book of Revelation. Both have the potential for Gnostic interpretation and could mislead Christians that there is a secret way to Heaven—one that the clever might learn, rather than just following Jesus' teachings and God's grace."

"I am not adamant about excluding the synoptic gospels. But, at a minimum, Revelation must be included. And Thomas' Gospel reflects the actual words of Jesus," Athanasius smirked mischievously. He was enjoying this. "I wouldn't shrink from including works that may confuse or mislead the less informed. That's why you have learned church fathers."

"Priests and bishops should be tending to their parishes, not explaining confusing scriptures." Ossius was getting tired of this discussion.

"Then we should restrict most of Paul's writing. He often goes on tangents that don't apply to, well, anything."

"I disagree. Paul was our original priest, the standard that we should all attempt to emulate," Ossius responded.

"I view Jesus as that example," Athanasius said in a rushed voice. He'd been waiting to say that. "This is the kind of discussion the broader council should have."

"As I said earlier, Athanasius, we need to develop a new Bible. But I think the complexity of its contents would likely consume more time than we have—as our brief conversation here has demonstrated. Let's make our decision about the creed first. Then we can grapple with the new Bible."

As Ossius left the meeting hall, Athanasius stepped toward him—but then hesitated and turned away. It was a nervous, fidgety maneuver.

Sirmium, Pannonia
Late January, 1078 AUC (325 AD)

Ossius arrived at Sirmium, having ridden directly from the Synod in Antioch. After some searching, he found Constantine at the city's hippodrome, testing his chariot racing skills against his original four palatini. The professional teams were not racing that day, so there were only a few pleasantly surprised citizens watching.

Chariot racing was the most popular spectator sport in the Roman Empire. Fans of the four major syndicates—known as the Red, White, Blue and Green Factions—spent substantial amounts of time and money to watch their favorite riders compete.

It was a dangerous sport. A rider's only protection was a leather helmet and vest; and he would balance precariously over the axel of a light, stripped-down version of a military chariot. A standard racing team was four horses, usually owned either by the Faction or a wealthy backer. In order to maintain control, the rider would wrap the reins of the lead horse tightly around his wrist, which often meant being dragged for hundreds of yards when an accident occurred. Which was often. And often fatal.

Constantine and his palatini were all proficient charioteers—but not as good as the professional riders employed by the Factions. Constantine had beaten Appius and Sevius but was in the process of losing to Titus.

Quintus, still injured, watched from the first row of the Stadium, next to the entrance to the stables. Ossius joined him there.

"How does the racing go, soldier?"

"Well enough for enthusiastic amateurs, our Priest."

Titus seemed to let up at the end of their race, as if to let the Emperor win. But he still ended up winning by a solid chariot-length.

After the race, Constantine rode toward the stable chute; he waved to Ossius, sitting next to Quintus, as he passed.

Appius and Sevius were standing on the track directly in front of them. Titus stopped in front of them and climbed off of his racer. Appius couldn't wait to get in the first word in: "Titus, my former friend! I look forward to your promotion to the front line of our next battle."

Titus grunted and rubbed his wrist—which had deep rein marks. "If your mouth hasn't gotten you to the front line in all these years, then one chariot race isn't going to do anything."

Constantine jogged out from the stables. "I had a line to get in front of you, Titus. But you closed it by cutting so close to the Turning Post Pillars. I thought you were going to hit one of them! Very nice job."

"Dominus, as a token of my accomplishment, may I cut Appius' viper tongue out of his head?"

"No. But, if you beat him in a three-lap race, I will order him not to talk for an entire day."

Appius snatched the reins hanging over Titus' shoulder. "Bet on! I will defeat Titus and talk only to him for 24 hours straight. But I want fresh horses for both of us."

"Done!" snapped Titus competitively. And the two guards led the horses to the stables.

Constantine walked up the steps to sit next to Ossius, greeting him warmly. Sensing a private conversation between the Emperor and the bishop, Quintus got up and walked with Sevius a few cubits around the track. But they kept Constantine in their sight.

"So, how was your trip to Antioch?"

"Imperator, I don't believe we will get a compromise from Athanasius. This synod was overwhelmingly partisan, as we suspected it would be. They want to excommunicate anyone who does not adhere to their concept of the nature of Jesus and God. Unrelenting. Of course, I'm sure that if I attended a Synod hosted by Arius the attitudes would be the same—from the contrary perspective."

Constantine pulled the towel draped around his neck over his head and dried his closely-cropped hair. Then he leaned back in his seat and looked up at the sky. "So much for the Christian concepts of tolerance and understanding!"

"Did you get my letter about meeting with Alexander before the Synod, Augustus?"

"Yes. And I read it. It will be a sad day when that old bird flies off to heaven."

Ossius nodded in contentment. "My conversations with him were revealing. We put together the draft of a Christian Creed quite easily. He obviously wanted his most important points to be included—but he was completely willing to leave room in wording designed for the followers of Arius."

"Good."

Now, Ossius shook his head. "Not so good. His deacon, Athanasius, was not so accepting and approached me after the Synod. He was critical of the omission of the word that ties the nature of Jesus and God as the same, 'homoousian.' It's evident that he will not agree to anything less than that word being included in the Creed."

Constantine scowled. "Why do you worry about the opinion of a deacon?"

Ossius nodded, seeing in the Emperor's reaction how Church politics seemed to an outsider. "I suppose to call him a 'deacon' isn't right. He's more than that. Alexander is an old man in poor health. Athanasius has been his secretary for over a decade. And my impression is that he acting as de facto Bishop. Which, in this case, means *de facto* Eastern Pope."

"Yes. Of course. These administrators...bureaucrats. So helpful. So willing to assume power by proxy."

Ossius knew this was a point of pride for Constantine. Unlike other generals—and certainly other emperors—he had never relied on a single, trusted scribe. Constantine read correspondence and wrote most of his own responses. As Emperor, the writing was so great that he had to rely on some clerks. But he rotated them regularly. Never became too reliant on any single one.

"By the way, Athanasius believes that Christians need a formal Bible. He's insistent that we need to develop one soon. So, on that point at least, you and he are in agreement."

Constantine laughed. "Well, good. We look for our points of common ground, eh? But the point of your meeting Antioch was not a new Book. It was this debate over 'homoousian.'" He over enunciated the word, to mock it. "And you really had only one army on the field there. Have the Western bishops developed any interest in this issue?"

"No. None. Sylvester writes me occasionally for updates. But, in general, he would like it to be over."

"And you know, Ossius that I agree with him on this."

"I know that, Dominus."

Constantine stood up and yelled a vulgar encouragement to Titus and Appius, who were positioning their chariots to start their race.

He was, at his core, a soldier.

When he sat again, he returned quickly to the subject of their conversation. "If the Western bishops were involved, would that change the direction of the debate?"

He'd asked this question before. Which meant he hadn't liked Ossius' previous answers.

Ossius sighed. "Possibly. But most of them consider it an intellectual matter with little practical meaning. If they were involved, they might argue that we are fixating on the something that has little to do with what Jesus taught—the same point you made in your letter. But these are bishops and priests, not generals. Confrontation is not part of their personalities."

After a lot of preparation, Titus and Appius were finally ready at the starting gate. And Ossius could see Constantine's interest in the theological debate waning.

"This controversy has gone on long enough, Ossius. Let's arrange a meeting of all the bishops—Western and Eastern—to decide this matter once and for all. And any other major theological questions that affect the Church's work. I will underwrite the cost. And we will all follow its conclusions."

"We once discussed having such a Council in Ancyra in May, is that still your wish?"

"No. We should have somewhere easier for the Western bishops to attend. Perhaps Nicaea. The central theater at the Palace there that can accommodate a large group. And the baths are well done."

"Yes, Imperator. And shall we include creating a New Testament Bible as part of that Council?"

"Seems like a good idea. Why do you ask in a doubtful tone?" Ossius shrugged. "The Book will be a debate unto itself. For example, in our brief discussion, Athanasius suggested two scriptures that he favors to be included. And, if we have discussions on those, the Council will never come to any conclusions."

"Which scriptures?"

"Thomas' Gospel and the Book of Revelation. Both have potential for Gnostic interpretation."

Constantine cocked his head. "There are mystical elements in all of the scriptures."

"It's more than that, Imperator. The Gnostics believe that there are clues in the scriptures to guide them to salvation. The rest of us believe that salvation comes from the grace of God, through worship and living by the teachings of Jesus. But many of our bishops in the East—especially in Egypt—have Gnostic beliefs."

"This is why you need someone above the bishops, Ossius. You have hundreds of fiefdoms; you need a single kingdom," Constantine stood again, to watch the race. "You should at least broach the subject of a new Bible and start the process during this Council."

"Yes. We could start the process. Over time, we could weed out the texts that don't conform. Eusebius of Caesarea might be the best person to put in charge of this."

"You know better than I, since you know who you are dealing with. But let's get it started." And then Constantine turned back to make eye contact, "And make sure Sylvester is there. We'll need some sense in that Council."

Ossius laughed. "I'll convey your message. But I strongly doubt he will attend."

"Why not? Can't be health. He will outlive me!"

"Just conjecture on my part, Augustus, that this is not Pope Sylvester's kind of Council...."

But Constantine was no longer listening. Ossius stood up with him to see Titus get a jump on Appius out of the gatehouse—a lead he never gave up.

Nicaea, Asia Minor
June 19, 1078 AUC (325 AD)

Constantine followed the bishops into the immense general hall. He wore an imperial purple tunic trimmed with gold thread. And a golden wreath meant to look like laurel above his ears. It was extravagant for his taste—the wreath, especially, seemed like a barbarian's crown. But he'd accepted the ostentatious outfit as a part of being Emperor. There was no mistaking that he was the most powerful man in the Roman Empire. And people would be confused or disappointed if he dressed like a soldier. Or even a general.

The hall was a huge covered building of stone and brick, with open sides and massive columns supporting the arched roof. There was bench seating for all. The more important dignitaries sat up front, close to the center podium.

His chair faced the crowd, behind and to one side of the podium. But he didn't sit right away. He was giving the welcoming remarks. "My fellow servants of Christ...."

He spoke to almost 250 bishops, plus attendant priests and deacons sitting in raised pews to the sides and back. He looked occasionally at a small page of notes that he'd hidden in one of his sleeves. His brief welcome was essentially the same text as the letter he'd sent the bishops some months earlier—minus the reference to their "trifling issue."

The politics here among the priests were almost as tense as any meeting in the Senate. Ossius was the chairman of the assembly, which helped. Prior to the grand entrance, Constantine had kissed the cheek of a bishop from the East who'd lost an eye during the persecutions. The priests knew, intellectually, that he was responsible for the new acceptance of Christianity and for the multitude of new churches being built. "But this gesture will underscore your good works on an emotional level," Ossius had suggested. And Constantine had seen the wisdom in it.

"Now, I turn the podium over to your learned brother—Eusebius, Bishop of Nicomedia—who will make some... introductory remarks. And later, Bishop Ossius will explain our agenda for the next few days. May God guide us to sound conclusions in this important work."

The Nicomedian approached the podium and made a very slight bow—a nod, really—and then pulled a larger set of notes from the sleeve of his tunic.

Constantine took his seat. Ossius and some of the more influential bishops sat nearby, but not close. The Emperor felt very much on display. So, he made a point to appear attentive to his cousin's remarks. But his mind drifted at several points. Try as he might, he could not muster much interest in these abstract points of theology.

After all the opening ceremonies ended, Arius, Eusebius of Nicomedia and Eusebius of Caesarea walked leisurely toward the baths.

"A good summary speech, my friend," The Caesarean said to the Nicomedian. "Although your partiality toward our cause was evident."

"Thank you." Eusebius was accustomed to compliments about his speeches or sermons—and he'd learned to answer praise with praise. "To return the compliment, I read the draft of the Creed you have developing with Ossius. It's very good. A bit stricter than I would like but, with minor revisions, I think this Council will approve it. And that will be an impressive accomplishment."

Arius scoffed. "Their work is fine. Very good, as you say. But don't count on anything from our camp being accepted by Alexander's camp. Athanasius has been preaching about the faults of the draft Creed to anyone who will listen. So expect changes. Lots of changes. By the way, my Caesarean friend, I saw you deep in conversation with Ossius and then Constantine joined the two of you. What was that about?"

The Caesarean shrugged. "Ossius wrote me some months ago, about developing criteria for a New Testament Bible. He wants to start a process of weeding out the questionable texts and those that don't reflect our true faith. He discussed that with me again today, indicating that Deacon Athanasius also has an interest—but favors some texts that may be problematic."

"Which ones, problematic?"

"Well, two that Ossius mentioned are the Gospel of Thomas and the Book of Revelation."

Arius seemed more enthusiastic about the New Testament than he'd been about the draft Creed. "A very good idea. And I agree about Thomas and Revelation—they're Gnostic and apocalyptic. Don't reflect the basis of our faith."

They walked a few steps in silence. Then Arius asked a question that had just occurred to him: "What was Constantine's interest in this new Bible?"

"Constantine wants 50 copies of the complete Bible, Old and New Testament, for his churches in the New Rome," Caesarea replied. "He wants me to include the Scriptures I feel most deserving for the New Testament.. Which will be those Origen recommended—probably minus Revelation."

"Agreed," Arius grunted. "Again, Revelation promotes mysticism. Not much different than sorcery and paganism. For that matter, I don't think John's Gospel should be included. Same reason."

"Hmm," the Nicomedian interjected—to contradict. "Revelation may not be worthy of inclusion in this New Testament. But the popularity of John's Gospel will require its inclusion."

"Yes," the Caesarean was siding with his counterpart. "Even Irenaeus, who only wanted the four Gospels as the New Testament, included John."

"You may have to include Revelation since Origen thought it should be part our sacred texts and included in a New Testament. In addition since Athanasius thinks it should be included, there are undoubtedly others that might dictate it being included. Plus, as we all suspect, the Gospel of John, the Epistles of John and Revelation were probably written by the same author. So maybe they all should be included in the New Testament. This assignment is truly an honor for you, my friend," the Nicomedian said. "I am very impressed. I hope that Emperor plans to pay you for all your effort."

The Caesarean blushed noticeably. "In a...manner of...speaking. Constantine is going to help pay for expanding our library. Which I very much appreciate."

"Well, you are full of surprises!" Arius exclaimed. "I am impressed too!"

The Caesarean tried to change the subject: "Do you have any idea how many bishops here may be aligned to our beliefs?"

"I counted 22," Nicomedia answered, precisely. "But I know of at least 30 more that have told me they would join us if we find a way to minimize Athanasius' intimidation. And those 30 speak for others. Only six bishops are from the Western Empire."

Arius groaned. "Only six! Let's see: 22 and 30 and maybe 30 more. Even with all of those, we don't have a majority. Not close. Perhaps we should concentrate our efforts on acceptable wording for the Creed."

"Don't think of the Creed as a consolation for losing the bigger question," the Caesarean chided the others. "It's a separate issue. What's important is that we expand our base within this Council—50 or even 85 won't be enough for us to negotiate on even footing."

"It's true. Our present numbers don't bode well," Arius said, again in a grunting voice. "It's too bad Sylvester isn't here. He could change the dynamic of this Council entirely."

"And that's the reason he, and the rest of the Western Bishops, chose not to come. It's not his controversy to resolve," answered the Nicomedian. "That practical reasoning is why the Emperor likes him so well."

Nicaea, Asia Minor
June 29, 1078 AUC (325 AD)

Ossius' mind drifted while one of the Syrian bishops argued that it was time to separate from the Jewish calendar for the calculation of the Easter celebration to make it independent of any Jewish celebration.

Keeping the bishops on point was proving to be difficult. Each wanted to demonstrate how much he knew. And each was used to being listened to. The first day, it had been chaos. They showed little respect for his instructions—that each speaker had to be identified first and then was to address all comments to the Chair. Very quickly, Ossius had lost control of the hall. Chatter rose from all sides.

And Constantine had to take charge. "Citizens! Citizens! Reverend Bishops! We must have order! Order! Thank you. We have so much to do. We must not waste each other's time. When the floor is open for comments, please speak one at a time. Ossius of Cordova is your Chairman. He will recognize each speaker first. And then you must direct your comments to the Chair. Not to one another."

Ossius noticed that Constantine's voice wasn't as deep or melodious as many of the bishops' voices. But the Emperor was used to seizing and keeping authority. He had no trouble quieting the room. In the days since, Constantine had been present every day— but usually only for an hour or so each morning. To see that order was maintained.

After 10 days, the only substantive issue they had resolved was the so-called "Meletian conflict." Meletius, an Egyptian bishop, wanted The Church to enforce a penalty for repentant Christians who had returned to the faith after fleeing during the persecutions. His position was rejected and Meletius himself was reprimanded.

Ossius snapped back to attention when an exchange between Nicholas of Myra and Arius grew heated.

Arius was practically yelling: "It is clear from the most respected Gospels that Jesus' Last Supper corresponds to the 14th day of the Jewish month of Nisan. The start of Passover. Jesus, being a devout Jew, would want us to use the dates established by his religion. So, we must rely on our Jewish brethren to set that date each year."

Without being recognized, Nicholas shouted back: "Brethren! The Jews aren't consistent in choosing their dates for Passover. Sometimes they choose a date prior to the equinox, sometimes after. Often in the wrong month. More important: Passover is of the wrong character to reflect the joy of Christ's resurrection. It is a festival of death!"

"Ach. It's a celebration of God's deliverance of the Jews from slavery! You are arguing to change a historical date based on your personal distaste for following Jewish custom." Arius responded.

Nicholas looked offended. "Not so! The date is arbitrary. The Jews follow a lunar calendar; we follow a solar calendar. Over 200 years ago, Pope Sixtus recommended that we establish our own dates for Holy Days. The time has come for the Church to heed his advice."

"And what else shall we change because you don't like it, Bishop Nicholas? Shall we change Jesus' name to Sol?" Arius asked the crowd, which groaned.

Nicholas glared at Arius with contempt—unusual from a man renowned for his jolly personality and generous gift-giving.

"Enough," shouted Ossius. "We have discussed the point sufficiently. We will return tomorrow to vote on the question: Whether to establish our own system of dates for scheduling Holy Days. A blessed evening to all."

As Ossius walked out of the hall, he saw Clodius and motioned for the deacon to join him. Once they were away from the crowd, Ossius said: "Deacon, have you been keeping notes of the proceedings as I requested?"

"Well...ah...yes, Holiness," Clodius replied—without making eye contact.

"May I see the notes?"

"Well...actually, Holiness, I have been coordinating with Athanasius on the notes. Alexander has requested the same thing."

Ossius stopped and looked hard at Clodius—forcing the deacon to make eye contact, which he couldn't hold for very long. Something bad was at work. "I wanted you to take notes, Clodius. Not Athanasius. I would like to see your notes from the last several days tomorrow morning."

"Yes, Holiness."

"I've noticed you in deep conversation with Athanasius. And also with the Emperor. What is that about?"

"Mostly small talk, Holiness. And I have given him answers to some questions he's asked me."

"What questions?"

"The Emperor wanted to know how certain bishops felt about the Arian controversy. I answered him to the best of my ability." There was an air of pride in his admission.

"Clodius, a Council like this is a heady experience. And your access to the Emperor is rare thing. But don't let these experiences flatter your vanity. You are a Deacon of the Church. You should listen more than talk. And be very careful about offering opinions."

"Yes, Holiness."

After supper, Ossius met with Constantine in his personal quarters of his palace. They spoke each evening, after the Council's business was completed. "Dominus, my apologies for any embarrassment my Deacon Clodius may be causing you during these proceedings."

Constantine smiled. "You don't trust him—do you, Ossius?"

"Trust is earned. As of yet, Clodius has not earned mine."

"He is a bit strange," Constantine nodded. "But I think he's harmless. Doesn't hold eye contact. He hasn't been an embarrassment to you. But...."

"I recognize that pivot, Imperator."

"Yes. The politician in me. So, let me say it plainly. Your deacon has extolled to me several times the piety of Alexander and Athanasius. Suggested that I declare Alexander a living saint. And he has been critical of Eusebius—so harshly that I doubt he realizes Eusebius is my cousin. Oh, and he suggested that I declare December 25 as the date of the Nazarene's birth."

"What?" Ossius almost screamed.

"It was a bit...incongruous. One moment he was praising Alexander to the sky, saying he already had the right answer to this debate, and the next moment he was suggesting when to celebrate the Nazarene's birthday. I don't remember how he connected the two. Perhaps he'd heard me say that the 25th is Fausta's favorite pagan holiday. Anyway, his idea was that I, as Emperor, could declare both matters resolved and be done with all of this."

Ossius felt betrayed. But he didn't want Constantine to see that weakness. Better to focus on Clodius' breach of protocol. "I will remove my insolent deacon your presence—and from this Council— immediately."

"You don't need to do it on my account, Ossius. As I said, what harm does he do? So, he's a bit...strange. Everyone who meets him knows that."

"The harm is that he represents me," Ossius said, hoping not to sound like a foolish old man who couldn't keep control of his underlings. "His assumptions and conduct could misrepresent what I stand for. I have not endorsed Alexander's position. It's not that I will not—it's just that, as we've discussed, some form of compromise would be best. For the Church and the Empire. I am frustrated with this, Dominus. I beg your leave—so that I can attend to it immediately."

Nicaea, Asia Minor
July 1, 1078 AUC (325 AD)

Nearly two weeks into its meetings, the Council decided to take a break for one day from official business. Attendees could take care of correspondence, pray or simply clear their minds of meeting protocols and procedures.

Ossius had spent the first part of the day considering what to do about Clodius. He read the notes that his deacon had given him— they were obviously Athanasius'. The inappropriate comments to Constantine were even a worse sign. The date itself wasn't the issue; some Christians already celebrated Christ's birthday on or near the winter solstice. Ossius didn't particularly care when Christ's birthday was celebrated. Like most priests, he felt the Resurrection was—by far—the most important episode from Christ's life. But, if asked, Ossius would have said that Jesus was likely born in the spring. The Gospel of Luke referred to "shepherds in the field," perhaps the spring lambing season.

But to link the date of Christ's birth with a suggestion that the Emperor override the Council showed weaknesses of judgment and temperament that Clodius would never overcome.

There was other business to resolve before the Council resumed. Most of the minor matters had been resolved, so the bishops were positioned to focus on the Arian controversy when they came back from their short break. Arius would have a day to present his position; Alexander would have the following day to present his. Ossius had stipulated that each man would present his argument personally—no proxies or advocates. Specifically, no Eusebius or Athanasius. Ossius expected that there would be another day (or perhaps two) of questions after each man had made his case. Then, the bishops would vote on which explanation of Christ's nature better fit the Church's goals and needs.

And they could move on to the wording of the Creed.

The break seemed to evaporate, it passed so quickly. And now Ossius was back in front of the Council, calling it back into order and describing how the next few days would proceed. He made eye contact with Constantine, who nodded in agreement, and invited Arius to come to the podium.

The great hall was packed with bishops, priests and their servants—but they came to a complete silence when the popular Arius walked to the front. "Thank you, Ossius. Thank you, my brothers. I salute you, children of God. We come together here, at this time, drawn by our shared love of Christ Jesus. And by our belief in His teachings. One of the necessary tasks that we complete in this Council is to determine how we teach the faithful about Christ's nature. And His relationship to God, Whom He called 'Abba' or 'Father' in our vernacular...."

Arius had been uneasy about speaking to the group. On the off-day, he'd complained to Ossius that he wasn't an orator. But he was doing well. As Ossius looked around, he saw quite a few heads nodding in agreement with what Arius said. And even those that Ossius recognized as siding with Alexander seemed to be listening attentively.

For the first few hours, Arius described Christ's nature in philosophical terms. He used the Socratic Method—rhetorical questions that he himself answered. Syllogisms. Abstractions. This kept the audience's attention. Even Constantine stayed in the hall longer than he usually did—in fact, he stayed for most of the day.

After a short lunch break, Arius shifted his argument to the practical matters of why his concept of a "complementary" Jesus, who was a "beloved Son" would be more effective for drawing people into the Church. And for keeping them inspired after they joined. That being a son of man, he was an example that other men could achieve, or at least to emulate.

When Arius was finished, he received some applause from the audience—a rare thing at a Church Council. He accepted the support humbly. Ossius reminded everyone that Alexander's turn would come in the morning and called an end to the day's business. A crowd gathered around Arius—asking questions, adding thoughts, offering encouragement.

But Ossius didn't stay around to listen. He saw Clodius—who'd spent most of the day milling around one of the side entrances—starting to leave the great hall.

"Clodius." At first, the deacon didn't respond. "Clodius! Wait a moment! I would like to speak with you." On the second shout, Clodius stopped.

Ossius pointed to a quiet, grassy hillock a few hundred cubits from the hall entrance. They headed that direction silently. Clodius seemed visibly anxious.

As soon as they reached the grassy area, well out of earshot from the hall, Ossius started: "Clodius, you mentioned to me a few days ago that you shared only 'small talk' with the Emperor. But, in fact, it appears your conversations were meant to influence him. Is that true?"

Clodius changed from looking anxious to looking confused. Had he been expecting something else?

"Influence? No, Holiness. I only…explained positions of people that he asked me about."

"And who might those people be?

Clodius shook his head slightly—still confused. "I explained— no, I mean, ah, I mentioned Alexander's and Athanasius' knowledge of the theology of Christ and God."

"And did you mention *my* knowledge of the theology concerning Christ and God."

"No," Clodius said slowly. "I mean I don't understand…."

"Do you *know* my position on this controversy, Clodius?"

"No. Not really. I believe you favor Eusebius and Arius. But that's my inference. Never heard you say it."

Ossius stared hard at his deacon. He believed Clodius was lying. The only question was: how much?

"And that would make you wrong, Clodius. You know not how I feel. You only see actions that may be there for the perception of what may be the good of our Church or the good of the Empire. And yet you work against my ends by conspiring with Athanasius and reporting to him my letters. That is true, is it not, Clodius?"

Clodius bowed his head "I may have misinterpreted and reported some of your statements, Bishop."

Ossius let that admission stand for a few moments.

"And what possessed you to approach Constantine about Christ's birthday?"

Clodius turned pale. "The Emperor was lamenting that he had other urgent business. I'd heard him talk earlier about how his wife favors the pagan solstice holiday—Sol Invictus. So, it occurred to me that he could easily fix both problems with one edict."

Ossius sighed. "The Emperor can do as he wishes. But to curry favor with him, in order to influence him to rule a certain way or take a certain action, invites serious trouble for the Church. I say this as someone who has known Constantine for many years. You overstepped here."

A few more moments of silence—during which Ossius noticed some priests coming their direction.

"Clodius, are you sure you wish to be a priest?"

"Yes, Bishop. It is the most important thing I can imagine. My great desire. I want to show people my dedication to the words of our Lord, Jesus Christ!"

Ossius shook his head slightly, ruefully. "But a priest helps people. He sacrifices his life for the good of others. He acts as an *illustration* of Christ's life. Having people see your dedication is secondary. Or less."

Clodius was starting to sweat. "Well, of course. That too. But I want those dedicated to Christ to see me as an equal."

"Clodius, I don't think I can help you be what you want to be. I don't think what you want is actually to be a priest. Your time with me must come to an end. I suggest you align yourself with another bishop. Or, better yet, a good Christian teacher. We will discuss this more after this Council has ended."

Nicaea, Asia Minor
July 6, 1078 AUC (325 AD)

Eusebius of Nicomedia felt that the Arian argument was not gathering the momentum it needed. There had been many favorable remarks about Arius' position. But Alexander's rambling two-day rant against Arius had been full of hell and damnation. Eusebius believed none of it—but some in the assembly did. Also, Athanasius was acting extremely smug. Overconfident. Eusebius wondered whether there was something he was missing.

This was the day when the session was supposed to open up for questions. But there had been some speculation through the evening and early morning that Alexander would refuse to give up the podium.

Ossius entered the great hall just moments before the session was supposed to start. He walked directly to the podium—and nodded to the head deacon, who called for order.

"Gentleman. I have a request from Alexander of Alexandria," Ossius looked uneasy. "He requests that, since he has summarized his position of faith, he be given the opportunity to begin the questioning of Arius." There were some murmurs of objection from the audience—but they died away. "Furthermore, Alexander requests that this Council grants him an additional indulgence. That we allow his deacon Athanasius to respond to the same questions."

Eusebius' first impulse was to disagree. He wanted time to figure out what Alexander and Athanasius were planning. But he didn't want to act from a position of weakness—and ignorance was weakness. So he remained silent and listened.

Ossius seemed a bit disappointed. "Unless we have objection to Alexander's request, will both Arius and Athanasius approach the podium?"

They did—and Alexander came with them. Ossius yielded to podium back to Alexander, who directed Arius and Athanasius to separate stools on either side of him.

Alexander pulled some notes from his sleeve and started the questioning. "Arius, my objective is to prove Jesus is identical in nature as God. I want to prove that They are homoousian. Do you agree that is my position?"

"I agree that is your position, Bishop. And my position is that They are not quite the same. That Jesus was begotten of God and is …lesser."

"I agree that is your position, Arius—faulty as it may be. And do you agree that, in the process of coming to your conclusion that Jesus is lesser than God, you have had to rely on blasphemous and heretical reasoning?"

Arius shook his head. "No, Bishop. I do not agree with that statement. I relied on accepted gospels and scriptures—books that I believe all here would agree are valid."

Alexander took a deep breath, which seemed to energize him. "If I were to prove to you that you have based your opinions on heresy, would you repent?"

Arius shrugged, "Yes. But my reasoning is not based on heretical scriptures. Or reasoning."

"I have several examples that I wish to share with the Council—which prove that you are misguided. But, before I begin, I will give you the opportunity to denounce your misguided opinions. As our Savior taught us, I pray that you accept your mistakes. So that we may embrace you back into the womb of the Church."

"Alexander, I sincerely believe my opinions are *from* the womb of the Church," as Arius said this, he realized that he sounded arrogant. "I look forward to seeing the illustrations that you feel prove the contrary."

Alexander nodded in agreement. "I ask the indulgence of the Council—to allow my deacon, Athanasius, to question Arius. This is due to his direct involvement in the events which will illustrate."

There was a general sound of agreement among the assembly to allow Athanasius to question Arius.

All eyes turned to Ossius, who looked to Constantine. Who shrugged very slightly. Ossius stroked his beard and the said: "We have allowed deacons and assigns to speak on other matters, so we will allow this now. But I'll remind all of the parties—on both sides of this issue—that the purpose of this exchange is to inform the Council's discretion. No one is going to be excommunicated here." He ended his warning by staring hard at Athanasius.

Alexander yielded the podium to Athanasius, who immediately asked: "Arius, do you recall a series of conversations you had with me, when I was but a student and a scribe? We discussed the teachings of Origen and your opinion of the Gospel of John?"

"Yes, I was thinking of that conversation not long ago. It was eight or 10 years ago. My impression was that you understood the concepts quite well, given your young age."

"Do you remember the letter you wrote me concerning that conversation?"

"Until this moment I had forgotten I sent you a letter. I vaguely remember I had included a verse."

"We will discuss the verse in a moment. But you agree you corresponded with me after our conversation on Origen?"

"Yes."

"Do you recall how you described the author of the Gospel of John?"

Arius was trying to remember the letter—but he'd written so many. "No, not specifically. But I suspect it was not complementary. I still have qualms about that book."

"You called him 'a Greek-loving deviant.'" The assembly was eerily silent.

"'A Greek-loving deviant!'" Athanasius repeated.

"I don't recall that wording...."

Athanasius lifted a piece of a scroll. "Here is the letter! Do you not recognize your own hand?" He walked from behind the podium toward Arius, still holding the letter up high.

"Yes. It appears to be my hand. But it is important to explain..."

"Explain how the most important document of early Christianity was written by a 'Greek-loving deviant'? Explain that this Gospel, inspired by the Almighty, was written by a deviant rather than the Apostle John?"

A crowd of deacons on the farthest edge of the hall started to chant "Blasphemy."

Ossius raised his hand for silence. And the chant died down.

Arius was still trying to find the appropriate words for his response. But he saw that Athanasius was about to say something more, so he spoke quickly: "My opinion is that the Gospels of Mark, Luke and Matthew are genuine. And the most authentic versions of Jesus' works and deeds. I believe the Gospel of John was written well after the others. And it reflects what its authors believed, not what the namesake Apostle witnessed."

Athanasius looked at Arius for a moment, and then asked," So do you not believe in the Gospel of John? Do you not believe that the Holy Gospel was written by the Apostle John? Not divinely inspired?"

"No. I believe much of the Gospel of John. I just believe the earlier Gospels…more," Arius answered.

"So, you do not believe the theme of John—that Jesus walked this earth as a divine being?"

"I believe Jesus walked this earth as the son of man."

More muttering and beginnings of chants. The audience was turning against Arius—and Athanasius would happily enflame the issue. Ossius saw Clodius, far to the right side of the hall, chanting something. He couldn't allow this. He stood and raised both arms: "Silence! This is not a circus! Or a political debate. This is a theological inquiry. Please listen quietly and with respect for all."

Ossius stared again at Athanasius—and nodded back to the empty podium. Athanasius returned and Ossius sat down.

"Arius, you did not answer my question. Do you believe in the Gospel of John, which reports that Jesus walked on earth as a divine being?"

Arius looked back at his questioner. He stood tall. And was ready to make a better answer. "Yes. Of course, I believe Jesus was divine while on earth. But I believe he was a man, too. A perfect man. But a man that we, as imperfect men, can imitate and follow. Not some distant god that we have no chance of imitating. A man who lived and died. Then was reborn by the glory of God's gift of Resurrection."

"So, you do not believe in Jesus as John describes him?"

"I believe in Jesus as Origen interprets the Gospel of John's description: *'Begotten by the Father after creation, not equal to the Father.'* This is like Paul's opinion, *'an example to follow, not a myth.'* I believe, as I have written in my *Thalia, that there was a time when the Son was not.*"

Athanasius made a haughty sneer. "Your poems are popular. They have made your name renowned. But, as Bishop Ossius reminds us, this is a theological inquiry." He was about to say more.

So, Arius jumped in: "True. Let us consider the Gospels as scholars, not as advocates. The Jesus described in the Gospel of John is not the same as the Jesus described in the Synoptic Gospels. John's Jesus is aloof and proud to declare that He is the Son of the Father. In the Synoptics, Jesus is humble and asks His disciples and those He cures not to tell anyone that He is the Christ. John's Jesus constantly tells His listeners 'verily, verily' and is impatient. "The Synoptics' Jesus asks simple questions to make profound points—and is understanding. Now, of course, this was in fact the same man. But two different portraits. I prefer the earlier portrait, from the three original Gospels."

The murmurs started again. The same group of deacons—and Clodius was one of them—were resuming their "Blasphemy" chant.

Ossius was about to silence the Council again, when someone else did it for him. A large Centurion appeared at the main entrance to the great hall. He didn't enter completely; but he didn't have to.

The crowd fell silent immediately. Many of them had been persecuted by Romans soldiers just like that.

The Centurion stayed by the entrance. Quintus, wearing a tunic, came in from behind him and walked directly to Constantine.
The guard whispered something to the Emperor, who rose and left
the assembly. Outside, Constantine recognized the tall Centurion—
the same man who'd found the crossing spot outside of Adrianople.
The Centurion tried to bow, but the Emperor shook his arm instead.
"My son, please, it is good to see you again. What brings you here?"

"Augustus, Dux Ablabius instructed me to deliver this letter to
you. Personally."

"Do you know what he writes, Centurion?"

"No, Imperator. He told me that it was important that no one
see the letter but you."

Constantine broke the seal and opened the scroll. He frowned
while reading it. And then he turned back to the centurion: "It is
better that you do not know what this letter concerns. There are elements in the Empire that would take your life to know its contents.
Let us meet before breakfast tomorrow by my quarters. I will give
you a response to be delivered to Ablabius. Go toward my villa and
ask for my Adiutor Aelius. He will get you a room, bath and dinner
for this evening."

As the Centurion walked toward the Villa, Constantine turned
to Quintus. Since his injury at Chrysopolis, Quintus could not
sustain significant physical activity. So, he'd become the closest
of Constantine's guards. Practically a companion. And, because
Quintus seldom spoke, secrets were safe with him.

"Ablabius writes that Licinius and Sextus have had conversations with the barbarians concerning building an army. He caught
two of the barbarians after a meeting with Licinius. They both
substantiated the treachery. He wants Licinius and Sextus both
executed. My concern is that Ablabius has always thought Licinius
should have been executed after Chrysopolis. I suspect he is looking

for every small infraction to prove conspiracy. What do you think, Quintus?" Constantine asked.

"They should both die, Augustus."

"Just like that? I promised my sister her husband could live."

"Battles for Empires are to the death. Licinius will never accept that he is not the rightful Emperor," Quintus replied.

"Your argument is compelling. You are a tough man to negotiate with, Quintus," Constantine said in mock humor. "But you are correct. Licinius and Sextus have lived too long, and that must include Licinius' son."

Nicaea, Asia Minor
July 14, 1078 AUC (325 AD)

Athanasius had been questioning Arius for several days.

The questions were based on letters and papers that Arius had written—in some cases, years or even decades earlier. Ossius had declared a couple of days of recess in between. During those days off, Eusebius of Nicomedia had spoken to several Council members whose opinions he respected. Athanasius had lost the crowd. The bishops and priests had heard more than enough of his prosecution of Arius. Some called it a "persecution."

At the beginning of the Council's day back from its break, Athanasius took the stage and his familiar place behind the podium.

As soon as Ossius called the Council into order, Eusebius rose and spoke. "Bishop Ossius, I have a point of order to raise before we begin our official business again."

"Yes, Bishop Eusebius?"

Eusebius walked up onto the stage, near Ossius and Constantine's seats. "Ossius," and then he turned to face the audience. "Brothers, we have listened patiently now for many days to this young man's vilification of Arius' writings. I've heard enough. I'm sure that, if a determined scribe were to scrutinize my letters from over a decade, he would find inconsistencies and imperfect opinions. And

I'm certain the same is true for most of you. The charge of this Council is to determine the Church's formal answer to the question of the nature of our Lord, Jesus Christ. It is not our business to scrutinize and ridicule one man's individual beliefs. Let us remove this one man from our consideration—and only look at the issue. I do not share Arius' opinion of the Gospel of John. I do not share his opinion of Paul's changing Jesus' message for one audience or another. But I do agree with Arius that God begot Christ at a time after God—that Jesus is the Son of God in the truest sense. I believe that God is timeless. So, I agree with Arius that God is the Mosaic God of the Jews—the God of the Ten Commandments, the God of Abraham. He is the 'God Almighty' that Jesus worshiped and gave reverence in all of His preaching. The God that Jesus states, even in John's Gospel, is greater than He. Now, you may agree with me—or you may not. But this is the issue of this Council, not to put the many writings of Arius on trial."

Loud applause was the Council's reply to Eusebius.

Alexander, as if anticipating Eusebius's argument, rose to reply: "What the good Bishop from Nicomedia says is true. Coming to a consensus on the nature of Jesus is our primary goal. To attain that knowledge however, we have to look to all our sources and decide their reliability. Arius has set the argument of Jesus being less divine. So, it behooves us to investigate the reliability of his opinions on a full range of theological issues. We must judge if he is a true and good Christian whose opinion we must value, or a tool of the devil sent here to mislead us."

The response to Alexander was not as strong—and was clearly coming mostly from deacons and younger members of the audience. Athanasius walked out from behind the podium and whispered something to Alexander.

Eusebius, still standing, answered: "Alexander, Arius holds a different opinion than you on this matter—that doesn't make him a 'tool of the devil.' He has been a devout priest for many years.

He studied with some of the most respected teachers of our time. Including you. Now he has become a tool of the devil? I share his opinion. Am I also such a tool?"

"The devil works in mysterious ways. Perhaps he is convincing you both that your argument is the correct one—in order to diminish the glory of Jesus Christ," Alexander said.

The audience groaned.

Eusebius sighed theatrically and then said, "Or perhaps he has convinced you that you are correct by appealing to your pride. Pride in having a position that allows you to intimidate others."

Alexander was noticeably uneasy. Athanasius whispered more. And gave Alexander a small scroll. Alexander looked at the scroll and then turned to the audience. "I have no such pride. I am merely a humble servant of the Lord. I believe my deacon's final question of Arius makes my earlier point. Arius, do you recall the verse you sent to Athanasius—similar to the verse you have in your *Thalia*? Let me read it to you and the Council."

God is inexpressible to the Son.

For he is in himself what he is, that is, indescribable, So that the son does not comprehend any of these things or have the understanding to explain them. For it is impossible for him to fathom the Father, who is by himself.

For the Son himself does not even know his own essence, For being Son, his existence is most certainly at the will of the Father.

All eyes turned to Arius, who nodded and said: "Yes. I recall that I have written that. It's from the *Thalia*. But my recollection of what I wrote to Athanasius is vague."

"Arius, by this admission, you believe Jesus can't comprehend God."

"I believe God is so inexplicably powerful, great and forgiving that no one in Heaven or Earth can comprehend him."

"Not even Jesus, our Lord, can comprehend his Father?"

The deacons again started chanting "Blasphemy." But, this time, the rest of the crowd hushed them.

Emboldened by Eusebius and the crowd, Arius responded more aggressively than he had before: "Alexander, do you understand God?" He paused momentarily for a response that didn't come. Then he continued: "I didn't think so. Nor do I think anyone here would claim he does. Jesus was divine. He could heal the sick and feed the poor. But could He create the cosmos? The moon, the planets, the stars? God's power has no limits. Nor his love. Nor his forgiveness. His qualities are boundless. Unimaginable to our human minds. You say the devil may be an influence on me. But my love for God leaves no room for the devil. I believe God's power and love will influence even the devil to repent and beg forgiveness. Some day."

"What??" yelled Alexander. "What did you say about Satan, the fallen angel?"

"God's capacity for forgiveness is so great that someday, perhaps Judgment Day, God could forgive Satan."

The assembly roared with calls of "Blasphemy!" and responses calling for silence. Ossius waved his arms for silence.

Ossius finally stood, quieting the uproar, talked to Alexander and then addressed Eusebius, who was still standing on the stage. "Eusebius, it's clear that many on the Council agree with your position that this exchange has become more about Arius than about the ideas about Jesus' nature that he has expressed. But Alexander has told me that he is near the final point of his questioning. I will allow him to complete his inquiry." And then he turned to Alexander, "But, Bishop, you must be the one who asks the questions. This Council is not a symposium for your deacon's training. Eusebius, Athanasius, please be seated. Alexander, you may take the podium. But, if your questions stray far from matters relevant to this Council's business, I will end the inquiry."

Alexander took the podium but was silent for a few moments while he gathered his thoughts. Finally he said in a deep voice with growing volume: "Arius, you are knowledgeable of the Synoptic Gospels; so, you must be aware that what you said a few moments ago contradicts the description of Judgment Day in those early books. And you completely ignore the description of Judgment Day in the Book of Revelation."

It wasn't a question, so Arius waited for more. When it became clear there wouldn't be, he responded: "The descriptions of God's Judgment in the Gospels and Revelation were written by a men with their opinions. In my opinion, God's forgiveness is best described by Jesus and his actions. He teaches us to forgive our enemies and He teaches us about God's limitless forgiveness. Origen was of the same opinion. His writings certainly have influenced me, as I suspect they have everyone on the Council."

"In believing such theories, you are denying the Gospel's words. Matthew, in his Gospel, writes that when Jesus returns He will separate those who have lived a Christian life from those that have not. He will send those that have not into everlasting punishment. You are committing blasphemy and—" Constantine coughed.

"Alexander, please stop. You are not to pass judgement, this is an inquiry, not a trial. I will not warn you again," Ossius said.

"Arius, do you believe that the Scriptures are the Word of God?"

"Yes, Bishop, I do. What we're talking about here are my opinions, my interpretations, of the works that God inspired men to write. We can debate their meaning. Only He knows for certain. I've stated that God may not have made His Son identical to Himself. Whether I am right or wrong about that, God's decision has already happened. I have stated that God may forgive Satan someday. God knows whether He will do that—or not. To Him, time is unimportant. But, to us, it is a future event that we cannot know. I don't believe even Satan knows. What we are debating here are human judgments and opinions. We cannot know God's nature or Jesus'. We base our opinions on what the Greek Philosophers called 'reason.' Arius turns to the crowd and continues. "Bishop Alexander also uses reason to conclude that Jesus has the same nature as God. He makes an interesting argument. But none of us really knows what God actually did."

"You are ignoring the very Word of God in the Scriptures that prove both of your opinions wrong," said Alexander, his voice again rising and shaking at the same time. "John's Gospel affirms our knowledge concerning the divinity of Jesus. And Matthew and the two other Synoptic Gospels are unequivocal that God will send Jesus to judge the unworthy and send them to eternal punishment in Hell. And Revelation describes it all!"

Arius looked at Ossius, who was looking down. And Constantine, who was looking up. Clearly exasperated, Arius moved away from the podium, then back. "Alexander' He yelled back. 'We have a library in your city that includes numerous editions of the early Gospels. In several languages. Many contradictory to each other. They are the texts that Origen studied. That I studied. And you studied. These texts are written by men—many with their own agenda, their own opinions, just as we have here today in this Council."

Arius continued still yelling. "The clearest picture of Jesus we have comes from the early Synoptic Gospels. In those, Jesus states in that He was a man, the Son of man. I take Him at His word for that." Arius literally screamed.

"Sinner, you are not heeding the very scriptures you so admire, that you have sworn as a Priest that you believe. You, my son, are going to Hell!" Alexander screamed, his angry, quivering voice rising in a crescendo.

A wave of objections and jeers—directed at both Alexander and Arius—flowed from the back of the hall to the front. Very loudly. Ossius rose and approached the podium, waving his arms for silence. After several minutes, the noise remained oppressive. So, Constantine also stood. And the Council quieted.

Ossius stared at Alexander, then spoke. "I think we have heard enough of this inquiry. Let us take the rest of the day for prayers and contemplation. We will meet tomorrow at mid-day and bring this matter to some resolution."

Outside in the bright afternoon sun, both Eusebiuses caught up to Arius at the same time. "My good friend," the Nicomedian started, "you are honest. Brutally so. I do not recommend a career in politics."

Arius, who had been walking to his room to get away from Council, laughed with some effort. "I apologize to you. To both of you. I have let you both down. I have let God down—by representing my opinions as I see them, rather than saying what needed to be said."

"You are only guilty of being human, Arius," laughed Eusebius of Caesarea.

The Nicomedian agreed. "Other than your opinions on Hell, everything you said was correct—as taught to us by Lucian so many years ago. But it is not what is accepted by today's Church. What Alexander is demanding is strict adherence to a new orthodoxy, not a debate."

"Though we know it's not Alexander who's pressing that rigid orthodoxy," the Caesarean added.

"Indeed not. But we know the Nazarene's teachings, His questioning, His acceptance to all walks of life. His forgiveness will be secondary to the method and manner in which we now must beseech Him," the Nicomedian said. All three echoed the last few words—which had been a favorite saying of their old teacher Lucian.

"Now that I have discredited our position, what will be the Council's next steps?" Arius asked.

The Nicomedian answered. "Ossius will talk to Constantine this afternoon and tomorrow morning. I suspect that the Emperor wants a resolution to this debate."

"You can see his frustration growing deeper every day he's here. He'd rather be killing barbarians or spending time with his young wife," the Caesarean said, smiling mischievously.

The Nicomedian laughed and then summed up their position. "His impatience for resolution favors orthodoxy. Rigidity has the advantage of being simple. Alexander will get most of what he wants. But I will try to make sure he doesn't get everything. And Ossius will move the Council on to the Creed, the only remaining item."

Nicaea, Asia Minor
July 15, 1078 AUC (325 AD)

In Constantine's private quarters, the Emperor, Ossius and Eusebius of Nicomedia were discussing the Council's next steps. Or, rather, Ossius and Eusebius were listening to the Emperor discuss them: "Cousin, the debate is over. Arius seems like a devoted priest but his beliefs about the nature of Jesus and God, and now Satan, are clearly out of step with the majority of the Council. I thought they were going to stone him yesterday. There is no way you can combine his views with the mainstream elements of the Church."

"But the Council is wrong—its conclusions are wrong. Arius is right about the early scriptures."

Ossius put a hand lightly on Eusebius' shoulder. "I agree with the Emperor, Eusebius. Dragging the debate on will only worsen the Council's discord. You're right that Alexander isn't making a much better case. But he has the majority on his side. And Arius will become only more of a scapegoat if he keeps making provocative arguments. We must move on to the final draft of the Creed."

Eusebius knew it was time to yield the point. But he decided to make one final appeal. "There are many within the Council who agree with Arius. They are the quiet ones—not the ones making vocal outbursts. If we don't reach some compromise, the losing group will be a constant division within the Church."

"I hope you aren't including yourself in that number," Constantine warned with a rising anger. "I am sick and tired of this whole debate. Those who don't follow the Church's doctrine will no longer be part of the Church and if I decide they threaten the Church, they will not live to do any damage."

Ossius interjected, fearing another debate would erupt, or worse. "Eusebius, how can there be compromise on this issue? What would it be? God and Jesus are either the same or they are not. They cannot be partly the same."

"God defies man's understanding. He exists beyond our sense of reason." Eusebius was quoting another of old Lucian's sayings. But, this time, there was no one to understand the reference.

"Eusebius, you can't build a Church on abstractions and philosophical epigrams. This has gone long enough, I have made the decision and this is what we will follow, do you understand." Constantine said in considerable anger directed at his cousin.

Eusebius turned his palms up and nodded to Constantine.

"Yes Cousin, you are undoubtedly right."

Ossius walked toward Constantine—so that he was literally standing with the Emperor. "More important, to the future of the Church, if a bishop or priest is so adamant in his disagreement that he would undermine doctrine, he cannot be part of that Church. He must be excommunicated." Trying to soften Constantine's earlier death threat.

Eusebius smiled ruefully. "Ossius, I understand. You sound, however, like Alexander's deacon."

"Those two hold no favor with me," Ossius said. "But we must do what is best for the Church. Long after memories of this Council have faded, our successors will agree that finding Jesus and God of the same nature is the strongest and clearest doctrinal conclusion."

Nicaea, Asia Minor
July 22, 1078 AUC (325 AD)

"Please, brothers, come to order!" Ossius implored from behind the podium.

The Creed was supposed to take a few hours—it had taken almost a week. The bishops had been politicking and wordsmithing every phrase. While the nature of God and Jesus was unknowable, the wording of a prayer was something that every Council member knew well.

To Constantine, the process was so boring that, after the second day, he'd joked to Quintus: "You should go out and start a war to get me away from out of this." His main role in these weeks of mind-numbing argument had been to keep order. Which he did, once again. He stood. And a hush fell over the Council.

Ossius nodded gratefully and read the final draft of the Creed.

> We believe in one God, the Father almighty, maker of all things visible and invisible; And in one Lord, Jesus Christ, the Son of God, begotten from the Father, only-begotten, that is, from the substance of the Father, God from God, light from light, true God from true God, begotten not made, of one substance with the Father, through Whom all things came into being, things in heaven and things on earth, Who because of us men and because of our salvation came down, and became incarnate and became man, and suffered, and rose again on the third day, and ascended to the heavens, and will come to judge the living and dead, And in the Holy

Spirit. But as for those who say, There was when He was not, and, Before being born He was not, and that He came into existence out of nothing, or who assert that the Son of God is of a different hypostasis or substance, or created, or is subject to alteration or change —these the catholic and apostolic Church anathematizes.

There was a smattering of applause—but not as much as Ossius had expected. "Brothers, our scribes have distributed several copies of what I just read. Please review our final version. We will gather again tomorrow morning to sign the covenant. And then, in three days, we will have a brief closing ceremony. May God bless us all."

As Ossius left the hall, Eusebius of Nicomedia joined him to walk toward the courtyard entrance.

"Ossius, I intend to sign this Nicene Creed for continuity of our faith. And in deference to Constantine. But I fear that others— Arius and perhaps Secundus and Theonus—may not. I have told them that they will likely be excommunicated. Is there anything we can offer them to encourage their agreement?"

Ossius rolled his eyes. "Eusebius, this isn't politics. I don't have anything to offer. They will be excommunicated and exiled if they don't sign. That's all."

"Where might they be exiled?"

"I haven't given the matter any thought. If I recall correctly, the three you mention are all from the African coast, near Libya. So we won't want them there. Too much opportunity for causing unrest. Perhaps Syria? No. Illyria might work."

"Yes. I know some patrons in Illyria that might accommodate them as guests. I would assume that they would be free to travel—as long as they were not to attend religious events?"

"Is this a negotiation, Eusebius?"

"Well, it isn't politics. Will you confirm this matter with Constantine?" Eusebius answered.

"I will mention it next time I see him."

After the signing of the Nicene Creed, Constantine issued a formal proclamation. Sent to all cities, townships and Churches throughout the Empire, he announced that the First Ecumenical Council in Nicaea had agreed to a Creed. His proclamation included the full text of the new prayer.

The proclamation went on to state that all Christians who did not pledge the Creed were to be exiled and excommunicated.

Finally, the proclamation stated that Arius of Alexandria, Secundus of Ptolemais and Theonus of Marmarica were all excommunicated and exiled to Illyria. All letters, verses or other literary works of Arius of Alexandria were to be consumed by fire. Possession of Arius' work was punishable by death.

Near Byzantium
December 31, 1078 AUC (326 AD)

The Christmas Holidays—between the winter solstice and Julian calendar New Year—were a mix of pagan-worship frivolities and the more serious but no less joyous celebration of Christ's birth. The New Year was a celebration of the two faced god, Janus. One face looked back at the past, the other forward to the future.

Constantine had his entire family in the partially-constructed Imperial Palace in the rapidly-growing "New Rome" section of Byzantium. They were having very good Spanish wine and eating honey figs, fruit and cheese when Eusebius of Nicomedia joined the family in the early evening.

Constantine had exiled his cousin to Gaul three months earlier, over the Creed matter. Eusebius had written almost immediately, asking for an audience around the holidays.

As usual, Helena made a commotion over him. Constantine's children were also happy to see their cousin. Eusebius had tutored most of them at one point or another. And Eusebius was still very close to Constantia, who was also with the family—but still in mourning after her husband's and son's execution.

Constantine walked Eusebius around the living quarters.

"Eusebius, you remember Crispus. And his wife Helena. I have no idea where their boy is."

"Crispus! It has been a long time. You should be proud—your reputation is outstanding." Eusebius said, shaking Crispus' arm warmly.

"Thank you, cousin. It is good to see you again."

They walked on, toward a balcony near the back of the house that had a spectacular view. There, they found Fausta, leaning against the railing. Eusebius hugged her and wished her a happy Christmas— and that he remember how well she liked the winter holidays. "How are you doing?"

"Better now. Just needed some air. I've been a little ill."

"She always feels ill in the early stages," Constantine added. "When she's closer, she feels fine."

Eusebius looked at Fausta, who nodded.

"My God! Congratulations, Fausta! This will be five? Stunning. You're increasing the population of the Roman Empire singlehandedly!"

"Well, not quite single-handedly. I'm going back in again, before I get a chill." She hugged Constantine and grabbed his shoulder in a way that conveyed genuine intimacy. Eusebius blanched a bit at that small point. "I'll leave you two out here to talk and enjoy this view. But don't stay away from us for too long." She said as she left.

When Fausta had gone back inside, Constantine took a deep breath and cleared his head of the wine's effect. Eusebius clearly wanted to speak of serious matters. For the moment, he seemed to be willing to look out at the city and port below. So, Constantine started the conversation: "I thought you were going to Sirmium to see your Mother?"

"I am. But I wanted to come here first to speak with you. About exiling me. And then I'll go see her."

"Don't complain, Eusebius. It's only been a few months. And Gaul is beautiful in the fall. I told you we needed to make it clear that the orthodox doctrine will prevail—but you kept pushing against it. So, we made an example of you. No one's above the law, not even the Emperor's cousin. Some of the other dissenters may not make it to next year's Christmas Holiday, I am tired of this discord."

They stood next to each other in silence for a few moments as Constantine cooled down. Then Constantine asked: "Have you heard that our old friend, Alexander of Alexandria, passed away? The day before Christmas?"

"No! God bless his soul. Who are the bishops going to choose as his successor?"

Constantine smiled, wearily. "Before he died, old Alexander sent a letter to his neighbors in the East, choosing Athanasius. And Athanasius quickly had three local bishops publicly support him. Mutatis mutandis," Constantine said. "He is young for that position, don't you think?"

"Yes. He's young—either 27 or 28. And our custom has been that no one should become a bishop before they're 30. Or 35, preferably," Eusebius responded. He was genuinely concerned at this news and wondered who actually wrote Alexander's letter of recommendation.

"Well, he is a pious man. Fervently pious," Constantine shrugged.

"Yes. Pious." Eusebius had a vision of decades of holy wars within the Church. It made his stomach clench up. "But I'm not certain that pious is always what the Church needs."

"I see your point, I think," Constantine said. "We should go back inside. If there's more you'd like to discuss, let's talk in the morning."

As the night progressed and the good wine flowed, Helena recounted to Eusebius her plans to leave for another trip to the Holy Land with Gaius as her bodyguard in a matter of months.

Fausta held court about many things, related to their plans for the remaining days before the New Year. Different groups of visitors were coming every day. She made sarcastic remarks to everyone—but picked on Crispus, especially.

This was a familiar pattern. At 36, she was only eight years older than her stepson. Yet their relationship had always been awkward. No one in the family paid much attention to their bickering.

After midnight, Eusebius said good night—and Fausta and Crispus were the only ones still awake. They wandered lazily toward their respective bedrooms.

Crispus made a joking remark about Fausta's clumsiness and expanding waist. "Every time I see you now, you're getting larger. And larger. Soon we'll have to get the construction people in here just to widen the doorways for you."

Fausta attempted to push Crispus in mock anger. But stumbled slightly and fell into Crispus' arms. Locked together, face-to-face, they kissed.

"Oh my God," whispered Crispus. "This is the stupidest thing…."

"Yes," agreed Fausta, as she pulled away from Crispus and got her bearings again. Then she whispered, "Too bad we both liked it."

They turned away from each other and went into their respective rooms, where their spouses were sleeping.

At the end of the hallway, Aelius had been quietly walking through the living quarters to evaluate what would need to be cleaned up first in the morning. He was used to seeing things he'd wished he had not. But this was the worst thing he'd ever seen.

Near Byzantium
April 15, 1079 AUC (326 AD)

Adiutor Aelius was extremely agitated, pacing in the kitchen of the Imperial Palace.

It was early in the morning, but he hadn't slept all night and he had no idea what to do.

During his rounds the night before, he'd realized Crispus was not in his quarters—his door was left slightly ajar. Later, he had seen Crispus cross the hallway leaving the Empress' room and go back into his own. Aelius had been watching Crispus and Fausta since he'd seen them together around the New Year. Their growing attraction was obvious to him but seemed invisible to the rest of the family.

He feared more than liked both Crispus and Fausta. He was not particularly close to either. And he didn't feel the loyalty to either of them that he felt to the Emperor.

Crispus' wife and child were visiting her family in Gaul. They would be gone for weeks, if not months. The Emperor was away, somewhere, on business. He was due back soon. Aelius decided to wait and tell the Emperor what he'd seen.

Or maybe he'd just keep quiet about the whole thing, His success as one of Constantine's trusted Adiutors was based on his discretion about family secrets. Maybe this was just one more matter that called for discretion.

This agitation was beginning to affect his work. He was snapping at other Palace workers and beginning to miss minor details.

Near Byzantium
May 25, 1079 AUC (326 AD)

Constantine got on his horse in the courtyard of his new Imperial Palace and waved to his seven-months-pregnant wife. "I should be back tomorrow night. I regret that I have to go to Nicomedia. But the plans for the 20th anniversary of the Milvian Bridge victory parade in Rome are…pressing."

"Not a problem, my love. I'll be fine."

As Constantine and his entourage went through the new gate through the walls of the city, he saw Crispus in a nearby field practicing with his trainers. He waved to him as well.

Crispus had returned from Gaul just two days earlier and was still adjusting back into city living.

Constantine rode south for about an hour. Rather than crossing the Bosporus straight into Nicomedia, he and guards stopped at a small waterfront town and had a leisurely lunch. Then they rode a short distance and he stopped the group and ordered everyone to make camp for the evening. As dusk approached, he called his four original palatini to walk with him along the water's edge.

"Quintus, you and I will leave alone this evening. The rest of you are to stay here until morning. At daybreak, I want the three of you to bring the others back to the Palace."

Appius as always was the most vocal: "Imperator, please. Any time you go without us, you are at tremendous risk. Quintus— no disrespect for you, brother—is not as strong as he was before Chrysopolis. It is best that the three of us join you. We can leave instructions for the others."

"Appius, I have thought this through. This is the plan we will follow. Quintus and I will go alone."

"Imperator—"

"Appius, no."

Constantine signaled for Quintus to prep their horses. They rode south, further away from Byzantium. Once out of sight—and certain they weren't being followed—Constantine made a wide turn, back toward the city and rode. Without haste.

When they re-entered through the same gate they'd passed through earlier that day, it was well after ten o'clock. But the gate passage was lighted with so many torches and lamps that it might have been noon. The Centurions standing watch were surprised to see Constantine again. One of the guards was about to sound the usual signal—but Constantine signaled for him to be silent.

As they approached the Palace, Constantine got off his horse and handed the reins to Quintus. "Either Aelius or I will be back to get you. Until then, wait in silence."

Constantine strode through the courtyard quickly and quietly, signaling for silence to all that saw him. Entering the Palace, he found Aelius—who was visibly shaking—waiting in the main greeting room. Aelius started to block his approach to the living quarters...and then thought the better of it.

Quietly walking toward his bedroom, Constantine picked up an oil lamp in the beginning of the hallway. The door to his bedroom was unlocked. Inside, he found his wife and his son in his bed. Crispus jumped out of the bed naked—and then fell awkwardly to the ground on one knee. Fausta started to whimper.

Constantine felt his face flush. At the same time, he felt a wave of overpowering sadness—even more than when he'd lost Vibius. He felt his eyes tearing. "I had expected I might find...this. I am disgusted. I hope you found it worth it. Neither of you will ever see me again."

As he turned to leave, he stopped. Facing the door and without looking back, he said, "Is that my child you are carrying?" A teardrop fell, hitting the back of his outstretched hand on the door knob.

"Yes."

"You are sure?"

"I have only been with Crispus once since the holidays."

Crispus, gathering his clothes, muttered: "I am so, so sorry father."

Constantine wanted to respond but his throat was too tight for him to speak. All he could was sneer. And leave.

He walked the halls for several minutes, trying to get control of himself. Finally, he came upon Aelius—still shaking—in the kitchen. "Aelius, how long have you known?"

"Two months. But I only suspected, Imperator. Only suspected."

"Why didn't you say something to me?" Constantine didn't really care. He was looking for something to wipe his face—and eventually settled on a dishcloth.

"I didn't know for sure. And I was afraid."

Constantine wiped away his tears and sighed. "You actually did tell me, Aelius. You have been acting so strangely, particularly when they were together. It made me suspect. Quintus is in the street just outside the courtyard, have him bring in the horses. And both of you join me in my study."

Aelius walked quickly through the courtyard. He felt pain—but also relief that the burden of secrecy had been lifted.

Near Byzantium
May 26, 1079 AUC (326 AD)

Before dawn, there was a knock on Crispus' door.

Four centurions walked in with a hood and iron manacles. Placing the thick canvas hood with eye slits over Crispus' head, they locked the manacles in front of him so that he could ride. Fausta opened the door of her room, in time to see Crispus being escorted out.

Before she could say anything, four other centurions approached her with the same hood and manacles.

Pola, Istria
May 30, 1079 AUC (326 AD)

It had been a four-day ride to Pola. Each day a new set of centurions would relive the prior set.

Crispus had not eaten by his choice. He was riddled with guilt, shame and was in disbelief at his stupidity. He looked forward to death, which he knew was coming. Throughout the trip, he had not spoken and he doubted—given the rotations—that these centurions had any idea who he was.

Once in Pola, he was immediately brought before Magistrate Cato, Constantine's senior judicial advisor.

Opening the stiff linen scroll with the Emperor's seal, Magistrate Cato looked at the hooded person in front of him. While reading, he motioned the guards to remove the hood. Looking up, he immediately recognized Crispus.

He ordered the guards to stand outside the room and finished reading Constantine's letter.

"Son, you have been accused of Treason and Moral Turpitude. How do you plead?"

"Guilty."

"These crimes are punishable by death. Are you aware of that?"

"I am."

"Because you have pleaded guilty, the letter states you have a choice of means of death. What is your choice?"

"Poison. But I am curious. What would my means of death be if I had pleaded not guilty?"

"You would be beheaded," Cato responded matter-of-factly. "Crispus, I know your father. There is some risk, but I can delay this proceeding. I can inquire to the accuracy of his request. He tends to anger quickly. I could try to wait for him to reconsider his decision."

"That would be a worthless exercise for both of us, Magistrate. My fate is sealed. My only request is that you include my regrets to my father for the pain I have caused him."

"I will include that in my response."

"Can we get this over with?"

"Don't you wish a last meal?" Cato asked.

"No. I want this over as soon as possible."

"I will arrange for it shortly."

An hour later, in a small room adjacent to the court room, Crispus drank a large cup of a bitter-tasting Cherry Laurel. Shortly after drinking it, he started twitching. Soon after the twitching, he was unable to talk, experienced difficulty breathing and felt severe abdominal pain.

Within 20 minutes, he was dead. His body was transported by ship and dropped into the Adriatic Sea.

Trier, Rhineland
July 2, 1079 AUC (326 AD)

Fausta kept pushing, even though the midwife had told her to stop. She was tired of being captive—even in a palace. She wanted to have this child and escape. She had warned Constantine years ago about her father's treachery—and Constantine was alive because of that warning.

Infidelity wasn't life-threatening. And it certainly wasn't uncommon among Roman Empresses. He could have forgiven. But seeing Crispus leaving that morning and then living in this captivity had convinced her that he wouldn't forgive.

And that made her even angrier.

She'd had time, more than a month, to plan an escape. With a trusted handmaid, she could get away from the centurions. She would switch clothing with one of the other handmaids—maybe a day or two after this child was born. It was just a few days on foot to the Rhineland frontier, where she could cross over to the unconquered Franks. Her father had lived there for a few years when she'd been a young girl. She was confident the plan would work.

Finally, after another hour, a baby girl was born. The midwife said that the child resembled her grandmother Helena. But that impression might have been influenced by suggestion: Constantine had ordered the baby to be named Helena, if it was a girl.

Fausta was bathed and slept fitfully through that first night, her new child by her side. And midwives watching.

Trier, Rhineland
July 3, 1079 AUC (326 AD)

Fausta was awaken early in the morning by her trusted handmaid, who tried to warn her that something was amiss. But by the time Fausta's feet were on the ground, two large women—dressed as bathhouse attendants—entered the room.

"Empress, the bath that you requested is ready."

"I did not request a bath. I have no desire for one. I just delivered my fifth child last night and want more rest." As she snapped at the two women, she began to realize what was happening. And adjusted her tone. "I can barely move. Perhaps I can take a bath tomorrow. So, let us postpone this."

"I am sorry, Empress. You are going to have your bath now," said the larger of the two women.

Fausta tried to think of some way to stall: "Well, can you give me some time to get ready?"

"No. You must come with us now," the larger women replied. It was clearly a command.

They were standing on either side of her. And they were so large that she couldn't move anywhere but in between them. And they were already pressing toward her, squeezing her up from the bed.

As the group walked toward the bathhouse adjacent to the middle of the palace, Fausta could see what she thought were two Imperial saddled horses. She thought one of them was Constantine's. She screamed "Constantine!" so the whole palace might hear it.

The smaller of the attendants simply responded, "He is not here."

Walking into the bathhouse, even the main pool room felt unusually hot. The boiler for the caldarium had been heated to a dangerous level. Fausta slowed down as her handmaid started to cry, behind her. As they approached the steaming caldarium, she turned and hugged her last friend—whose name she couldn't even remember.

Then, without a word, Fausta walked into the hot room.

She thought that it was strange—women who didn't want to be pregnant would often go into hot caldariums to lose their babies. She had a baby she wanted and was going into a hot caldarium to lose her own life.

In less than an hour she was found dead in wooden stall by the small boiling pool.

Constantine had both Crispus and Fausta "damnatio memoriae." All records of their lives were destroyed including any public proclamations, statues or paintings.

Constantinople
May 2, 1089 AUC (336 AD)

Alexander of Constantinople was in Friday morning prayers in the Hagia Irene, the main church in Constantinople, when he received the letter from Constantine. The Church was adjacent to the Imperial Palace and Constantine frequented it on a regular basis.

Alexander had been given to the Church by his Italian parents over 90 years earlier. A devout Christian, he had once fasted for 20 days. Later, after moving to Greece and Asia Minor, he had gone four years without wearing clothes as a sign of his devotion to his faith.

Constantine's letter to Alexander was simple. Given the Synod of Tyre and Jerusalem a year earlier, it was time to accept Arius back into the Church with a celebration and communion this Sunday. Quoting from the Synod, Constantine wrote:

> "We believe that yourselves also, as if recovering
> the very members of your own body, will experience

great joy and gladness, in acknowledging and recovering your own bowels, your own brethren and
fathers; since not only the Presbyters, Arius and his
fellows, are given back to you, but also the whole
Christian people and the entire multitude, which
on occasion of the aforesaid men have a long time
been in dissension among you."

Alexander feelings could not be any more opposite than
Constantine's letter predicted.

Constantine had changed significantly in the ten years since
he'd ordered the death of his son and his wife. Some of the change
became noticeable at the twentieth anniversary celebration of his
triumph at the Milvian Bridge in Rome. Four months after Fausta's
death. The parade, the parties, the meetings were awkward, and
Constantine was unprepared. He had taken his mother, Helena, to
try to divert attention from his missing son and wife, but Romans
would shout question as to their whereabouts. He was noticeably
angry and often appeared confused. Helena handled her role per-
fectly but was still cool towards Constantine because of the death
of her favorite grandchild. After the festivities he left Rome and
never returned.

From that point on he tended to listen to the last person talking
rather than form his own opinions. His dress became more extravagant, as he favored more expensive and elaborate clothing. He'd
taken to wearing a blond wig over his thinning hair. He no longer
practiced martial arts with his palatini.

In fact his original palatini were all dead. Constantine began
to develop a deadly obsession after the Rome celebration. The hollowness of his earlier years was replaced with the twin cancers of
paranoia and indecision. The paranoia was extreme and rampant.
He feared, if his son's and wife's affair were known, it would expose
the very core of his manhood. That he would be revealed as a fake,

a charlatan, nothing more than another aging aristocratic cuckold. Anyone who might have any knowledge of what they had done, with the exceptions of Bishops, were slowly eliminated. Adiutor Aelius was the first to disappear, without a trace less than a year after Constantine's son's and wife's death. Aelius had a sister who he was close to who was unexpectedly murdered in a market by an unknown assailant several months later. Almost every servant in the new residence in Constantinople had died of some fatal encounter in the five years after their deaths.

Even his original palatini appeared targeted.

Quintus unexpectedly died in his sleep a year after Aelius, and Appius died soon after. Titus and Sevius were lost when a ship they were aboard sank in the Black Sea. This purge by death continued for almost ten years. Like so many of the Emperors before him, the human lives of subjects had become of little concern. In spite of his promises years earlier. Unlimited power brings assurance of abuse and corruption. In this case to protect the dark cloud of the secret.

Constantine successfully built the sleepy town of Byzantium into the modern bustling central city of the Empire, Constantinople. He was also still effective at solving the Empire's fiscal, administrative and building projects, particularly churches—but politically and militarily, he was a weaker version of his former self. He did lead successful campaigns against his old enemies the Goths and Sarmatians, but the Persians under Shapur II had begun to capitalize on those weaknesses by taking some Christian territories near their frontier. And on the Arian theological issue, he waivered dramatically.

After Crispus and Fausta's deaths, Ossius had immediately returned to Cordova. He had no communication from Constantine again. He wrote him several times but the letters went unanswered. Ossius suspected that Constantine knew that he was very critical of his execution of his wife and child, although Ossius had never expressed that opinion to anybody

Ossius' waning influence allowed Eusebius of Nicomedia to assume a larger role in Constantine's spiritual life. In time, Eusebius and Constantine's sister, Constantia, convinced Constantine that Arius' theology was sound. And that the Council of Nicaea had treated a provocative— but devout—thinker unfairly. The Emperor invited Arius to Constantinople, his "New Rome." Arius now lived in a small, two room apartment within the Imperial compound, a short distance from the Hagia Irene. Thus the convenience of the letter 'suggesting' that Arius be brought back into the Church through the Eucharist, sent to Alexander of Constantinople.

Alexander of Constantinople was distraught about Arius being admitted again into the Church. But there were also other reasons for his concern. Bishop Athanasius had recently been exiled to Trier, due to charges of having an opponent murdered, illegally taxing parishioners, sorcery and treason. Athanasius still wrote frequently to Alexander and his deacon, Clodius. Letters from a sorcerer and traitor could be grounds for exile themselves.

After several hours, Clodius and the rest of the staff realized that Alexander was missing. After some searching, Clodius and Macarius, one of Alexander's assistants, located their bishop in his bedroom, behind a locked door.

Clodius inquired: "Holiness, are you ill?"

"Yes!" Alexander answered through the door. "The Lord has struck my heart with sorrow that cannot be healed."

"Pray, my Bishop, open the door so that we can see the nature of your illness," Macarius pleaded.

There was a click. But the door stayed closed. Uneasy, Clodius and Macarius looked at each other, slowly opened the door and inched in. The old man was on his knees, praying at the side of his bed. Macarius stayed standing; Clodius sat in a woven chair, closer to Alexander.

"What is the cause of this sorrow, Holiness?"

Alexander had been weeping. His eyes were wet and puffy. His lips, trembling. "I have received a letter from the Emperor. He instructs me to accept the Infidel into the Church with communion this Sunday."

Clodius and Macarius looked at each other again, knowing that an inevitable day had come.

"Holiness, we knew this was coming. Athanasius mentioned it after the Synod last year. He believed that it would be sometime after Easter that this filth would try this. To feign acceptance of our Creed. And request a return to the Church. My anger is that the time has come so soon. It's an injustice. What shall we do?" Clodius responded.

Alexander nodded and started to weep again. "I had hoped that Constantine would remain immune to the poison of his worldly cousin. As he was for years. But he has given in. I am on my knees now, praying that the Lord will take me before Sunday. Or I pray the Lord to take that serpent Arius. Any way that I might be excused from committing this blasphemous act. Please, God! I pray to you, relieve me of my earthly role. I have not the strength. Please deliver me from this evil!"

Clodius had become accustomed to talking the old man through his spells of weeping. "Holiness, I promise you—I promise you emphatically—your prayers will be answered. The Blessing of our Sacred Eucharist shall not be bestowed to that demon."

Constantinople,
May 3, 1089 AUC (336 AD)

Arius finished his usual fig juice and grain cereal breakfast, which had come late this morning. He was getting ready to go out with Mastiff.

Both Mastiff and Arius were getting on in years—Mastiff was nearly 16 and Arius, 80. Of the two, Mastiff was showing her age more. Although she still got excited at the prospect of going for a walk, she moved slowly and often required the return in Arius' arms.

Arius was a celebrity in Constantinople—and it would be common to see him walking with a group of admirers. This Saturday, it was even more so. The entire community was aware that he was going to be reinstated with the Church. Crowds of well-wishers greeted him as he started his walk, congratulating him.

A longtime critic of Arius, Socrates Scholasticus, described what followed:

> It was then Saturday, and Arius was expecting to assemble with the church on the day following: but divine retribution overtook his daring criminalities. For going out of the imperial palace, attended by a crowd of Eusebian partisans like guards, he paraded proudly through the midst of the city, attracting the notice of all the people. As he approached the place called Constantine's Forum, where the column of porphyry is erected, a terror arising from the remorse of conscience seized Arius, and with the terror a violent relaxation of the bowels: he therefore enquired whether there was a convenient place near, and being directed to the back of Constantine's Forum, he hastened thither. Soon after, a faintness came over him and, together with the evacuations his bowels protruded, followed by a copious hemorrhage, and the descent of the smaller intestines. Moreover portions of his spleen and liver were brought off in the effusion of blood, so that he almost immediately died. The scene of this catastrophe still is shown at Constantinople, as I have said, behind the shambles in the colonnade: and by persons going by pointing the finger at the place,

there is a perpetual remembrance preserved of this extraordinary kind of death.

As the crowds grew around the privy where he lay, one of his crying admirers went to pick up Mastiff. She was sitting by the entrance, sensing that her master would not be coming out.

As he picked her up, she whimpered. And then went limp.

The large crowd grew even larger as Arius' body was identified and removed.

Alexander received the news and was overjoyed. He was greatly relieved. He rejoiced, praising the Heavens that his prayers were obviously answered by God.

The huge crowd that had gathered by the privy knew, however, that such an "extraordinary kind of death" was not the answer by God. It was the product of poison.

Nicomedia, Asia Minor
May 21, 1090 AUC (337 AD)

Eusebius looked at Constantine, as he fitfully slept on the couch in the Palace's great room. Daylight was waning and most of the visitors had left. For the moment, the two were alone.

That morning, the Emperor had removed his Imperial purple and gold robes and had been baptized by Eusebius in the company of three other bishops and his daughters. He was now clothed in the white robes of a learning Christian, a catechumen.

The pain Constantine described in his stomach was identical to what his father had described in the weeks before he had died.

Constantine said he had no doubt that he would die soon.

Eusebius started to plan what course the Church would take, now that its most powerful supporter was dying. Constantius II, Constantine's favorite son, was leading an army on the frontier in Persia to regain some of the territory lost to Shapur. A detail had been sent to notify him about his father. Eusebius was closer to

Constantius than he was to Constantine's other children—but that didn't guarantee anything.

Suddenly Constantine awakened.

"Eusebius, why is it I fear I am headed to Hell and I awaken to see you?"

"My apologies, cousin. I've always had that effect on people."

"Any word from Constantius?"

"No. He is south of the Jordan River with the army. So, quite a distance from here. But we've sent word."

"I had hoped to join him. And to be baptized in the Jordan River. That is where the Nazarene was baptized," Constantine grimaced while he spoke.

"Shall I get you some opiates?"

"No. Perhaps later tonight, to help me sleep. I watched my father die of this same thing. He had no opium and didn't complain. I should be so strong."

"I remember him well. He was a good man. He would be so proud of you," Eusebius said.

"I hope so. I hope to see him soon."

Eusebius tried to change the subject. "Tell me, cousin. How did you get out of Galerius' court to rejoin your father? Galerius was so brutal. I've often wondered what you did to avoid getting yourself killed or maimed by him."

Constantine nodded. The spasm of pain seemed to be ending. "He did try to kill me. He threw me in a room with a lion once. Thank God, he gave me armor and a sword. How I escaped from Galerius was simple, really. I got him drunk. He thought he was going to seduce me—but he just passed out after I had him sign my transfer to my father's army. Then I rode all night. Switching horses at…five…roadhouses, I believe it was, before dawn. By the time he awoke, surely disoriented and uncertain of what had happened, I was too far away for him to catch."

"His guards didn't stop you?"

"No. They hated him as much as everyone else did. Maybe more," the Emperor laughed. "I was with my father's army three days later. Where was it? Somewhere north. Anyway, that was when I saw Vibius really fight for the first time. What a soldier."

"And Galerius didn't seek revenge?"

"I'm not sure he knew what had happened. He wasn't really a sodomite. But he did take boys once in a while—and, sometimes, those boys just vanished. He probably didn't remember and thought he had had me in return for my release. He was one of the last real pagans. Hated Christians. He burned down the palace of his co-emperor and blamed it on Christians."

"Co-emperor. I'd almost forgotten about those."

"Yes. Like trying to take an army into battle with two generals. Or build a Church with two popes. Bad idea unless they are directly related." Constantine grimaced again. The spasms were coming more quickly. "Old Galerius hated Helena, too. And he would have nailed her to a cross—but he was afraid of my father."

"Even though your father had married Theodora by that time?"

"Yes. But he always showed kindness toward my mother."

"How did Galerius even know your mother?"

"She lived very close to where we are now. And his Imperial Court was right there," Constantine sat up for a moment and pointed out a window across the room, "in the center of town. She would enter his court, uninvited, to see me. I think she believed that, if he saw her constantly, he'd think twice about doing harm to me. He may have feared her, too. Not just my father. Bullies often fear women."

"Well, Helena was fearless. It's amazing to me that she went to Bethlehem and Jerusalem when she was nearing 80. And was a still full of so much energy," Eusebius said. "She was one of the truly most fearless people I've ever known."

"Yes. Fearless and relentless about encouraging me to build more churches. In the Holy Land alone, she authorized four—the

Church of the Nativity in Bethlehem, Mount of Olives in Jerusalem, Burning Bush in Sinai and…the last one…St. Catherine's in Sinai. She would start those churches, then come back and tell me I had to pay for them. Such will! I wish…I'd found a wife like her. The children we might have had."

"Your children are good and loyal, cousin."

"I suppose. But they've had lives of privilege, which does not make strong metal. I think of the years in Naissus—after my father left. The abuse and ridicule of the soldiers. That ridicule made me stronger, more determined. My children have never had that. Constantius is a good son—he will probably do best. But even he…. I wish I could help him grow and mature, make him a better soldier. I didn't do enough of that with him. If only I had Crispus."

"That is the first time I've heard you mention his name since… you told me what happened."

"I am haunted by it. Constantly, cousin. It never leaves my mind. I have such fear, of them, of people that know, that…. I look forward to death, if only to stop that which haunts me. Such immorality. And needless. They each could have done…other things. God forgive me, I was so angry."

Eusebius rested a hand on Constantine's shoulder. "If your regret and repentance are genuine, then God will forgive. You know that."

"I beg His forgiveness, Eusebius. Of my children, Crispus was the best leader. The Empire would be stronger now, if he were alive. I prayed that evening—and every evening since—for God to tell me whether fierce justice was right. But I never heard an answer. And, in my pride, I also prayed that their sin would never be known, fear so much fear, I have never feared death, but this…" Constantine's voice trailed off.

"That prayer has been answered, cousin. I've never heard anyone speak of it."

"Good. My mind is full of conflict. But I'm ready for sleep, cousin."

"Then sleep. We all feel conflict and doubt when we face death. It is part of the human condition," Eusebius said, in an assuring tone.

And he watched his cousin slip back into sleep.

Nicomedia, Asia Minor
May 22, 1090 AUC (337 AD)

Constantine had gone into a coma the night before and his breathing had become erratic. A huge crowd of people had surrounded the villa on the outskirts of Nicomedia. Most of his ranking officers, important magistrates and his daughters were present, as he remained on the couch in the Great Room.

At mid-day his breathing became worse and then just stopped. He had passed.

The news spread throughout the Empire in record time, the only subject people wanted to talk about. Constantine had been the only Emperor that many citizens of the Empire had ever known.

Soldiers came and lifted the Emperor's body into a golden coffin covered by his purple standard. They transported it to the Imperial Palace in Constantinople. It lay in state for several days, while dignitaries and common citizens from all over the Empire came to pay their respects.

Constantius II arrived and led the procession of a military guard, followed by masses of people, to the Church of the Holy Apostles— where a High Mass was dedicated to his father's life.

Constantine's body was interred in a mausoleum within that Church, causing significant disappointment in Rome that the Eternal City would not be his eternal resting place.

EPILOGUE

Those wanting a compromise in the wording of the Nicene Creed were correct given the conflicts that followed. The debate continued for centuries. Eventually, the Creed was modified in the Second Ecumenical Council of Constantinople in 381. The new creed removed the specific clauses aimed at Arius and added references to the Virgin Mary and the Holy Ghost.

> I believe in One God, the Father Almighty, Maker of Heaven and Earth, and of all things visible and invisible.
>
> And in one Lord Jesus Christ, the Son of God, the Only-Begotten, begotten of the Father before all ages; Light of Light; True God of True God; begotten, not made; of one essence with the Father, by Whom all things were made; Who for us men and for our salvation came down from Heaven, and was incarnate of the Holy Spirit and the Virgin Mary, and became man.
>
> And He was crucified for us under Pontius Pilate, and suffered, and was buried. And the third day He arose again, according to the Scriptures, and ascended into Heaven, and sits at the right hand of the Father; and He shall

come again with glory to judge the living and the dead; Whose Kingdom shall have no end.

And in the Holy Spirit, the Lord, the Giver of Life, Who proceeds from the Father; Who with the Father and the Son together is worshipped and glorified; Who spoke by the prophets.

And in One, Holy, Catholic, and Apostolic Church.

I acknowledge one baptism for the remission of sins. I look for the resurrection of the dead, and the life of the world to come.

Even with these changes, conflicts within the Church over Arius' theology would continue. In the nearer term, the Arian conflict caused considerable trouble among Constantine's own heirs. After Constantine's death, the Senate voted that the Roman Empire would be divided into five administrative districts—each controlled by one of his three surviving sons or two nephews.

Within a few months, both nephews were killed by their own troops—reportedly on the orders of Constantius II. As a result, the Empire was ruled by the three sons. One of those sons, Constans, was only 14 at the time; so control of the Empire fell to the two older brothers—Constantine II and Constantius II.

Constantine II supported the Nicene Orthodoxy and recalled Athanasius from one of his exiles in Gaul and restored him as Bishop of Alexandria. Constantius II, a supporter of the Arian Theology, was offended.

Like his older brother, young Constans was generally more inclined to the Nicene Orthodoxy. However, he was offended by Constantine II's, his guardian, reluctance to allow him to rule when he came of age. He also didn't like his brother's demands for territory based on primogeniture claims.

As a result of those issues, Constantine II and Constans began to feud in 340. It ended quickly. Constans' troops ambushed Constantine II and killed him.

Constans was betrothed at one point to Ablabius' daughter. But the marriage never took place—which was best for Ablabius' daughter. Constans had an attraction only for young pagan boys and his extreme cruelty and inconsistency eventually turned even his own army against him.

In 350, one of his generals, Magnentius, led a rebellion. Magnentius' soldiers assassinated Constans in a pagan temple, exactly 10 years after they'd helped kill his brother.

Ablabius, one of the most powerful senators in the Empire and a Nicene believer, was assassinated by Constantius II, an Arian.

Constantius II was the most successful of Constantine's heirs. He ruled 24 years, as either Emperor or co-Emperor. He pursued and killed Magnentius in the course of two major battles. He tried—but failed—to encourage a compromise theology between the Arian and Nicene orthodoxies. He died in 361 at the age of 44.

Constantine's daughters didn't fare much better. The elder, Constantina, was married to her cousin, Hannibalianus, until his early death on Constantius II's orders. She later married another cousin, Constantius Gallus. Together, they ruled some Eastern portions of the Empire—but, after reports of mismanagement and cruelty, Constantius II ordered them to come to his Palace in Italy to explain. Constantina died on the trip. And Gallus blamed her for the mismanagement. Constantius was outraged and sentenced Gallus to death. Helena, Constantine's youngest child, was married to Jullian the Philosopher, another cousin and the successor to Gallus in ruling parts of the Eastern Empire. She died in childbirth in 360.

Athanasius was expelled five times from Alexandria by four different Emperors for a period of seventeen of his forty five years as Bishop. He is a Church Father and is venerated as a Saint in both the Roman Catholic Church and the Eastern Orthodox Church. In his Easter Letter of 367 AD he listed the 27 books of the New Testament which he regarded as canon. Of those 27 books he included John's Revelation. It is generally agreed that these books were accepted as canon at the Synod of Hippos Regius in North Africa in 393 AD.

Constantine and his mother, Helena, are also venerated as Saints by both the Roman Catholic Church and the Eastern Orthodox Church. Constantine is often referred to as the Thirteenth Apostle.

About the Author

John R. Prann, Jr. is the former CEO of a NYSE-listed company and past member of several corporate boards. His interest in Christian history first began developing when he was a graduate student at the University of Chicago. John lives with his wife, Cheryl, and their ferocious miniature Schnauzer, Pepper, on Sanibel Island, Florida. *Imperator, Deus* is his first book. He is working on his second novel.

.CPSIA information can be obtained
at www.ICGtesting.com
Printed in the USA
BVOW03s0807120217
475971BV00001B/313/P